Advance Praise for *There's Cake in My Future*

"Charming, heartwarming, wry, and whimsical. Kim Gruenenfelder is at her very best. This is better than double chocolate fudge cake."—Beth Kendrick, author of *Second Time Around* and *Nearlyweds*

"A delicious read! *There's Cake in My Future* takes us on a great ride with characters who are easy to love. Funny and touching, Kim Gruenenfelder's latest is her best book yet! You really can have your cake and read it, too."—Jennifer Coburn, author of *Tales from the Crib* and *The Wife of Reilly*

"Kim Gruenenfelder has done it again! A laugh-out-loud book filled with warmth and insight, and women we can all relate to. This captivating cakewalk is not to be missed."—Nancy Redd, *New York Times* bestselling author of *Body Drama* and *Diet Drama*

"A delightfully witty story about friendship and love, *There's Cake in My Future* sparkles from start to finish!"—Liz Fenton, coauthor of *I'll Have Who She's Having*

"With sparkling dialogue and a fun-as-all-get-out story, you'll want to grab the book, a glass of your favorite something, and settle in for a very happy night."—Quinn Cummings, author of *Notes from the Underwire*

ALSO BY KIM GRUENENFELDER

A Total Waste of Makeup

Misery Loves Cabernet

There's Cake in My Future

KIM GRUENENFELDER

ST. MARTIN'S GRIFFIN
NEW YORK

To Brian and Alex—as always

This is a work of fiction. All of the characters, organizations, and events portrayed in this novel are either products of the author's imagination or are used fictitiously.

www.stmartins.com

Library of Congress Cataloging-in-Publication Data

Gruenenfelder-Smith, Kim.
There's cake in my future / Kim Gruenenfelder. — 1st ed.
p. cm.
ISBN 978-0-312-61459-1
1. Brides—Fiction 2. Female friendship—Fiction. 3. Magic—Fiction.
I. Title.
PS3607.R72T47 2010
813'.6—dc22

2010037787

10 9 8 7 6 5 4 3 2

Acknowledgments

First off, I'd like to thank Matthew Shear, my publisher, and Kerry Nordling, in Foreign Rights. If you guys didn't sell my books, I could never sit in my pajamas writing my books, and for that I am eternally grateful.

Many thanks to Jennifer Weis, my editor, for supporting my books and helping steer me through the whole writing process on project after project.

To Kim Whalen, my agent. Again, how do you thank the person who has guaranteed that pajamas can be work clothes?

To Jennifer Enderlin, for coming up with the title for my book. (I still believe it every day!)

To Dorothy Kozak, for saying, "You should write a book about a cake pull."

To the people I trust so much that I let them read the "crappy first draft": Carolyn Townsend, Brian Smith, Jennifer Good, and Anne Bensson. I don't know how I got so lucky to have found a group of people who have enough faith in me to tell me the truth about what doesn't work in my books and what needs to be fixed. I do know that it's easy to lie to the people you give up on. It's harder to plod through with those you know have more in them. I treasure you.

To Erin Dunlap for helping me so much with Mel's "Am I happy?" monologue. You should be writing novels—I'm just sayin'.

To Seema Bardwaj and Reena Singh, for letting me take your names for my character and giving me tidbits of info about Indian American culture. Obviously Seema isn't either of you (you are both much more fabulous), but I'd like to think a few of your cracks and quips made it in.

To my family: Brian and Alex, of course. Carol, Edmond, Janis, Jenn, Rob, Haley, Declan, and Maibre. And on Brian's side: Caryol, Walter, Eric, Sonia, Eric Jr., Kyle, Emily, and Korie.

And one other family I have to thank: the friends my son Alex thinks have the first name "Uncle" or "Aunt": Jeff Greco, Brian Gordon, Robert Sexton, and Suzi Hale Sexton. To "the winetasters": Dorothy, Missy, Gaylyn, Jen, Nancy, Reena, Christie, and Marisa, for all of your encouragement. And to Laurie, for her encouragement.

Finally, I want to thank a particular group of writers whom I've met since *A Total Waste of Makeup.* These writers don't all know each other, and they're not all in the same field of writing. But they have one thing in common: they are all artists who are also incredibly good and supportive people. That's hard to find—and somehow I found you. Joe Keenan, Bob Daily, Jennifer Coburn, Beth Kendrick, Quinn Cummings, Jeff Greenstein, and Nancy Redd. Whether it's coming to book signings, sending me a picture of my book on a bookstore front table, bantering about agents and editors, or letting me pitch asinine ideas at you until something interesting came out, I am grateful.

And if I missed anyone—you know who you are—yell at me and I promise you will be in the acknowledgments for Book 4.

There's Cake in My Future

Prologue

Melissa

Is it a *really* bad sign when the bride has locked herself in the bathroom? Or is it just one of those things that all brides are secretly tempted to do right before the ceremony?

I am standing in the back room of a beautiful old church in Santa Monica wearing a sparkly satin aquamarine dress with a giant bow at the hip, dyed-to-match aquamarine pumps, and an aquamarine hat so ostentatious it could make Liberace climb out of his grave just to tell me to tone it down a bit.

Obviously, I'm the bridesmaid. An honor that currently affords me the task of knocking politely on the bathroom door of my good friend Nicole (aka The Bride) and begging her to come out.

"Nic? Honey," I say gently, tapping lightly on the door. "Do you want to talk about it?"

"No," she whispers to me through the locked door. "I'm an awful, selfish person who doesn't deserve a wedding, or a marriage, or happiness. And I am going to die alone with a bunch of potbellied pigs."

"Pigs?" I ask, confused but trying to sound understanding and sympathetic. "Why would you end up with pigs?"

"I hate cats."

I can't tell if she's overreacting or not. I mean, when you think about it, a wedding is an astonishingly big leap of faith. Any ceremony that specifically mentions "sickness," "poverty," and "death" as part of the agreement—that should at least give a girl pause. Right?

Maybe that's why society has encouraged women to focus more on the glittering diamonds, the gorgeous dress, the flowers, the presents, the cake. . . .

Oh . . . the cake. After this past week, I'm pretty sure the bride doesn't even want to hear the word *cake*, much less look at one.

Our friend Seema, Nic's maid of honor, opens the front door of the bridal room and backs her way in, careful to keep the door as shut as possible while she slithers through the doorway. Seema wears the same ridiculous ensemble as I, but her luminous Indian skin can handle the hideous shade of blue Nic has picked for us. And her hourglass figure easily pulls off the lacy décolletage of the V-neck top and the stupid bow at the hip.

"No, no problem at all," Seema insists with forced cheer to someone out in the hall. "We just need a few more minutes. The bride . . ." She glances over at me as she struggles to finish her sentence. ". . . smaid!" Seema continues. "The *bridesmaid* is depressed that it's never going to be her and has locked herself in the bathroom. We'll be right out."

Seema slams the door shut, locks it, then runs over to me, still camped out at the bathroom door. "I think I bought us a few more minutes," Seema whispers to me hurriedly. "I don't think anyone suspects anything yet."

My eyes bug out at her. "Who was that?"

"The church lady. She wants to know why we're behind schedule."

"Why did you tell her that *I* was the depressed one?" I whine to her in a whisper. "Like I'm not having enough problems today.

Do I really need three hundred people thinking I'm holding up a wedding because I can't get my love life together?"

"I panicked," Seema admits in a whisper. "Besides, it *could* be an excuse."

"Did it ever occur to you to use *your* sorry excuse for a love life as an excuse?" I challenge her. (An outburst that is completely out of character for me but I believe well within my rights.)

"Fine," Seema concedes, her tone of voice clearly brushing me off. "So next time, you can go out there, and use me as the excuse." Seema begins rapping on Nicole's bathroom door several times. "Nic, drama time's over," she says firmly, but ever so quietly. (Can't have the wedding guests hear anything in the back room, after all.) "Now come on out."

"No!" Nic whispers back urgently through the door.

"Don't let my whispering fool you," Seema warns Nic. "I swear to God, I will kick down this door! Put me in an aquamarine skullcap in front of three hundred people. Oh, you *will* get married today! I don't care if I have to drag you down the aisle with a chair and a whip."

"First of all, it's not aquamarine—it's aqua," Nic begins with a hint of condescension. "As a matter of fact, if we're getting technical, I'd say it's more of an electric blue."

"Really?" Seema responds dryly. "This is what you want to do right now? Lecture me on your chosen bridal color palette?"

Nic whips open the door to haughtily tell Seema, "Well, you make me sound like some tacky little bride from 1984. And, secondly, it is *not* a skullcap. That is a lovely—vintage!—forties hat and veil."

Nicole looks exquisite: the quintessential California girl ready for her wedding at the beach. Her sun-kissed skin glows, her emerald eyes sparkle, and her platinum-blond hair practically shimmers under her long veil. She looks flawless in her gorgeous

Monique Lhuillier strapless princess A-line gown in ivory satin. A vision, ready to walk down the aisle. . . .

Until she slams the bathroom door shut again before we have the chance to ram our way in and force her to get married.

I let my head fall into the palm of my hand.

Seema tries the door, but it's locked again.

"It's a costume for an extra in an Esther Williams movie," Seema yells as much as possible while speaking in a stage whisper. "Now get your butt out here!"

There's a polite knock on the front door. I walk over to it. "Yes?" I ask through the door in the most carefree and breezy tone I can muster.

"It's Mrs. Wickham," the lady from the church says on the other side of the door. "People are starting to ask questions. Is everything okay in there?"

I watch Seema stand up, determinedly walk back a few steps, then run like a bull right into the bathroom door.

It doesn't budge.

"It's fine," I lie. "I was . . ."

Seema grabs her shoulder in pain, and starts rubbing it. "Son of a . . ." She pounds on the door with both fists and stage-whispers, "You get out here, woman!"

I open the front door as little as possible, then squeeze through the tiny crack and step out into the hallway. As I do, I take my left hand and push Mrs. Wickham away from the door and farther out into the hallway while simultaneously closing the door behind me with my right hand. "I've been vomiting," I lie. "And crying. Nic was just helping me clean up my mascara." I grab her by the collar and whine, "Oh God, Mrs. Wickham, why isn't it me? Why is it never me?"

Suddenly I hear a loud, rhythmic pounding inside the room. I quickly let go of Mrs. Wickham's collar, open the door a crack, then peek in to see Seema holding a fire extinguisher and ramming it repeatedly into the locked door.

I close the door quickly to block anything unseemly from Mrs. Wickham, and force a toothy smile. "But I'm good now."

POUND!

I continue to smile, "You go make sure the groom is okay . . ."

POUND!

My cheeks hurt, I'm smiling so hard. "After all, without a groom, we don't have a wedding."

POUND!

PSSSSSSSSSSSSSSSSSSSSSSSSSSSSS!!!!!!

"Oh shit!" I hear Seema roar on the other side of the door.

I open the door a crack for a second time to see Seema covered in fire extinguisher goo.

I slam the door shut again, then turn around to the church lady and force myself to admit, "Okay, we might be having a little problem with Seema's dress. We're gonna need two more minutes."

One week earlier. . . .

One

Seema

Date not bad. She's pretty cool actually. Can't wait to see you tonight. Have drinks ready. ;)
Love ya!

I stare at the text on my phone.

My God, men are just glorious in their ability to send mixed signals. I look over at my friends Melissa and Nicole, both scurrying around my kitchen, setting up an assortment of food and drinks for Nic's bridal shower.

"Okay, this is the last text, I promise," I say, showing the screen to Nic as she pulls a giant glass pitcher of peach puree from my refrigerator. "What do you think Scott meant when he wrote this?"

Nic takes a moment to read the words on the screen. "That he's a typical guy who wants you to carry a torch for him but doesn't actually want to kiss you, make out with you, or take any responsibility for leading you on."

"I hate it when she minces words," I joke to Mel, who laughs and nods as she diligently wraps prosciutto slices around melon wedges.

"Okay, I give up," Nic admits to me in confusion as she holds up the glass pitcher. "What is this?"

"Fresh peach puree," I tell her, with just a hint of defensiveness. "For the champagne."

Nic looks horrified. "Since when does perfectly good champagne need to be sullied with sugared fruit?"

"Since every bridal magazine and online article I read told me that proper bridal showers need to have peach Bellinis," I answer her, with just a hint of "Bring it on, Bitch" in my voice. (I have spent the last week perusing wedding magazines and online wedding sites getting ready for this damn shower. I'll admit, reading about all of these deliriously happy fiancées has made me a tad sullen.)

"Seriously?" Nic asks. From the scowl on her face, I'm going to guess this is the first she's heard of it.

"Tragically, yes," I say. "I also bought orange juice for mimosas. Apparently destroying twenty dollars' worth of sparkling wine with fifty cents' worth of sugar during a bridal shower is as traditional as the bride throwing the bouquet, unmarried wedding guests having a fight on the way home about why the guy won't commit, and a bridesmaid waking up on top of someone horribly inappropriate the next morning." I hand Mel my phone to read Scott's text. "What do you think this means?"

Mel clutches her chest. "Oh my God! The poor guy. He liiiikes you. Why don't you just let him be your boyfriend already?"

I shrug. "I don't know. Is it worth jeopardizing a really good friendship just because I want to have sex with him?"

Mel answers with, "It would be so romantic. The best relationships start out as friendships," just as Nic talks over her with, "Absolutely. Pin him to a wall and show him who's boss."

Mel glares at Nic disapprovingly. Nic shrugs. "What? I didn't say *she* had to be the boss."

They're both right in their own way, of course. I desperately and achingly want to have sex with Scott. I think about it all the time.

Actually, that's not true.

What I desperately want is to have that first six-hour make-out session where you just kiss and dry hump on someone's couch until one of you falls asleep and the other one sneaks off to the bathroom to wash off her makeup, brush her teeth, and prepare to look radiant when you both wake up three hours later. At which time, hopefully he suggests brunch, and you both keep sneaking kisses all day.

But I'm afraid what would happen instead would be the morning that has haunted every girl for months or years after the actual event. When, the next morning, the man that you have finally caught, the man that you have dreamt about kissing for so long, now has that look on his face that men get when they want to find a way to nicely let you know that you were a giant mistake, and that they wish the night had never happened. But it's not you, it's him. Really. And can you still be friends? Because he just loves you so much . . . as a friend.

And what do we girls typically do when presented with this humiliating situation? Most of us stupidly pretend that nothing happened, that everything is okay, and that we can go back to being "just friends."

But not one of us has ever really felt comfortable around the guy again. How can you relax around someone who doesn't think you're enough?

In my experience, the breakup goes one of two ways: either you pretend to stay friends and slowly drift apart—canceling on dinners or not scheduling movie nights anymore. Or, worse, you do keep seeing each other. And while a taste of honey is worse than none at all, a taste of tequila is deadly. Someone inevitably makes a move, someone says no, you both start yelling, and you never see each other again.

Oh, or I guess there's the third dreaded kind of breakup: the one that happens three months later, after you've declared your undying love for him, he has said he loves you back, everything's going incredibly smoothly, you're picking out wedding china in your head, and Bam! He breaks up one night. Doesn't even give a good reason, just doesn't "feel the sparks" you feel.

This is the biggest reason for why I haven't kissed Scott. I've already felt the heartbreak of him breaking up with me hundreds of times—all in my head. Depending on the night, I either go to bed fantasizing about him kissing me or I think about the breakup that would inevitably follow.

It *would* happen. I know this logically. We are completely wrong for each other.

I am a key fund-raiser for the Los Angeles Museum. It's a job I kind of fell into, but I like it very much, and I'm pretty good at it. I organize sophisticated parties and showings for the well-to-do in Los Angeles, and try to get them to become patrons and donate money to the various programs and exhibits within the museum. I have no artistic ability whatsoever, but I am the biggest fan of a good exhibit. I'm stable. I have a steady job, a mortgage, and a 401(k). I get my teeth cleaned twice a year.

On the other hand, Scott—sexy, delicious Scott—is a walking disaster. He's an artist: like a real *painting, sculpting, honest to God that's his job* artist. As such, some months he can barely cover his rent. He goes to the dentist only when a tooth is exploding in his head. Getting him wrangled into a suit for a fund-raising event usually requires negotiations, flattery, and bribery. He sleeps until noon, then works until three in the morning. I get "booty calls" from him at 2:00 A.M.—because he actually wants to *talk*. (And, like an idiot, I always take the call. Then we stay up until four or five in the morning talking, and I spend the next day at work exhausted and inhaling Diet Monsters and plain M&Ms to get through the afternoon.)

I met Scott about ten months ago at a show a curator from the museum had put together on modern life. I'll admit, contemporary art frequently escapes me.

Scott had done a piece everyone was raving about that night called *The Conformity of Imagination*. The piece was a white couch from a thrift store, a dark blue table, and some red, white, and blue tissue paper ribbons strewn from a red painting to the white couch.

I didn't get it.

So, when the incredibly sexy guy with wet hair and freshly washed Levis walked up to me and asked what I thought of the piece, I diplomatically said, "It's crap."

He laughed. "Don't let the artist hear you say that."

I looked around the room nervously. "Where is he?" I ask Mr. Hotness. (One thing I've learned as a fund-raiser is never to discount an artist in public. You can say you "don't get" a piece. But don't cut them out completely—that may be the next Hockney or Picasso you're dissing, and you will pay for it later when his pieces show up in Paris and three billionaires call you wanting to sponsor him in L.A.)

"Oh, I have no idea," he who could be Orlando Bloom's hotter brother said to me at the time. Orlando took two glasses of champagne from a passing waiter and handed me one as he asked, "So why don't you like it?"

"Well, it's so unoriginal," I said to the insanely handsome man. "It's like the artist was on deadline, knew he needed to turn in a piece, and had nothing. So he looked around his living room, and said, 'Got it! Fuck 'em if they can't take a joke,' gave the piece a good title, and turned it in."

The man smiled at me. "Wow. You're even meaner than the art critic from the *Times*. She said she thought I went to IKEA to pick up some cheap wineglasses, and when I was looking at their display modules, decided to duplicate one and call it art."

My face fell. "Oh. Shit. You're not . . ."

"I am," he admitted with a glint in his eye.

I let my shoulders fall. "I'm so screwed."

"I would love to take you up on that, but unfortunately I'm here on a date," the man told me flirtatiously. Then he flashed me a sexy smile as he put out his hand. "Scott James."

I reluctantly put out my hand as I tried to figure out a way to apologize. "Seema Singh."

Scott cocked his head. "Seema Singh? How do you have a Northern Indian first name and a Southern Indian last name?"

I was impressed. Not only that he knew that I was Indian (you'd be amazed how many Americans think I'm black, Asian, or related to Tiger Woods), but that he knew that my name was wrong. I smiled at him, immediately smitten. "I had parents who fell in love despite themselves. How do you know so much about India?"

"Took a trip there last year. I was dabbling in watercolors, trying to become less postmodern. More classic." Scott looked over at his piece and said in an easy, self-deprecating tone, "Clearly I failed."

I tried to backpedal. "You know, it's not bad at all. I was just trying to be clever."

Scott seemed amused. "Never apologize for your opinion. All notes are legitimate." Then he winked at me and said breezily, "Just promise me that you can love the artist, even if you don't understand his art."

That statement was the first of hundreds of flirtatious remarks Scott makes that to this day throw me off my game.

That night, I wasn't sure if Scott hated me or saw me as a worthy adversary to be conquered.

But I did know that I could have been conquered.

I stared at him off and on all night, and we ran into each other a few more times. Maybe he was hitting on me? I'm still not sure. His stunningly beautiful model date never allowed me to find out—she hung all over him for most of the evening, then dragged him home early.

At my behest, Scott and I exchanged cards and began meeting for lunch to talk about work. Lunch eventually led to drinks, which led to dinners, late-night games of pool or darts, and finally middle of the night phone calls.

But no make-out sessions, and no sex.

You see, our timing has always been off. By the time he was done dating the model, I had moved on to a very nice guy named Conrad. Who turned out to be a jerk, which I couldn't wait to tell Scott one night, only to discover he had started dating a sitcom writer. By the time he broke up with her, I was with Alan, who I dated until last week. And now that I'm free from Alan, it sounds like Scott might be dating again.

Sigh.

Despite our poor timing, I think a few times we've come damn close to a Love Connection.

Maybe.

I'm not sure.

Times like when we were in the kitchen at a party and just started staring at each other, and I wanted to kiss him, but I didn't. Or one of the many nights when we would order takeout, watch a Blu-ray, hug a bit, and fall asleep in each other's arms. Hugs good night that lasted forever. Kisses hello that might have lingered a half second too long.

Or maybe this is all my imagination. Who the fuck knows?

And it doesn't help that he constantly says stuff that could be interpreted a million different ways. Things like:

Date not bad. She's pretty cool actually. Can't wait to see you tonight. Have drinks ready, ;)
Love ya!

I stare at the text. "Have drinks ready." What does that mean? Let's get drunk so that I can take advantage of you?

I'm being silly. Scott is crucial to my life. With Nic engaged and living with Jason, and Mel almost engaged and living with Fred, Scott's the only single friend I still have left to play with. He's the one who can go out on a Saturday night at a moment's notice. He's the one I can call after 10:00 P.M. without a lecture from the other side of the king-size bed.

And lately, he's the one I want to call when I have news. Any kind of news: good, bad, big, small. Anything from booking a hundred-thousand-dollar donation to my finally finding that vanilla-bean porter from that local brewery in bottles.

He's the one I called right after my grandmother died. (It was 2:45 in the morning. I didn't want to bother the girls.) He's the one who dragged his ass out of bed to pick me up in the middle of the night, drove me up to San Francisco, then stayed with me while I dealt with my crazy family during her Indian funeral. He's the one who listened to me as I talked through tears about this gold bell that she had on her mantle, and why it meant the world to me. At one point, I was crying so hard, Scott pulled the car over, took me in his arms, and let me sob until I started heaving.

I think back to that moment when I was just a big pit of needs, and he was there for me unconditionally, unquestioningly, and unwaveringly.

I take a deep breath.

Right.

When I'm being lusty, I forget about what's really important. You don't find guys like him every day. Why would I want to jeopardize that unconditional love and support just for a one-night stand, no matter how fun and tempting it might be at the time?

I delete Scott's text. "I'm being silly," I say aloud to the girls.

"Scott is a good friend. I love him. If something was supposed to happen, it would have by now."

"You're not being silly," Nic assures me with a look of determination. "What you need is a chili pepper."

I furrow my brow at her. "Please tell me that's not something else I'm supposed to mix with champagne."

"No. It's the charm you're going to pull," Nic tells me in a firm voice. "I'm telling you, this is going to change your life."

Two

Nicole

I can tell Seema is suppressing an urge to roll her eyes at me.

"Don't give me that look," I tell her. "The first time I was ever at a cake pull, I pulled the silver heart, which meant I'd be the next woman to fall in love. I met Jason that night."

Mel looks up from her melon tray. "What's a cake pull? What are we talking about?"

"Glad you asked," I say, beaming, as I walk to Seema's refrigerator. As I open the door, I hear a loud pop of a champagne cork. I turn to see Seema opening a bottle of Taltarni Brut Taché, my favorite sparkling wine.

"Ah," Mel says happily. "I love that sound."

Seema pours some champagne into flutes for us. "Good. You'll need booze to hear this."

"Stop that," I say sternly, as I pull a large circular cake with white frosting out of the refrigerator and place it in the middle of Seema's kitchen table. Radiating from the cake are twenty-four white satin ribboned loops, evenly spaced around the circumference.

"Okay now, you see these ribbons?" I ask Mel.

"Yes," Mel says, taking a sip of champagne as she fingers one of the ribbons.

"Each ribbon is attached to a sterling silver charm, which gets pulled out before we eat the cake." I continue. "I stuck twenty-four charms in here, one for each woman at the party. Some of the most common charms include the engagement ring, the heart, the baby carriage, the money bag, the hot air balloon, and the wishing well. The charms are like fortune cookies. Whatever charm you pull, that's the next stage in your life coming up."

"How on earth did you get these in here?" Mel asks me.

"It's easy, but messy. First, I bought the charms at therescake inmyfuture-dot-com. Next, since I can't bake to save my life, I went down to Big Sugar Bakeshop on Ventura and had them bake a two-layer chocolate fudge cake with buttercream frosting. Then I stuck the silver charms in between the layers of the cake, careful to leave the ribbons hanging out in full view but the charms hidden."

"How long did it take you to do that?" Seema asks me with a hint of disapproval.

"And make it look pretty? About three hours," I am forced to admit.

The girls widen their eyes at me. I shrug. "What can I say? Since losing my job, I've discovered the joys of making a mess in the kitchen, needlepoint, and doing vodka shots at noon."

As Seema snags a finger full of frosting, I watch Mel inspect the ribbons closely. Mel's interest is clearly piqued. "So if someone picks the engagement ring, does that mean they're the next to get engaged?"

"Right," I tell Mel as I point to her. "That's the one you're going to get. And I'm making sure the baby carriage goes to Heather . . ."

"Is she the one at your old job doing the IVF?" Seema asks.

"Yeah. Poor thing has gone through three cycles already. Oh, and speaking of people from my old job, my friend Carolyn was fired during the latest round of layoffs, so she gets the typewriter."

"Wait. How do you know which charm everyone's going to get?" Seema asks.

I look at her like that's the stupidest question I've ever heard. "I rigged the cake."

Mel eyes me suspiciously. "How do you *rig* a cake?"

I proudly point to a red toothpick at the bottom of the cake, ever so slightly hidden by gobs of vanilla buttercream. "See that toothpick there? When we put out the cake, I'll make sure the toothpick faces me at the table. Since everyone has a place card, I know exactly where each woman will be sitting. With that chart in mind, I slipped the perfect charm for each girl's future into the part of the cake closest to her."

I grab my purse from the dining room table and pull out a folded paper map. I unfold the map to show Seema and Mel a giant circle with twenty-four spokes radiating out of it. On the outside of each spoke is a guest's name and inside the spoke is the charm they will get. I point to where Mel will sit. "For example, Mel, here you are . . . ," then I point to a ribbon on the cake, "and here is your corresponding charm: the ring. Seema, you're here. And here's your charm: the red hot chili pepper. Which means you'll be the next one to have a red hot romance."

Mel promptly pulls her assigned ribbon from the cake.

"What are you doing?" I exclaim.

She looks at the silver solitaire ring attached to the ribbon. "Just making sure your map works."

I grab the charm from her. "It works!" I insist as I carefully slide the ring back between the cake layers. "I spent a long time on this. Don't mess it up."

Seema laughs to herself. "So that's what you think I need most in my life? Hot sex?"

"Don't all people need hot sex in their lives?" I counter.

"Fair enough. But why can't I pick which charm I want?" Seema asks. She takes the list from me and reads, "Like the wishing well, why can't I have that?"

"What would you wish for? Scott?" I ask knowingly.

I can tell from the way Seema shrugs her shoulders that I'm right about that one.

"Okay," Seema concedes. "But what about the hot air balloon? I've always wanted to go to Napa and take a ride in a hot air balloon."

"No," I say, shaking my head determinedly. "The hot air balloon is for my friend Julia. It symbolizes adventure and travel. She's never been out of California. It's time."

"Why wouldn't *you* want the hot air balloon?" Mel asks me as she looks over Seema's shoulder to read the chart.

"I'm already spending two weeks in Italy for my honeymoon. I don't need more travel," I tell her. Then I let them in on my dream. "No. What I want is the shovel."

Mel furrows her brow. "What's the shovel stand for?"

I smile proudly. "A lifetime of hard work."

Seema and Mel exchange a concerned look. Seema shakes her head. "Sometimes I worry about her."

"Seriously, I have to get back to work. I'm going nuts at home."

Seema nods, then says sarcastically, "Yeah, it must be terrible having to sleep past five in the morning."

I cross my arms. "Actually, for me it is—"

I'm about to begin a diatribe when Seema's doorbell rings.

My guests have arrived.

I point to the toothpick, then to Mel. "When you bring out the cake, make sure the toothpick faces me. You'll get your ring, I'll get my shovel, Seema will get her pepper. Be diligent. I don't want to leave anything to chance."

• • •

Two hours, three new toasters, four place settings, and one obvious regift later, my gaggle of female guests are tipsy, well fed, and (most importantly) sitting in their assigned seats.

Mel brings out the cake for dessert. I am treated to a bunch of "ooohs" and "aaahs" from the group.

Mel places the cake about three feet from me, in the center of the table. As we planned, she is careful to place the covered red toothpick dead center in front of me.

I give everyone a brief history of the cake pull: an old Southern tradition, charm reveals your future: blah, blah, blah. Then I hold up a sheet of pastel-pink paper. "Each of you has a chart like this one under your place cards. The list will tell you what your charm means. Okay, now, everyone, I want you to loop your finger through the ribbon *closest to you* . . ."

They all do *exactly* as I instruct, each girl putting her index finger into the correct satin loop. I do a quick mental scan of the table to make sure everyone has their finger in the right loop. Then I put my finger through my assigned white loop, and say, "On your mark. Get set. PULL!"

I hear a cacophony of laughter and delight as we all pull out our charms.

And I pull . . . the baby carriage.

Shit.

As the women begin licking the cake crumbs and frosting off of their charms and reading their pink charts, I hear our friend Ginger squeal, "Oh my God! I got the diamond ring! That means I'm the next to get engaged, right?"

That can't be right. Ginger's been dating her boyfriend Jeff for all of three months. She was supposed to get the fleur-de-lis, which means "Love will blossom."

I look over at Mel, whose face has fallen as she watches our friend Ginger show off the exact same ring charm Mel pulled out two hours ago. I lean over to her and whisper, "What did you get?"

Mel glares at me. "The red hot chili pepper."

"But then what did See . . ." I start to ask, turning to see Seema holding up the shovel, then draining the rest of her peach Bellini.

Shit, shit, shit.

My friend Carolyn gleefully says, "Hey, I got the money bag. Maybe I should go buy a lottery ticket tonight."

"No, no . . ." I blurt out. "Didn't you get the typewriter?"

"No. But why would I want the typewriter?" Carolyn asks, genuinely confused.

"Because you're a journalist. I figured with all the layoffs, you'd want good luck getting a new job."

Carolyn's having fun with the pull, not taking it seriously at all. She shrugs. "Well, if I win the lottery, I'll just start my own paper."

"I got the typewriter!" Jacqueline, Jason's ex-wife, cheerfully says. "Which is awesome, because I'm up for a speechwriting job for the governor."

"You're up for a job with the governor?" I ask her nervously. "As in the guy who lives in Sacramento?"

She's thinking of moving Jason's daughters to Sacramento? When was she planning on springing that news on us?

"It's a long shot," Jacqueline assures me. "The mayor put in a good word for me. Still . . ." She holds up the silver typewriter. "Nice to have a good luck charm."

I open my hand, clenched tightly in a fist, and stare at the baby carriage.

A good luck charm. Yeah . . . that would have been nice.

I close my hand around the charm again, force a smile to my

guests, and excuse myself to the kitchen. Once I'm in the sanctuary of Seema's kitchen, I open my clutched fist once again to reveal the baby carriage.

A baby carriage. WTF?

I can't have a baby! First off, I have no desire to ever touch diarrhea or spit-up. Plus, I like sleep. And I like spending my money on whatever I want. (What mother in her right mind would spend three hundred dollars on a pair of suede pumps with a college fund to worry about?) But the most important reason that I can't have a baby is a nonnegotiable . . . I like being able to hyperfocus on my career as a newspaper reporter, a job which has stalled enough in the past year without a mewling infant on my hip taking away any shot I have of ever writing again.

It's not that I don't like babies. I do. I love holding them, playing with them, being an auntie, and then SENDING THEM HOME. It's why I make such a great stepmother but would make a lousy mother.

I almost didn't date Jason after I found out he had children.

When I first met Jason at a museum fund-raiser Seema had put together, I thought he was gorgeous, charming, and smart. Wickedly smart, which sort of surprised me for a former NBA basketball player, who was now an NBA assistant coach here in L.A. The first hour we talked, I was totally smitten. He was thirty-seven at the time (six years older than me, a bit past my comfort zone), but he was a very in-shape and smokin'-hot thirty-seven. As we talked and laughed, I started thinking about fate, and the silver heart charm I had pulled earlier that day, and how you just never know when the right one is going to come along.

Then he mentioned his two daughters, who at the time were four and eight. *Damn*, I thought to myself—*I knew there had to be something wrong with him.* Within minutes, I had politely excused myself and started scoping out other men at the party.

But I kept running into him: he was at the bar getting a drink when I popped by for a refill, later I turned a corner to see him admiring one of the Monets. At the end of the night, he was behind me in line for the valet.

He asked for my number. I told him I was seeing someone.

After the valet pulled up with my car, we stood by my open car door talking for so long, the valet actually asked us to move it along. Jason asked for my number again. I politely declined.

Then he asked Seema for my number. She called me right after she gave it to him to declare that I was an idiot, that she had overruled me, and that he was perfect for me.

When Jason first started calling, I used the accepted code of those not interested: I couldn't do this weekend, I would be out of town. I was really busy with work during the week. My weekend was completely booked as my cat, Mr. Whiskers, had died, and I was planning his funeral. There was no Mr. Whiskers, and I'm allergic to cats. But I figured nothing turns off a guy faster than a crazy cat lady. (By the way, he was onto me. He sent flowers and asked if he could attend the service.)

Despite my rebuffs over the next few weeks, I always stayed on the phone a little too long and thought about him a little too much the next day. So, after he asked me out for the tenth time, I agreed. I mean, for God's sake, the guy wasn't proposing, he was asking me to dinner. And what was wrong with dressing up on a Saturday night to gaze at an elegant man with poreless caramel-colored skin and clear hazel eyes?

During our dinner I discovered (to my astonishment) that this guy was a real guy. He actually pursued me: a rarity in Los Angeles. I was used to typical L.A. neurotic guys. Men who would call once every eight to ten days, with no rhyme or reason to when or why they would call. Men who asked me to go dutch at dinner. Men who were incredibly attentive until they got sex, then talked ad nauseum about how they weren't sure if they had time for a relationship. (At which point they, too, would call at random times, although at least then I knew the reason.)

But this guy asked me out again before the first date was even over.

He knew what he wanted and—like everything else in his life—he planned to go after it until he won. If other men in Los Angeles are like toy poodles—yippy and useless—this guy was a Labrador: hardworking, loyal, a bit slobbery, and beautiful.

A month later, I agreed to meet his kids. And I fell in love with them immediately. Megan was a gorgeous eight-year-old (now nine) who cracked me up with a knock-knock joke and had fun polishing my toenails. Malika, four at the time, had the cutest voice I'd ever heard. There was (and is) nothing she says that I don't want to repeat to all of my friends, because it's just so damn cute.

That said, it took me a while to feel comfortable in my role as stepmother. And frankly, I screwed up sometimes. Like when I snapped at Malika for repeating the same sentence for the sixth time, or when I drove Megan to her school for her dance recital instead of to the auditorium the school had rented, thereby giving us all of four minutes to run from the parking lot to the correct stage to begin her dance.

This summer, the girls have been living with us full-time, per the custody agreement. I love it, but I am ready to rip my hair out. I seriously don't know how mothers do this full-time. We can't go out to dinner without Malika insisting on sitting next to me (never her father) and screaming in my ear the entire time. And I can't insist she sit next to her father, because then I'll look like a mean stepmonster.

Oh, and on the subject of food: what is it with kids and not eating anything? Malita is the picky eater to end all picky eaters. We had an argument last week because I used tomato sauce on my homemade pizza rather than "pizza sauce." It wasn't worth the fight—it's just pizza—so I nuked her some fish sticks instead.

The same thing happened with the gourmet mac and cheese I slaved over one night. It was baked. It was white. It was pronounced "wrong," "weird," and "yucky."

We have been eating neon-orange mac and cheese from a box ever since.

And don't get me started on all the driving! Whatever happened to summers off? This summer the girls have had a combination of ballet camp, museum camp, zoo camp, and music camp. Of course, neither girl has the same camp as her sister, and inevitably each week's camp is at least ten miles (meaning forty-five L.A. driving minutes) from the sister's camp.

Jason has had a full-time job all summer prepping his team for the next season. I currently have no job. Guess who does 90 percent of the driving?

I love these kids. I really do. But in one week, they go on a Caribbean cruise with their mother, and then it's back to school for them—and back to weekend parenting for me.

Politically incorrect though this may be, I am not only counting down the days until my honeymoon, I'm counting down the days until I get my life back.

I look down at the silver carriage again.

Nope. I'm barely hanging on as a part-time stepmonster—there's no way I'm ready to have a baby.

Seema and Mel walk into the kitchen. Seema hands me a Bellini, then says, "Sweetie, it's a cake, not an augury. It doesn't mean anything."

Easy for her to say. Ever since we were in college, Seema has lambasted me for my belief in fortune-tellers, good luck charms, and fate.

"Yes it does!" I say, almost crying. "You don't understand. At the last two showers I've been to, every woman's fortune came true. There was this woman who couldn't have a baby, who got the carriage. Pregnant two weeks later. One person got the wishing well—said out loud she wanted a new job in New York, totally got an offer."

"Okay," Seema concedes, "but, with all due respect: the woman who got pregnant could have been doing IVF for the past year. And the woman who wished for the new job had probably been working on getting that job for a while."

"You gotta admit," Mel says, opening her hand to examine her pepper. "It is a pretty big coincidence."

"No, it's not," Seema counters. "It's people having enough faith in their lives to work hard and go after their dreams. Here," Seema says, taking Mel's pepper. "Give me this. Nic, give me your charm."

I hand Seema my charm. She places it and the other two charms in the palm of her right hand, covers her hand with her left, and shakes her hands like she's about to roll dice. "Supercalifragilisticexpialidocious."

Seema opens her hands, then gives the baby carriage charm to Mel. "You take this. Nic, you get the shovel. And I'll take the chili pepper."

"Why do I get the baby carriage?!" Mel practically howls.

Seema glares at Mel. "I thought you didn't want the chili pepper."

"Well, I want it more than a baby carriage!" Mel whines.

Seema rolls her eyes. "Fine. You want the engagement ring, right?"

She waits for a response from Mel, who looks down and shrugs self-consciously.

"Be right back," Seema says.

As she leaves the kitchen, I look down at the shovel. "Maybe since she hid it in her hand, it could kind of count. . . ."

"What the Hell is wrong with you?!" we hear someone screech in condemnation from the other room.

Seema comes racing back in, with my friend Ginger running in after her. "Mel! I got you your engagement ring. Quick! Throw the carriage at her!"

Three

Seema

That night, Scott keeps me company while I clean up all of the shower refuse scattered about my house.

Or, I should say, Scott comes over so we can get drunk on left-over champagne and hors d'oeuvres, then watch a double feature of wedding movies together. We each picked one: he picked *Wedding Crashers*, I went with *27 Dresses*.

Okay, so we're not the most romantic couple in the world.

"What the Hell is this?" Scott asks, picking up a stainless-steel serving platter from the pile of gifts Nic had left behind to pick up tomorrow.

"What's what?" I yell from the kitchen, as I collect some freshly washed champagne flutes from my dish rack. I look through my kitchen doorway to watch Scott as he holds up the platter and scrutinizes it.

"It looks like a giant . . . comma?" Scott says questioningly.

"That might be the weirdest gift of the day," I say, as I emerge from my kitchen with my flutes and an open bottle of just-popped Taltarni sparkling wine. "Someone at the party said it's a *traif* dish."

"A what?" Scott asks, as he turns it slightly in his hands to examine it further.

"A *traif* dish," I repeat. "You know . . . for serving *traif*."

"And that would be what?" he asks me.

"Um . . . shrimp I think?"

Scott shakes his head as he puts down the platter. "Okay, you can make fun of us men all you want for wasting money on lap dances during a bachelor party, but wasting money on a *traif* dish you'll never use is just as sinful. Maybe even more so."

"How do you figure it's 'more so'?" I ask, as I put the glasses down on my coffee table.

"At least the twenties we're handing out at the strip club will help pay for the girls' college education."

"They're never really going to college," I say with a tone of disgust, as I reach for the pitcher of peach puree, left largely untouched by my guests.

"So says you. Let me keep my fantasies. Oh, honey, please don't put peach glop into my drink."

He called me "Honey," I happily think to myself, as I stare at Scott examining all of Nic's shower gifts. As I fill his flute with bubbly, my imagination immediately rushes to the fantasy of what it would be like to have him here in my living room, looking through all of *our* wedding gifts. I hand him his glass. "One glass of champagne, sans peach glop."

"Thank you," he says, taking the glass as he makes himself comfortable next to me on my sofa. "So next week—'black tie' doesn't really mean I have to go rent a tuxedo, right?"

"Not if you already own one, no," I answer him teasingly.

This is one of our running gags with each other. I love clothes and shoes. Scott could not care less if he tried.

Tonight, for example. Once the shower was over, I changed out of my perfect "bridal shower" long pastel-peach A-line skirt with matching top, and into dark jeans cut at just the right waist level for this season, a purple Graham & Spencer crew top I just picked up at Fred Segal, and Giuseppe Zanotti sparkly flat sandals that were full price, and in my mind worth every penny. I put a lot of time and effort into my look. Buying the pants alone took at least three hours, and included two runner-up pairs and me turning around in the dressing room to stare at my backside at least five times while asking Nic if they made my butt look big.

Scott, on the other hand, is wearing a wrinkled "Stone Brewing Co." T-shirt with blue jeans: one of his many "pick out of the clean laundry basket because God forbid I should ever fold anything and put it in a drawer" ensembles. It took him all of two minutes to get ready. Five, if you include a shower. The "just laid" look is one that no woman could ever pull off but one that guys like Johnny Depp and Scott will probably get away with until well after they hit the nursing home.

I hate men. More pay for equal work, no labor pains, and they can be ready to go out in two minutes flat. So unfair.

Anyway, despite the frat boy look, I still want to pounce on him, right here and right now, and take advantage of his virtue. But God knows it's not because he's trying. He's never trying. He just *is*.

Scott smirks. "I could rent an aquamarine tuxedo to match your dress."

"You do and no one will give you a blow job that night," I warn him.

"Like I would have a shot at meeting anyone anyway. I'm already going to be with the prettiest girl in the room. The others will be too intimidated to talk to me."

"Aw . . ." I say. Then I reiterate firmly, "You still need a tux."

"Now, are you sure you really want me to rent one? What about that guy you're seeing? Conrad. Don't you think it would be better to take him?"

My shoulders tense up. I've been avoiding this subject all week. "Um . . . actually, we broke up."

Scott furrows his brows. "What? When?"

"Last week," I say, trying to use a light and breezy tone. "It's good, really. It just wasn't quite right. And, you know, it was getting to that point where we were either going to sleep together or not, and I just . . ."

I pause. *I just kept thinking of you. And comparing him to you. And even though he was way more appropriate for me, all I could think about was you.*

Scott is staring deep into my eyes, and I worry he can see right through me.

So I make a joke of it. "Quit looking at me like that. I'm fine. Besides, I really did not want to take a date who I knew was temporary just so that I could have well-meaning people embarrass me all night with questions like, 'So, have you two talked about marriage yet?' "

Scott laughs. Tension diffused. "Why do people do that at weddings?" Scott asks, shaking his head appreciatively. "It's right up there with asking a single person if they're seeing 'anyone special'. I always want to answer, 'No. Is your prostate still giving you trouble?' " He glances at a pile of pastel-pink index cards on my coffee table. He looks at the top card. "Brad Pitt. What's this?"

"Oh, that's this game we played called fantasy Date/Date from Hell. Everyone had to write down who their ideal celebrity date would be, and then their celebrity date from Hell. Then we all had to guess which girl picked which dates."

Scott shoots me a mischievous look as he picks up the pile. "Oooo . . . I'll bet I can guess who you picked."

I grab the cards away from him. "No, you can't. Besides, I don't want you making fun of me."

Scott playfully tries to grab the cards back. “I’m not going to make fun of you.”

“You can’t help it. It’s in your DNA.”

“No. Seriously—I’ll be good.”

Off my dubious look, he continues. “Come on, it’ll be fun. I’ll show you how well I know you.”

He puts out his hand for the cards. I eye his open hand wearily.

“Fine,” I say, about to hand him the cards. “But first you need to tell me your ideal celebrity date.”

Scott looks up at my ceiling, seemingly giving my question serious thought. “Um . . . I guess my ideal would be Drew Brees,” Scott answers. “And that stupid blond chick with the reality show—she’d be the worst.”

“The quarterback?!” I exclaim. “But you’re not gay! Wait, you’re *not*, are you?”

“No,” Scott assures me. “And neither is he. But if I get to go out to dinner with any celebrity in the world, why waste that on a first date that will inevitably lead nowhere?” He rubs his fingers together. “Cards please.”

I reluctantly hand him the pink cards. Shit—when he sees the name on my card, he will so obviously associate it with himself. Fuck! That name is about to give away my crush, and then he’ll never see me the same way again.

Scott leafs through the cards. “Ben Affleck,” he guesses.

I am tempted to lie, say *yes* and get it over with. But I know the other side of the card is Hugh Hefner and, while the old man is gross, he can’t be the worst guy in the world to be on a date with. So I am forced to admit, “Not a bad choice, but no.”

He continues to fan through the cards. “Jason Washington is obviously who Nic chose . . .” Then he guesses, “Bradley Cooper?”

"What? Him? No."

"John Krasinski."

"No."

"It's not the actor on *Heroes*, is it?"

"Dr. Suresh? No. Why do you assume just because I'm Indian, I'm going to go for an Indian?"

"I don't," Scott says triumphantly, proving how well he knows me as he turns around the card to show me Zachary Quinto's name (Sylar on *Heroes*).

I shrug, and concede, "Actually, Zachary Quinto's kind of hot in a 'take your damn Spock ears off' kind of way."

" 'Take your damn Spock ears off.' Sexy," Scott deadpans, as he leafs through the cards. "Fabio?"

"He's from the dates from Hell side of the card, you moron."

Scott stops at one card. He cocks his head to one side. "Orlando Bloom?" he guesses.

"Yeah," I admit quietly.

Scott looks up at me, looking a bit perplexed. "Seriously? He doesn't seem like your type."

Considering Scott is a dead ringer for Bloom, you'd think he'd pick up on the hint. Oh yeah, right—he's a guy. They pick up on hints about as well as magnets pick up seashells.

Now I'm defensive. "Why wouldn't he be my type? He's cute. I know people who have worked for him, and he's really nice. . . ."

"It's not that. It's that he has dark hair. You normally go for blonds."

"No I don't. Why would you say that?"

Scott shrugs. "Your last two boyfriends are blondish. Both had blue eyes. I figured that was your type. Who was your hell date?"

"Antonin Scalia," I respond, still reeling from Scott's obvious misinterpretation of me and my "type."

"The Supreme Court justice?" Scott asks, as he finishes looking through the cards. "Not really a celebrity. Who picked Stephen Colbert?"

"I don't have a type," I continue. "There's no type."

"Please," Scott says, flashing me a patronizing look. "No offense sweetheart, but you like the westside type: blond hair, or had blond hair as a kid at least, a little bland, has some sort of nonartistic job that he's a bit bored with, but which is stable. You know, like an actuary or a strategic planner. Lives in a condo west of La Cienega . . ."

Now I'm fuming. "That is so not true. I dated an actuary *once*, and I have dated a lot of artists."

"Not for more than a date or two. Then you find something wrong with them, and move on."

I have nothing to say back, but my feelings are hurt. He doesn't see it: he genuinely has no idea how much I like him. And the only way for me to ever let him know how much would be to go so far out on a limb that my weight could easily shatter the branch.

Scott smiles. Tickles me under my chin. "There's nothing wrong with it. I don't like dating artists either. I'll admit I'd rather have a downtown lawyer than a westside computer geek, but we're pretty much the same."

I still look sad. Scott knows this, but he has no idea why.

My phone rings. Saved by the bell. I walk over to my landline and answer. "Hello?"

"Is Scott there?" Nic whispers into her end of the phone. "Am I disturbing anything?"

"Never," I say, maybe a little too brightly. "We're just drinking champagne, going through your gifts, and figuring out which ones you won't miss."

"Ginger just called me," Nic tells me in full panic mode. "She got engaged tonight."

The guest who pulled the ring charm.

Shit.

"And it's all my fault!" Nic continues. "If I hadn't tried to get Mel hitched, none of this would have ever happened. I wouldn't be checking my birth control pills to make sure the pharmacy didn't accidentally switch them with mini SweeTarts, you wouldn't be doomed to a life of hard work, and Karen wouldn't be avoiding going to Oklahoma City next week."

"Oklahoma City?" I ask.

"She got the tornado charm," Nic tells me, her voice getting more anxious and high pitched. "Which was supposed to go to Samantha to guarantee a whirlwind life. I fucked everything up."

"Okay, take it down a notch," I advise. "Don't go off all half cocked, it's just a coincidence."

"It's not a coincidence, and I am completely cocked," Nic insists, sounding more frightened than the babysitter in a slasher movie. "It's happening."

"You say that with a tone of voice like we're in the middle of Armageddon."

"I can't have a baby right now," Nic says. "I have no job."

I resist the urge to point out that she's thirty-two, has found the love of her life—the holy grail for all of us singles out there still searching—and that he has money and wants to fill their house with their laughing babies. Right now is the perfect fucking time to have a baby. I have a job—they're not all they're cracked up to be.

Instead, I cover the phone's mouthpiece and whisper to Scott, "I need cake."

"I'm on it," he says, standing up. "Fridge?"

"Cake stand on the counter," I tell him.

He makes a show of closing his eyes, shaking his head, and opening his eyes again. "Cake stand? Another thing women don't really need."

I playfully push him. "Just get me cake." Then I turn my attention back to Nic. "No, I'm still here. Just talking to Scott for a second."

"I would *not* be a good mother," Nic insists. "Even the idea of changing a diaper disgusts me. The *Teletubbies* bore me. I'll admit, I like *Sesame Street,* but a Snuffleupagus fan does not a mommy make."

I sigh. "Are you still taking your pills?" I ask her.

"Religiously. I'm starting to wonder if they come in extra-strength."

"Then you have nothing to worry about," I assure her. "I'm not saying that I believe in the magic of the charms. But even if I did, maybe the carriage just symbolizes that you're about to have children in your house part-time. Maybe it's just about the girls."

Nic takes a moment to consider that possibility. "Yeah, it could be that, I guess . . ."

As Nic continues talking, I watch Scott in the doorway of my kitchen. Man, he is so cute. And he's here with me on a Saturday night. To watch wedding movies. Why won't I make a move?

"Malika's calling for me to read to her," Nic says, "I gotta go. Any chili pepper hotness going on?"

"Not yet," I admit. "But the night is young, and he's still sober. Give me time."

Nic laughs. "Remember, it's that or you have to revert to your original shovel."

"Thanks for the incentive."

"I love you," Nic tells me.

"Love you too. Bye." I hang up the phone just as Scott appears with two slices of chocolate cake. "I cut big slices, as there really is no such thing as too much cake," he says, as he hands a massive slice to me.

"A man after my own heart," I (half) joke as I take the cake and settle in on the couch to take a huge bite.

Scott sits down next to me. "Who was that?"

"Nic. She's a little stressed."

"Cold feet?" Scott asks, as he takes a bite of cake.

"No. It's silly, really. We just played this game where—"

"Ow!" Scott yelps, grabbing his mouth. He sticks out his tongue and pulls something silver out of his mouth. "What the . . ."

The charm is not attached to a ribbon, and I can't see which one it is. Scott opens his hand to examine it. "There's a heart in my cake."

The heart charm: the next one to find true love.

Four
Melissa

I hate to be a bad friend, but really, is there any woman over the age of sixteen who actually *likes* going to bridal showers? I mean, besides happily married pregnant women who can gloat, and tell us in excruciating detail how their husbands proposed.

I'm sitting with my boyfriend, Fred, in a ridiculously romantic restaurant, with an incredible view of the city lights. He looks positively dapper tonight: his swimmer's body looks fantastic in his new navy-blue suit; his brown eyes sparkle as he tells me a story about his day, and he seems to be in a really good mood. We're having lovely wine and fantastic sushi. But instead of focusing on what I do have (a boyfriend who showers me with romantic dinners), I am paying attention to what I don't have (a ring on my finger).

I can't believe Ginger got the ring charm. Of course she'll be the next one to get married. She's one of those beautiful women who always has ten doe-eyed suitors doting on her at any given moment. Women like that don't need to force the issue of marriage—it's just part of the natural course of things for them. Like having exactly one boy and one girl, so you don't miss out on the experience of parenting either one. And being supported by your husband if you choose to quit your job to go be a mom for ten years. And by that I mean supported both financially and emotionally—like having a guy around who loves you enough to want to have kids with you.

Fred doesn't want kids. Or at least not with me. I'm a high school calculus and physics teacher, and any time I mention kids, he counters my hints by pointing out that boys with mothers who are freakishly good in math have a much higher incidence of autism and Asperger's.

Which might be true. I wasn't the easiest kid to raise, and maybe these days I'd be diagnosed with one of those disorders. I have to force myself to look people in the eye—I hate doing it. Always have. That's a sign of both Asperger's and autism. Plus I have a high IQ: 177. That's frequently another sign.

Fred's laughing as he finishes his story about someone at his law firm. (He's a divorce lawyer. Which might be why he's so anti-marriage.)

Instead of laughing with him, I'll admit I'm kind of in my own world tonight. Fred takes my hand and asks me sweetly, "Are you okay? You seem . . . distant."

"Sorry," I say, sad but trying to cover.

Should I tell him about the ring charm? Ruin a perfectly good evening by bringing up marriage again? Maybe. I mean, honesty is supposed to be the cornerstone of a good relationship. Why shouldn't I let him know how much his actions are hurting me?

I chicken out. "I was just thinking about how happy Nic and Jason looked earlier today. Like they've never not known each other. Pretty amazing after only one year together."

Fred starts chuckling. He says playfully, "Here it comes."

I know very fucking well what he means, but I still ask in irritation, "Here what comes?"

"Oh, isn't marriage wonderful?" Fred says in a dreamy voice.

"We should think about getting married. We'd have the cutest children."

He playfully touches my nose and jokes, "Trying to give me ideas."

God, I am so sick of this. I push his hand away from me. "I wasn't doing anything except telling you how happy they looked."

"Okay, I'm sorry. Now you're mad."

"I'm not mad. I'm tired," I say. "It's been six years. A girl gets tired after six years."

Fred gets a pained expression on his face. "Mel, I'm just not there yet."

"Six years," I repeat, my voice rising. "When are you going to be there? Seven? Eight? Twenty? Just give me a number, so I know what my options are."

Fred looks around the restaurant self-consciously, then leans in toward me and lowers his voice. "Honey, please don't do this."

I make a conscious effort to keep my voice low, but can still hear myself getting angrier. "Seriously, what is it going to take? What event has to happen that you suddenly realize that you love me, and that you want to spend the rest of your life with me?"

Fred looks down at the tablecloth, and away from me. "I don't know," he says sadly. "But can't we just have a nice evening? Do we have to have this fight again tonight?"

I sigh, too. I hate not getting through to him. He either doesn't know how important this is to me, or doesn't care.

And I know exactly what's going to happen tonight. First, I will have a fleeting thought in my head of how I will live without him. About how I'll go home, right after dinner, pack my bags, move out of his house, and move back in with Seema. I'll think about how I will finally have the courage to get on with my life. I'll daydream that I'll find a new guy who can make a commitment. Who loves me enough to make a commitment. I'll imagine what it'll be like and wonder whether or not I am strong enough to do this—to be by myself after six years. And by the time dessert comes, in my head we'll be broken up. It will just be a matter of saying it aloud.

And then, over dinner Fred will become the sweetest, most attentive boyfriend ever. He'll tell me how much he loves me, hug me, passionately kiss me, give me the best sex of my life, and then fall asleep, with me fitting perfectly in his arms.

The next morning he'll do something incredibly romantic: breakfast in bed, complete with champagne. Or an impromptu trip to Santa Barbara for the day. And I'll be happy again (for the most part) and feel loved and treasured (mostly). And I won't bring up marriage again.

Until the next event happens that breaks my heart.

Fred gently takes my hand. "I have an early birthday present for you," he says.

Yes—I am an idiot. As he fishes in his pocket, I feel a rushing surge of hope that he will pull out a square-shaped, velvet box.

Instead, he pulls out a travel magazine. "Here. Go to the page with the Post-it on it."

I flip through to page ninety-seven, where I see a yellow Post-it over an article about Bora Bora, and a picture of overwater bungalows looking out over a large mountain. "It's beautiful," I say, confused.

"We're going," Fred says, flashing me a wide grin. "For ten days. Tahiti, then Bora Bora. Starting the day after Nic's wedding. Check out the next page—it shows what our room looks like."

I go to the next page to see the inside of a bungalow built right over the turquoise-blue water. It is stunning: there's a high ceiling with a thatched roof, teakwood furnishings, a king-size bed with a fluffy white comforter, and plenty of cushy pillows everywhere. In the step-down living room part of the suite is a glass coffee table that you can flip open to feed the tropical fish swimming beneath.

"You got off work?" I ask him incredulously. Fred works all the time. We haven't had a vacation together in two years, and even then it was a four-day weekend to see his family in New York.

"I thought I needed to take some time for us to just be alone together and reconnect," Fred tells me. "As much as I love you, it seems like we've been drifting apart lately."

I smile as I read about ladders that take you from your room right into the warm turquoise waters of the Pacific. "You can swim with dolphins at this hotel?" I ask, happily surprised. I look up from the magazine. "I've always wanted to swim with dolphins."

Fred is clearly excited to elaborate about his surprise. "I've signed us up for that. And we're going to do this picnic on a private island that's only accessible by boat. Plus there's snorkeling and water sports. And this amazing gourmet restaurant . . ."

I smile, stand up, and give Fred a big hug. "I love it. Thank you."

Fred hugs me back. "I love you so much," he says softly, then kisses me.

I give him another kiss, then sit back down.

Life is pretty good. I look at the pictures dreamily again and sigh. "I'll bet they have a spa there. Maybe the two of us could get a couple's . . ."

And then the strangest thing happens. Fred looks over my shoulder, and all of the color drains from his face.

I turn around to see a strikingly beautiful woman staring at him from the maître d's podium. She is stunning. Looks like Bar Refeali's way cuter sister.

I turn back to Fred. "What?"

"Uh . . . nothing," he barely manages to squeak out. "Just a client. I did her divorce a few months ago. I'll be right back."

Fred throws down his napkin and quickly rushes up to the

woman. She looks beyond thrilled to run into him, quickly giving him a tight hug and moving in for a kiss. I watch Fred pull away from her uncomfortably. He then kisses the woman's cheek demurely. She looks a little thrown by his reaction—not angry, just puzzled.

Then she sees me. And she's pissed. Fred gently takes her hand, and the two of them talk. Eventually, Bar looks at me inquisitively, kisses Fred good-bye on the cheek, then leaves the restaurant.

Once she is out of my sight, Fred walks back up to our table, and takes his seat. "I'm sorry I didn't get a chance to introduce you. She was just leaving. Where were we?"

I stare at him. "You're fucking her, aren't you?"

Honestly, I don't know why I said that. The words came tumbling out of my mouth before I could think about them.

But suddenly I can't breathe. It's as though my entire body instinctively knows what's happening, and my brain is struggling to catch up.

"What?" Fred says, unconsciously looking around the room for a moment. "Why would you say that?"

I take a deep breath, throw down my cloth napkin, and look him dead in the eye. "Fred, do you want to get married or not?"

"Wow," Fred says, clearly stunned by my outburst. "Because I'm not ready to get married, somehow I'm now cheating on you?"

I'm about to answer him with, "Yes. Why else would a man wait six years, unless it's to sample what else is out there?"

But before I can say anything, from the corner of my eye I watch a tidal wave of red wine fly past me and hit Fred dead in the face.

I turn to see Bar, the beautiful blonde, with an empty glass in her hand. "Knulla dig! Farväll lögnare!" she spits out angrily at Fred, then turns on her heel and marches away.

I'm stunned. My jaw drops. I want to get up from the table, but my legs are frozen.

Fred begins calmly wiping his face clean. "I guess she didn't like the settlement I got for her."

Five

Seema

"So you're saying this means I'm about to find my true love?" Scott asks me as he plays with his new charm and smiles so wide that I can't tell if he's fucking with me or genuinely thrilled to hear such news.

"I'm saying *Nicole* thinks it does," I clarify. "I know it's completely bogus, but you should have seen how she flipped out when—"

"How do you know?" Scott interrupts.

"How do I know what?"

"How do you know it's completely bogus? What scientific proof do you have?"

My shoulders drop. "Stop that."

Scott smiles and shrugs his shoulders. "You just said her friend Ginger just got engaged. Maybe the universe is trying to tell you something."

I make a point of sighing loudly and rolling my eyes. "There were twenty-three girls at the party today who pulled charms. One of them pulled a charm that coincided with her future. Twenty-two others—twenty-three, if you include your heart—did not. Mel isn't suddenly going to have a wild sex life with her boyfriend of six years, Nic won't get pregnant if she doesn't want to, I'm not going to work any harder at my job than I already have to, and you're not falling in love anytime soon."

Scott looks me in the eye and seems to genuinely ask me, "How do you know?"

I cross my arms, irked. "How do I know . . . which one?"

He shrugs and smiles. "Pick one. Any one. How do you know I won't be the next person to fall in love?"

It's at that point that I realize—maybe he's already fallen in love with the girl he just started seeing two weeks ago.

Damn it. Why didn't I break up with Conrad sooner? Better yet, why didn't I make my move on Scott sooner? I had almost a fucking year, and I blew it. I should have just kissed him that first night and gotten it all out in the open. Either he would have been interested—in which case I wouldn't be in this Hell (not even Hell—limbo. At least in Hell, you know who your enemies are), or he wouldn't have been interested, in which case I could have had him as a coffee friend but never allowed myself to fall for him.

I look at his beautiful face. He's smiling, and his sparkling eyes seem to be dancing. His lips are pink and plump and sexy, and I desperately want to kiss him. I do. I ache for it. Even though I know it's no good for me, I will dream about it a hundred times tonight before I go to sleep. I'll fantasize about the perfect place, the perfect time, how he'll kiss me back, and how my life will be changed forever.

But this isn't the perfect time or place. There never has been a perfect time or place, and now that he's dating someone new, there probably never will be.

Scott jokingly wags his eyebrows up and down like Groucho Marx in an old black-and-white film. My eyes narrow, and I eye him suspiciously. "You are totally fucking with me, aren't you?"

Scott laughs. "Of course I'm fucking with you." He lifts up his silver heart to inspect it in the light. "I'm constantly amazed that women, particularly intelligent women, believe this crap. When was the last time you heard of a guy reading his horoscope or having his tarot cards read?" He slips the heart into his pocket. "I do want to keep this, though. I have a piece I'm working on that I want to put it in."

I smirk "Please don't tell me you're calling the piece, 'Crap Women Believe In.'"

Scott laughs. "THAT would be an awesome piece! I could totally get some bachelor to buy that!" He pulls a small notebook from his pocket, and a black ink pen. "The battle of the sexes always fascinates me," he says, as he begins sketching his new project. "I could do it all in powder-pink and white, like a wedding . . ." I watch him as he quickly (and flawlessly) sketches a three-layer wedding cake as the centerpiece, then surrounds it on all sides with a series of shelves. "For the top shelf, I'd intersperse diet books like *The Zone* and *Ten Days to Skinny* with self-help relationship books like *Think Like a Lady, Act Like a Man* and *He's Just Not That Into You*."

"It's *Think Like a Man, Act Like a Lady*," I correct him.

Scott looks up to give me a pitying look. "You disappoint me, Singh."

"I didn't say I bought it, I just know the title. Knowledge is power. And I actually think I like that *Ten Days* diet book. I was leafing through it at the bookstore—it had some interesting ideas."

Scott continues to draw ferociously, a man possessed. "No woman needs a diet book. Every woman I know knows enough on the subject to write a diet book herself. And it would be a short book, too. Page one: walk every day. Page two: if you're wicked serious, go to a gym three times a week and lift a few weights. Page three: quit eating all that crap. Whether your crap is Zingers every time life throws you a curveball, Twinkies hidden in your desk drawer, or eating a two-thousand-calorie 'salad' loaded with dressing and meat, knock it off!" He turns the notebook around for me to scrutinize his work. "What else do I need?"

I look at the drawing and decide to betray my own sex in the name of flirting. "A Christian Louboutin shoe."

"Which a woman believes will help her catch a man. Perfect!" he says, drawing an insanely high heel.

"Plus a DVD of *Sex and the City,* an eyelash curler, maybe a deck of tarot cards . . ."

"You are on fire, girl!" Scott says happily, taking a quick sip of champagne, then going back to his sketch.

My home phone rings. "Hey, can you do one of these about men?" I ask as I head to the phone.

"No," Scott answers me firmly.

"What? Why not?"

"I wouldn't know what to put in the display."

"Under 'Crap Men Believe'?" I exclaim. "You're kidding, right? How about a Knicks jersey, a letter from *Penthouse,* a porn DVD, and an old pizza box."

"Hey—the Knicks have a shot this year. And a porn DVD is clichéd."

"No more clichéd than a diet book," I insist as I sip my champagne. "Oh! And for the center of the piece: a pillowtop mattress thrown onto the middle of the floor, with no box spring or headboard in sight."

Scott laughs at my joke as my phone continues to ring. I look at the caller ID. It's Mel. Damn it. She knows I'm seeing Scott tonight.

I pick up. "Hello."

"I don't think I'm getting the ring or the chili pepper fortune." Mel says, and she sounds like she's been crying. "Do you think there's a toilet charm? Because that is where my life seems to be headed at the moment."

"What happened? Are you all right?"

"No," she says quietly. "If I were all right, I'd be in a romantic restaurant right now planning a trip to Bora Bora with Fred, dreaming of his proposal to me while we're there, and being completely oblivious to where my life was headed. Instead, I am stunned, ready to throw up, and parked in front of your house."

I'm confused. "Wait," I say, walking to my front window, and pushing back my curtains to see her bright blue Prius parked out front. "You're outside? Why aren't you coming in?"

"Because Scott's car is parked in your driveway, and I don't want to bother you," Mel reasons. "But I don't know where else to go. Fred's cheating on me."

Six

Melissa

Seema and Scott run out to get me and bring me inside.

I quickly catch them up on the last hour of my life and have just finished the part about some strange Swedish woman throwing a drink in Fred's face.

I then fill them in on what happened next: Fred wasn't stupid. I saw a woman throw a drink in his face—he wasn't going to get off without a full-blown explanation.

Svetlana, that's her name—as if I could ever compete with a Svetlana—had been a client of Fred's for three months. She was the trophy wife of a seventy-eight-year-old studio head who she caught getting head one night from an even younger woman than herself. Fred was her divorce attorney.

I had actually heard about her. Her husband had forced the final arbitration to be in Manhattan—so Fred was stuck there for a week and a half while both sides hammered out whether a five-year marriage to a decrepit guy was worth one hundred million dollars or one hundred and fifty million.

I remember Fred asked me to go with him to New York, but my high school was in the middle of state testing, and I didn't want to leave my students.

I guess I should have.

I sit on Seema's couch, numb, as I continue my story. "Fred told me, in a moment of tearful confession, that the night the case was settled, he took her out for drinks at the Oak Room. They had too much wine, he walked her back to her suite, she kissed him, and they made out for a few minutes."

"Oh, good Lord . . ." Scott mutters under his breath.

"She's not done with her story yet," Seema tells him.

"Yeah, but obviously . . ."

"Scott . . ." Seema says warningly.

"Fine," Scott says to Seema, crossing his arms. Then he turns to me. "But you do know he's lying about that, right?"

I take a deep breath before I answer, "Honestly, I have no idea."

"Finish your story," Seema tells me sympathetically.

"Yes, you do!" Scott insists to me. "They did NOT just make out for a few minutes. You *do* know that, right?"

I look over at Scott, surprised at his vehemence. I shrug. "He says that's all that happened."

"Oh please. What's he going to say? 'I fucked someone in a hotel room three thousand miles away. I never thought I'd get caught. Oops.' "

His statement makes me burst into tears. Now I'm sad *and* embarrassed. Seema gives me a hug. I can't breathe. I'm feeling sick, my nose is clogged, and my life is over.

I take a Kleenex from a box Scott brought into the living room, wipe my eyes, and gauge Seema's and Scott's reactions.

Seema's eyes are wet as well, she is so shocked and saddened to hear my news. She looks almost as heartbroken as I feel.

Scott, on the other hand, looks angry. And the longer he listens, the angrier he gets.

I take a deep breath, and end my story. "Honestly, I don't know what the truth is," I tell them. "Fred's called me at least seven times on my cell, and left texts. I haven't picked up, because I don't know what to say to him. I'm not ready to go home yet. I'm not even sure if I have a home to go to anymore." I tear up again, but don't cry. "I just have no idea what to think or what to do."

"He's a chode," Scott states matter-of-factly. "You're better off without him."

I stare at him blankly. Seema glares at him. "Don't say things like that!" she chastises Scott.

"Why?" Scott rebuts. "The guy's not only cheating on her, but he's lying about it with some insipid, 'Strange girl only stuck her tongue in my mouth for a couple of minutes' lie! He's a total chode!"

"Because you don't say things like that to someone who doesn't even know they're broken up yet," Seema admonishes.

"What? You're going to tell her to forgive the chode and marry him?" Scott argues.

"Of course I'm not going to tell her to marry the chode," Seema counters. "But there's a time for venting and a time for constructive advice. Check your watch."

"Excuse me," I say quietly. "What's a chode?"

"Chode," Scott repeats. "He's a dick, a knob, a prick—"

"Thank you for the anatomy lesson," Seema interrupts, cutting him off.

"He's also an asshole," Scott can't help but add.

Seema throws down her hand on her coffee table as she asks firmly. "Will you stop that?"

Scott ignores her. Asks me with complete sincerity, "Do you want me to go beat the crap out of him? Because I am so there."

Seema tries a different approach. "Scott, can you go get us some drinks please?"

"She hasn't answered my question."

"She doesn't want you to beat him up," Seema insists. "How is landing yourself in jail going to help her?"

"Actually, I would kind of like him to beat Fred up," I admit to Seema.

She looks mildly horrified.

"I didn't say I was actually going to have Scott do it," I tell Seema. "I know that would be wrong." Then I turn to Scott. "That is so sweet of you to offer, though."

Scott looks a bit disappointed.

Seema takes my hand gently. "What *do* you want?"

"That's the million-dollar question," I tell her. "I want to find a way to get past this. I want it to have never happened."

Seema doesn't say anything—just nods her head knowingly. She gets what I'm saying. She pulls me into a hug, and we just sit there in silence.

Which is broken by the unlikeliest of heroes. "Nooooo!" Scott booms in his masculine voice. He gets up and begins pacing around. "I don't get women sometimes." He flips around to me. "Aren't you *pissed*?!"

Scott's clear green eyes stare right at me. I take a moment to collect my thoughts. "I . . . well, of course I am. I mean—"

"No, no," Scott interrupts. "That's not the sound of an angry woman. That's the sound of a woman who thinks this is somehow her fault."

I think about that for a moment, then admit aloud, "Well, you got me there."

Seema's jaw drops. I try to explain myself to her. "I keep trying to figure out what I could have done differently to make Fred not cheat on me. Maybe if I had gone to the gym more. I'm a runner, but I never lift weights. Or maybe if I had had that nose job—he always teased me about my nose. Or if I had just stayed on a diet—"

Scott interrupts my thoughts. "Jesus—do you realize how ridiculous you sound? You have a smoking body . . ." He turns to Seema. "Wait, I'm allowed to say that, right?"

Seema and I look at each other. "Um . . ." Seema debates. "Can he say that?"

Duh. I nod my head yes.

Scott continues, "Don't be sad. Get angry!" He walks out of the living room and into Seema's office, where he yells, "Sweetheart, where do you keep your notepads?"

"Top right drawer," Seema yells back. Then she looks at me. "Can I get you something? Something with sugar in it? Something with booze in it?"

"Actually," I say, "I would kill for a peach Bellini the size of a small horse."

Seema pats me on the knee, then heads to her kitchen as Scott walks out of her office carrying a legal pad. "Here's what I want you to do," he says, handing me the pad. "I want you to write down one hundred things that you hate most about him."

Seema emerges with a champagne flute just as Scott clarifies his assignment to me. "Not things that are going to make you blame yourself. You can write, 'Number one, he won't marry me.' But only if you realize that that's *his* fault—not yours. Only if the statement means, 'He's an asshole!' Not, 'What could have I have changed about myself?' Personally, I would start with 'He likes Nagel.' And not as an ironic or a kitschy eighties thing; he actually likes him." Scott stops talking as he notices Seema carefully pouring peach puree into the flute. "What the Hell are you doing?"

She looks up at him. "I'm making Mel a drink."

"Are you out of your mind, woman? You're going to give her a bridal shower drink on the day she finds out her boyfriend cheated on her? My God, it's amazing we ever breed with you people. You make no sense."

Scott walks out of the room and into her kitchen. I lean in to Seema. "Where's he going?"

She shakes her head. "I don't know," she sighs. "But I'm sure he's making some testosterone point." She then whispers to me, "Why do I like this guy? He's a total freak."

Scott reappears with a bottle of Gentleman Jack and a shot glass. He opens the bottle, pours a shot, and hands it to me. "Here. Drink this."

I hate whiskey. I look at Scott. "I'm not really a . . ."

"Drink it," he says, in a low, commanding voice.

What the hell?—I drink the shot.

"Well?" Scott asks.

"It's dreadful," I sputter. "Like drinking broken glass."

"For the next hour, if you want a drink, promise me you won't drink overly sweet girlie drinks that will get you drunk, make you cry, and make you long for weddings, true love, or Fred. Drink a man's drink—a hideous drink, if you will. Use it to get angry."

He scribbles *Why Fred is a Chode* on the top of the notepad, then underlines it. "Okay, what's your number one?"

I suddenly feel put on the spot. I have spent the last six years cultivating an image of Fred for all of the world to see. A happy image. A loving image.

An image that might not necessarily have been completely 100 percent true.

I mean, it was true when we met. Fred really was amazing. He was still in law school, and I had just started teaching, and we were both wildly in love, and absolutely sure about what we wanted in life.

Then, somehow, life got in the way.

It wasn't just his high salary and seventy-hour workweeks crashing against my small salary and wanting to keep my summers off. Although certainly not agreeing on how much money and free time you can live with is big. It was sex that slowly got routine, and less and less frequent. And not being able to agree on a place to live together for so long that I finally had to move into his place, which I hated every day. Or not agreeing on a place to go on vacation, which led to not going on vacation together at all.

Sometimes, a relationship withers, and by the time you realize how close it is to death, you don't know what to do to save it.

I desperately want the guy who brought silver roses to me on our second date back. I miss the man who lay in bed with me all day every Sunday, equipped with a *Sunday Times,* a few rented Blu-rays, and breakfast delivered to our door. I want my buddy back who watched *BBC America* with me every Thursday night.

I miss him, and I know he's still lurking somewhere inside the too-sleek yuppie who crawls into bed with me every night. I know he's still there.

Or, at least until tonight, I thought he was still there.

As I stare at the blank sheet of lined paper, I am at a total loss as to what to write.

1. Nagel.

Scott reads my number one upside down. "That's cheating," he says. "I totally served that one up for you. Show some originality."

"But I can't stand Nagel," I point out.

"And I don't like wet socks. Who does? Movin' on to number two."

I'm not really comfortable telling my friends the real reasons my relationship isn't working. So I start by writing down some of my minor grievances:

2. Works too much.

Scott smiles. "Good."

3. Cannot see a dish in the sink to save his life.
4. Will not shop for Christmas presents until December 24th.

Seema reads that one. "Hmmm . . . so basically number four just makes him male."

Scott turns to Seema. "You loved your gift card." Then he turns to me, "Keep going, sweetheart."

5. Blares U2 at 8:00 A.M. on Saturday morning while getting ready for his softball game.
6. Accidentally deletes my DVRed Monday-night sitcoms every time a game is on that night.

Then I brace myself, take a deep breath, and write down the really painful ones.

The ones that sometimes do make me hate him.

7. Wouldn't let me move in.

Seema's eyes widen. I never let on to anyone that he didn't want me to move in. Never admitted to her (back when she, Nic, and I were roommates) that I gave him an ultimatum one night: let me move in, or we're over. He did—eventually. But he kept all of his furniture exactly where it was. All of my stuff went into storage. So I always felt like a guest in my own home.

8. Wasted six years of my life.

I scribble angrily.

"Great start," Scott says. Then he puts out his hand. "House keys."

I am confused for a moment. "I'm sorry?"

"You're moving out," Scott says matter-of-factly. "What do you need most between now and Monday?"

Seema sighs again, then says to Scott, "Um . . . honey? With all due respect, you're pushing too hard here—"

"No, no," I interrupt quickly, giving him my keys. "I either need a pair of Banana Republic blue jeans or the ones I bought from Target. My fat jeans, not my thin ones. And my flat Steve Maddens, my gray Ann Taylor long-sleeve T-shirt, a long T-shirt to sleep in, preferably the one with the Grinch and Max the dog on it, a toothbrush, and my Kiehl's moisturizing lotion."

Scott looks at me blankly.

I clarify, "I need pants, shirts, shoes, and a toothbrush."

Scott smiles at me. "I'm proud of you. Most women would be curled up in a ball right now."

He gives me a kiss on the forehead, kisses Seema good-bye, then takes his leave.

The moment the door closes behind him, Seema warns me, "Just so you know: he might very well come back with a pair of Gap blue jeans from 1993, tennis shoes, and your beat-up old Spice Girls T-shirt. I've gone on weekend trips with him: there is no rhyme or reason to what he packs."

"I don't care," I say, feeling myself smile. "He could come back with a box of Tampax, a pair of pantyhose, and a flashlight. Tonight, I have a hero taking care of me."

And as awful as this night has been, how politically incorrect and wonderful is it to be able to say that?

Seven

Nicole

"And chances are," I gleefully read to Malika, my soon-to-be stepdaughter, "if she asks for some syyrruup . . ." I drag the word syrup out five syllables to wait for Malika to finish the sentence.

Malika looks up at me, her face brightening as she squeals, "She'll want a pancake to go with it!"

"Yes, she will! Won't she?!" I say, tickling Malika, who giggles as she squirms her little body beneath me.

We're both in our pajamas, lying in her bed, and I have just finished reading her Laura Numeroff's *If You Give a Pig a Pancake* while Jason reads *Harry Potter* to her nine-year-old sister Megan in the other room. On alternate nights, Jason reads to Malika, and I get to read *Harry Potter.*

"Switch!" Jason, clad in his nighttime ensemble of his team T-shirt and gray shorts, yells happily from the doorway.

I rapidly kiss Malika on the cheek five times. "I love you," I tell her.

"I love you too."

"I love you more. Who's the cutest five-year-old?"

"Me!"

I smile, stand up, and walk past Jason. "Tagging out!" I say, making a show of high-fiving him.

"Tagging in!" Jason says.

I head to Megan's room and catch her reading the next chapter of *Harry Potter.*

"Hey, that's cheating." I pretend to lecture.

"I just have to know how it ends," Megan says, as I walk over and sit on her bed. She looks up at me and whispers, "Do you think I could use my flashlight? Just for a little bit?"

How can I resist that angelic smile and those pleading eyes? I lean in and whisper, "Okay, but just one chapter."

Megan smiles and pulls a flashlight from under her pillow. "Don't tell Dad."

"Your secret's safe with me," I assured her conspiratorially. I give her a kiss on the forehead and say, "I love you."

"Me too."

I take my leave and watch Megan throw the covers over her head, turn on her flashlight, and begin reading again as I turn out the light and close the door.

Jason closes Malika's door and meets me in the hallway. "Did she have the flashlight?" he asks me under his breath, amused.

"Of course," I say, my heart melting at how cute she is. "So, you mentioned something about wine?"

"Indeed I did," Jason says, taking my hand and walking down the hallway, toward the stairs. "I want to hear about all those wedding gifts we got today."

Our home phone rings as I joke with him. "Well, I know you had your heart set on a *traif* dish."

We ignore the phone as Jason continues with the joke. "Not nearly as much as the fingertip towels."

"We didn't register for fingertip towels," I tell him.

"Yes, we did," Jason insists.

"No, we didn't," I assure him.

He actually looks confused by this. "Yes, we did," he insists.

"That must have been for your first wedding," I joke.

Jason mock glares at me for my joke as our answering machine picks up.

"Well, then, what were those tiny purple towels in the linen department if not fingertip towels?" Jason asks me.

"Those were washcloths."

"No. I called them washcloths and was strongly chastised by the woman at Bloomingdale's."

"That was because you were looking at fingertip towels at the time—the ones in tea rose. We went with another manufacturer, so that we could get them in aubergine. But the other manufacturer didn't make fingertip towels, they made washcloths."

"Okay, you know the next time I talk about the differences between a zone trap and a pressing man to man, you are allowed to say nothing."

"Hi Jason and Nicole, it's Jacquie," we hear Jason's ex-wife say happily on the machine. "Listen, I know it's getting kind of late, but I have some stuff I want to run by you both when the girls aren't around. I was hoping I could just drop by tonight for ten minutes."

Jason and I share an inquisitive glance.

"You know what?" Jacquie continues. "You might still be out with the girls. I'll try you on your cell. But call me back the second you get this. Or Nic, call me back the second you get this. Whoever. Just someone please call me back."

The machine beeps. About thirty seconds later, Jason's cell phone begins ringing in our bedroom.

"What's that about?" Jason asks me.

I shrug. "I have no idea."

Jason makes a detour to our bedroom. "Are you sure she was okay being at your shower today? Did she seem weirded out at all?"

"No," I say. "She seemed cheerful. As a matter of fact, she . . ."

I stop talking.

The charm. She got the typewriter.

Jason picks up his cell. "Hey, Jacquie," he says into the phone. "What's up?"

Jason looks at me in confusion as he talks to her. "No, Nic didn't mention anything. . . . Yeah, I guess so. Is everything okay?"

I watch Jason as he listens to the voice on the other end of the phone. He occasionally looks in my direction in total confusion. I try to stare blankly back at him, like I don't know any more than he does. Which, really, I don't. But I have a nagging suspicion Charm #2 is about to come true.

"No, come on over," Jason says tentatively. "Okay, we'll see you in a few minutes. Yeah, bye." Jason hangs up the phone. "Did Jacquie mention a job offer to you today?"

Shit! I knew it! I just knew it. Seema may think I'm half cocked, but I'm onto something here. "She said something about being up for a speechwriting job," I tell Jason. "But she said it was a long shot, so I didn't think too much about it."

"Huh," Jason says. "Well, she got the job. And she told me to tell you not to say anything until she came over. What doesn't she want you to tell me?"

I open my mouth to answer him. But before I can say, "Your ex-wife wants to move your girls five hundred miles away," the doorbell rings.

Jason quickly heads downstairs and over to the front door, with me half a step behind him. He opens the door to his beautiful ex-wife, Jacquie, who is beaming. "I got it!" she screams, then slips past her ex to pull me into a hug.

I look over Jacquie's shoulder to watch my confused fiancé widen his eyes (couple shorthand for "What the hell is going on?"). Before

I can answer him, Jacquie pulls away from me, then excitedly grabs Jason. "I start Monday!"

"Um . . . congratulations," Jason says, feigning enthusiasm. "You start what Monday?"

Jacquie pulls away from him. "Didn't Nic tell you?"

Shit.

"I didn't think anything was definite," I say weakly.

"Tell me what?" Jason asks. "What job did you get?"

Jacquie proudly tells him, "I am the new junior speechwriter for the governor." Then for added emphasis she happily screams, "Ah!"

Jason's face falls. "Of California?"

"No. Of Rhode Island," Jacquie jokes. "Of course, of California. He announces his candidacy for the U.S. Senate in the next week or two, so he's expanding his staff. The mayor put in a good word for me. I didn't think I had a shot in Hell, but I flew up there yesterday, and I guess I made an okay impression, because I got it!"

Jason looks shell-shocked but like he's trying to cover. "You flew up to Sacramento?"

"I did!" Jacquie says, looking so happy she might burst out of her own skin. "I didn't bother telling you because I didn't think it was going to happen. But senator. Can you believe I have a shot at working in Washington, D.C., next year?"

"But what about the girls?" Jason blurts out. "We have a custody agreement."

"Yeah, what about the girls?" I hear from the staircase. The three of us look up to see Megan standing at the top of the stairs. "I'm not moving to Sacramento," she states firmly as she walks downstairs.

"Oh, honey, you don't have to," Jacquie says, walking halfway up the stairs and hugging her daughter. "I've got it all worked out.

Sacramento is only an hour's flight away. You girls will live with your father during the week, I'll fly home every Friday night, pick you up, then drop you off on Sunday night, and fly back up. It'll be exactly the same schedule you had before, just with your dad and me having you on opposite days than we did last year."

"But what about our family cruise?" Megan asks. "It's next week."

From the look on her face, I can tell Jacquie hadn't thought that one through. "Well . . ." she stalls. "We can still go. Just not next week."

Megan gets a look of disgust on her face that should be reserved for teenaged girls and Simon Cowell. "Malika has been looking forward to that trip for six months!" she nearly screams at her mother. "You already postponed it once. How can you do it again?"

"Honey, I have to work," Jacquie tells her apologetically. "We'll find a different time." Jacquie looks over at us. Her face lights up as she says, "And you'll love Italy."

Say what now?

Jason and I have the conversation that only couples can, which consists of no words and fleeting looks.

First look, a pleading expression from Jason: *I'm sorry.*

Second look, a shrug from me: *It's okay. It'll be fine. They can come.*

Third look, relief from Jason: *I love you so much.*

"Who goes with their dad on his honeymoon?" Megan asks in disgust.

"Lots of kids go on honeymoons with their parents," Jacquie assures her. "I've read about the trips. They're called familymoons. Why, I'm sure your dad and Nic could find you guys amazing things to do in Venice. They have gondolas, and pizza, which you love. Plus there's . . ."

As Jacquie continues to sell her firstborn on the idea of Italy, I look up to see Malika, standing at the top of the stairs, silent and devastated. "But why can't they just come on the cruise with us?" she begs her mother.

The girl looks heartbroken. Utterly heartbroken. As her mother walks up to her, she bursts into tears.

How can I enjoy the romance of Italy, knowing it came at the expense of a five-year-old's happiness?

I immediately walk up the stairs and kneel down to be at eye level with Jason's little girl. Then I muster up all the enthusiasm and excitement I have in me and tell her, "You know what would be really cool after the cruise is if the four of us went to Epcot. I hear they have a pretend St. Mark's Square that's even better than the real thing."

Eight

Melissa

By 3:00 A.M., Scott has gone home, Seema is in her room, and I'm in my old bedroom at her place, the one I lived in before Fred and I moved in together.

My old room.

God damn it. I loved living here—don't get me wrong. I love my friends, I loved feeling like part of a family that I picked out, and being surrounded by people who loved me and accepted me for who I really am.

But, at the same time, when I moved out, I felt a little smug. Not smug—that might be the wrong word. But I was the first one of us to move in with the love of her life. And, at the time, I thought I was just months away from being the first of us to get engaged.

Back then, I was absolutely giddy that my life was moving forward. I had been sure that I was the smartest and the luckiest of the three of us. In my mind, I was the chosen one, because someone had literally chosen me! I wasn't quite thirty yet, but I had managed to figure out the secret to having it all: a job I loved and a boyfriend who wanted me to move in. (Fine, allowed me to move in. But I'm not the first woman in the world who ever gave an ultimatum. I'm not even the first one today.)

And now, at thirty-two, my life has just taken a giant fucking U-turn, and there's not a damn thing I can do about it.

I feel completely powerless, helpless, and useless.

And as much as I know I have to leave, my mind is racing for something he can do to win me back.

The rest of the evening wasn't too bad. Fred called a bunch of times but, with the help of my friends, I had the strength not to answer the phone. Scott went to Fred's house and packed a whole suitcase for me. I have no idea what he said to Fred, but somehow he managed to convince him to give me a night or two to cool off.

Then Scott came back to Seema's and tried to cheer me up as I continued writing my list of things I hate about Fred.

I had written sixty-two things down and left room at the bottom of the last page for more. The list zigzagged from petty to huge: his blaring U2 I guess is minor—his lying and cheating is gigantic.

And now, sitting in bed alone, I look through my list and add number sixty-three.

63. Knew if I ever found out that he had an affair, it would break my heart. Did it anyway.

I begin to cry again. Soon, my crying turns into loud sobbing, and my stomach hurts again from my violent hyperventilating.

Seema is through my bedroom door in no time flat and pulls me into a hug. "I know . . ." she says gently. She hands me a box of Kleenex, and I quickly pull out a fistful of tissues.

After a few more minutes, I stop crying enough to blow my nose and dry my eyes. "I think I might be running out of tears," I tell her through my stuffed-up nose.

"Do you want me to get you some water?" Seema asks me. "Or a cocoa or something?"

"Water," I say weakly. She stands up. "You want to try and get some food into you too?" Seema asks. "I have tons of leftover cheese and crackers."

I shake my head. "If I eat, I'll throw up."

"Booze?" she asks.

"If I drink, I'll throw up."

"Cigar?" Seema asks.

I raise one eyebrow. She found my weakness. I might be pathetically clutching at straws for any way to make myself feel better, but I do love cigars. They are decadent, and bad for me, and Fred hates them on my breath.

Perfect.

Two minutes later, we're on Seema's front porch, sitting in her side-by-side white wicker chairs. As she lights my cigar, I suck in deeply, attempting to enjoy the intoxicating caramelly aroma of a good smoke. I can taste it, but I still feel like crap. I hold the smoke in my lungs, then slowly exhale out.

"I just didn't even see this coming," I say to Seema, as she lights her cigar. "I mean, I knew he had a problem committing, but I just figured it would happen eventually. I figured if I could just stick it out long enough, he'd realize he couldn't live without me."

Seema gives me a sympathetic look. She doesn't say anything. How could she? What can you say when your best friend gets cheated on?

I take another puff of my cigar and try to savor this treat that usually brings me such joy. "God, I'm such a fucking idiot," I say angrily.

"You're not an idiot," Seema assures me, as she sucks on her cigar to get the whole thing lit. "You're a woman in love. It happens to the best of us."

"You've never been this stupid," I point out to her.

Her cell phone beeps a text. She lifts up the phone so I can see Scott's text. "Wanna bet?"

"What's it say?" I ask, unable to focus through my watery eyes.

She reads the screen, "Just got home. Is she okay?"

"Nice someone cares," I say.

"A lot of us care," Seema says while texting something back.

"What are you writing back?" I ask.

"Just telling him we're smoking cigars," Seema says. She hits send, then tosses the phone onto the white wicker table between us. "So when do you want to move your stuff in?"

I love that it's not even a question, it's a statement. It's not an offer, it's a given. I'm family, I'm wounded. And I'm home now.

Nonetheless, Nic just moved out six months ago. I feel guilty for intruding on Seema's new life without roommates. "I don't want to cramp your style," I tell her. "What happens when you finally begin your torrid affair with Scott? How's it going to look that first night? I can just see it: the two of you are making out in a frenzied heat on your front porch. Clothes are unbuttoned, but still on. Tongues are flying everywhere. You unlock the door, bursting into the living room ready for a night of passion . . . and the two of you see me, in my pink fuzzy bathrobe, watching bad TV, a spoon of ice cream sticking out of my mouth and my face tearstained and red."

Seema takes a moment to paint the picture in her mind. She shrugs. "I'll just tell him Friday's your self-pity night. I get Mondays, Wednesdays, and Valentine's Day."

I try to laugh. It comes out more as a loud smile.

Seema pats me on the back. "Come on. It'll be fun. We could have your old room decorated in about a day."

I casually look around my old neighborhood. "It would be nice to move back in here," I admit. "It feels safe here."

"Of course it does," Seema agrees.

Her cell beeps again. She reads the text, then smiles sheepishly.

"What's it say?" I ask.

"He says that watching a woman smoking a cigar is one of the sexiest sights on the planet, and that watching two should be illegal."

I try to smile, but I think those muscles have atrophied. "He's a good guy," I tell her.

"You think?" Seema asks me, smiling from my approval.

"Yeah," I say with absolute certainty. "Complete wimp in terms of what he's going to do with you, but a really good guy otherwise."

"If you listen to all those self-help books, they'd say he's not interested," Seema tells me as she frenetically flicks her fingers over her BlackBerry's minikeyboard.

I shrug. "Not necessarily. You're with someone, then he's with someone. At some point, if it's meant to be . . ."

"Oh, God, I hate that 'meant to be' crap," Seema says as she tosses her BlackBerry onto the table again. "If it were meant to be, one of us would have done something about it by now."

"Fair enough," I say, not wanting to fight about it. Seema's BlackBerry beeps again. She can't help herself—she's like a kitten staring at a flickering thread of yarn. She picks it up and reads as I take another puff of my cigar. "Although I must ask: if it's not meant to be, what's he's doing texting you at three A.M. on a Saturday night?"

Seema looks over at me. Gives me a *I have no fucking clue* look with an accompanying shrug.

"Ah, men," I say. "A mystery."

"Wrapped in sharp spikes," Seema continues.

"And covered in chocolate," I finish.

Seema reads, "He says to tell you that he's making filet au poivre at my house Tuesday night, and that you need to tell me you're moving in or he's not going to make you one."

"He cooks?" I ask.

"He finds it soothing."

"Look, if you don't want him, can I have him?"

"Oh, honey, I love you," Seema tells me warmly. "But if you touch him, I'll break you like a twig."

I try to laugh. It is funny. I take a big puff of cigar. "All right, you got me," I say. "I'll move in."

"Good!" she says cheerfully. "With someone chipping in for rent, I might be able to afford those filets."

Nine

Nicole

Chester ripped off Penelope's bodice. Her nipples hardened. But was that from the cold air, or the promise of his

I drum my fingers on my desk. What's a new word for penis?

the promise of his shaft of love

I actually saw that in a book once. Ick. I highlight *shaft*, and use my computer's thesaurus. Rod of love, stick of love, pole of love, shank . . .

Good Lord, I'm scraping bottom here.

I highlight my passage and hit delete. So much for trying to make it as a romance novelist.

It's three in the morning, I can't sleep, and I'm not getting anything done either. I throw my legs up on the desk in my home office and stare at my computer screen.

Man, I hate writing. I mean, you know, I love being paid to be a writer. I love reading what I've written. I love telling people at parties that I'm a writer. I just don't so much like the writing part.

As a matter of fact, lately I hate all of it. Seriously—why do people ever want to become writers?

It's a weird thing when your job is everyone else's hobby. Writing's certainly not the only job like that. It's just like any other job that, if done well, looks effortless. Jobs people are sure they would be great at (and get rich from) because they do it so well at home. There are the home chefs who make the perfect risotto who want to shuck it all and open a restaurant. The community theater actors in small towns around America who secretly want to shuck it all to try to become the next Cate Blanchett. The bakers who have perfected a red velvet cupcake in the privacy of their own kitchens and dream of opening a little shop. The bloggers who think they're the next Bob Woodward. Or the people who are sure their lives would make a fascinating screenplay and who even buy a copy of *Final Draft* and begin typing:

INT. COFFEE SHOP—DAY

BLAKE CONNORS, good-looking but doesn't know it (think John Krasinski), sits at a table drinking his coffee. A beautiful woman rushes in, wearing a wedding gown.

WOMAN
You need to hide me!

Seriously, I have read that opening line in a script on three different occasions. Once the character was described as (think George Clooney). Once it was (think Gerard Butler). Once it was (think Dane Cook). Which is just wrong on so many levels.

Anyway, I think the reason that most people never actually follow through on their dreams is because on some level they know that it's not as easy as it looks, it's not as fun as it looks, and it's never as lucrative as we see on TV.

Case in point: actually being a working writer. That sounds

pretty glamorous, right? Or at least fairly easy. You get up at noon, have your coffee, tell the world what observations you've made about your life. Very Carrie Bradshaw.

Unless you're a screenwriter. In which case you get up at noon, go to a studio meeting or two, then hang out with your screenwriter friends in a coffeehouse or bar and talk about what you should be writing. Very . . . um . . . well, there are no famous screenwriters I can think of, but you get the point.

Most of my paid writing has been as a newspaper columnist. Which to most people conjures up a fantasy of traveling the world, putting one's life in jeopardy while digging up stories, effortlessly speaking to the locals in any of the seven languages one is fluent in.

God, I wish. I am fluent in one language: English. And at seven in the morning, I wouldn't even go that far.

Up until six months ago, I worked for a local Los Angeles newspaper. I was overworked and underpaid. I frequently worked for the Metro section, which meant I was the woman who showed up at City Hall early in the mornings, then wrote about anything from a contentious city council meeting to what was going on at the LAUSD to what zone ordinances were threatening the city's water supply.

In short: I had the most boring writing job in the city. And I miss it every day. I worked way too many hours. I was paid so little that up until recently I was still living with a roommate. And I was constantly worried that my job was going to go away because people are more interested in reading about the sex lives of Jon and Kate than whether or not their local charter school license would be granted, or if the mayor would raise the parcel tax another hundred dollars annually.

Six months ago, during the third wave of layoffs in as many years, the company bought me out, and I was out of a job.

I was devastated. I was thirty-one and had spent the last ten years of my life building a career that was gone in a ten-minute meeting with my boss. And forget about going to another paper: circulation was down everywhere and no one was hiring.

So there I was, smack dab in the middle of a midlife crisis, at the ripe old age of thirty-one. I supposed I would die early.

I called Jason, who was, as always, perfect. He always knows when to listen to me vent, when to ask questions, and when I am emotionally spent and ready to listen to his advice. And that day was no exception.

"Okay," Jason said calmly the morning I was let go, after listening to me monologue for at least twelve minutes straight. "How about if you take a few days off and regroup? You can come with me to Portland this weekend and think about your options."

(Side note: Since Jason is an NBA assistant coach, he travels with his team on road games from October until as late as June. That weekend in February they were in Portland.)

"I have no options," I remember whining to him from a locked bathroom stall. (I had gone to the ladies' room to hide, cry, and use my cell phone to track down moral support.) "I don't know how to do anything else."

"The *L.A. Tribune* isn't the only paper in the world," Jason had said. "Why don't you update your résumé and see what else is out there?"

"Nothing else is out there," I said. "Circulation is down everywhere. And besides, I love you, and I don't want to leave you. It's not like I can move to Seattle or New York or anywhere else. You're here."

Jason proposed to me that night. And as far as everyone else knew, I chose to take the buyout from the paper because I wanted to plan my dream wedding, then get pregnant and become a housewife.

Everything sounded so perfect when I said "Yes."

And, for the most part, it has been pretty damn perfect these past six months. Yes, I have been trying to get work as a writer (my latest botched attempt being this romance novelist idea), but honestly I've been a bit lazy.

The politically incorrect thing is, for the most part I rather like being a housewife. I like not having to get up until nine in the morning. I like helping Jason's girls with their homework during the school year, when they stay with us on weekends. I like having a maid come in once a week to clean the toilets. And I really like having enough money to pay my electric bill *and* my cable bill in the same week.

But I'm not so sure I'm going to like helping with homework every day, and I'll admit I'm disappointed about Italy.

I pull the silver baby carriage out of my desk drawer and stare at it.

Babies. Motherhood.

When do you know you're ready to start the rest of your life? How do other women know? And is something wrong with me that I'm so terrified of the thought of a person on this planet thinking my name is "Mommy"?

Everyone says motherhood is incredibly fulfilling. No one I know seems to have ever regretted having kids. Plenty of people I know regret becoming reporters. Why is looking at this damn charm filling me with such paralyzing fear?

I stare at the baby carriage. Is this my future? Is someone trying to tell me something?

Jason knocks lightly on my open door. "You working?" he asks me as he yawns.

I smile at him as I toss the charm onto my desk. "Trying," I say. Then I turn to my computer screen and sigh. "I think you're right. I'm not cut out to do romance novels."

Jason smiles at me. "I'm not cut out to play point guard. That doesn't mean I'm not a good basketball player."

He walks over to me and gives me a kiss, then pulls me into a hug. "You'll find your niche."

"I found my niche," I tell him sadly. "Newspapers. I just lost it."

"You'll find another niche," he says, rubbing my back. He pulls away slightly to look me in the eye. "I really appreciated what you did earlier tonight."

I smile at him, then give him a kiss on the lips. "It wasn't a big deal."

"It was a *very* big deal," Jason assures me. "And it makes me love you even more that you're acting like it's not a big deal." Jason notices the baby carriage and picks it up. "What's this?"

I shrug and try to downplay it. "Oh, it's just the charm I pulled at the shower yesterday."

Jason's eyes widen slightly. He smiles at me. "You got the baby carriage? I thought you wanted the work charm."

"I did," I say. "But I rigged the cake wrong. I got this instead."

Jason looks at it. "Hmm."

"Hmm," I repeat. "What does 'Hmm' mean?"

Jason does some downplaying of his own. "It just means, 'Hmm.'"

"No, it doesn't," I argue. "That 'Hmm' is fraught with subtext."

Jason cocks his head, smiling at me in amusement.

"What?" I ask suspiciously.

"I love that you think that anything I do could be fraught with subtext. I'm a guy: we are rarely, if ever, fraught with subtext." He wraps his arms around me and gives me a big bear hug. "You want to talk about it?"

I lean my head into his chest and say apologetically, "It kinda freaked me out."

"Why?" Jason asks me, in a tone of voice that lets me know he suspected as much.

"I just don't know if I'll make a good mother," I admit. "At least not yet."

"Need I remind you, you just cancelled your honeymoon—"

"That's different," I interrupt. "Changing two weeks of your life isn't the same as changing twenty-four/seven."

"That's true," Jason agrees. "It's a good start, though."

I'm starting to get uncomfortable. I know Jason would like another kid. We've talked about it: buying a cute crib, getting the baby a little basketball, loving each other so much that we want to make a new life. But . . . I'm just not there yet.

"Can we talk about something else?" I ask.

"Sure," Jason says. And I love him for that. "So what charms did everyone get? Did Seema get her red hot chili pepper?"

"No, Mel pulled that."

"What's Mel going to do with a chili pepper?"

Ten
Melissa

It's Tuesday night, and I'm finally starting to feel like maybe I did the right thing.

I think.

I've just read an article about surviving breakups that instructs you to "journal" how you're feeling about the breakup. You start by writing down three pages of whatever gibberish goes through your brain. It can be anything from, "I'm hungry," to "Fred's a jerk," to "Why do men cheat?" to "Man, now I really want a cookie."

After completing the three pages of non sequiturs racing through your brain, you should begin writing specifically about your relationship, your man, and any questions and fears you have about the breakup.

The process is supposed to help you see clearly what scares you about being alone, then help you find ways to deal with your fears and move on with your life.

I'm sitting in my room by myself, listening to deafening silence. Seema and Scott are out getting us filets. They've been great, and when I'm with them I can get through the hours, the minutes, the seconds of this hideous week. But when there's no one else around, I immediately sink back into feeling desperate, sick, and rudderless.

I grab a blank yellow legal pad from my home desk and fiercely scribble down:

> What's wrong with me? Why didn't he want me? Maybe I'm wrong. Maybe that really was just a client. Maybe I'm an idiot for even entertaining that notion. Maybe if I had just

My cell phone rings. I pick it up from my nightstand and stare at the caller ID. It's Fred again. He's been calling nonstop for days.

Now I know how addicts feel. I'm sick to my stomach and miserable. I know it's better for me not to have him around, but I'm not sure how much longer I can stand feeling this way. Fred is my drug. I know he's bad for me, but I just want to be out of pain at this exact moment. I pick up the phone, succumbing to my fix. I'll deal with the consequences of my actions later. I'll have willpower later. Right now, I just desperately need to be out of pain.

"Hello," I answer.

There's silence for a few seconds on his end. "You picked up . . ." Fred finally says, a little startled. "I was going to leave you another message. How are you?"

"I'm fine," I lie. "What were you going to say on the message?"

"That I happened to be in the neighborhood, and I wanted to know if you'll have dinner with me. Any place—you choose."

Fred lives and works in Brentwood. We're all the way out in Hollywood. "What are you doing so far from home?" I ask him.

"Driving around your block over and over again, hoping you'd pick up the phone," Fred tells me.

Inwardly, that rock that's been in my stomach for days slowly begins to dissolve.

Fred continues, "I have a bouquet of roses resting on the passenger seat for you too. Can we go somewhere and talk?"

The tension in my body slowly, but continually, begins melting away. "Are they silver?" I ask him.

"Of course they're silver. But you can't have them unless you have dinner with me."

I glance over to look at the mirror on my wall. I don't want him to see me like this. My eyes are puffy, my skin is blotchy and red. "I can't really go tonight. Scott and Seema are out getting us steaks."

"And you want to be the third wheel watching Seema not make her move again?" Fred jokes. Then he boy-whines, "Come on. Go out with me!"

They are going to be so mad if I go out to see Fred. Still—I do need to get the rest of my stuff out of his condo, and it would be easier if I had a bit of closure. "Actually I wasn't hungry for steak—I was just being polite to Seema. I could go for some seafood, though."

"What about the Water Grill in downtown?" Fred suggests.

It didn't take long for me to brush my hair, throw on a nice dress (the place is rather formal by L.A. standards), and leave a note for Seema and Scott.

Within the hour, Fred and I are sitting at a beautiful table against the wall in the dark, clubby, Art Deco dining room at Water Grill. We start with some drinks: Fred gets his usual dirty martini made with Grey Goose. I opt for a glass of Ariadne, a wonderful mix of sémillon and sauvignon blanc that Nic introduced me to.

Water Grill is known for its oysters, so Fred starts with half a dozen Beau Soleil oysters, then orders the Wild Skeena River king salmon. I start with the Long Cove oysters, then have the spiny lobster tail.

On the drive over, conversation was stilted, but safe: he told me how nice I looked and asked about my preparations for the coming school year. I asked him about his work. We talked about the Dodgers's chances of clinching a spot in the playoffs and the latest U2 album.

But once we had ordered, and each of us had a drink in front of us, the real conversation began.

"I didn't sleep with her," Fred tells me softly but firmly as he stares into his martini glass. "I know what I did was really wrong, and I know that you'll probably never be able to forgive me. But I just wanted you to know the truth. I would never do that to you. I would never hurt you like that."

I look down at my glass of wine. "I know," I say, and I think I mean it. "But you have to understand how humiliating that was for me."

Fred nods his head almost sheepishly. His eyes flit around the room. I continue staring at my wine. Finally, he asks, "So . . . where are we?"

"I don't know," I answer honestly. "And I have to ask you some questions before I will." I take a deep breath and begin. "I know we dated without a commitment for the first few months. Were you sleeping with anyone else at the time?"

My question is a little like the base question, "What is your name?" on a lie detector test. I already know the answer—I found out years ago that he and a girl named Lisa were not completely broken up when he first started seeing me. And what man isn't having breakup sex with the woman he's trying to stop dating?

If he admits to Lisa, I'll know he's telling the truth. If he doesn't, I'll stand up and walk out of his life forever.

Fred takes a deep breath. He doesn't look up from his drink. "Yeah," he finally tells me. "I was. Actually, I was dating her when I started going out with you. Which is a track record that's not really helping my case here. Her name is Lisa."

I remember how to breathe. "Okay. Anyone else?"

Fred looks up at me and shakes his head. "I didn't want anyone else. I wanted you."

"Until you met Svetlana," I say, maybe a little too bitterly.

"I didn't want her either. It's just . . . it's complicated."

I'll bet. I realize I'm clenching my jaw as I say sternly, "I'm listening."

"I wasn't really ready to take the next step with you," Fred admits. "You've been talking about marriage for a while, and you've been really making me feel pressured and . . ."

My eyes bug out at him, "Wait, so it's *my* fault you had an affair?"

"No, that's not what I'm saying at all," Fred says quickly, taking my hand. "I love you. This is all my fault. You did nothing wrong. Absolutely nothing . . ."

He looks at my left hand and begins stroking it. "You know, you have every right to be mad. But all I did was kiss her. Things could have been much worse."

I quickly pull my hand away. "You're losing me here."

"Mel, I love you, but I need to tell you this my way. If you want me to be honest, you have to listen."

I sigh heavily. Grab my glass for a huge gulp of wine. Force myself to tell him, "Okay, go on."

"That night in New York you and I had just had a big argument about the couch, remember?"

I do remember. I had found this amazing red couch that I totally fell in love with, and that was 60 percent off. But it was a first-come first-serve thing, and the couch would be gone by the end of the week. I called Fred, bursting with happiness over the couch.

He hesitated. Said stuff like, "Let's not jump into any big purchases right now." And "We're happy. Why can't we just leave things the way they are?" Which quickly led to an argument about him never wanting to commit to anything. Which led to my version of "Why haven't you put a ring on it?"

"I think that was our worst fight ever," Fred told me.

"It was certainly our loudest," I am forced to admit. I'm getting nauseated as I think back to that fight. That night, I screamed at him, then hung up on him. I spent the next few hours packing then unpacking. Eventually, I collapsed in a corner and cried off and on until sunlight started to seep through our curtains.

Apparently Fred found more appealing ways to deal with our fight. "So after you hung up on me, I went down to the Oak Room, got a Scotch, and really started to think hard about marriage. And what I concluded was, I didn't want to get married. Not to you, not to anyone."

I think I just dry heaved. Fred continues, "Then Svetlana showed up. She was beautiful. She was flirty. And, most important, she was low maintenance. This was a woman who had no intentions of ever wearing a diamond ring again. She just wanted to have fun."

I look down at the table and can feel the tears begin to well up in my eyes.

Fred finishes his story. "When I walked her to her suite, she kissed me, and we made out. And it was wrong. And I felt like the worst human being on the planet then. So I said good night to her. And that was all that happened."

I don't respond at all. I can't. My body is frozen, my mind is frozen. I want to stand up, throw my drink in his face, and storm out. But I can't move.

"I called you the next morning to apologize," Fred finishes. "And I told you to go buy the couch."

Wow. This is so over. He doesn't want to marry me. I force myself to stand up. "I have to go," I manage to eek out (although in a much weaker voice than I had hoped for).

Fred takes my hand again, "Mel, please stay. Please, please, please. I am so sorry. I'll never do anything like that again, I promise." I watch him a moment. Tears also start to well up in his eyes. "Please let me make this up to you."

In the six years we've been together, I've never seen Fred cry. I don't know how to process this information. I slowly sit back down.

"You don't want to marry me," I say, shaking my head. "How are you going to make it up to me? You don't want to marry me. It's over."

"I said I didn't want to marry you that night," Fred corrects me. "But these last few days have made me realize that I can't live without you. In the past five years, you've constantly asked me what it was going to take to get me to realize that I wanted to marry you."

Fred stands up from his chair and gets down on one knee. As other patrons turn to watch, he takes a Tiffany & Co. robin's-egg-blue box out of his jacket pocket and presents it to me. "Will you marry me?"

Eleven

Seema

I am in the middle of a perfect date.

A gorgeous man (who can cook—natch!) is standing in my kitchen, preparing a gourmet meal of filet mignon, freshly mashed potatoes, and baby peas. Things are going incredibly well. He's told me twice how beautiful I look tonight. We not only have yet to consummate our relationship, we haven't even shared our first kiss yet. So I still have all of those "Oh my God! What a great kisser!" and "Should I or shouldn't I let him take off my bra so early into the relationship?" moments of titillation to look forward to. We are sharing a fabulous bottle of cabernet, and the half glass I've already consumed combined with his presence and flirtations are the perfect elements to make a girl feel relaxed, confident, and just a little bit giddy.

Except it's Scott, I've yet to make a move, and I am still steaming over Mel's ridiculously stupid note, which she left on my kitchen counter.

Hi guys,
Having dinner with Fred. Things might be turning around.
Wish me luck!
Love, M

"I don't get it," I say to Scott, taking a sip of my wine as I watch him peel a clove of garlic. "Mel is a beautiful woman with a killer body. She could have any guy she wants. Why would she go see that loser after all he's done to her?"

"First of all, you don't know for sure that she's seeing him to rekindle things," Scott tells me, as he opens my top drawer to leaf through my kitchen gadgets. "Where's your garlic press?"

"I don't think I have one," I say, as I look over his shoulder to see what I do have in there.

"You don't have a garlic press?" he asks derisively.

"You don't have a cake plate?" I answer back in the same tone of voice.

"Yeah, but you could actually *use* a garlic press."

"Dude, I go through a lot of cake."

"Fair enough," Scott concedes. He walks over to my block of kitchen knives and pulls out a paring knife. Then he walks to my cutting board and begins to perfectly chop the clove of garlic into perfect tiny cubes. "So how much garlic do you want me to rub into your steak?"

"Depends. How much making out are we planning to do tonight?" I say, throwing him a relaxed smile.

Scott looks up and flashes me a wicked smile in return. "I'd toss this knife over my shoulder, shove everything off your kitchen counter, and take you now, but the pan is heating."

Rats. But I'm used to the ubiquitous rejection, so I continue with my rant on Mel. "I just don't understand why beautiful women make such foolish choices."

"This from the beautiful woman who in the past year has dated a tormented writer living with his mother, the owner of a comic-book store with autographed pictures of William Shatner and Leonard Nimoy, and a Flying Wallenda."

"Do you think I'm beautiful?" I ask him, flaunting my ongoing insecurities.

"Yeeees . . . ," he says, stretching out the word like he thinks the question's stupid and the answer obvious. He finishes chopping and begins sprinkling chopped garlic on the filet mignons that we got from an actual butcher shop. "Should I put some on Mel's steak?"

"Why not? I doubt she'll be back tonight, we might as well eat it."

"She could be back," Scott says. He grabs his wineglass and takes a sip. "Not likely, but . . ."

"How can you say that?!" I blurt out at him.

"What? I'm agreeing with you," Scott points out defensively. "You know men—when we're done, we're done. But women, they think they need closure. They have to sleep with us one more time, some have to talk to us one more time. You know the drill. All women do it."

"You've slept with a woman one more time, even though you know you were going to stay broken up?"

Scott looks crestfallen. "Oh, honey, you can't be pushing thirty and still be that naïve." He grabs the open bottle of cabernet from the counter and refills my glass. "I just slept with an ex recently because she needed closure—and she called me, like, six months after our breakup."

I stare at my glass as he refills my wine. Of course, I cannot focus on the fact that he mistakes me for twenty-nine. No, no . . . much bigger news was dropped just now. "You slept with an ex-girlfriend? When? Who?"

Scott shrugs as he takes the lid off a pot and checks the boiling potatoes. "I don't know. A few weeks ago? Before Britney. Remember that girl Sherri from earlier this year?"

I do indeed. I was so jealous of her at the time that I couldn't see straight. "The one with the on again/off again boyfriend?"

"Yeah. Well, I guess he was off again when she called me, then on again by the weekend. Point is, she needed *closure* with me. That's what she called it. Closure. Mel's no different—she has to have a seriously unfulfilling time with Fred to remember why she broke up with him in the first place. All women do it."

Scott had sex recently.

And not with me.

And *before Britney*. What's up with that? Is Britney the official BIMY girl (where everything is "Before I Met You")?

I take a big old gulp of my wine. "So, how was it?"

Scott cocks his head. "What?"

And another gulp of wine. Liquid courage. "Sex with the ex. How was it?"

He shrugs. "Eh. Nothing to write home about."

He flashes me one of his meltingly wonderful smiles.

So many questions I want to ask: *What's "Eh"? What kind of sex would you write home about? What kind of woman would you write home about?*

And, most importantly, *What do you mean, "Before Britney"? You just met her! What does she have that I don't?*

The ringing of my telephone interrupts my thoughts. I decide to let the machine get it.

Scott turns around to walk toward my spice rack. "We need cracked black pepper."

As he brushes past me, I grab his arm. "Wait."

Scott stops. Again, he cocks his head, curious. I look into his clear green eyes and try to get the words out of my mouth: "I love you. Pick me instead."

I try, but no sound comes out. Instead, we stare at each other for at least ten seconds. I could stare at those clear green eyes for the rest of my life. Since I can't get out the words, I decide to finally just make my move. I lean in for a kiss . . .

When I hear my machine go off.

"Hey, it's me! Pick up, pick up, pick up!!!!" Mel yells into the phone.

Ignore her, I tell myself. *Just force yourself to move forward.* I move my mouth closer to his luscious pink lips, part my lips slightly, and . . .

"I'm getting married!" Mel screams excitedly.

That jolts me back into reality. "What the fuck?!" I blurt out before making a beeline for the phone.

Scott grabs my arm. "Don't answer that."

Is he nuts? "But I . . ."

"You're just going to say something stupid," he warns.

As Mel continues talking, saying things like "Gorgeous diamond" and "Water Grill," Scott and I continue arguing. "As opposed to something smart like, 'He's a chode,'" I retort.

"He is a chode," Scott agrees. "But nothing you say tonight is going to change anything. You need to pick your battles here."

More words from Mel: bridesmaid, Bora Bora, black bridesmaids' dresses (well, since I'll be in mourning over their marriage, at least the color's appropriate).

"I can't just stand idly by while . . ."

"Yes you can," Scott tells me firmly. "Idly by. Good words. Now, which do you need more right now: wine or ice cream?"

I am torn. I look over at my machine just as Mel is saying, "Okay, you're really not there. I'll try you on your cell. I love you very much, and I really appreciate you taking me in these past few days. But . . . um . . . well, just in case you're staring at the phone right now not knowing what to say to me . . . just . . . please be one tenth as happy for me as I am right now."

There's a long pause. I almost pick up. "Okay, I love you," Mel continues. "Bye."

And she clicks off. I feel Scott stand behind me and begin to rub my shoulders. "You did great."

"I'm going to need a lot of ice cream," I say.

Scott puts his arm around me and leads me toward the refrigerator. "The perfect appetizer to my filet mignon."

"And wine. I will need a lot of wine."

"The perfect dessert."

Scott's phone buzzes to let him know he has a text. He pulls out the phone. "Who is it?" I ask him, thinking it might be Mel.

Scott reveals a shy smile as he reads the text. "No one."

I can't help myself. "It's not Sherri, is it?"

Scott's smile widens. "No," he says, grinning like a Cheshire cat. "You'll be happy to know Sherri's out. I've moved on."

Fuck. Now I definitely need ice cream.

Twelve

Nicole

I used to fantasize about family dinners. Seriously. As a child of divorce, I always had this rose-colored dream of everyone sitting down to a nice home-cooked meal (made by me, of course), talking about our days, sharing our dreams, and being each other's biggest supporters against the trials and tribulations of life.

I wonder where those families are. Colorado maybe?

Seriously, after a day like today, I am exhausted, overwhelmed, and feeling like a total failure at this whole stepmotherhood business.

Let's start with that home-cooked meal. I spent the morning shuttling kids back and forth to their various "enrichment" classes, everything from Spanish for fourth graders to Chemistry for Tots—a title that scared the Hell out of me when I first read it. Then I raced over to the school for Malika's kindergarten orientation, only to learn that my lovely husband-to-be was stuck at a meeting and would not be able to attend, and could I please collect all of the required paperwork, sign anything necessary, then write down any important school dates on the master calendar? Back to the Valley to pick up the girls from their classes, then over to a kids' clothing store that specializes in school uniforms, where we picked up the assorted skirts, shorts, logoed shirts, and cardigans needed for the coming year.

Next was a trip to the toy store for not one but two birthday presents for the birthday parties this week (just this week!), a trip to Target for school supplies, and a trip to the pharmacy for drugs. The drugs (sadly) were not for me but for Malika, who needed a refill of a liquid antibiotic that I spilled all over her bedspread last night when she accidentally kicked my arm as I was pouring the fruit-flavored syrup into the teaspoon, thereby splattering the filled spoon and open bottle all over everything and making her bedspread look like a Rorschach test.

By the end of the day, all I had time to make was a phone call to the local Thai restaurant for takeout. Dinner consisted of twelve assorted white boxes filled with various exotic dishes. We all grabbed a plate and scooped out what we wanted.

Side note: I want to know where that mom is who successfully cooks only one meal at night—take it or leave it, she's not a short-order cook. Because that bitch is making me feel bad, and I want to go to her spotless house, with her gourmet kitchen and her perfectly behaved children, and tell her to fuck off. Between Malika's refusal to eat meat or anything with sauce on it, Megan's abhorrence of anything even vaguely resembling a vegetable, and a fiancé who absolutely refuses to have any of his food touching any of his other food, dinner in this house has become more of a train wreck of late than a bonding experience.

Well, there is talking. That part is very nice. I get about ten minutes every day to feel like we are an actual family. We do a version of thumbs up, thumbs down, in which we tell each other our favorite part of our day and our least favorite part. For example, today I learned that Megan hates her new skirts and wishes the school would allow free dress days on Fridays, a policy a few other private schools have recently adopted. Which led to a discussion on freedom of expression and freedom of speech, which was interesting. And I learned that Malika wants to be a veterinarian when she grows up, provided that she doesn't have to give shots to dogs or clean up their poop. (Note to self: make sure we don't get a dog.) Finally, I learned that Jason needs me to pick up his tuxedo tomorrow.

Of course he does.

That was his thumbs down. His thumbs up was that he gets to marry me on Saturday.

Big happy face. He sure is cute tonight.

"Wanna play Rock Band, Daddy?" Malika asks her father right after dinner.

"Okay," Jason says, standing up from the table, "but only for a little bit."

"Yay!!" the girls yell excitedly, before bolting out of their seats and running to the living room. Jason stands up, walks to my seat, and leans down to give me a soft kiss on the lips.

"Are you up for a video game?" he asks me.

I smile at him sweetly. "Hi! My name is Nic, and I'll be your fiancée today."

Jason laughs. "Are you going to try and get some work done?"

"Probably," I lie. (In reality, I will most likely head on over to my computer, stare at a blank screen for ten minutes, then hit Facebook, latimes.com, wwtdd.com, and the Web site that shows my favorite daily comics.)

"All right," Jason says, smiling and giving me another kiss.

As he heads over to the living room, I gaze at the wreckage of tonight's meal and sigh. Dirty plates, uncleared, plus dirty serving spoons and empty cartons of pad see ew, pepper and garlic shrimp, and chicken panang.

I know this is my fault: I have gotten into the habit of clearing the table by myself. At first, I did it because I wanted Jason's night to go smoothly. We were still in our early stages of dating, back when the girls were only here part-time. I didn't want him wasting precious daddy time cleaning. So cleaning up was my way of quietly helping him get all he could out of what little time he got with them.

But now the girls are here most of the time. And I find myself quietly resenting them for being so messy. It's not something I would ever say aloud. I don't want to be the wicked stepmother or the imperfect wife. I like my role as the cool "bonus mom," as they like to call me. And I know that Jason does appreciate how effortlessly the house seems to run these days. And he is working, and I'm not, blah, blah, blah. . . .

And yet . . . I don't know . . . I'm starting to feel unappreciated.

I yell from the dining room table, "Before you guys start, can everyone please clear their plates so that I can begin cleaning up and winding down for the night?"

I can hear Rock Band's opening blare from the T.V., but I hear no children coming toward me. Nor do I hear my soon-to-be husband. I walk into the living room and yell, "Can everyone . . ."

But then I stop. Megan is sitting at the drums, Jason is on fake guitar, and Malika is standing in front of the T.V. screen with her microphone. She turns to me. "Hey Nic, can you please come play bass?"

"No, honey. I just want to—"

"Please . . ." she begs, giving me the desperate puppy eyes.

What grown-up can resist the desperate puppy eyes?

I absolutely hate video games, but I seat myself on our plushy red couch, grab the pretend bass, and get ready to jam.

Three songs in, my fingers are cramped, and I already have a headache. I love Malika, and she is a gorgeous girl. But let us just say that she does not have a voice to match her looks. It's a good thing she wants to become a vet, because her growing up to be a mezzo soprano is about as likely as my growing up to be a gymnast.

I excuse myself, and head back to the dining room to clean up.

Cleaning is a little like good newspaper reporting: if done well, it is invisible. A good article focuses on the subject, not the writing. A clean kitchen focuses on the beauty of the granite countertops, not the wife being taken for granite. (Little joke there. Not making me feel better.)

As I rinse off the dishes, our home phone rings. I walk over to the phone and check the caller ID to see it is Mel. I pick up. "You know, there are some advantages to being single," I tell her without so much as a "Hello."

There's a pause on her end before she asks, "Like what?"

"For one thing, if you clean your house at night, and you go to bed . . . when you wake up, it's still clean."

Another pause. "Yeah. That's true, I guess," Mel concedes.

"And you get a first kiss. I'll miss those," I think aloud as I rinse off a large serving spoon and put it in the dishwasher. "First glance, first touch, first heated make-out session where sex isn't just *expected* . . ."

"I'm getting married!" Mel practically screeches to me over the phone.

Whuh?

"Oh my God! Honey—that's great!" I force myself to say in the cheeriest voice possible. Even though the poor girl has been hysterically crying about Fred's affair since Saturday. "So the cake charm was wrong," I add. "Good news for the rest of us."

"Well no," Mel tells me. "Technically, it was right, because Ginger got engaged first. But it's also right about the red hot chili pepper! He bought me flowers, took me to the Water Grill, and is out at the store right now buying a bottle of Cristal!"

"Wait, you're not with him?" I ask her, confused.

"No! I wanted to take a few minutes to call my best girls. So, will you be my maid—no wait, matron—of honor?"

The three of us made a deal years ago: since we all love each other equally, we'd take turns being the bride, maid of honor, and bridesmaid. Seema is my maid of honor, I am going to be Mel's maid of honor, and Mel will be Seema's maid of honor. "I can't wait!" I say, filling my sentence with forced glee. "So, have you set a wedding date yet?"

"No," Mel says excitedly. "I need to see if my parents will cover any of it, and if they want it in Oregon, things like that. But I already know that I want my colors to be black and white!"

Ick. I'll have to work on her about that. Actually, there's a lot of stuff I need to work on her about. For example, her choice of groom. Or, as I plan to refer to him from now on: Fuckface.

Mel continues, "Fred and I don't want to steal your thunder, so we're going to wait to announce the engagement until after you leave for your honeymoon."

My honeymoon. There's a loaded word these days. I haven't told anyone about my change of honeymoon plans yet. And now is definitely not the time.

"Honey, that's such good news!" I lie. "Don't worry about stealing our thunder. Shout it from the rooftops!"

I could not sound more fake. Hopefully, she's so obliviously happy, she won't notice.

My phone beeps. "That's my other line," I say. "Can you hold on one sec, and I'll get them off?"

"No, no. I should go anyway," Mel tells me happily. "I have so many more people I need to call. I love you."

"I love you too."

"And Nic?" Mel says, suddenly striking a more serious tone.

"Yeah?"

"I really want to thank you for not saying anything bad about Fred these past few days. I know what he did looks really bad on the outside, and it would have been so easy to condemn him. Your not judging him or me has made me feel so loved and accepted. And it . . . well, it just means a lot to me."

Well, I guess I can't say anything now. "No problem," I tell her. "I love you very much. You know that."

"I love you too," Mel says. "Fred's home. I'll call you tomorrow."

"Okay, have a wonderful rest of the night."

I hang up the phone and click over to the other line. "Hello."

Seema opens with, "What the fuck?"

"I know! Right?!" I concur. "Did you tell her what you really thought?"

"Scott says I'm not allowed to," Seema tells me. "The phone rang, and I let the machine pick up. When Mel screamed her news into the machine, I ran to the phone to pick up and start shouting, 'Wrong!' But Scott wouldn't let me answer. He says I can't say anything now, and that their relationship will either blow up on its own or there's nothing we can do about it . . . Did you tell her?"

"No," I admit. "I couldn't figure out how to work 'You're making the second biggest mistake of your life' into the conversation without looking unsupportive."

"Second biggest mistake?" Seema repeats.

"Her biggest mistake would be if she breeds with him," I reason.

"Indeed," Seema agrees. Her mouth sounds full as she says, "I thought I'd open with, 'How can you even think about marrying Fuckface?' "

"Jinx! That's my new name for him too. What are you eating?"

"I'm sublimating my rage with a pint of Ben & Jerry's while Scott cooks us dinner. What are you having?"

"Oooohhhh. . . . Good idea," I say, opening the freezer door and pulling out a box of Trader Joe's vanilla bon bons, which are these delicious little bite-size ice cream cakelets covered in dark chocolate. They are heaven in a box, and just the thought of popping one in my mouth makes me feel better.

I think for a moment, then reluctantly put them back into the freezer. "Wait no, I have to fit into my dress on Saturday. Anyway, I think rage is a little strong. She's old enough to make her own choices. . . ."

"I'm not sublimating my rage over Mel. I'm sublimating over Scott."

"Wait. Why?"

Seema's mouth is even more stuffed as she says, "Because he's having sex, and not with me."

I'm confused. "Right now?"

"No, not right now," Seema tells me like I'm an idiot. "He recently had sex with Sherri. Remember that awful—"

"I remember."

"Yeah, well, apparently she called him a few weeks ago for revenge sex. Only he doesn't even realize it's revenge sex, and it was meaningless to him, so she gets to have him instead of me. But even worse, he just told me she was, and I quote, 'Before Britney.' "

"Wait. There's a Britney? Who's Britney?"

"Um girl I ate . . . Oo are so uggy . . ."

"Your mouth is full, I can't understand you," I tell Seema.

I hear Seema swallow. "Sorry." Then she lowers her voice and clarifies, "Some girl I hate. You are so lucky. I mean because you're getting married Saturday."

I hear the dryer buzz, alerting me that it's done with my latest load of darks. Oh goodie—more clothes to fold. Before I can say anything else, Seema says, "Scott's yelling for me. Dinner's ready. Gotta go. Love you."

"Okay, love you too," I tell her. "Good luck tonight."

"Schyeah right."

Seema hangs up.

I look back down at the dishes and decide I've had enough for the night.

I am exhausted. I've had a hard day. Maybe not the way I used to have a hard day when I was a reporter, but a hard day nonetheless. I deserve a little treat. I return to the freezer and take out the bon bons.

The box has already been opened.

Dammit! I just bought them yesterday.

I pull the plastic container that houses my goodies out of the box, my gut telling me that though there should be twelve inside, I'll be lucky if I find six.

One.

I sigh. Why would anyone leave only one piece and stick it back in the freezer to get my hopes up?

I pop it into my mouth. I think about going out to the living room to loudly and derisively ask who ate most of my ice cream, but then that strikes me as a bad message for the girls about sharing. I should be able to share my ice cream without the hissy fit currently playing in my head. I'm being petty. Next time I will know to buy two boxes of bon bons. Or seven boxes.

Yes—seven would be better.

I toss the empty box into the trash, and head upstairs.

I just need five minutes of quiet. I pass Jason and the girls playing "I Wanna Hold Your Hand" in the living room, then quickly and stealthily walk upstairs to our bedroom, shut the door, and collapse in a heap on our bed.

Man, what an exhausting day. I had no idea motherhood was this tiring back when I thought it was temporary. When I look at all of the other families around me, the kids always seem so well groomed and cheerful. And no one ever seems tired or overwhelmed. But, I mean, there have to be some mothers out there who are just faking it, who are just as clueless about this whole parenthood thing as me, right? Even the ones who have had the kids since birth must feel overworked and underappreciated occasionally, right?

Right????

Clearly, I'm lazy. Everyone else manages to raise their kids without the use of Diet Monster drinks and venti lattes. What's wrong with me?

Shit. I can hear Jason coming up the stairs. *No, no, no.* I have known that man for over a year, and yet I still cannot get across to him that when I head upstairs and CLOSE the door, it means I need a break. I need silence. I need to hear myself think.

I shut my eyes tight and pretend I'm asleep.

Jason walks in and immediately begins droning on about his team. "If Rabinovitz starts drawing fouls toward the end of the games, that might help us. He can be like a buzzing little flea, annoying the other player on defense so much that they foul him. But his free throws have got to get better. I swear, I got the kid just shooting free throws two hours a day now, and he's just not improving enough, you know?"

What? Were we having this conversation earlier, without my knowledge? Is he asking my opinion about something?

I say nothing, keep my eyes closed, and hope he'll pick up on the most obvious of clues. I mean, isn't it blatantly apparent that if someone leaves the room you're in, shuts the door of another room, and closes their eyes, they might want some privacy?

Jason looks down at me. "Move," he says in a playful voice.

I open my eyes and look over at him. "Why?"

"That's my spot," he says cheerfully.

"It's your spot when we're sleeping. It's my spot now."

Jason gently pushes me while saying in his cutest voice, "Come on. Move. I want to spoon."

I sigh, but move over. I love that he loves to spoon with me so much. Just not right now. Right now, I want a few minutes to myself.

Jason climbs in behind me. His knees touch the backs of my knees, and his right arm donuts around my stomach. This would be nice if the sports monologue didn't continue. "Now Johnson is a great free-thrower, but we prefer that he be resting toward the end of the game. Plus that he was in foul trouble way too much toward the end of post season. . . ."

Now I hear the pitter pounding of five-year-old feet on the steps. Malika has realized her daddy has left the room and has come to find him. She bursts through the door. (Five-year-olds never knock. It's in the handbook.) "What are you doing, Daddy?"

"I'm cuddling with Nic," Jason tells her.

"I'm famous for my cuddling!" Malika yells gleefully, running to the bed, hurling herself up into the air, and landing with a thud on my stomach. She interrupts Jason's insanely boring monologue to begin one of her own. "Wanna know what happened on *iCarly*?"

I want to say, "No. I do not have the slightest bit of interest in *iCarly*. I love you, but please be quiet." Of course, the question is rhetorical, because Malika continues before I can answer. "Sam and Freddie kiss. But they don't want Carly to know, so they . . ."

"What's everyone doing in here?" Megan asks in her *I'm so over you* voice.

"We're cuddling," Malika tells her happily, then gives me a big hug.

"I thought we were playing Rock Band," Megan complains.

"Come on girl. Since when don't you like family bonding time?" her father asks.

Megan sighs heavily with tween disapproval but climbs into bed with the pack anyway. She then climbs over me to get the remote on the nightstand, and flips on the TV.

Oh good—*High School Musical 17.* I was afraid I'd missed that one.

If everyone wasn't so happy with this family moment, I would hide in the bathroom. Except that I found out just last week that the bathroom doesn't lend itself to privacy any better than my bedroom. It leads to Malika walking in and happily chatting with me while I am in the shower.

As the girls move to the foot of the bed to watch TV, I watch Jason turn to me and smile. I smile back.

Jason gives me a gentle kiss on my cheek, then leans over and whispers in my ear, "I can't wait to marry you."

I smile. I love him so much.

Maybe even enough to have his baby.

So I can go hide in her crib.

Thirteen

Melissa

The sex was perfect. Everything a girl would expect it to be on the night she gets engaged: romantic, sexy, fun.

And the romance beforehand was perfect. Fred was absolutely amazing, from the start of the evening until its delicious conclusion. I hung up with Nic just as he was pulling into the driveway. Not only did he bring home Cristal champagne, but while he was at Gelson's he also picked up my favorite Vosges dark chocolate candy bar (the one with bacon—don't judge) and a stack of bridal magazines: *Bridal Guide, Brides, Martha Stewart Weddings*! We fooled around the first time, then sipped our champagne in bed, naked, as we leafed through the magazines and shared our opinions on dresses, cake designs, and china patterns.

For the first time in our relationship, I was able to tell him all of the things I had dreamed about for our wedding: the colors, the style, the kind of china I wanted to register for. And no matter what I told him, he seemed charmed by my choices and amenable to all of them.

And when we made love again, it was with the same kind of passion that we had had for each other when we first started dating. None of the old resentments that had crept into the bedroom recently (the ones about marriage and babies and future) were there anymore. I'm not sure I even realized how heavy those resentments had weighed on me and my libido until they were gone. I felt free and uninhibited with Fred again. The way I had felt when we first started dating. Free and truly happy.

So when we fell asleep in each other's arms, postcoital, I should have been blissful.

But instead, that knot in my stomach came back full force.

Something's wrong.

I look at the clock: 2:34. Fred has been sound asleep for over an hour. I've been lying in our bed, naked, and staring at the ceiling.

Maybe I'm just determined to be unhappy. For the first time in my life I have everything I want: I should not be feeling like this. I am allowed to be ecstatic. Maybe I'm just one of those superstitious people who fears that if she has everything and is happy about it, it will all be taken away from her suddenly.

I look at my ring: glittery, polished, and new. I move my hand from side to side, watching it sparkle in the moonlight coming through the window. It's a beautiful ring: a one-and-a-half-carat center stone, set in platinum, and surrounded by a pavé of shimmering smaller diamonds. It is absolutely stunning.

Nope. Something is not quite right. I can feel it in my gut. I can't put my finger on it yet, but it's . . . something.

I look over at Fred, out cold, and snoring ever so slightly.

His phone. That's it! His phone hasn't rung all evening. This is a man who gets at least twenty calls and texts from work every night. Why didn't his phone ring or buzz?

I silently sit up in bed, watching Fred to make sure that I don't wake him. Then I drop my feet to the floor and tiptoe over to his suit jacket. I notice I'm wincing as I pull his phone out of his jacket pocket. I keep an eye on Fred, still sleeping, as I check his phone.

It's set to vibrate.

Okay, so this is our engagement night. A normal woman would think getting rid of all work distractions was just one of many romantic gestures her man would make to guarantee a perfect evening.

I wish I was normal. I wish I could totally forgive him for his dalliance and not be suspicious. But that's going to take time.

Time and a few checkups.

I tiptoe out of our room, and quietly shut the door. I wait to hear a stir from him, but nothing. I check his phone:

A text from Svetlana:

Hej sötnos
I miss you. Good luck with your meetings tonight.
Jag älskar dig

I would say my heart sinks, but I'm too much in shock for that to happen. My head takes over, and I am determined to learn the truth.

I walk into our office, flip on the light, and turn on his computer. I don't even bother being quiet anymore: if anything I am loudly pacing the room as I read through the rest of his text messages and check his phone logs. Not only is her number listed a million times, but there are other women on his call log as well. I have no idea if they're coworkers, clients, or mistresses. But, again, time to find out.

My first step is to find a Swedish-to-English translator online, which is easy enough. I start typing in various phrases she has texted him, beginning with *Hej sötnos* and *Jag älskar dig.*

Hej sötnos: Hi, sweetnose
Jag älskar dig: I love you
Hjärtat: Sweetheart

Snigging: Handsome
Min alskling: My darling
Pojkvän: Boyfriend
Sot som en gris: Sweet like a pig

Oh, he's a pig all right. I hurl his phone full force across the room, hoping to break it into a million pieces and wake him with my rage.

I wait a few moments, wanting to hear our bedroom door open, and preparing to have Fred walk into the office so that I can pounce on him and hit him with my fists over and over again until I'm worn out.

But all I am greeted with is silence. Deafening silence.

He hasn't budged. Which is a blessing in disguise. Because it gives me one last chance to learn the truth. No filters. No explanations. Just the facts.

I click onto his e-mail and spend the next hour reading.

He doesn't just have Svetlana. He has a girl in Chicago he sleeps with occasionally and an ex-girlfriend from high school who may or may not be sleeping with him (no mention of a husband or kids on her part, no mention of me on his).

I decide to go on Facebook to try and collect more information about the ex and the others. At this point, in my heart I know it's over. But I want the truth—all of it. You can't get rid of a cancer until you know how badly it has spread.

I click on his page.

I start by looking through his old Facebook e-mails. I click on the ex-girlfriend's first message to him:

My God—why didn't we do that back in high school?! I'm still all tingly. When will you be in D.C. again?

Fred responded with:

I wanted to do that back in high school—you said no! Probably for the best. I've gotten better over the years. I'll be in D.C. next month, and can't wait to see you.

But I meant what I said about you coming out here. My door is open anytime. (And my bed.)

As I continue reading, yet another woman, Ashley, ropes him into chat:

Hey, Hot Lips. Boyfriend is in town this weekend, but I should definitely be able to hook up some weeknight next week. Do you actually want to try for dinner this time?

I write back:

This isn't Fred. This is his fiancée. Or should I say, ex-fiancée. And I'm about to break up with him, so he should be available any night next week, and for the rest of his life.

I calmly click him off Facebook and turn off his computer. I call a cab and request a pickup in twenty minutes. Then I walk into our room, quietly grab my two suitcases from his closet, silently open my closet and dresser drawers, and stuff everything I can into them.

Finally, I open a lipstick and write on the mirror:

Min alskling—I know everything

Then I say good-bye to my old life forever.

Fourteen

Seema

So, this past week has been . . . different.

Let's see, where to start.

Scott has been pretty much AWOL since Tuesday: no middle-of-the-night phone calls, a few noncommittal texts. Which can only lead me to assume he's having hot monkey sex five times a day with mystery girl Britney, who I hate with the fire of a thousand suns.

Mel has spent the week waffling between being heartsick over Fred and wanting to rip out his lungs with nothing but her bare hands and a pair of nail clippers.

Nic has been getting more and more agitated about the details of her wedding, to the point where the calm bride that I knew up until the shower has now been replaced by a Bridezilla who suddenly gets worked up over every little detail of her wedding—from the Clos Du Val red wine being cabernet and not merlot to the confetti being thrown after the ceremony being exactly the right shade of aqua and shaped like squares—not little boy babies. (Although I see her point on that one, what with the cake charm she pulled and all.)

Speaking of cake charms: I've also spent the week watching everyone around me have their cake charms come true. First, there was Ginger's engagement. Then our pregnant friend Joyce, the one who got the Noah's Ark, found out that she was having twins. Finally our screenwriter friend Jean, who pulled the wishing well, had jokingly said aloud that she wished she'd sell one of her scripts to Disney. She sold one to Disney on Monday, then a different script to Paramount on Wednesday.

And now I am at Nic's rehearsal dinner, standing in the middle of the restaurant with Nic and Mel, and talking to Nic's friend Carolyn.

And I may have a stroke from her news.

"So you actually *won* the lottery?" I ask Carolyn.

"I know!" Carolyn exclaims. "It was the strangest thing. I never play. I mean, never. But I was driving home after the shower and just thinking about how kooky it would be if I bought a lottery ticket that won a buck. You know, like I got one number of the six. I thought it would be funny. I didn't even know how you played, picked numbers, anything. So I just picked the birth dates of me, my brother, and my sister, bought the ticket, and here I am!"

"What are you going to do with all that money?" Mel asks her, with a smile that looks genuine to the untrained eye.

Carolyn beams as she tells her, "I leave for Paris first thing Sunday morning. Gonna just hang out for a few months in Europe with my boyfriend at all the five-star hotels, come home, buy a house, then figure out what I want to do with the rest of my life. No more fucking newspaper jobs. I am *done*!"

I smile. "That's awesome," I lie. "I'm so happy for you."

"I know! Isn't it amazing!" Carolyn exclaims. "I'm gonna go find a drink. Got a limo tonight, so I can have whatever I want! Can I get anyone anything?"

We all answer with versions of "No" and "I'm good."

The moment Carolyn is out of hearing range, my smile drops,

and I turn to the girls. "She's begging us to push her face in the cake tomorrow."

"It's a cry for help really," Nic says dryly.

A thought occurs to me. "Maybe the shovel I pulled is the weapon I am supposed to use on all these bitches with their perfect runs of luck."

"Oh, come on," Mel chastises us. "How can you guys not be happy for her? Someone had to win the lottery. Might as well be one of your friends, right?"

Nic and I turn to each other to think about Mel's statement. True: someone did have to win the lottery. And, logically, it doesn't really affect my life one way or another if Carolyn won, and I should be happy for Nic's friend.

Nic starts to shake her head. "Nah, I'm still jealous as hell."

I nod. "It's amazing how petty and small I can be," I concur.

We hear Pink belt out "So What" on Mel's cell phone. Fred. Mel reaches into her purse, yanks out the phone, and begins her latest tirade. "May you rot in Hell. What is it now, Fuckface?"

Nic looks at me in surprise. "You told her you called him that?"

"Of course not," I say quickly. "I told her *we* called him that."

This is followed by Nic's phone chiming "It's My Party and I'll Cry if I Want to" by Lesley Gore. She picks up. "If you tell me one more kind of flower has frozen in the middle of August, I swear to God I'm going to climb through the phone and strangle you."

Over the years, I've learned to hate the ubiquitous cell phone. I mean, besides the obvious: oh goody, I get to perpetually wait by the phone since if the bastard was interested in me at all he would call, e-mail, text, or Facebook me, all of which I can access now on my phone. (Side note: not feeling constantly rejected—is there an app for that?)

But, also, because it just encourages people to ignore you.

Even if you are a much more supportive and pleasant person than the dipshit on the phone.

"Oh no!" Mel yells into her phone. "The Britney Spears CDs are mine! You gave them to me! This is just your pathetic attempt to blackmail me into seeing you again. . . . Because heterosexual men *look at* Britney Spears. They don't actually *listen to* Britney Spears!"

I shake my head. "Mel, just let him have the CDs. You can get all the hits you want on iTunes for twenty bucks," I advise, as I snag a flute of Taltarni Brut Taché from a passing waiter.

Nic covers the phone. "Are you talking to me?" she asks me distractedly.

"No."

"Because I'm on with my florist," Nicole tells me. "Just give me one more minute." Then she returns to her latest wedding adversary. "But I didn't order the Biedermeier bouquet, I ordered the Cascade bouquet. It's in the contract."

Mel covers the phone to answer me. "I don't want to go on iTunes, because I don't just want her hits. The whole point of an album is to hear the lesser known, more artistic songs."

"Of Britney Spears?!" I blurt out.

Mel takes my flute, gulps a huge mouthful of sparkling wine, then continues yelling at Fred, "No we are not talking about this in person . . . Fred, you show up at the wedding tomorrow, and I swear to God, I'll castrate you with a butter knife."

"Yes, I know the difference!" Nic yells in exasperation while grabbing a sourdough roll from a nearby table and stress eating. "How do I know the difference?" she says incredulously through a mouthful of bread. "Because up until today I'd never heard of a Biedermeier bouquet!"

"You miss me?!" Mel says incredulously. "*Fan ta dig!*" she hisses in Swedish.

"No, no. Not lilacs—lilies!" Nic says urgently into her phone. "What do you mean, 'There's really no difference'? I'm sorry: are you a gay man or a straight man? Because a man who sucks cock knows the difference!"

I jolt at that.

"You know what? Suck my cock!" Mel growls at Fred.

And I jolt at that. (I thought I was the one in this group who said raunchy, shocking things.)

Nic slams her phone shut. "Honestly, if you had asked me anything about bouquets six months ago, I would have said, 'I don't know. They're pretty, and they usually come with a plastic thing you can hold when you're walking down the aisle.' Now suddenly I'm arguing about lilies freezing in summer."

"Oh yeah, right!" Mel yells into her phone. "That's about as likely to happen as lilies freezing in summer."

Nic grabs my flute from Mel and downs the rest of my drink. She turns to me. "You know, for some stupid reason, I always thought my wedding week would be romantic. I pictured being so in love with my Prince Charming that we would spend the week making plans about our future: talking about our future babies, our future jobs, where we wanted to buy a house, dreaming of where we'd live in retirement. Maybe picking out a new sofa: our sofa. Instead, I have spent the entire week stressing out over stupid things like whether my parents can be in the same room together without killing each other and if anyone will notice if I'm carrying a Biedermeier bouquet."

Mel covers the mouthpiece of her phone and returns to her normal voice. "That's why I told you to get a wedding planner."

"Do you have any idea how much a wedding planner charges in Los Angeles?" Nic tells her. "We're already spending way too much on this wedding. Besides, it would be one thing if I had a job filling my days. But ever since I became a lady of leisure—a term I'm quite sure a man coined, by the way—I apparently have nothing better to do with my life than discuss fondant and fillings with cake bakers, argue with the caterer about the differences between crab cakes and ahi tuna sushi appetizers, and wonder why the Hell I ever agreed to go on a cruise."

I eye Nic in confusion. "I'm sorry. Is the team going on some basketball cruise?"

"No," Nic says, shaking her head. "We are. We're not going to Italy. The honeymoon has been canceled. Or redirected or . . . something."

Mel turns around to Nic in alarm. "I have to call you back," she says to Fred, as she immediately flips her phone shut.

The two of us shoot a barrage of questions at Nic: "What? Why? When?" and "Wait. Does that mean you're eloping on the ship, and we don't have to wear the dresses?"

Nic glares at me for my last question, then tries to rush through her answers so that we can move on to another topic. "Seven days ago. It's not Jason's fault. And yes, you still have to wear the fucking dresses. Do you think ahi tuna is an appropriate appetizer?"

"I didn't say 'fucking,'" I point out.

"It was implied," she assures me.

"Actually, it was inferred," I say.

"No. What I said was inferred. What you said was implied. The difference is—"

"Are you two seriously deflecting the real issue here with a grammatical argument?" Mel chastises. "What happened? Why aren't you going to Italy?"

Nic eyes the other guests mingling about in the room. She takes a new glass of bubbly from a passing waiter, then gestures with her head for us to follow her to a quiet corner, away from everyone. We each grab a glass of champagne as well, and follow her.

Once everyone is out of hearing range, Nic whispers to us, "Jacquie—she of the typewriter charm—got a job as a junior speechwriter for the governor. He'll be announcing that he's running for the Senate in the next few days, so she had to go to Sacramento immediately. Jason and she agreed that they didn't want to pull the girls out of their school in Los Angeles. So we now have them full time. The plan is we'll take them on weekdays, and she'll fly home on Friday nights, and have them on weekends."

"Is that all?" I ask. "You don't need to cancel your honeymoon. Just take the girls with you to Italy."

"I can't," Nic tells me. "The girls have to be back in school soon. And they've been promised this particular family cruise for the last year, followed by a trip to Disney World, which Jacquie now can't take them on, because she's already started her job in Sacramento. So we have to take them. No Venice. No Florence. Instead I'm going to be retching my guts out for seven days, then taking pictures with Mickey Mouse. We leave for Florida tomorrow night, right after the wedding."

I shake my head. "Honey, I'm sorry their mom flaked on a trip she promised them, but this is your honeymoon. Their needs don't automatically trump your needs."

"Spoken like a single woman," Nic retorts. "What kind of parent would cancel their kids' trip to Disney World?" she asks me harshly.

"Um . . . their mom, off the top of my head," I rebut.

Mel, of course, tries to play diplomat. "I think what Seema is trying to say is that this is only a few weeks out of everyone's lives, but that these few weeks are crucial to you. You only get one honeymoon."

"Familymoon," Nic corrects her.

"Fam . . ." Mel begins. "I'm sorry. What is that??"

"It's a honeymoon for blended families," Nic explains.

I snort a suppressed laugh.

Nic gives me the stink eye. "Oh come on! What was I supposed to say? 'I'm sorry, Jason. I know you would kill to have the girls live with you full time, and that we have this amazing opportunity that's been handed to us on a silver platter. But I have to go see Italy, and I'm afraid that's much more important than you getting to be a full-time dad, your daughters getting to continue in the school they love, and your ex-wife getting the dream job she's been shooting for these past ten years.' "

"You still do all those things," Mel points out gently. "And it's great that you want to. But you have to insist on your honeymoon. You can't let a man walk all over you."

"Whoa," Nic snaps. "Did I judge you when you got back together with Fred?"

"No," Mel concedes, a little surprised by Nic's outburst.

"Even when getting back together with him was a really *stupid* idea?" Nic continues.

Mel looks down at the carpet sheepishly. "Okay, I'm sorry."

I open my mouth. "We're not being judgmental. We're merely pointing out—"

"Five words for you," Nic tells me sternly, as she puts out her fist, thumb up. "Michael," and then up come the rest of her fingers. "Ken, Greg, Paulo, Pierre. Did I ever say *one* bad word about them when you were dating?"

Well, that's just harsh, bringing up my worst five choices in men so succinctly like that.

I shut my mouth immediately.

"Nic!" we hear Jason call from across the room. Nic smiles, and waves to him. "I have to mingle. Please, guys, I'm sorry I'm being a bitch right now, but I just need your unconditional support for the next two days."

And she's off. Mel turns to me sympathetically. "Pierre wasn't so bad. You know, other than the bisexual thing." Before I can respond, Mel's eyes bug open. "Wow. I *so* need to leave you two alone tonight."

I follow her gaze to see Scott walking into the room.

My jaw drops.

I'm not kidding, my jaw is dropped. I am stunned.

I have never seen him look so fucking sexy. Mr. Jeans-and-a-T-shirt is wearing a gray wool suit, with subtle pinstripes, a matching gray-and-white shirt, and a purple tie.

He has figuratively and literally taken my breath away. All I can think about is pulling off his jacket, undoing his tie, undoing those buttons, and getting him naked as quickly as possible, because he is just so spectacular, I can't wait one minute longer.

I stare at him, dumbfounded, as he rushes up and kisses me on the cheek. "I'm sorry I'm so late."

"It's okay," I say, barely able to put words together. "You look AMAZING."

He smiles as he looks down at this outfit. "You think? I feel kind of silly in it."

"Don't," I assure him. "You look . . . the best I've ever seen you."

Scott smiles, and looks away from me in an uncharacteristically bashful way. "Thanks. You look really good too."

I walk around him, my jaw still in dropped position. I put out my hand to feel his gray suit. "Seriously. I can't get over how amazing you look. Have you always had this suit?"

"No. I just bought it today at Nordstrom. Britney helped me pick it out. I've been so busy with work this week, I totally forgot to go clothes shopping. When Britney called this morning to ask me what I was doing today, I told her in a panic, 'I have this rehearsal dinner tonight, and I need to impress my date by wearing a great suit.' So we hit the malls, and I got this."

My mind is racing. He called me a date, but he was out getting dressed (and undressed?) with a girl all day? And he's been working all week? Does this mean he hasn't been having hot monkey sex five times a day with Slutella?

"Well, you look amazing," I repeat to Scott. But I can't help but be confused. "So you told this girl you were going on a date, and her response was to help you pick a suit to . . . impress your date?"

Scott looks up at the ceiling for a moment. "Man, that would make me an asshole. No. I've told her all about you. She knows we're just friends."

I plaster on my best smile. "Oh."

"Hey, and if you think I look good in this, wait 'til you see the tuxedo I bought," he tells me proudly.

"With Britney?" I accuse.

Scott knits his brows at me. "Are you okay? You're acting . . ." He searches for the right word. "Weird."

I shake my head, clearing the cobwebs. He's right. I am acting weird. Yes, he looks fucking phenomenal in his suit, but that doesn't change anything. As he just said five seconds ago, we're just friends.

And my thinking about leaning in and kissing him right now is beside the point.

As it frequently is.

I hear Scott's phone beep. He pulls it out of his pocket, reads a text, then laughs out loud. He quickly starts typing back as he says to me, "Britney wants to know if you and I want to go grab a drink with her later tonight."

I feel like I've been punched in the gut.

Why do I stay friends with this person? I am never going to get what I really want. Never. So all that happens when I'm around him is that I end up feeling bad about myself, and like I'm not enough. I eat too much to deal with my self-loathing after seeing him. I drink too much when I'm around him just to drown out all of my feelings.

I'm not happy this way. I need to either make a move or quit seeing him. I can't live with this beautiful creature in my life one minute longer without knowing he's mine.

"Maybe a quick one," I tell him. "We'll see how the night plays out."

Jesus, I'm pathetic.

Fifteen

Melissa

I wake up and see his face every God damn morning. Literally—I wake up, and I think I see him. Fred's face staring at me, watching me sleeping. Something he used to do that drove me absolutely nuts that now I miss desperately.

And then his face dissolves, and I am looking at my old wall. In my old room. From my old life.

I don't pretend to know how widows feel, but I wonder if they also go through this the first few months after their husbands die. I'm so used to Fred being around that every single morning I wake up thinking of him, then have to remind myself of our breakup. It's like when I sleep, my brain tells me to go back to that time when everything was fine, and we were still together, and I was happy. Really happy. And then . . .

And then I wake up, and I experience the death of our relationship all over again.

It has happened every morning since we broke up, and this morning is no exception.

I sit up in bed and try to motivate myself to face the day.

God, he's probably with one of those women right now. Waking up in their bed, belonging to one of them. If I had to guess, I'd say he's probably with Svetlana. From now on, she gets to be the one who wakes up, rolls to her left, sees his naked form, and snuggles up next to him for another twenty minutes of contented shut-eye.

My God, the thought makes me so sick to my stomach that I want to run into my bathroom and dry heave.

"Are you up yet?" I hear Seema yell from the other side of the door.

I force myself to breathe, and try to fake my way through a normal voice as I yell, "Yeah."

"I made coffee. Can I come in?"

"I'd love coffee. Yeah."

Seema opens my door and walks in. "It's already eleven," she says, as she hands me my coffee: cream, no sugar. "Are you okay?"

"Not even vaguely," I admit, as I take the coffee. "When is this pain going to go away?"

"Oh, honey. You'll start to feel better in a few weeks. I promise."

"A few weeks?" I stammer out. "I need to feel better *now.* I'm the one in the right here. He should be hurting every morning, not me. He should be alone, not me." I look over at my silver chili pepper, which I have put on my nightstand to give me hope for my future.

So far, it's not working. I pick it up and look at Seema. "You know, I'm trying to tell myself, 'Everything happens for a reason.' But I just don't see it."

She gives me a hug. What more can she do? I hug her back. When we break away, Seema asks, "Are you going to be able to get through the wedding today?"

"I'll be fine," I say offhandedly, as I take a sip of coffee. My body immediately rebels. Any time I've put food in my stomach in the last few days, I feel like someone has punched me in the gut. This has led me to not bother eating at all, or eating two bites of food, then calling it quits.

I've lost almost ten pounds in a week. I know it's water weight, and a very bad thing for me to do to my body. But I must say, at least I look good. Getting through Nic's wedding day will be hard enough without feeling fat or being tempted to drink. My stomach has taken care of any chance of that.

I give up, and put down my coffee. "So how did the rest of your night go? How was Britney?"

"Very perky, and very blond," Seema says, sighing a bit. "Just another painful reminder to me that a surfer-looking dude like Scott is never going to want an exotic-looking girl like me."

"That's not true," I insist.

"It is true," Seema tells me matter-of-factly. "You know, I was thinking about this last night, as I lay in my bed, alone as usual. I have met a few of the girls Scott has dated, and all of them have been white, and most of them have been blond. It's not like I can compete."

"That's not true."

"Clearly it is true."

"He hit on you the night you met, remember?" I remind Seema.

"I thought so at the time," Seema concedes. "But it's probably just wishful thinking on my part."

"Oh, please. I was there," I remind her. "He hit on you that night. He was so obvious about it that your date was getting annoyed . . . what was his name?"

"Greg. . . ."

"Greg. Right. . . ."

"If it was so obvious, why didn't he ask me out?"

"He *did* ask you out," I argue. "He asked you to lunch."

"Work thing. Doesn't count," Seema insists.

"Unless it wasn't a work thing initially, but you turned it into one, so he didn't push it."

Seema shrugs.

"And Greg was a jerk," I continue. "Maybe you and Scott should have gotten together that first night."

"You of all people are telling me I should have cheated on Greg?"

"Please. Greg and you were only on your third date. He barely kissed you good night on the first date, and after date two you told me he was good on paper, but totally not your type. He was only your date that night because you needed an escort for the event. And I'm not saying you had to sleep with Scott the first night. But, if you had such chemistry with him, you should have shown interest. Or then, fine, if you didn't want to flirt in front of your date, you could have called Scott the next day to ask him out to dinner."

"I don't believe in asking men for dates," Seema declares firmly.

"Do you believe in showing any interest at all in them when they're around?" I ask, raising my voice in exasperation.

Seema waves me off with her hand. "I show plenty of interest . . ."

"Really? What's his favorite color?"

Seema furrows her brow. She doesn't know. "Well, he knows yours," I tell her. "And he knows exactly how you like your steak done. And what spice company to go to for the crushed garlic you like. Last week he bought you season four of your favorite show on DVD. Do you even know his favorite show?"

"He liked *Damages* a lot," Seema tells me triumphantly. Then she mutters under her breath, "Why, I don't know."

"And then there's that . . ." I begin.

"Incredibly well written," Seema continues. "But who wants to spend that much time with characters you don't like?"

"That's another thing," I exclaim, pointing my index finger at her. "Your constant criticism of the things he likes. When Scott is around, you make fun of his apartment, you make fun of his clothes, and you make fun of his choices in women. Who the Hell wants to date someone who doesn't even seem to like them that much?"

Seema defends herself. "I complimented him last night. I told him over and over again how handsome he looked in his suit."

"That was picked out by another woman who he was determined to introduce you to. I got a theory about that. Wanna hear it?"

"Not really . . ."

"He wants you to know he has other women interested in him," I continue. "Beautiful women. Stunning women. Women who are so head over heels for him they help him buy clothes for another date! I mean, for Christ's sake, woman!"

Seema seems jolted by my rant.

I gently back off. "Sorry," I say quickly. "I am the last person who should be giving dating advice. I just . . ." I stammer.

I can't help myself, I know I should shut up now, but . . .

"Scott's a really, genuinely good guy. And I would love it if you two got together, because he makes you happy. But, I don't know, he just also . . . he makes you really sad too. And I hate seeing you sad all the time. So, either let him know you're available or let him go."

I can tell from the look on Seema's face that I have gotten through to her, but that she doesn't know what to say.

"He has a girlfriend," she mopes.

"No. He has a girl who's been around for a few weeks. You could take her."

Seema laughs. "I could *take* her?"

I smile and shrug. "What can I say? I'm trying to be a tough girl for the new chapter of my life. At least I didn't say, 'It's on, bitch.' "

Seema laughs.

"Limo's here!" I hear Nic's voice yell from the living room.

Nic tears into my room as I drag myself out of bed. "It's eleven o'clock! Why are you guys still in your pajamas?"

Before we can answer Nic throws up her arms and starts dancing around. "I'm getting married today!"

Sixteen

Nicole

"Come on out!" I urge Seema through the dressing room door. We are in the bridal area in the back of the church, a few minutes from my big moment. "I'm sure you look fantastic!"

"Unnhhhh . . ." I hear Seema grunt. "Just trying to lose twelve pounds in the next minute and a half."

"What is that sound?" I ask in alarm. "Are you okay in there?"

"I'm fine," Seema assures me through the door. "The zipper and I are just having a rather heated debate. Damn, I should not have dealt with my Scott depression with Twinkies, potato chips, and peach Bellinis."

"At least you *can* eat," Mel says from behind the door of the bathroom, which she uses as her dressing room. "Any little bite of food makes me want to hurl. I think I've dropped ten pounds in the past seven days. I've completely lost what little I had of a chest."

"I'm pretty sure those pounds migrated to my ass this week," Seema tells her through the door. "I'm happy to give them back."

We are standing in the back room of a beautiful church in Santa Monica, and have just finished putting on our gowns. Our makeup is done, our hair looks great (I mean, I assume it looks great. I'm in a veil, how bad can it look?), our bouquets are on the table, and in five minutes I will become Mrs. Jason Washington.

"I'm sure you both look amazing!" I insist. "You looked fantastic at the bridal salon two weeks ago."

"Two weeks ago, I was still happily in love," Mel says through her closed bathroom door.

"You were never *happily* in love," Seema points out from her room.

"Fine, I was mildly dissatisfied in love," Mel concedes. "Which leads to stress eating and weight gain. Now I'm miserably in love, which leads to no eating, and rapid weight loss."

"Guys, we're on in five," I remind them. "Will you just get out here?"

Both girls walk out wearing beautiful satin dresses in my favorite shade of blue. I smile. The dress style was a perfect choice: the same cut somehow emphasizes Seema's hourglass figure (damn, I wish I had her 36Cs) while also showing off Mel's petite little body (I wish I had her runner's legs).

"You're both perfect," I declare, beaming with pride. "And we found the holy grail of dresses: ones you can actually wear again."

Seema looks genuinely horrified. "Honey, I'm thirty-two years old. I kind of hope no one asks me to prom at my age."

I glare at her. "Be glad I didn't put you in an orange micro-mini and white boots."

"Fair enough," Seema concedes, walking to the table to grab her bouquet. "All right, let's get this show on the road."

Suddenly, I get a queasy feeling in my stomach. It's sort of like what happy people call "butterflies in the stomach." Except it's more like angry bumblebees buzzing madly and looking for a way out.

I think I'm going to be sick.

Oh my God. Shit. I'm getting married. For real. There's no

turning back after this. In ten minutes, I will be someone's *wife*. I will never again be able to check the "Single" box on a government form. Suddenly, this decision strikes me as overwhelmingly life changing and permanent.

Very permanent.

Disturbingly permanent.

"You're grabbing the wrong bouquet," I try to tell Seema.

Only no words are coming out of my mouth, and I can't breathe.

Seema doesn't hear me. She takes the white lilies that Mel is supposed to carry, opens the front door, and heads out into the hallway.

I can feel my heart beating. I can actually HEAR my heart beating! Am I too young to have a heart attack? What does a heart attack feel like? An elephant landing with a thud on your chest maybe?

Oh God, and I think my vision is starting to go black.

I can hear Mel cheerfully say, "Here we go!" as she passes me on my right, takes the white rose bouquet meant for Seema, and follows her out into the hallway.

I'm definitely going to throw up. I quickly turn around, run to the bathroom, and slam the door shut so they don't have to watch me in my beautiful gown dry heaving from nerves.

I fall to my knees so that I can vomit into the toilet.

Only nothing comes out. I haven't eaten since last night. Of course nothing's coming out.

Still . . . this nausea can't be a good sign.

I stare at the toilet water in front of me.

What am I doing?

This isn't right. A bride is not supposed to hurl right before she walks down the aisle. I know this week hasn't gone as planned. I know next week is going to be a disaster. But this . . . this has to be bad.

I hear a knock on the door. “Honey, are you all right?” I hear Mel ask, her voice dripping with concern.

“I'm fine,” I yell through the door. “I just need a second.”

And then I crawl on my knees to the door and turn the lock.

Seventeen

Melissa

It's been five minutes since I told Mrs. Wickham (aka the church lady) that we'd be down in two. Seema has managed to clean off most of the fire extinguisher goo from her dress and has promised not to try and bash in the door with any more blunt objects.

I look through the keyhole of the bathroom door. It's an antique door that probably hasn't been replaced since the church was built in the 1930s. I pull out a bobby pin securing my forties hat to my gelled-down hair. I carefully slip my bobby pin into the lock as I say to Seema, "This is an old lock. I think maybe if I can push down on the . . ."

Suddenly, a sparkly aquamarine satin high heel four-inch pump whizzes past my face, and Seema successfully kicks down the door. I blink several times, the bobby pin still in my hand. "Or we could just try the approach that will cost us five hundred dollars in repairs. . . ."

I see Nicole, looking flawless in her gorgeous Monique Lhuillier strapless princess A-line gown in ivory satin. She is breathtaking.

Well, okay, other than the fact that she's sitting on the toilet, resting her now-shoeless stockinged feet on the dresser across from her, and has an unlit cigarette dangling from her lips.

We all have that half second, where no one can think of what to do next.

"I know what you're thinking," Nic sighs. "You might as well say it."

Seema and I exchange a look. Neither of us knows what to say.

Seema goes first. "How come Melissa gets the hot surfer dude for an usher and I get an eighty-year-old who keeps telling me I look like, and I quote, 'That girl with the scar on her face from *Slumdog Millionaire*'?"

Nic looks at both of us for a moment. Rather than answer Seema's question, she changes the subject. "Do you realize that, as of today, I will never get to date Prince William?"

Seema and I exchange another look. What is she talking about?

Seema shrugs. "Well, you'll never have to date a Jonas brother either, so it all evens out."

As Seema grabs a towel from the rack to wipe off more fire extinguisher slime, I walk over to Nic and yank the cigarette out of her mouth. "Honey, you don't smoke."

"Not now," Nic says as she watches me throw the cigarette into a dainty lacy trash can. "But, as this week has clearly shown, nothing in my life is going as planned. Maybe I should take it up to lose weight."

"Yup. Nothin' drops those pounds quite like chemotherapy," Seema quips. She shows me the towel with more white glop from the extinguisher. "What is this stuff made out of? Should I be breathing it?"

"You'll be fine," I tell her as I lift Nic's left foot, and put her five-inch satin heel back on. "How on earth are you ever going to walk in these?"

"I have white ballet slippers for later," Nic answers me. "When I was a preteen, I had a huge crush on Luke Perry. But then, as the years went on, I always kind of wondered about Prince William. And now, today, I'm admitting to the world that I will never date either Prince William or Luke Perry."

Seema looks at Nic in disgust for a moment, then turns to the mirror to examine the mess on her dress. "Luke Perry? My God, there's no accounting for taste."

"Oh, and who did you like when you were twelve?" Nic asks. "Jason Priestley?"

"Will Smith," Seema answers. "And yes, I know: rumored Scientologist. But have you seen him in *Bad Boys,* runnin' with his shirt off? Paws up, baby!"

As I lift Nic's right foot to put on her other insanely high heel, she says to Seema, "Fine. Then you're never dating Will Smith."

"Shocking as it may seem, I've come to terms with that . . ."

"Well I haven't . . ."

"Well he's married to Jada Pinkett, so you're gonna have to."

"I liked Paul Reiser," I say, eager to get into the conversation (although I don't know why).

Both of them turn to me, dull eyed.

"What?" I ask defensively. "A girl can't like a guy with a sense of humor?"

Nic deadpans, "Shudder, shudder . . ."

"Cringe, cringe," Seema finishes while she continues to clean up. "Man, you were even a nerd at twelve."

I decide to ignore Seema's dig, and return my attention to Nic. I rub her arm sympathetically. "Honey, what are you saying? You want to hold out for Luke Perry?"

"No. I just . . . I thought finding my Prince Charming was going to be different than this. I thought it would be wildly romantic all the time. I didn't think everything was going to be this hard this soon, and require so much compromise so early on." Nic sighs.

"I love Jason so much. But I don't think I should marry him. I just . . . I don't think I'm ready yet."

Before I can talk Nic off the proverbial ledge, Seema states authoritatively, "I'm on it!" then starts to march out of the bathroom.

I grab Seema's arm. "What do you mean you're 'on it'? What are you on?"

"Right now, just a little champagne," Seema tells me. "I'm holding, though. What do you need?"

"I need you to tell her she's being ridiculous!" I instruct Seema. "I need you to tell her that Jason is amazing, and that most of us would kill for a chance at happiness like the one she currently wants to throw away."

"That's not my job," Seema states unequivocally. "I'm the maid of honor. My job is to make sure that her Uncle Ted doesn't hit the bar too many times before his toast, that her father doesn't come within ten feet of her mother, and that if she decides she can't get married to hail her a cab and not ask questions."

We hear a knock on the outer door that leads to the hallway.

A moment of silence as we exchange looks of panic.

Seema wails, "I'm never going to be the one in the white dress either!"

"It's just us," Nic's soon-to-be stepdaughter Megan says in a bored tone through the door. "Can you let us in?"

We turn to Nic, looking for an answer.

Nic stands up, walks out of the bathroom, through the bridal suite, and over to the outer door. She unlocks it, and lets Malika and Megan walk in.

They look achingly adorable in their white dresses with satin teal (electric blue?) bows around their waists, carrying little baby roses in small bouquets.

Nic melts. "You look gorgeous. Both of you."

Malika flashes us a proud grin. Megan just glares at her possibly soon-to-be stepmother.

"What the Hell is going on?" Megan asks Nic.

"Language," Nic reminds her.

"Fine," Megan concedes. "What the fuck is going on?"

Nic looks over to us for inspiration, although I'm not sure why. We're single, one of our dresses is covered in the remnants of fire extinguisher slime, and we're both convinced she's crazy. How much help are we going to be?

Nic sighs. She doesn't know what to say. She takes a knee to be at eye level with Megan, and begins. "Girls, you're too young to understand this now, but relationships are complicated. It's nothing that you did, I promise, but I—"

"Oh dude!" Megan declares. "You're too old for cold feet drama. You're never gonna do better than Dad. Suck it up, grow a pair, and let's go!"

With that, Megan turns on her heel and marches out of the room. Malika flashes her eyes toward Nic apologetically. "You look really pretty," she says, then runs out the door to follow her sister.

Nic blinks several times in stunned silence. She stands up, takes a deep breath, then turns to us. "She's right. I'm ready."

Nic grabs her bridal bouquet from the side table and walks out of the room, into the hallway, and onto the next phase of her life.

I quickly grab both bridesmaids' bouquets as Seema tells me, "She's a fucking lunatic."

"Right," I say quickly, handing Seema her bouquet and shepherding her out the door. "Go, go, go. Before she gives it any more thought."

Eighteen

Seema

The ceremony was going off without a hitch.

I was a little worried about Nic for the first few minutes after we busted her out of the bathroom, but she absolutely glowed as she walked down the aisle. And now the priest is done with his minisermon on marriage and has just begun with the "Dearly Beloved" part. Nic and Jason are stealing shy glances back and forth and looking like what they are—made for each other.

I glance over to see Scott, in a pew about halfway back, between a little old lady in a pink wool suit and one of the girls from the bridal shower. I keep glancing back to check him out.

He is wearing a tuxedo and looking the best I've ever seen him.

Ah, very debonair. Very James Bond. Very . . . wait . . . who the Hell is that girl? Because she totally looks like she's flirting with him! Why that little Jezebel! And in a church, of all places!

Nic smiles at me as she hands me her bouquet.

Right. Pay attention to the wedding. This is a beautiful moment for one of my best friends, not to mention a crucial one. I should not be thinking about my current lust.

They exchange their vows, which they've written themselves. This is usually the part of the wedding that makes me want to gag. Do I really need to hear that Nic has pink fuzzy bunny slippers or that Jason's favorite soup is split pea?

But it's actually kind of funny, and includes vows such as Nic's "And I promise to never use your razor."

I wonder what Scott's favorite soup is. I think he ordered clam chowder once at this divey beach restaurant we went to. I look over to see the little slut leaning over and putting her hand on Scott's knee.

Scott smiles and points to the front of the church, clearly telling her to pay attention.

Good.

I think. Unless it was a coy, "Pay attention to the ceremony. You had me at cleavage."

He waves to me. I smile girlishly and try to give a little wave back.

Jason and Nic recite their final *I dos* and exchange rings.

"I now pronounce you man and wife," the priest tells them. "You may kiss your bride."

I can see Jason smiling wide as he leans in to kiss Nic. She throws her arms around him and plants a long kiss on him. Then she takes her bouquet back from me and triumphantly walks down the aisle with her husband.

When the ceremony is over, I take the arm of my eighty-something companion and walk down the aisle after Jason and Nic.

I smile at Scott as I pass him. He gives me a wink and mouths, "You look gorgeous."

I can't help it. I smile shyly, then mouth, "So do you."

He makes a point of smiling as he puts his hands on his heart to show me how much he likes my compliment.

• • •

We in the wedding party spend about an hour having our pictures taken, then we take a limo over to Shutters, an incredible five-star hotel right on Santa Monica Beach. Nic had opted not to have us in the receiving line. (Yay! Another wedding annoyance of mine is having to greet three hundred people with feigned excitement each time: "Hi! How are you?" "Hi! You look great, what have you had done?!" "No dear, it'll be your turn soon, I can feel it.")

Mel and I walk into the cocktail area, just outside of the hotel's Grand Salon. The area has been decorated to look like a glam nightclub: very sexy, very modern. Guests have been here for a while, so the party is in full swing.

"How bad do you think the fire extinguisher residue is?" I ask Mel.

"It really just looks like you spilled some water on your dress," Mel lies. "I'm sure no one will even notice."

Scott walks over to us, holding a silver tray filled with champagne flutes. He gives a slight bow and presents us with the tray. "Ladies."

"Thank you," I say, as Mel and I each take a glass. "How did you snag a whole tray?"

"The head of catering thought I was one of the waiters," he says as he puts down the tray and takes a glass for himself. "And I'm going to kill you for making me wear this tuxedo."

I bend my knees slightly and whine, "Oh, but you look so good!"

He bends his knees, and answers me in my same pleading tone, "I look like a waiter!" Then he returns to his normal voice. "No one else is wearing a tuxedo, except the groom and his party. The guests are all in suits!"

"Then they didn't pay attention to the invitation, which clearly stated, 'Black Tie Optional.' "

"You didn't tell me that!" Scott says, a bit jokingly. "You said the invitation said, 'Black Tie.' "

"I said, 'Black Tie Optional,' which means a proper guest dons a tuxedo."

"Optional. Key word there, Singh. Optional."

" 'Optional' means the bride wants you in a tuxedo, but doesn't want to be rude and demand it of her guests," I insist.

"I can have you out of that thing in three minutes flat," Mel almost challenges him.

We both turn to her. Scott looks amused. I am not. I glare at her.

"Sorry," Mel says, taking another sip of champagne. "Must be the booze talking."

"You've had one sip," I point out.

"Okay, I'm sorry. I know it's completely inappropriate, but weddings make me horny."

"That is a most excellent mating call," Scott says.

"Time to get over Fred by getting under a wedding guest," Mel declares.

"Good point," Scott agrees. "You know what they say—weddings beget weddings."

"I'm sorry?" I say.

"Weddings beget weddings. You know, like in the Bible: 'Abraham begat Isaac' and 'Isaac begat Greg.' Weddings beget weddings." Scott motions to the rest of the room with his champagne flute. "Everyone's in a romantic mood, and hopeful about the future. The women are looking beautiful. The men are horny, but vetted . . ."

"Vetted?" Mel asks.

"If a man is here tonight, he is friends with either the bride or the groom. That means that you can find out all you need to know about him after a few minutes of carefully placed questions to the wedding party. Bonus, he's not going to screw you over later, because if he does he'll either have a six-foot-six athlete who will pummel him or, worse, your friend Nic."

"I don't need to vet anyone," Mel insists.

"This from the girl who used to Googlestalk her first dates," I blurt out derisively.

"No. I am a changed woman. I don't need to view a man as my future husband anymore. I need to view him as a hottie and just get laid."

I stare at her. "You cannot be serious."

"I am indeed. I've been giving this some thought. The cake charm said I was going to have a red hot chili pepper future. Right?"

"Oh, Christ, we're back to the cake charm," I mutter.

"I got the heart," Scott says happily.

"You did?!" Mel says, clearly envious. "Oh my God, you're so lucky. That means you're about to fall in love. Can I see it?"

"Nah, it's in a piece I'm working on for next month's show. It's pretty cool though. You're coming next month, right?"

"Do you think there will be easy men there?" Mel asks him in all seriousness.

"Of course," Scott answers with a look of abject confusion. "There are easy men everywhere. Men are, by definition, easy."

I ignore Scott for the moment, keeping my attention focused on Mel. "What is with you? This morning, you could barely get out of bed."

"That was this morning," Mel says with unabated excitement. "Grieving is like drinking poison and hoping your enemy dies of it. What's the point?"

"Actually, that's resentment," I point out.

"Oh, don't worry. I have a lot of that too," Mel assures me. "But listening to Nic when she was locked up in the bathroom made me realize something: unlike Nic, I'm not married. I can go have sex with Luke Perry! And Prince William! And even a Jonas brother if I want to!"

I turn to Scott. "What do you think? Do I go with a gay joke here or one about a purity ring?"

Before he can answer, Mel continues, "Back to my theory. I've decided to listen to what the cake charm has been trying to tell me. I'm thirty-two years old, and I've never been a slut." She pauses for effect. "It's time."

I stare at Mel, in shock. What the Hell? I don't even know where to begin. How can someone so intelligent come up with a plan so gloriously dim-witted?

I see Scott's fingers snap in front of my eyes. "When they go into a trance, you need to just shake them out of it," he says to Mel.

I turn to Scott. "Can you please tell Mel what men think when they pick up bridesmaids at weddings?"

"If they look like Mel?" Scott asks me in a normal voice. Then he changes his voice to a celebratory tone. "'Yippee, I'm going home with a bridesmaid!'"

"You're not helping."

Scott continues in the same thrilled tone, "That was totally worth the hundred and fifty dollars I spent on throw pillows!"

"Nic wanted the throw pillows. Let the throw pillows go," I say sternly to Scott. Then I turn to Mel. "Honey, the whole one-night-stand thing—way overrated."

Scott smirks at me in amusement. "Do tell."

"Oh, come on," I say defensively to him. "What single thirty-two-year-old woman hasn't made at least one incredibly bad decision in her sex life?"

"Me!" Mel says quickly. "I have not made any bad decisions in my sex life."

"You chose Fred," I point out.

"Duly noted," Mel says. "But I am a serial monogamist. I went from my college boyfriend to Jeff in my early twenties to Fred up until this week. I've only been with three men in my entire life. I have done exactly what society has told me to do, and where has it gotten me? Alone, in my old room, and able to fake orgasms better than a porn star. It's time to try something else." Mel takes another sip of her champagne as her eyes wander the room. "There. That's the one. I've spotted my prey."

"What, you're a cougar now?" I ask her.

"Too young for that. I'm thinking of myself more as a sex kitten."

"Meeeoooowww . . ." Scott says approvingly.

Mel subtly nods her head toward the corner of the room. "See that guy over there? Do either of you know him?"

Scott and I turn to see five men standing in the corner. "Which guy?" I ask her.

"The guy in the gray suit," Mel tells me.

"They're all in gray suits," Scott points out to Mel while he glares at me.

"What?" I exclaim. "You look great!"

Scott narrows his eyes playfully. "Grrrr . . ."

"The tall guy," Mel clarifies.

"Jason works for a basketball team," I point out. "Half the guests here are tall."

Mel leans into us and nearly whispers, "The black guy."

"Why are you whispering?" I whisper back.

"I don't want to offend any of the guests here."

"Why? Don't they know they're black?" I say kiddingly.

"Tall guy approaching. Shhh . . ." Mel says.

A rakishly handsome, tall black man in a gray suit walks right past us and over to a gaggle of giggly girls who immediately surround him.

"Okay. Well, men who look like that have a lot of options," Mel says, not missing a beat. "I'm going to go look at the table assignments and try to accidentally on purpose run into either him or some other twelve on a scale of one to ten."

She takes her leave.

"Personally, I am a cereal monogamist," Scott tells me. "I always eat Rice Krispies."

I smile at Scott's joke. Scott waves to someone over my shoulder, so I turn around to see the bitch from the church. "Who's the girl?"

"Eh, some ex-girlfriend of Jason's," Scott tells me in a brushing-off tone.

"Was there a love connection?" I ask him, trying not to sound too interested.

"Didn't you hear me?" he says, taking a sip of champagne. "Ex-girlfriend. She'll be fucking him tonight, not whatever poor sap becomes her one-night stand." He takes my right hand with his left, and begins holding my hand as he says, "Seriously, no sex is worth dealing with tears or anger the next morning."

"But you just told Mel—"

"Mel is a good girl," he interrupts. "She might talk the talk, but she'll be going home—alone—with us tonight. Let her feel like a sex kitten for a few hours. It'll make her feel like she's in control of her dating life. Which, really, she is. Most women are—they just don't know it."

I look down at our hands, and our intertwined fingers. It feels very nice, and I feel those familiar butterflies in my stomach. But I don't know how to react publicly. Happy? Curious? Flirty?

"You know, if we hold hands, I can't find anyone tonight either," I tell him.

I mentally kick myself. *Good, Seema: go with suspicious and aloof. Men love that.*

Scott makes a show of whispering sweet nothings into my ear

as the girl approaches him. "I can have you out of that dress in three minutes."

I giggle, then take a sip of my champagne. "Is the extinguisher goo that bad?"

"No, no," he assures me, then shrugs and smiles flirtatiously. "But I'll still use it as an excuse to get you out of your dress."

We continue to hold hands as I respond sarcastically, "Right. Like you couldn't have done that by now."

Scott visibly jolts at my statement. Clearly, I've made him uncomfortable. I take a nervous sip of champagne. Here I go again with the nervous drinking. I see the girl from the church make an abrupt left away from us and toward the bar.

Well, at least I won that round.

I notice that even after she's gone, Scott continues to hold my hand.

"So how was the rest of your date with Tiffany after I left last night?" I can't help but ask, although I'm not sure I want his answer.

"Britney."

I quickly apologize. "Sorry. Right. Britney." Then I notice the strangest look cross his face. "What's wrong? Why the look?"

"Huh? Oh, nothing," Scott says cryptically. Then he gets another look that I can't quite read and says, "It's going really well. Surprisingly well, actually." And then he zings me with, "And you really like her, right?"

Crap.

I try not to hedge as I say, "Yeah. She—"

"Because she liked you," Scott interrupts. "And not very many of the women I date like you."

Wow. Okay.

"And I think this girl could really be in my life, so I want you guys to like each other. You did like each other, right?"

I force a smile, and lie through my teeth. "Yeah. She's great."

He smiles back, relieved. "Good, good."

"So who didn't like me?" I can't help but ask.

"Sherri. She thought you were secretly in love with me."

Before I can react to that bombshell, Mel walks up and urgently announces, "Nic put you guys at the singles' table. Switch with me."

Oh, good Christ. "Okay, I know you have this whole 'I'm going to be a slut' idea going for you right now," I tell her. "But trust me, no one wants to be stuck at the singles' table for the evening. Trying to find a bangable guy there is like going to Antarctica for a tropical vacation."

"I'm sorry. Did you just say 'bangable'?" Scott asks me.

"What can I say? The term 'smokin' hot' has become cliché," I tell him.

Mel continues, "He Whose Name Shall Not be Spoken and I are at table sixteen, also known as the *happy couples who have been together for a million years* table. I just really can't deal with that tonight." She takes a moment to register that Scott and I are holding hands. Then she shakes the thought out of her head and begins to beg, "Pleeaaasse let me take your table thirteen seats . . . I need to be with the beautiful people tonight."

Scott and I exchange a look of horror. This is followed by my exclaiming, "You think the singles' table has the beautiful people?"

"Of course," Mel insists with vigor. "They're the ones who have the time and the money to work out, get plastic surgery, and spend money on expensive dinners without boyfriends telling them they don't make enough and shouldn't be spending so recklessly."

Before I can say, "What a loaded sentence," Mel continues, "And they can have sex with whomever they want, whenever they want, so finding someone's easier."

Scott responds to Mel with, "Speaking as one of those people,

I can have either one of you out of that dress in three minutes." He reconsiders his statement, then turns to me with a wicked smile. "Or both of you."

I hit him on the arm, then insist to my friend, "Mel, I think you're missing the point of the singles' table. It may sound like fun, but in reality there's a lot of desperation that you don't want to be a part of. . . ."

"Desperation mixed with alcohol is an aphrodisiac at a wedding," Mel counters. "Haven't you been paying attention?"

Just as I am about to stand firm that, no, we will not change tables just to accommodate Mel's harebrained scheme, Bitch (I mean the girl from the church) walks up to Scott. She flashes an ivory card with the number thirteen calligraphied in aqua-colored foil. "So, will you be anywhere near me tonight?" she asks him in her sultriest voice.

And the plot sickens. "No," I say, trying to sound disappointed that we won't be joining her. "Honey, I think we're at table sixteen."

Nineteen

Melissa

Once the Grand Salon opens up to oohs and aahs, I quickly head to table thirteen to begin my night of wild passion.

Just as soon as I find a guy to have it with.

I happily have a seat in the middle of the round table and prepare to hold court.

Unfortunately, all I get are the jesters.

"What's your favorite quadratic equation?" a middle-aged, pencil-necked geek to my left asks me as he sits down next to me.

"I'm sorry?" I ask.

Geekozoid smiles at me. "I took the liberty of asking Jason what you do for a living. He said you are a math teacher. So what is your favorite quadratic equation?"

I narrow my eyes at him. "How was Comic-Con this year?"

Urkel's face lights up. "Dude, it was rad. Even better than last year! There was a hot girl there dressed as Princess Leia when she was Jabba the Hutt's slave . . ."

I put up my palm. "Thanks for playing. Buh-bye," I tell him, then get up and make the long journey to the opposite side of the round table.

A balding man with a ponytail soon walks up to me and takes a seat by my side. "I'd like to buy you a car."

"I'm sorry?" I say, convinced that I must have heard him wrong.

"I'm Joseph Potter," the old man says, putting out his hand for me to shake, "and I'd like to buy you a car."

I shake his hand, eying him warily. "I've heard that name before. Aren't you some kind of movie producer?"

His face swells up with pride (or maybe Scotch). "I am. My film *Wolf* grossed over a billion dollars last year. Perhaps you've seen it."

The girl who I can tell Seema wants to stab with a fork walks over to our table. I practically pounce on her. "Hi, I'm Mel, and this is my friend Joe," I say to her quickly.

She puts out her hand for me to shake. "I'm Janet."

"Hi Janet," I say, shaking her hand quickly. "Are you an actress?"

"Why, yes I am."

I throw her hand into Joe's. "This is Joe. He's a movie producer, and he'd like to buy you a car."

As the two begin their love connection for the night, I stand up and head to the midpoint between Geekozoid and *Rich Old guy who thinks he's still thirty* to have a seat.

An incredible hunk of a man with short blond hair walks up to the table, debating where to sit. I make eye contact for a few seconds—then smile and turn away shyly.

He walks over to me. "Hi," I say, "I'm Mel."

He puts up his index finger to shush me. "So then I told the bitch—look, either take me as I am, or I am out of here!" he yells into his headset. "And you know what that cunt of a woman told me . . ."

And I'm up again and onto the nine o'clock position of the table (since midnight, three and six are all zeroes in my book).

It takes about three minutes for a fat guy with garlic breath to sit next to me. He turns to me and says, "Hi, I'm . . . Achoo!"

And he sneezes right into my lap.

Perfect.

I politely excuse myself and head to the bar.

Okay, maybe Scott and Seema had a point. I always saw the singles' table as less pathetic than this. The singles I had always noticed at weddings were happy, flirty, and in great shape. Everyone seemed to be laughing and drinking. No one was secretly glaring at their boyfriend, angry at him for not proposing.

"White wine, please," I tell the bartender.

As the bartender pours me a glass of Clos Du Val chardonnay, the gorgeous man I saw earlier sidles up next to me. The bartender asks him, "What can I get you, sir?"

"Sam Adams, when you get a chance," Gorgeous Man tells him. Then he turns to me. "Okay, I gotta ask: are you a dancer, a runner, or a soccer player?"

I turn to face him. Oh my God—he's even better looking up close: flawless mocha skin, not a pore in sight, clear brown eyes, short dark hair. And it looks like there's a nice little body underneath his pinstriped suit.

"I am a runner," I say, a little confused. "Although I was on a soccer team in high school. How did you know that?"

"I'm a personal trainer, so I pride myself on body types," Adonis tells me. He puts out his hand. "I'm John. I'm Jason's cousin."

Perfect. He has a hot body, he's someone I would never normally go on a date with (a personal trainer with a math teacher?), and he's Jason's cousin, so he won't be a jerk to me tomorrow morning.

I take his hand and smile. "I'm Mel."

John gently brings my hand up to his lips to give it a gentle kiss. "Charmed," he says, flashing me the sexiest of smiles. "So I take it you're a friend of Nicole's."

"No, I just like to go to weddings in really ugly dresses," I deadpan. "I've been thinking about getting a trainer. Do you work around here?"

"No. I live in Washington State. Just down for the weekend."

Perfect. I want to start tapping my fingers together and letting out a wicked laugh as I say, *It's all coming together according to plan* when he tells me, "I have to admit, I have an ulterior motive for talking to you."

Uh-oh. Please don't ask me to introduce you to one of my hot friends. "Um . . . okay."

He looks over at the losers at table thirteen. "I have been put at the dreaded singles' table. I have already been yelled at by a guy talking to his therapist on his headset, hit on by an actress, and sneezed on. Actually sneezed on. I saw you sitting there a minute ago—I was wondering if I could sit next to you and pester you all evening."

"Any of them mistake you for a hooker?" I ask him dryly.

"Who mistook you for a hooker?"

I jerk my chin toward the balding fat guy. "That guy over there had the opening line that he wants to buy me a car."

John laughs uncomfortably and shakes his head. "Wow. As a guy, I have to ask: has that line ever worked?"

"Probably, or he wouldn't be dumb enough to use it."

"Hmm," John says, taking a sip of his beer the bartender has put down. "So what line does work on you?"

I immediately come back with, "So far I'm liking, 'I was wondering if I could sit next to you and pester you all evening.'"

John smiles at me as though he's completely entranced. "Now how is it a girl like you got stuck at the singles' table?"

I decide to say the next words flirtatiously. "Now, see, *that* line won't work."

John seems surprised. "I haven't fed you a line."

"Yeah, you have," I enlighten him. "'How did you get stuck at the singles' table?' is another way of saying, 'How is it a girl like you isn't married?' Which is really just a nice way of saying, 'What the Hell is wrong with you?' "

John laughs. "I cannot imagine anything is wrong with you."

He seems to genuinely say that to me.

"Yeah, well, I got lots of stuff wrong with me," I say lightly. "So, what about you? What the Hell is wrong with you that no one's snapped you up yet?"

John looks up at the ceiling as though he's really giving my question some thought. "Well, I live in Seattle. I'm not sure girls here are digging someone who leaves tomorrow night."

I make a show of considering his statement. "Still only a two-hour flight. Go on."

"I have a dog," he admits.

"Hmmm . . . If it's a Chihuahua, we're done."

"He's a Dalmatian."

"And we're back!"

"I'm not great about cleaning up my apartment. . . ."

"That would make you male . . ." I point out.

"And, for the most part, I am too shy to go up and talk to extraordinarily beautiful women." He flashes me a sexy smile. "But, like the Wizard to the Lion, weddings have been known to give me courage."

I smile and blush a little as I let that sentence dangle in the air a moment. "Do you dance?" I finally ask him.

John seems amused but confused by my question. "I have been known to cut a rug, yes."

"I think if you want to hang out with me tonight, it's going to cost you two fast dances, one slow dance, and a bunny hop."

"A bunny hop?"

"Nic and Jason really want everyone to do the bunny hop. Don't ask."

"Don't tell," he quips immediately. "But promise *me* you won't raise the roof."

"I can't promise you that," I tell him. "Nor can I promise not to break out a Roger Rabbit. I do promise not to moonwalk."

"Well, that's something," John concedes. "Can you do the moves from Beyoncé's 'Single Ladies'?"

"If the DJ is stupid enough to play, 'If you like it then you should have put a ring on it' at a wedding, I will body slam him to Tuesday."

John bursts out laughing.

I like making him laugh.

He puts out his beer bottle to toast, and we do.

Is it possible that there really are handsome men out there who find me attractive?

And, if so, where have they been hiding themselves?

Twenty
Seema

It's now ten o'clock. Dinner has been served, toasts have been made, the cake has been devoured. (I had two pieces.)

Scott has been witty, attentive, and charming all evening. As usual. I have once again filled myself with nervous cocktails. As usual. And I am now obsessing over Scott's body, and trying to figure out how to kiss him.

Well, I'm nothing if not consistent.

Why is it that every time I'm drunk, all I can think about is how to figure out a way to sleep with him? When I'm sober, I can push the thought out of my mind. I think about his other women, his flighty nature, his not wanting to settle down.

But right now, sitting at table sixteen and holding hands off and on all night, I can think of nothing else. As he talks to a mutual friend, I find myself staring at his pink lips and desperately thinking about how much I'd like to kiss those lips. I glance down to check out his rocking body (rocking—a term I never use, and yet every time he takes off his shirt in front of me that's the word that pops into my brain—rocking).

Maybe tonight I can get him to spend the night. He would take off his shirt, and this time would be different. This time I would put my hands up to his chest. I'd caress his perfectly toned belly.

I'd kiss his neck and see if I get any reaction. I'd learn once and for all if he is more of a neck guy, or possibly weakened by ears? Could I make him go crazy by kissing his ears? Blowing in his ears. Putting my tongue . . .

I lean over and blow into his ear. He turns to me, furrowing his brow but smiling. "What?"

"Nothing," I say, quickly sitting back. "You have a little something on your chin."

Scott furrows his brow at me a bit more, wipes his chin, then goes back to talking to our friend Karen, who's in midstory. "So I got the camera charm. I'm thinking, how depressing, I'm never going to direct a film, and BAM! I get a grant to do this documentary in Beijing for the next four months."

"That's amazing," Scott says, genuinely happy for her. "And you shoot such great stuff! I can't wait to see it."

"Thanks!" Karen says to Scott. She beams as she looks over at the dance floor, then says to me, "I see Mel's hot little chili pepper is coming true, too."

I turn to look at Mel and her guy du jour (de soir?) dancing sexily with each other to Lady Gaga's "Bad Romance" as Karen happily asks me, "So what charm did you get?"

I force a smile. "The shovel."

Karen's face falls, and she looks embarrassed. "Oh," she says. "What's that mean again?"

My cheeks hurt with forced frivolity as I say, "A lifetime of effort and hard work."

Karen actually winces. It was a small wince, but I'm sure I saw it. "Well, it's probably all a bunch of hooey anyway," she assures me. The three of us share an uncomfortable moment before she says, "I should get back to Gerri. It was great seeing you guys."

And off she goes. I must have had a sad look on my face,

because Scott starts rubbing my shoulders. "It's not real," he reminds me.

"I know," I say, sighing.

"Of the twenty or so people who got charms, I'll bet more than half haven't had anything come true."

I watch Mel shimmy a little for John, and John smile as he watches her. "Mel's is coming true," I point out.

"One of the reasons Mel is acting the way she is tonight is because she believes in that stupid charm, so she's going to make it come true."

I shrug, halfheartedly agreeing with him.

"Come on," Scott says, rubbing my shoulders. "Do you really think you're going to be stuck toiling away for no reason for the rest of your life?"

What the Hell am I doing with you right now? I think to myself.

I shrug noncommittally again.

Scott shoots me a look of mock disapproval. "You think I'm gonna find true love next?"

I try not to look sad as I ask him back, "Why not?"

He smiles at me. Moves his hand up and down. "Who's going to want this? I'm a mess."

"I think you're pretty great," I say sadly.

"Eh, so I got you fooled," he says humbly.

I look over at the dance floor, desperate to be as happy and flirty as Mel. I turn to Scott and smile. "Do you want to dance?"

"God, no."

"Come on."

"I don't dance—you know that."

"But it would mean a lot to me."

Scott looks over at the dance floor. He seems to entertain the idea for a moment, but then shakes his head. "I don't know—maybe for a slow dance."

I cross my arms, and I guess I pout.

"What's that look for?" he asks me.

"Nothing," I say. "I just want to dance."

"You've been dancing all night," Scott points out.

My face falls. "Hardly."

"Oh, come on. You danced with Mike, you danced with Nic's dad, you danced with that boyfriend of Carolyn's, you actually samba'd with Nic's gay cousin, you bunny hopped with the guy Mel likes, *and* you danced with Nic when all of the girls got on the floor to dance and sing along to Gloria Gaynor's 'I Will Survive.'"

"You could have joined me for that one."

Scott looks horrified. "A GUY dancing to 'I Will Survive'?! You gotta be kidding. And there is no way I could ever samba—that guy rocked."

"But I haven't danced with you, and I really want to dance with you," I say, maybe a little pleadingly.

Lady Gaga finishes, and the music dies away. Nic takes the microphone from the DJ as couples make their way back to their tables. "First of all, my groom and I would like to thank you all for coming tonight. It has truly been the most wonderful night of my life, and I am so grateful to all of you for traveling, buying new dresses and suits . . ."

Scott leans into me and whispers, "Did you notice she said suits?"

"And spending waaayyy too much on our gifts," Nic continues.

Everyone laughs.

"Jason and the girls and I have to leave the party now so that we can to get on a plane and begin our familymoon . . ."

Cue the polite applause.

"But I want to assure the drunks out there that the bar will be open until one . . ."

Laughter.

"And the band will be playing until one, as well. Also, the hotel is happy to arrange any cabs or rooms you might need at the end of the evening. So get home safely." Nic holds up her Cascade bouquet. "And now it's time for my favorite tradition, the tossing of the bouquet."

"Oh great," I mutter, hearing a collective groan of *ughs* and *oh, shits* from the crowd.

Scott smiles, wildly amused. "Go on. It'll be fun."

Against my better judgment, I slowly stand up. "Like the cake charms weren't a bad enough harbinger for my future."

"Hey, at least she's not throwing a shovel at you," Scott jokes, his face shining with glee.

Mel and I meet halfway between our tables, then trudge up to the dance floor for the traditional spinster mockery. "So are you going to try and catch it?" Mel asks.

"No-oo!" I say, knitting my brow and looking like I smell a skunk. "You?"

"I can't decide," Mel tells me as we line up behind two blond girls in four-inch heels who have their arms held up high. "On the one hand, it would be fun to catch. I've never caught the bouquet before. On the other hand, you have to dance with the guy who catches the garter, and I don't want to let John out of my sight."

"Ladies!" Nic says into the microphone, as she turns around so as not to see us.

I look at Mel. "Back row?"

She nods quickly. "Back row."

We walk farther behind the flock of women and wait for a delighted scream to emanate from one of them.

"One . . ." Nic begins. "Two . . ."

"So things seem to be going pretty well with John," I say to Mel.

"Yeah," Mel says, pleasantly surprised. "He hasn't tried to kiss me yet, but he certainly seems interested."

"Three!" Nic yells.

And I guess she must have thrown the bouquet, because I looked up just as it was going over my head.

I turn to see the bouquet land right behind me on the ground, so I turn and bend down to pick it up.

And promptly get tackled by a million other women trying to grab the bouquet.

Once I realize that I am at the bottom of a scrum, I decide to hold onto the flowers fiercely. I mean, seriously, this pile is embarrassing. I'm not rewarding their behavior by giving up my flowers.

Disappointed girls slowly peel off of the pile and let me stand up with my bouquet.

I glance over at Scott, who can't stop laughing.

"Ahhhh!!!" Nic screams gleefully as she runs up and hugs me. "So you're next!"

Um . . . yeah. "I thought Ginger was next," I tell Nic grumpily as I look at the bouquet.

"No, no, she's already engaged," Nic tells me. "Maybe Scott's going to propose."

"I can't even get him to propose brunch," I point out.

"And now it's time for the garter toss!" Jason says into the microphone. "Gentlemen, I need you up here."

Scott stands up with the other single gentlemen. We pass each other on the way to and from the dance floor.

"Good luck," I tell him.

"With all of the basketball players here, I'm gonna assume you'll have a new dancing partner in moments," Scott teases.

Nic sits down on a chair Jason has provided. She lifts her dress hem ever so slightly to reveal a blue garter, which Jason takes off to fling at the bachelors.

Such bizarre customs we Americans have when you think about it.

Jason makes a big show of turning around so that he can't see the other guys.

And the next thing that happens makes my heart skip a beat.

The garter flies over the group of men, just like the bouquet had flown over us. Only, to my surprise, Scott steps back and catches it, throwing his left hand back and up in an insanely lucky catch.

Not that anyone else was trying to catch, but still—it was inspired.

I am stunned. My eyes must look like saucers. Scott smiles as he walks up to me, puts out his hand for me to take, and asks, "May I have the honor of this dance?"

I smile, put the bouquet down at our table and give him my hand. "I thought you hated dancing."

"Oh, I do," he says. "But I knew you weren't going to shut up until I danced with you once, and at least with this I'm guaranteed a slow dance."

We walk onto the dance floor, and Nic and Jason's guests applaud. The lights dim as Etta James's "At Last" begins to play. Scott donuts his arm around my back and pulls me in close. I lean against his chest, completely content.

We dance for all of thirty seconds before I get self-conscious. "Isn't anyone else going to join us up here?" I ask, looking around at the sea of faces watching us by our lonesome on the dance floor.

"I'm not sure," Scott answers, pulling back from me a bit to look around. "Are they supposed to?"

"I don't know," I say. I spot Mel watching us from table thirteen.

I motion for her to join us with a slight wave of my hand. She shakes her head.

I motion more obviously. Then I look past Scott's shoulder to yell, "Everyone come join us."

A few people join us on the floor, and I relax into his chest again.

This is nice. I could get used to this. I lift my chin up to look into his eyes, and I almost kiss him.

But I don't. Instead, I turn away and watch the crowd.

Coward.

I hate myself for this. If I'm not going to make a move, I should try to stop obsessing.

I know logically that he doesn't want me, or he would have tried to kiss me by now. Whatever reason he may have for not kissing me (loyalty to another woman, worry about rejection, thinking I'm too fat, whatever), I cannot combat that reason.

But, in my heart, I guess I just keep hoping. And wonder what I can do differently this time that will make him want to kiss me. How can I act? What can I say? What thing can I do differently than before, that will make him want to make out with me for the next six hours? Hell, make him want to rip off my clothes—the relationship be damned—because I am just too enticing for him to resist?

And suddenly something he said pops into my head.

Weddings beget weddings.

I've never been to a wedding with Scott before. That's what's different. He was trying to tell me that earlier: Weddings beget weddings.

I look back up at Scott again, and this time I move in for the kiss.

I kiss him on the lips.

Just a tap kiss really. He kisses back though, and smiles.

Now what?

Does a tap kiss count as a real kiss? Should I lean in and open my mouth? How pathetic would that look at a wedding?

Or maybe it's romantic. As he said, "Weddings beget weddings."

I lean in to kiss him again just as his phone rings.

I pull back a few inches but continue the dance.

The phone rings again.

"You gonna get that?" I ask as we move around the floor.

"In the middle of a slow dance?" Scott asks me incredulously. "What am I, mental?"

He spins me around with a flourish, flinging me out, then spinning me back. And just as Etta belts out her final sultry, "For you are mine . . . at last," Scott lowers me into a slow dip.

The audience applauds as he lifts me back up and pulls me into a hug.

After the hug, I keep my arms around Scott's neck. "One more dance?" I ask flirtatiously.

Scott smiles, almost shyly. "Okay."

And the two of us begin our slow dance again.

Until the bass starts kicking in from Eminem's "Without Me." Bah-nah-nah-nah-nah.

The slow dance is over, and possibly so is my only shot at romance for the night. Scott smiles, takes my hand, and leads me away from the dance floor.

Heavy sigh.

His phone beeps a text. Scott opens it to look. His brow furrows.

"What is it?" I ask.

"It's from the owner of the gallery that sells my stuff. The place has been robbed."

Scott's phone rings again. He immediately picks up. "Dude, what happened?"

His face falls as he listens. "Well, are the cops there now?" He looks at me as he says into the phone, "I can't. I'm at a wedding right now . . . Well, I can't just announce to my date that I have to leave. Let me just tell you which pieces I sent over: *Chode, Requiem for a Hershey Bar, True Love in a Cucina,* and oh . . ."—he starts snapping, trying to remember—"the one with the high heel and the bright red paint . . . crap, what's it called . . . ?" He snaps again.

"*Wedding,*" I remind him.

"*Wedding,*" he repeats into the phone. He winces at the irony. "No, *Chode* wasn't a painting. It was an installation, a collection of things over a painting . . . You know what? I took photos of everything. Just . . . let me know who's investigating the robbery, and tomorrow I'll bring them everything they need."

"You should go," I whisper to him as he continues to insist to the person on the other end of the line, "No. I can't abandon my date. I'm her ride home."

"Abandon your date," I insist in full voice. Scott looks at me. "Really? But I . . ."

I start waving my arms toward the door. "This is your livelihood. Go!"

"Okay, Jack, I'm in Santa Monica, but I'll be right over."

Scott hangs up the phone. "Thank you. Do you want me to come pick you up at the end of the night?"

"No, I can cab it home," I assure him. "Do you want me to come with you?"

He looks around the room. "No. Nic hasn't left yet. I don't want you to get into trouble." He kisses me good-bye quickly. "But can I call you late tonight?"

"Of course."

"Okay. I love you."

"I love you too."

And Scott runs out the door.

Damn it.

Damn it, damn it, damn it!

Twenty-one

Melissa

Have you ever been on one of those perfect dates that is only perfect because you didn't know you were on a date? That's what it has felt like being with John all evening. He has been funny, attentive, ridiculously attractive, and, for some reason, all mine.

Up until ten minutes ago, when everything changed. I don't know if he got a text message that I didn't see, or saw an ex I haven't heard about, but John has gone from being interested to distant, flirty to quiet. And I have gone from being a confident seductress to an insecure mess.

I have just finished the single woman's rite of humiliation (wait—I mean passage), and tried and failed to catch Nic's bouquet, and have come back to the table to see John with this weird look on his face.

Did it seem desperate to want the bouquet? I think to myself. *Did it look like I was too marriage minded? Or make me look like one of those girls who constantly jumps ahead in a relationship?*

"Are you going to go up for the garter toss?" I ask John, determined to scoot past this awkward moment.

"Um . . . no," he says, looking over at the dance floor as the single men gather around to do something men hardly ever do: avoid lingerie.

"Are you okay?" I ask him, concerned.

"Yeah, I just . . . Will you excuse me for a moment?" John asks me.

"Sure," I say, not sure what I did wrong.

John quickly walks out of the Grand Ballroom. I sit there, stunned, wondering what to do to salvage the situation.

I watch Scott catch the garter, then head over to Seema for their romantic "First Dance."

Okay, I can't go talk to them to get advice. They're having a nice moment. So I sit at table thirteen by my lonesome, and try to dissect what I did wrong.

I spend the next few minutes running through all of the causal possibilities for the change in dynamics. That's a math teacher's way of saying I try to figure out where I screwed up.

A drunken twenty-something comes up to me. "That is one ugly dress," he slurs at me.

"I'm sorry?" I say to him.

"I said that is—"

"No. I meant I'm sorry," I say firmly, then wave good-bye. "Off you go. Chop, chop."

I decide to take matters into my own hands. I grab my purse, and head out of the ballroom in search of my new infatuation.

I walk around the lobby. Various couples are flirting with each other, people are starting to pull out their valet tickets and prepare to go home.

John is nowhere in sight.

Damn it. Is he secretly on his cell phone with his fiancée, telling her not to wait up? Did he head out to the lobby bar to trade up for the evening? Has he gone up to his hotel room to tuck his four children into bed for the night?

Dejected, I start to head back to the ballroom just as John

emerges from the men's room. "There you are," I say, very happy to see him.

"Oh, hey," John says to me awkwardly. "Miss me?"

"I did," I tell him sweetly. "Say, do you want to go out and take a walk on the beach?"

John takes a moment to think about my suggestion.

That can't be a good sign.

"Um . . . sure," he tells me, taking my hand. "Let's go."

We walk hand in hand out onto Santa Monica beach. The night is wildly romantic. It's late August, so it's not cold yet. I smell the salty air, and listen to the ocean's waves pounding against the sand mixed with the sound of a bass pounding out from the ballroom.

I look up into John's eyes, then I lean in and kiss him.

He politely kisses me back. (That's bad.) And when I pull away from him, he has an almost pained expression on his face.

I try to give him a hopeful expression. "Shall we try again?" I joke, and lean in just as he looks down at the ground and . . .

Bwahh . . .

He throws up wedding cake all over my dyed-to-match shoes.

"Oh God!" I yell, involuntarily stepping back in horror as he grabs his stomach and says, "Jesus! I'm so sorry. I . . . Bwah . . ."

And there goes the filet mignon with Roquefort, all over the sidewalk.

Ew! Ew! Ew!!!! What kind of a red hot chili pepper is this?!

I rub John's back as he stays bent over, ready for the next assault on his system. "Are you okay?" I ask him. "What happened?"

John starts hyperventilating as he tells me, "I thought the ice cream I picked up at the airport tasted funny, but I figured, 'Oh, I don't eat much ice cream, I guess this is how it tastes. And now . . . Bwahhhh . . ."

I bring John over to a nearby chair and help him take a seat. He clutches his stomach as he finishes his story. "For the last hour I've been feeling queasy, but I was hoping it would go away."

I rub his back for a few moments. After the next wave of vomit, I ask him, "Do you have a room here?"

John painfully nods yes.

Twenty minutes later I have helped get John into bed and returned to the ballroom, where I see Seema sitting at a table, looking forlorn.

"Hey," I say, throwing down my purse. "Where's your date?"

"He's with the police." She sighs.

I do a double take.

Wonder if there's a cake charm that can predict that?

Twenty-two

Nicole

A writer has to write. I can't help it. I am going nuts on this family cruise, and I need to vent.

I am sitting at the teeny tiny pool on the cruise ship, a watered-down mai tai at my side, watching the girls slide down the water-slide and into the pool over and over again.

Any mathematician who insists there is no such number as "umpteenth" has clearly never had kids.

Today, I have to write.

And by that I don't mean real writing—I mean sending e-mails to my friends to complain.

I place my portable computer on my lap, click online, and begin writing to Mel and Seema.

To: Seema@atotalwasteofmakeup.com, Mel@atotalwasteofmakeup.com
Subject: Are we there yet?

I will not, WILL NOT, at $0.55/minute Internet cafe rates, click on the Hotel Danieli live cam in Venice, Italy to see what I'm missing. Nor will I look up pictures of the Tuscan villa that Jason and I should be staying at later this week.

I am in the first ring of Hell—there are no real criminals here, but I am in Hell nonetheless.

First off, I had forgotten that I am my mother's daughter. As you both know very well, this means that I get seasick in spite of my love of water sports, and that water from any country other than my own makes me . . . oh, what's the word I'm looking for? Sick on both ends.

But wait, I'm getting ahead of myself.

So, as you two know, my darling husband (all right, I'll admit I am LOVING that word) and I had to leave our wedding reception early to take a limo over to the airport for a red-eye flight to Orlando. (By the way—both of you seemed to be doing very well when I left. What's the latest with each of you? Am I going to be an aunt anytime soon?)

The kids were great on the plane. Malika fell asleep almost immediately upon takeoff. Megan watched movies. Myself? I had two of those little airline bottles of Scotch and a valium I snagged from my dad. Because I'm worth it.

We got to Orlando. I had this vision from watching too many thirtie's musicals that someone was picking us up. Instead, we were entering the Sheeple Mover. We had to wait, overtired and unshowered, at Orlando Airport for three hours before we got on the bus. During this time we met a nice couple, Jeff and Brian, with two small children, one of whom would scream at the top of his lungs for no discernible reason every ten seconds or so. The five-year-old, I mean. Although Brian was threatening to do so on at least two occasions. Me compadre! I bonded with him immediately.

We also met a honeymooning couple going on their—wait for it!—twelfth cruise. It is a cult. The honeymooning couple had the system down. They were the first ones on the bus. They have Caribbean cruise–themed webbed necklaces with plastic covers for their room cards. We, of course, after three hours of waiting, almost missed the first bus because of a potty emergency.

On to the terminal! Where we had another long wait under overcast skies with tropical humidity. The words "one hundred" pop to mind—as in one hundred degrees, one hundred percent humidity.

And then we boarded. Upon each family's arrival, someone introduces them by name in the grand lobby, and then a paid staff of crew members cheers wildly. We are all special here.

We started at the buffet. The buffet is big. Since we're off to the Caribbean, naturally they featured a wide array of tropical items, including macaroni and cheese, hamburgers, and mini-corndogs. There is margarine and Cool Whip in abundance.

Also, you are immediately pressured into joining the wine program.

And here is my first official observation for the week: people are here because they do not actually want to spend time with their children. They are here to dump the kids and drink. (As Malika so succinctly put it on our third day here, "What kind of parents force their kids to play basketball just so they can go drink?")

Out of the mouths of babes.

But back to that first day.

Lest I be considered a teetotaler here, the parents are not wine tasting. God knows, I love a good wine tasting. No, no. They drink heavily, and with an air of desperation and in this mock hilarious way that seems more common on the East Coast than the West. And they eat. There are many obese people here whose idea of a vacation is moving from one mediocre buffet to the next. We Americans are not a pretty people.

We got through the buffet. Megan felt sick. She didn't actually vomit. We checked out the kids' areas, which the girls seemed to like. Then we finally got to go to our stateroom. It is the tiniest room I have ever seen. Truly. There are bunk beds that come out of the walls at night. Let us just say there can be no "classic honeymoon activities" when your five-year-old stepdaughter accidentally shoves her foot off of her bunk bed, and into your nose.

We changed to go to the pool.

The pool deck is like the line at Disneyland. The big children's pool, the one with the water slide, was closed because some small child had pooped in it. It would not be open again until we got to sea. The other pool, which is ten feet by thirty feet, must have had fifty people in it. The smell of chlorine makes your eyes water. Elbow to elbow with the Coney Island crowds, I tried, to the tune of "Celebrate Good Times Come On," to pretend that I am enjoying this.

Then we needed to leave the pool to have our emergency evacuation drill. You have to go to your stateroom, put on your life vest, and then go to your lifeboat. A great way to start a trip, packed together, everyone, like sardines on the fourth floor.

And then we took a nap, so we missed the bon voyage party. I was lying in bed with Megan and Malika when I heard the engines start. I fell back asleep only to be awakened by severe nausea as soon as we were under way.

We wake up the girls for dinner. This was a mistake. Malika spent the entire meal at the lovely pseudo-French restaurant crying, "This place sucks. I want to go home," in various forms, over and over again.

And so do I.

Would it be really bad form to fly to Tuscany for one day, then fly home?

Love to all,

Nicole—aka, the Wicked Stepmother ☺

I hit send and close my computer.

"Nic! Nic! Watch me!" Malika yells as she races down the slide—and splashes water all over my computer.

Sigh. I throw a dry towel over my computer and place it on the clear plastic table next to me. Then I give her a thumbs-up, and encourage her to go again.

"They're really loving this vacation," Jason says from the chaise next to me.

"They're definitely getting into the spirit of things," I say with false cheer.

Jason smiles and takes my hand. "Do you need another mai tai?"

I lightly kiss his hand. "No, I'm good."

We share a calm moment just before the cruise director yells over the loudspeaker, "Okay, everyone! Get ready to Macarena!"

I squint at the cruise director as Jason stands up. "I'll make it a double."

"Thank you."

I'm starting to rethink that wine club.

Twenty-three

Melissa

They're having sex right now. I'm sure of it. It's around one in the morning, Fred's favorite time of day for seduction. And it's Friday night, when he's done with his workweek and ready for some recreation.

My imagination is doing terrible things to my heart. I am convinced that at this very moment he is having the best sex of his life, and he doesn't ever want it to end. He's kissing her neck, she's rubbing his thighs. They're doing things I would never do, and then reloading with Gatorade and doing it all again. He's glad I'm gone. He's happy to be free.

I look over at my clock radio, and wonder if I'll ever sleep again. How many more nights do I have to wonder what I could have done differently to save my happiness? I play in my head not believing him the first time he said that men on business trips didn't sleep around as much as women thought. Would it have changed anything if I had quit my job to join him on lengthy business trips? Would that have helped? What if I had changed my physical appearance? One of the lies men say is that they don't understand plastic surgery—and yet they love bigger boobs, fewer wrinkles, and skinny thighs.

I'm not only mourning the old relationship, I'm mourning the future I thought I was going to have. The future I'd been planning for. Fighting for. Counting on.

I counted on something, and I lost. I fought hard for something, and I lost.

I lost, and Fred won.

I don't understand why the universe is allowing Fred to be rewarded for his betrayal. For his lies. Why should he be loved when I'm alone? While he gets off scot-free, I suffer the heartbreak. He smokes—I get the lung cancer.

And then out of the blue . . . like, in a matter of seconds . . . the thought that I should continue suffering just because he is a jerk makes me so angry.

I know I should still be grieving but, at least in this moment: I'm. Just. Pissed. Off.

What the Hell ever happened to karma? What does it say about our society that we let our men regularly cheat on their women, and we never do anything about it? Why are advertisers still willing to pay spokespeople like Kobe Bryant and Tiger Woods? Why does Hugh Grant continue to make *romantic comedies*, of all things? David Letterman's ratings went up when he not only cheated on the mother of his child, but cheated with a subordinate who worked for him? Physical abusers like Chris Brown go down in flames (as they should)! So why not psychological abusers?

I once read that betrayal can only happen if you love someone. Fair enough. So by that logic my happiness is as simple as not loving the schmuck who did this to me. To not let the psychological abuser get away with his actions.

Without thinking, I get out of bed, march over to Seema's room, and knock on her door. "Are you awake?"

She starts to mumble, "Not really. I was sort of staying up, because Scott sometimes calls in the middle of the—"

I open the door, and turn on her light. "They're passive-aggressive motherfuckers, and we can do better!"

Seema is lying in her bed, possibly asleep. She opens her eyes. "And I guess, 'Not really' could be construed as 'come on in . . .' "

"Seriously, it's been almost a week!" I tell her angrily. "Why the fuck hasn't Scott called you?"

Seema blinks several times, forcing her eyes to stay open. She sits up. "He's holed up in his loft, working. He's got less than four weeks to re-create everything that was stolen last Saturday, plus he needs to turn in several extra pieces—"

"That's passive-aggressive bullshit!" I yell accusingly. "He's just such a . . . MAN! They ALL are." I turn on my heel, and march back to my room. "I'm going to get the rest of my stuff," I announce, going into my room to grab my car keys and purse from the dresser, then passing through the living room and over to the front door.

"Wait. What?" I hear Seema yell from her bedroom. She quickly races out of her room, throwing on a robe as I open the front door. "What are you going to do? Go confront Fred while he's with the other woman?"

"I think I am," I say, feeling in control of my life for the first time in days, weeks, months, possibly (six) years. "I'm gonna go get my life back."

And with that, I'm out the door. Seema runs out after me in her pajamas and robe. "Wait. This is a bad idea. . . ."

"Why? I have no furniture there—I had to put my major stuff in storage, remember?"

The look on Seema's face shows me she does remember, but that she thinks that's beside the point. I head to my car. "I need my stuff out of there. It's only a few carfuls. I can be out by dawn. And when I am, I will officially have my life back."

"Wait," Seema says quickly.

I turn around to face her. We engage in a staring contest. I don't blink. I'm not going to be swayed. Seema finally rolls her eyes and sighs, "Let me follow you in my car—then we'll have enough room to get everything out in one trip."

I smile. "Thank you," I tell her quietly.

She gives me a quick smile, then goes back into the house to get her keys and purse.

I pull out my cell phone, and hit the speed dial. "Hey, it's me," I say to Fred. "I'm coming to get my stuff . . . Yes, now. . . . Well, if she or you are anywhere near my vicinity when I get there, you will see the difference between a dumb woman's anger and a smart woman's wrath." Fred forces me to explain, so I do. "I say that because she only threw a drink in your face, and then stupidly took you back. That's dumb. I, on the other hand, am smart. I would never take you back. Oh . . . and if you're stupid enough to be at home when I get there, I'm smart enough to make what happens to you look like an accident."

Twenty minutes later, I am standing on my old doorstep, Seema by my side, listening for voices, footsteps, or perhaps sirens.

All I hear is silence.

"Are you insane?" Seema whispers. "I know you're mad, but he could call the cops after a threat like that."

As I pull out my old house key, I shake my head knowingly. "That would mean he'd have to admit to the policemen, or policewomen, that he was afraid of a little five-foot-two wisp of a thing. Never gonna happen."

I use my key to unlock the door, then slowly push it open. Fred is nowhere to be found. I smile triumphantly. "All clear," I say as I walk in.

"Wow," Seema says in amazement. "You actually got him to clear out in the middle of the night with no notice?"

"Be very impressed," I say to her, feeling like a force to be reckoned with as I walk into my old kitchen.

"I am," Seema says. "Remind me never to cross you."

We walk through the house, and I make a mental note of what's mine and what's his. Hideous plaid couch: his. Tasteful sterling silver frames with pictures of the two of us in happier times: mine.

Seema surveys the scene with me. "So, what do you want to take back first?" she asks me.

"Well, I've taken back my dignity, and my life. So let's start with those Britney Spears CDs."

Twenty-four

Seema

I am so fucking tired.

Although I was happy to help Mel get everything out of her old place, I wish she would have put a little more thought into the timing. We were packing and loading up until five in the morning. By the time we got home, Mel was completely hyped up on a combination of coffee, Diet Monsters, and adrenaline. I, on the other hand, could fall asleep on a bed of nails. I yawn as we each carry in Glad bags of her clothes.

"Isn't this just the best day?!" Mel announces, beaming. "Where do you want to go for brunch? I'm buying!"

"Sweetie," I say. "I can barely keep my eyes open. We've got our cars locked in the garage, so your stuff is safe. Let's just take a nap, and . . ." I yawn so wide that my ears pop, "leave the rest of the unpacking for later in the day."

"We need to join an online dating service," Mel tells me purposefully.

My eyes are stinging. At what point does someone slip from a really good friend into a codependent? "You've had too much ginseng and caffeine. Go to bed."

"I know a lot of success stories," Mel insists to me as she tosses her Glad bags of clothes onto her bed.

"No, you don't," I counter, throwing my Glad bags next to her closet.

"Yes, I do," Mel insists.

I heave a big sigh. "No. You know people who dated someone who wasn't all that into them for three months, maybe a year. Or, worse, you may know some people who were never in love but who married their safety net—because they weren't getting any younger and at least this person was nice to them. But you do not know anyone who actually fell in love on a dating Web site."

"I don't need to fall in love," Mel says to me passionately. "As a matter of fact, I specifically don't want to fall in love. I want to have indiscriminate sex with gorgeous men who I toss aside the next day. I want all of the benefits of being courted without the costs of being caught."

Our phone rings. Mel picks up on the first ring. "Forget it. It's not going to work this time," she says proudly. "I'm out, and I'm going to have better sex than you ever dreamed!"

Mel listens to the caller a moment, then hands me the phone. "It's for you."

I furrow my brow as I take the phone. "Hello?"

"I take it you've been out with Mel all night," Scott guesses, sounding amused.

"We've been moving," I say, walking out of her room with the phone. "What are you doing up so early?"

"Working, feeling guilty for not having called you all week," Scott says. "I miss you. How have you been?"

He misses me! Yay! There is a God!

"Fine," I say. "Other than the fact that Mel is trying to talk me into participating in the idiocy of online dating."

"I heard that!" Mel yells from her room.

"You were meant to!" I yell back.

"I tried to call you around one," Scott tells me. "But no one picked up, so I tried again at two, three, four, and now. Does that make me a needy loser?"

"Depends. Were you updating your profile on every matchmaking Web site out there while splitting your time between a tub of full-fat ice cream and a fifth of cheap whiskey?"

"No."

"Then you're fine."

Scott laughs. "What are you doing later tonight?"

"Avoiding putting my profile up on every matchmaking Web site out there," I tell him.

"What are the hot new clubs these days?" Mel asks me loudly from her room.

"And nightclubs," I continue into the phone. "I will also be avoiding nightclubs, and men half my age trying to bed me by challenging me to beer pong."

"I read church is a good place to meet men," Mel continues to yell toward my direction. "What religions have services on Saturday night?"

"Hold on," I tell Scott. Then I yell to Mel, "I only go to church for the hatch, match, and dispatch!"

"The what?" Scott asks.

"Baptisms, weddings, and funerals," I explain to Scott. "So what's going on later tonight?"

"It's kind of boring, but do you feel like coming over and helping me with my work?" Scott asks. "I have a bunch of digital pics I took before I turned in the pieces. Maybe you can help me compare them to what I've done so far? Let me know what you think?"

Yay! He asked me out for Saturday night! Things aren't weird between us! I still have a shot!

"Will there be steaks, grilled just the way I like them?" I ask flirtatiously.

"No," Scott says. "But there will be takeout. I figure we work until we're both punchy, then argue over the virtues of Thai versus pizza, then watch a video or something."

"Oh. Netflix just sent me *When Harry Met Sally*. Any interest?"

"None in the least," Scott admits cheerfully.

"*Four Weddings and a Funeral?*" I ask, knowing full well that his answer will be . . .

"Good Lord."

"*He's Just Not That Into You* . . ." I continue.

"Woman, are you out of your mind?"

"I'm about to say *Twilight* . . ." I threaten in a singsong voice.

"I'll take *When Harry Met Sally*," Scott answers me. "I've never seen it."

"You've never seen it?!" I exclaim, reveling in the possibilities of being able to discuss whether men and women can ever truly be platonic friends with my frustratingly platonic friend. "You're going to love it. It's really funny. What time do you want me there?"

"Six," he tells me, letting out a big yawn. "Now go get some sleep."

"You too," I say. And then my voice catches as I say to him, "I love you."

Scott yawns again. "I love you too," he says through his big yawn. "Good night."

"Good night."

And he hangs up, and he is gone. I stare at my phone for a second before clicking it off.

Well, he did say he loves me back. He always says he loves me back. But does that mean anything?

I head back to Mel's room. "Do you think it's true that Inuits have a bunch of different words for 'snow'?" I ask her.

I walk back in to see Mel, passed out on her bed, using one of the Glad bags as a pillow.

I'm pretty sure I hear snoring.

So maybe she didn't have too much ginseng after all.

I know I should be a good friend and let her sleep, but I can't help myself. I'm obsessed and need an answer. I shake her shoulder softly. "Mel . . ." I whisper.

"Farmers' markets!" Mel says, sitting straight up in bed. "Another target-rich environment to meet men."

I take a second to process that. "Duly noted," I say, and then repeat my question. "Do you think it's true that Inuits have a bunch of different words for 'snow'?"

"I think it's true that Americans do," Mel says, yawning, and collapsing back down on her bed. "Slush, sleet, flurries, blizzard, powder, hardpack . . ."

"I'm going somewhere with this . . ." I say, eager to get to my point before she passes out completely. "But I like that you came up with six. Shouldn't there be six different words for love?"

Mel doesn't even have to think about it. "There are. Adoration, worship, fondness, devotion, adulation . . ."

"*My point* is that when I tell Scott 'I love you,' I don't think it's fair that he can say 'I love you' back, when clearly my 'I love you' means 'I adore you and want to rip your clothes off and keep you in bed until a week from Thursday,' whereas his 'I love you' means . . ." I look Mel in the eye as I desperately ask, "What does it mean?"

She looks at me sympathetically and shrugs. "Honestly, if I knew how to read men, do you think I'd be here with you?"

Of course she doesn't know either. What did I expect? She's a girl. In order to read a guy, I need another guy to translate. The problem is, the only guy I can think of who can answer these questions would be . . .

Ding, ding, ding. Right.

Who's never watched *When Harry Met Sally* before. Huh. I wonder which question from the movie I'll start with. And how much wine I'll encourage him to drink before he gives me his answer.

Twenty-five

Melissa

It's amazing how much information you can find on the Internet these days. When I Googled "How to Meet Men" I got more than a million results. If only I had an available man for every available result . . .

I settled on five different articles from five different dating gurus. Then I did another search to make sure all of these people were married and threw away the single one because—though you may not need to be a chicken to judge an egg, it helps your credibility if you've proven you can catch a rooster. (Also, she suggested dance classes, and I think we all know that the man I meet there is going for the same reason I am—to meet a man.)

Each article gave me a top-ten list of places to meet men. A few of the places were on all or most of the lists, so I threw those out due to lack of creativity. (Grocery stores? Really? You know, I've been going to the grocery store since I was a baby. I occasionally pick up things I hadn't gone in for. Once I went home with a twelve-pound watermelon. Once I went home with a lawn chair. Not once have I gone home with a man.) Then I threw out some suggestions because they would require too much time and money on my part. Dog park shows up a lot on these types of lists. I don't own a dog. One suggested hanging out at an animal shelter, which I just found depressing. Several suggested joining a co-ed softball league or scuba club. That would require even a smattering of interest in learning softball or scuba diving.

Later that Saturday, I dress up in new jeans and a cute red top, put on a little makeup (enough to look better, but not so much that the men know I'm putting on makeup), bring my silver chili pepper charm for good luck, and begin my man hunt promptly at noon at Home Depot.

Why noon? According to one of the dating sites, I don't want to come in the morning unless I want a Type-A personality who wakes up too early and has a list of things to do for the day, because this is not a man who will be swayed from his mission, even for a chance to hook up. And I don't want to go too late in the day, because then I get the men running in to buy one can of Glidden paint in antique white or a General Electric 20-amp one-inch single pole circuit breaker because they're almost done with their fucking project and just need one more random item in order to finish their day.

Noon. Noon is when the homeowners come in to look at new countertops. When they saunter in to compare and contrast flooring options. When they come in to pick the new drill they need to finish the bookcases they're making by hand.

I begin my search in the kitchen area, right by the granite. I lean my elbows down against a gray marble counter and try to look casual.

That looks stupid.

I stand up.

Look around.

Exactly what am I supposed to do during the time I wait for Mr. Right Now to approach me?

"Can I help you?" a good-looking dark-haired twenty-something wearing an orange vest asks me.

"Oh . . . um . . ." I look around nervously. "Actually, I'm waiting for someone."

He smiles. "Okay. Well, let me know if you need anything."

I flash him a nervous smile. "I will. Thanks."

He walks away, and I begin my search again.

A fine-looking blond wearing jeans and a Beatles T-shirt is perusing a dark blue laminate countertop. He's gorgeous: glowing tan skin, light eyes, a swimmer's body. I could get used to looking at that. And no wedding ring—very important.

He runs his fingers over the counter thoughtfully, and I see he has a pianist's fingers: long and thin, and indicative of someone who knows how to run his fingers over just about anything. "I was looking at that one myself," I say aloud.

Is that a good opener? What the heck is a good opener for laminate?

The blond looks up, and smiles at me, "Yeah. Do you know the difference between this one and that beige one over there?"

"Oh, you don't want to go beige," I advise him. "It's your kitchen, not your office."

He smiles at me, amused. "Huh. You might be right. You're a woman—what do you think a woman would want in a perfect kitchen?"

"Bright white with lots of colors," I happily tell him. "What's your favorite color?"

"Red."

"Then I'd go with a white tile countertop with a mix of various red tiles interspersed with the white. Then I'd get a backsplash of mostly white, a few red, and a handful of hand-painted tiles. Or if you really want to go bold, go for a quartz counter in bright red."

"Wow. You know your stuff," Adonis tells me, visibly impressed. "Do you work here?"

"No. I'm just looking to remodel my kitchen," I lie. "So do you live around here?"

"I do. I just relocated from Minneapolis. Got this fixer-upper that seemed like a great deal at the time, but it's led me here pretty much every weekend. I've even started to take the classes here."

"They have classes here?"

"Yeah. Everything from plumbing to electrical. You should come sometime. They help a lot."

I smile. He's invited me out (sort of). "I might do that. I'm Melissa, by the way," I say, putting out my hand to shake.

"Steve," he says, shaking my hand.

"So when and what's the next class?" I ask him.

As he opens his mouth to answer, a California blonde with perfect white teeth walks up to him. "Sweetie, I found the chandeliers. There's this one that's so cool—it's kind of silvery and kind of crystally, and it would be perfect for the dining room."

Needless to say, Mystery Date #1 did not work out.

I quickly say good-bye to the perfect little surfer couple and head over to Paint. There have to be some single men who need to paint. I walk over to the Glidden section, where a major cuteness with dark hair is looking over paint card samples. His body is stunning—muscley, but not overly so. The biceps are there, but not in a Governor Schwarzenegger obnoxiousy way. I walk over, leaning over him to take a sample of dark pinks to peruse. "Oh, honey, you don't want that," he insists to me as he points to the shocking pink square on my card. "The Barbie dream house was fun at eight, but you're a grown woman now."

I laugh out loud. Turns out I got the Mystery Date who in the children's game was wearing the purple tuxedo. "I just broke up and moved into a new place," I admit to him. "And I want my bedroom to scream, 'No man lives here.' "

"I know just how you feel," the young Liberace tells me. "Mine was cheating on me. How about you?"

"Oh my God! Same thing," I say, happy to have an immediate bond, even over something so awful. "How are you holding up?"

"In the last month, I've dropped fifteen pounds, bought a dog, and taken up sobbing inconsolably. You?"

"I've decided the best way to get over someone is to get under someone," I tell him. "You wouldn't happen to know anyone looking, would you?"

He thinks about it a moment, then shakes his head. "Not unless you want a guy who still lives with his mother, a former heroin addict, or a clown."

"You mean like a comedian?"

"No. I mean an actual clown. Like in the circus. He's gone a lot and makes no real money."

Eek.

"Oh!" new man in my life says to me. "What about . . ." New man looks down at the ground, thinking to himself. "Oh wait, no. I set him up once, and it turns out he's an asshole." He looks up at me. "When did we get to the age in our lives when we know why all of our single friends are still single?"

"Thirty," I answer without hesitation.

New man and I talk for a bit, then I head to gardening. There's a hot Latin number near a ficus tree who I might be able to have a love connection with.

Until he tells me, *"No habla inglés."*

I go for broke with my broken Spanish, "*Quisiera usted* . . . um . . ." I try to think of the word for "sex." Damn it! I start making kissy noises at him.

He squints his eyes, looking at me in confusion.

Trying a more subtle approach, I throw my pelvis out toward my new Latin lover.

Now he looks vaguely terrified. "*Por favor,*" I say as sweetly as possible.

He shrugs and shakes his head.

Oh well.

I begin perusing the aisles, and settle in at lighting fixtures. "Excuse me?" I hear a voice crack behind me.

I turn around to see a pimply-faced teenage boy smiling awkwardly at me. "Hi, I'm Greg," he says.

"Hi, Greg, I'm Mel."

"Do you want to go to my house and have sex?" he squeaks at me.

I close my eyes and shake my head a bit. I must have heard that wrong. "Excuse me?"

"Since you were asking my dad's gardener to have sex, I'm thinking you're pretty desperate. I'm kind of desperate too, so I figured, you know . . ."

I left the Home Depot so fast I looked like I was being chased by a giant tidal wave.

Twenty-six

Seema

"Your penis was larger than this," I say authoritatively to Scott that Saturday night.

"You're wrong," Scott argues, slightly out of breath.

"I'm right," I insist. "You're not looking at it from the right angle."

"How many angles are there?" Scott whines. "And besides, a different angle won't make it smaller."

"Yes, it will," I insist. "You're several feet from it. If you got up close like me, you'd see it needs to be bigger."

Scott finishes securing a large engagement ring that's been cracked in half onto a navy blue canvas, then steps down from his ladder and walks over to where I am standing, in the center of his living room. He knits his brows as he stares at the big penis sculpture in the center of his dark blue canvas. He scrutinizes the picture on the digital camera I hold in my hand. It's a picture of *Chode,* one of his installations stolen from the art gallery last week. "You're right. It was bigger before," Scott concedes.

"I'm sorry," I tell him sympathetically.

"It's also the wrong shade of red," Scott says, exhaling a worried sigh.

I look at the picture again, and debate, "Oh, I think that part's fine."

Scott shakes his head. "Right now it's not red. It's pink."

"Penises can be pink," I say to him reassuringly.

"In real life, they can be. But in my last version of this piece, it was bright red."

I look at the picture again. Scott leans over my shoulder to stare at it for the millionth time. I don't mean to, but I inhale the sweet scent of his cologne as he debates, "Well, maybe it could be pink."

As I hand Scott his camera, all I can think is, *What is that scent? It's new. Oh, he smells good tonight.*

Scott shakes his head as he looks at the camera's screen. "No, I gotta redo it. It's gotta be red."

"It's fine now," I assure him. "Just keep going."

Scott shakes his head. "I want the piece to be angry."

"Oh, I think you have a pretty angry penis there," I joke. "Seriously. If you think it's big enough, move on and focus on the broken promises section in the back left."

"Nope," Scott says, rushing over to a massive bookcase filled with a variety of sculptures—everything from penises of assorted sizes to butterflies to guillotines to wedding cakes. "I can't move on until I think it's perfect," Scott says. He puts his camera down and pulls two penises from a shelf. "Pick one. How big should we go?"

"The piece is called *Chode.* Go as big as you can."

Scott scrutinizes both penises. "What do you think the ideal size penis is?" he asks me out of the blue.

"Excuse me?" I ask him back, shocked by the question.

Scott looks up from the penises. "The ideal. Women say size doesn't matter, but of course it does. So what's the ideal?"

"I don't know." I stammer. "What's the ideal breast size?"

"Thirty-six C," he answers without hesitation.

I look down at my boobs. How the Hell did he know that? I look up to see Scott smirking at me. "If you guess my weight, I'm leaving," I warn him.

"One hundred and two. Soaking wet," he lies, shooting me a teasing smile.

That was definitely flirting. I'm sure of it.

"Take these," Scott says, handing me the two penises.

I am clearly not thrilled to be holding these. As he backs away from me, I say to him "I don't see why you can't just—"

"Smile!" Scott says to me brightly. Then he lifts up his digital camera and snaps.

"Oh, you did NOT just take a picture of me holding penises."

Scott turns the camera around to see the shot. "Well, I don't have kids, and it's important to get a good shot for Christmas cards." He shows me the picture—a candid of me talking to him, and holding a penis in each hand. "Look at it as a composition. Which is better?"

I look at the digital shot and concede, "The smaller of the two."

Scott nods. (I'm getting better at this whole art thing.)

He takes the slightly smaller of the two penises from me, grabs a small can of bright red paint from a corner, flips open the top, gets a brush from another section of his studio, and begins placing and painting the centerpiece of his work.

I can't get that other penis out of my hands fast enough. I practically throw it back onto the shelf. "Yuck."

Scott laughs. "You're acting like you're holding a snake. Wait . . . forget I said that."

"Yeah," I agree. "Too easy, even for you."

I walk over to my glass of wine on his kitchen counter and take a sip.

It's Saturday night, and we are in his loft downtown. I always like being here: it feels like a completely different world, even though it's just in another part of the city. The loft itself is basically a giant room—sort of like an apartment with no walls. (Except for the bathroom—obviously he has walls for a bathroom. He's not that eclectic and bohemian.) The apartment, and the building, could not even vaguely be described as a starving-artist-looking kind of place: the living room/bedroom/art space is gigantic, with amenities like polished hardwood floors, high-end lighting fixtures, and floor-to-ceiling windows with amazing views of the city lights.

Scott has divided the mammoth space to make a distinct area for each part of his life. When you first walk in, you'll notice his installations, and other artwork: they take up what would normally be a living room.

To the left of the "living room" is his "bedroom." Which in this case is just a mattress thrown on the floor with a nightstand on each side of the bed: to the left of his bed is an electric blue nightstand resembling a clown's head, and to the right of the bed is a bright canary-yellow nightstand that he's had since he was four years old. A bright red dresser rests against the wall, with a pile of clean laundry lying on top, waiting to be folded. (Or, in Scott's case, waiting to be leafed through and thrown on.)

The living space to the right looks like a fraternity boy's idea of a bachelor pad. A four-thousand-dollar red leather sofa, a glass coffee table with a shelf in the middle to display coffee table books (or in his case postcards from all the cities he's traveled to), and a monstrously large sixty-five-inch plasma TV mounted on his brick wall.

The kitchen takes up the back of his cavernous apartment. It is ultra modern, with black granite countertops, stainless steel Sub-Zero appliances, and checkerboard black-and-white linoleum flooring. It's very pretty—my idea of a perfect kitchen. And right now, it is the perfect backdrop for enjoying my glass of wine. I take a sip as I watch Scott continue to paint his penis. "So, have you heard from Nic?" he asks me.

"She sent a few e-mails," I tell him.

"How's it going?"

I laugh. "Well, let's see. The e-mail she sent me yesterday began with: 'Greetings from the newlywed, the nearly dead, and the overfed!' "

Scott laughs. "Yeah, she doesn't seem like the cruise ship type."

"No," I agree. "Apparently, earlier in the week, she met a crew member with the name tag 'Charon.' Which she found either really funny or really depressing . . ."

Scott laughs again. "Charon? Like the ferryman who gets paid to take people down the River Styx and into Hades?"

I'm visibly impressed. "Well, look at you. I had no idea who Charon was. And apparently no one else on the boat did either, because she made a 'Boat to Hell' joke that just withered on the vine and died."

Scott smiles at my story as he continues to paint. "She'll be home soon. How's Mel?"

"Oh, God," I exclaim. "On a rampage. Don't get me started."

Scott looks up from his work and makes eye contact with me just long enough to let me know to continue.

"She's a complete nut job," I declare, shaking my head. "We got her stuff out last night, which was great. But then she woke up this morning after all of two hours of sleep to research the newest ways to meet men. It's like she's on a mission with this; she even wants to start online dating. And, get this, she wants me to do it too."

I wait for a reaction from Scott. I'm curious about what he thinks of online dating. And, more important, what he thinks about me online dating. But he seems so focused on his work, I'm not sure if he even heard me.

After several silent seconds, I ask him, "So what do you think?"

"Of what?" Scott asks while brushing his penis.

"Of online dating. You didn't say anything."

"You're telling me a story," Scott says, as he pulls open a nearby bottle of blue paint. "There's nothing for me to say. I'm listening."

"Oh. Sorry. Let me rephrase: what do you think of online dating?"

Scott considers my question for a moment. "I'm not a fan. But it doesn't matter what I think. What matters is what she thinks."

"Do you think I need to get online?" I ask him.

Please say "No." Please make it sound like that's the most ridiculous idea you've ever heard. Tell me something—anything—to hint to me that I don't need to go out looking because you're right here.

Scott looks up at me and locks his eyes with mine. It's one of those moments that always make me yearn for him to lean in and kiss me. A moment where I nervously keep staring, because I don't want to break away first and look like I'm not interested.

Scott shrugs. "If you want."

If I want? What kind of an opinion is that?

But before I can get him to elaborate, his buzzer to get in the building goes off. Scott turns to it, a bit confused. "Hold that thought."

Scott walks to his front door, and presses the button on his intercom. "Speak to me."

"It's Britney!" I hear a girl's voice cheerfully yell on the other end. "I thought you could use some food!"

Scott quickly shoots me a nervous glance (or was that my imagination?) then presses the buzzer to let her into the building.

He turns to look at me. We make eye contact again. He says nothing.

"Should I go?" I finally ask him. "Give you guys time alone?"

"What? No," Scott says, still by the door. Scott puts his hand on the doorknob, then stands there a moment, clearly debating his next move.

"Can you excuse me for a sec?" Scott says, opening the door and heading out.

I start to shout after him, "I really can go if you . . ."

"No. I'll be right back," Scott yells from the hallway.

And then there's nothing but silence.

I look around his cavernous space. Twiddle my thumbs. Step up on my tiptoes. Bring myself down on the balls of my feet. Take a nervous drink of wine.

Man, it's quiet. I've never noticed how quiet it is here. You'd think in a giant building of artists, there'd be a lot of noise on a Saturday night. But no. Just . . . awkward silence.

I slowly tiptoe across the room and toward his open front door. I'm not hearing anything from the hallway. Which probably means he's not unhappy to see her. Or it means he's kicking her out before she can see me.

I lean my ear toward the hallway, trying to pick up on any recon.

Still silence.

Maybe she doesn't even know I'm here.

Or maybe she does know I'm here and came by to have a pissing contest, let me know he's her man now, and that he won't be making any more midnight phone calls to the likes of me.

That little blond bimbo bitch! I'll bet that is what she's trying to do! She's just a controlling, manipulative little heifer who wants to eliminate his female friends one by one so she can . . .

"I can go," I hear Britney say from down the hall. "I have friends waiting for me at Library Bar anyway."

"At least have dinner with us," Scott tells her. "Seema would love to see you."

I quickly (and silently) run back to my spot near his work as the two of them continue walking down the hall.

I can still hear the two of them talking, and Britney continuing to apologize. "But I don't want her to think I'm some weird possessive girl who just shows up unannounced like some bunny boiler."

"She's not going to think you're weird. She loves you. Just come in," Scott says.

He pushes his open door wider and walks in with Britney. Beautiful, blond, ridiculously happy to be alive Britney. Jesus Christ, where does he find women like this? She carries in two white plastic bags filled with white paper cartons, and Scott carries in a BevMo! bag.

"Seema, you remember Britney," Scott says, as he closes the door and walks across the room to his kitchen.

"Hi," I say, forcing my face to light up. "Good to see you again."

"Hey girl!" Britney says to me brightly, walking up to me and giving me a big hug. "Sorry to intrude. I know you guys are working, so I thought I'd bring over some food. You know how he forgets to eat when he's working."

"Yeah. It takes a special kind of stupid to forget to eat," I say without thinking.

Great. She's bringing him food, and I'm calling him stupid.

Scott places the BevMo! bag on the counter, then opens his kitchen cabinet to get some plates. Britney puts the white bags on another part of his kitchen counter, and I smile awkwardly as I sniff the food. "That smells great," I say. "Thai?"

"No, it's this great little Japanese place we found on Third," the perky little bitch tells me as she opens the correct drawer to retrieve his cutlery. "They have sushi, of course, but also a bunch of other interesting cooked dishes." She turns to Scott. "Oh, baby, I brought you this beer I think you'll like. It's an IPA with double hops."

Scott opens the bag, and pulls out a six-pack of bottled beer. "Oh, this looks cool. Do you guys want one?"

Yuck. I hate the kind of beer he drinks. "I'll stick with the great wine you got me. Thanks."

Yup. While you were out shopping for him, he was out shopping for me!

Okay, even I know I'm being petty.

"I'll take one," Britney says happily to Scott, completely oblivious to any verbal strategic maneuvering on my part.

"You got it," Scott says to Britney, pulling two pint glasses from a cabinet as Britney effortlessly moves around him to grab a bottle opener out of a different drawer. (How many times has she been here that she knows where the bottle opener and the utensils are kept, and that she can flawlessly choreograph her way around him in his kitchen?)

Britney pops the top off the first beer as she insists, "I'm gonna have one beer and a little food, and then I'll go."

"I told you, you don't have to go," Scott reiterates to her.

"No. You're working," Britney says. "Besides, I'm meeting Roger and Roger for drinks. It's kind of a work thing."

"Roger and Roger?" I ask.

"Yeah, they're the co-owners of the gallery that carries most of my pieces," Britney tells me.

"Roger and Roger . . . Wait, is your stuff at R and R Gallery?" I ask her, surprised.

Britney nods, then turns her face away from me almost demurely.

"Wow," I say, impressed and hating myself for it. "That's a good gallery."

Scott takes the bottle of red he bought for me at Trader Joe's, and refills my glass. "Her pieces rock," he brags. "Britney has a show coming up there in six weeks. You must go."

"Oh, it's a group thing," she says humbly to me as she pours her beer into one of the pint glasses. "I'll only have five pieces in the show. I'm not like Scott or anything."

"She's being modest," Scott says proudly as he opens a carton filled with tempura. "Her pieces are insane. Vibrant, energetic. I wish I had that kind of talent."

"My God!" Britney guffaws as she hands him a pint of perfectly poured beer. "You are so much more talented than I am!" She slaps him on the arm playfully. "Mr. 'I've had my stuff on display at a museum!' "

Mr. what??? What is he? Five?

"You're young. You will," Scott insists, as he chuckles at the pretend smack on the arm.

And she's young, too. Perfect. How young? 27? 15? What?

Britney turns to me. "Seema, tell Scott how talented he is."

Oh, am I still in the room? Thanks for noticing.

"You are incredibly talented," I say to Scott in all sincerity.

Scott makes a show of dropping his jaw at me. Then he practically rolls his eyes at me and turns to Britney. "Seema hates my stuff."

"That's not true," I say, shocked that he thinks such a thing.

Scott turns back to me, and smiles an amused smile. "So true," he counters with a light tone. Then he turns to Britney. "I told you how we met, right?"

She giggles, as though he's the wittiest man she's ever met. "Oh my God, that was Seema? The one who hated your *Conformity* piece?"

"I never said I hated it," I say quickly.

Scott laughs good-naturedly. "No, you just said it was thoroughly unoriginal."

I'm not laughing. "I didn't mean it like that."

"Yes, you did!" Scott says, still smiling at me warmly, as if he doesn't hold it against me at all.

I don't know how to take that. What am I supposed to say?

Britney's phone beeps a text. She pulls her phone out of her pocket. "Okay, they're at the bar now. You guys wanna meet up there later?"

Yeah, I'll bet it's us *guys* she wants meeting her later.

"We'd love to, but we can't," Scott tells her apologetically. "Seema saw my pieces before they were stolen. She's the only one who can help me re-create them exactly, and I only have her for tonight, so I gotta finish at least two pieces before the night's over."

"No worries," Britney says. "I'll be back around two."

And with that, she kisses him good-bye.

It's a hot, passionate kiss, with tongue and the tiniest bit of moaning. And if I was a more suspicious woman, I would say it was more for my benefit than his.

Can I officially hate her yet?

Twenty-seven

Melissa

Next on my carefully cultivated list of ways to meet men (a list that I am about to rip into a million pieces I might add) is a Scotch tasting. I've never had Scotch before, and frankly I'm a little intimidated by the idea of it. But the author of one of the lists seemed to feel very strongly that because Scotch is considered a man's drink, more men will attend a tasting than women. And I seem to feel that after the day I've had, I could use a drink.

Man-wise, this looks promising. As I walk up to the line of people waiting to check in, I see there has to be about eight men for every woman here. The men range in age from early twenties to late sixties, but many of the guys here seem to be my age, and most don't have wedding rings on. (Although today I have learned that this is not necessarily indicative of anything other than an intense dislike of jewelry.)

The Scotch company has rented a stage at a local studio in Hollywood in order to teach potential customers the ins and outs of a good Scotch. So, even if the evening is a total bust, I still get to lurk around the studio lot for a bit in the hopes of spotting George Clooney.

I arrive at 8:30 that evening, wait in line for a few minutes, then get to the door of Sound Stage Nine. I give my name to the perky girl at the front desk. She checks my name and I.D., then reminds me that the tasting and lecture is set to begin promptly at nine. She hands me a coin for a free drink at the bar, and I head inside.

Nice. Where have these tastings been hiding? The studio has been decorated to look like a sleek, sexy nightclub, complete with mood lighting and loungey overstuffed chairs. I walk up to one of the three bars in the room and look at the drinks menu. I have a choice of a Scotch and ginger ale; a glass of twelve-year-old Scotch, served straight up, over rocks, or with a splash of water; or what looks like a Scotch mojito, mixing the Scotch with mint, sugar, and ice cubes. Since I will be getting straight-up Scotch in the next room later, I go with the mojito.

As the bartender pours the ingredients into a cocktail shaker, I glance around the room to peruse my selection of men for the evening.

I check out a rocker type who looks paler than a sick person and who wears skinny black jeans and a funky black T-shirt. He has tattoos running up and down his arms. No. I don't mean to be judgmental; people can do whatever they want to their bodies. But there is something unsightly to me about a giant Marilyn Monroe plastered on someone's arm. Rocker guy smiles at me when he notices me looking at him, and I realize he's fifty if he's a day. I immediately avert my eyes.

My drink is ready. I hand the bartender my free drink coin, along with a one-dollar tip, then sit down on one of the plush chairs.

Absolutely no one approaches me. I make eye contact with the cute half-Asian guy in the gray wool suit. Nothing. He either doesn't think I'm looking at him, or finds me so repulsive that I don't even warrant a polite smile. I give the five-second stare (you know, when you look at a guy for one, two, three, four, five seconds straight) to a redhead in a button-up shirt and jeans. I do get a polite smile back, but then he turns to his friends and continues conversing with them.

Damn. Zero for two.

Next, I try a ten-second stare on a tall, dark, and handsome stranger who just invokes the word "delicious."

Zilch. He almost looks confused by my interest. Although his girlfriend, a ridiculously hot redhead wearing a black minidress and black knee-high boots to show off her perfect legs, did suddenly appear next to him with two drinks in her hands.

Damn it. I look over at a group of older guys. Oh fuck it—maybe I should just flirt with one of them.

"Excuse me. Girl in the sexy red dress," I hear a girl say to my left.

I look over to see the hot redhead walk up to me. "Hi! I'm Candy," she says brightly to me.

"Hi, I'm Mel," I say back, a little confused.

"That's Dave over there," she says, jutting her head toward the cute guy with her. "So what do you think? Cute, right?"

"Delicious," I say out loud.

Oh God! You dork. You are not nearly cool enough to pull off "Delicious." Knock it off.

"Perfect!" Candy declares. "Because he'd like to know if you're single."

"Really?" I ask, surprised a guy like that would even notice me, much less send his friend over to go bond with me.

Dave raises his drink and smiles at me as Candy says, "Would you like to join us for a drink?"

"Sure," I say, standing up.

"Great. Because we both think you're really cute . . ."

I put up the palm of my hand. "Wait. We? What do you mean *we*?"

"Oh come on," Candy says playfully. "He is an amazing lover, and all I do is stand by with the camera."

Eek!

"Wow," I blurt out as the man starts to walk toward us. "No, no, no," I warn him over and over again as I wave my hands around like I'm trying to swat flies away from a picnic. "You go away. Shoo!"

"Honey, this is a perfect opportunity to expand your microcosm," Candy tells me. "When was the last time someone completely catered to your fantasies?"

"About ten years ago, when Häagen-Dazs came out with their dulce de leche ice cream," I answer.

Candy smiles at my joke. She seems to really like me. "No worries," she tells me genuinely, then pulls out her business card. "If you change your mind, just call or text me. I think the three of us could have a lot of fun."

"Thank you," I respond awkwardly, taking her card and reading it.

Wow. Her name really is Candy. Dr. Candy Horowitz. And she's a dentist.

A dentist?!

I'm not sure which throws me more: that dentists look like that, or that they have sex lives like hers.

Ten minutes later, the hostesses announce that the Scotch tasting will begin, and to please segue into the next room.

I slowly walk in with the crowd to a large room that looks like a weird combination wedding reception/high school laboratory: throughout the large room are circular banquet tables that each seat eight. In front of each of the eight chairs is a collection of test tubes: five tubes hold Scotch, five hold other ingredients. In front of the ten test tubes are three glass snifters. Two of the snifters have Scotch in them, one is empty. Behind the test tubes is another glass containing what I assume is water.

Huh.

A hostess at the door asks me how many are in my party.

"One," I say, proud of myself for heeding the advice of the dating guru who insists that men hunt in packs, but they don't hunt them.

The hostess seats me at a table near the front. Seven men, ranging in age from about thirty to about sixty, are already seated. One of the men, a white-haired gentleman who looks like a college professor, stands up as I approach. "Finally, a lady in our presence."

"Thank you," I say, as I sit between the white-haired guy and a cute thirty-something I hadn't noticed before while scanning the bar area.

Thirty-something is nerd cute: something about him seems so approachable. Like a young Jon Stewart—good looking, but not so much that you say stupid things and look at the ground the entire time you're with him. A man who might not fill me with self-loathing for the next few hours.

"Jimbo, didn't I tell you?" the white-haired guy says to the Jon Stewart look-alike. "What's your name, sweetie?"

"Mel," I say, quickly flitting my eyes back and forth between white-haired guy, who looks victorious, and approachable guy, who seems a bit embarrassed. "What? What did you tell him?"

"I'm George," white-haired guy tells me. "And I told Jim that we should sit a seat apart from each other, just in case Angelina Jolie comes in alone looking for a drink. And, instead, we got her much prettier sister."

This guy is so charming that his statement didn't sound like a pickup line: it sounded like one of those things dads say when they're trying to boost your ego.

"Take it down a notch," young Jim tells George as he gives him an indulgent smile. "Obviously, a woman like this is taken."

"Are you taken, Mel?" George asks me without hesitation.

"Um . . . no, actually," I say. Then I give both of them the line I have rehearsed in my head a hundred times just on the car ride over. "I recently dumped my boyfriend of six years. And I'm excited to get back out in the world and try some fun things on my own."

Then I decide to throw in for good measure, "I thought it was time to expand my microcosm."

"Really?" Jim says, visibly impressed. "I just broke up too. Well, actually she broke up with me. But I gotta say, *that* is the attitude to take. Just get back out there. Have fun. Meet some new people."

I smile at Jim, glowing a bit from his approval. Not that I should care what a total stranger thinks, but it's nice to hear someone say aloud that they think I'm on a good path.

The perky blonde who checked us in takes a microphone and introduces us to the company's "ambassador," a delightful Scotsman who tells us about the history of Scotch in general, and his company in particular.

I spend the next twenty minutes sneaking glances at Jim, who smiles easily and effortlessly, and learning a bit about Scotch.

Actually, learning about Scotch is a little like learning chess. You can spend an eternity learning, but all you really need to know to get started are some basics. For chess, it's that the rook only moves horizontally and vertically, the bishop only goes diagonally, and the queen can go almost anywhere. You don't need to start off knowing Bobby Fischer's favorite moves.

For Scotch, we learned that a single malt is a Scotch that is distilled in a single distillery. Blended Scotch, on the other hand, can be a mix of forty or more different types of single-malt

Scotch. We also learned that Scotch has been around for hundreds of years, and that based on where and how it's made, it can smell and taste like a variety of things.

Our ambassador tells us that we have five single-malt Scotches in the test tubes in front of us. Each one has a unique scent and flavor to it. The trick is to only smell the Scotches, not drink them (not drink them?!), to see which one we like the best.

We are instructed to open the first test tube, and sniff.

It smells like honey. Not surprising—there's an amber goo on the bottom that I assume is actual honey. Then we smell the first test tube of Scotch. I'll be damned, the Scotch smells like honey. Who knew?

We open the next test tube, which smells like oranges. Also not a shock, as there is an orange peel at the bottom of the tube. I smell the corresponding Scotch, and it does indeed smell citrusy. I wouldn't say it smelled exactly like oranges, but it smells of fruit.

Next we were onto the lavender test tube. "What do you think?" Jim asks me as we smell the corresponding Scotch.

"Smells like bubble bath," I say happily (and a bit flirtatiously).

The next test tube is easy, since I can see the vanilla bean inside. But I open the tube and take a giant whiff of my favorite scent. Smells like ice cream.

Finally, we open and inhale the scent of the peat test tube.

Ick. Ew. This is supposed to smell "smoky," but I think that's a Scotch drinker's version of what wine tasters call "dung."

I brace myself, then open the last test tube of Scotch. Ick. Ew. Repeat.

"I think that one's my favorite," Jim tells me. "What do you think?"

"I think I don't want to be licking the bottom of a fireplace anytime soon," I say, then stick out my tongue for emphasis. "Ew. Ew. Ew. You like that one?"

"I do."

"You have no taste," I jokingly argue.

"Maybe not in booze," Jim admits. "But my taste in women is excellent."

I smile at him, not knowing how to take that. "Really?" I say, almost giggling. (Is it okay to giggle when you've just met someone?)

"Well, if the last half hour is any indication, then absolutely," he assures me, flashing me a masculine yet subtle smile.

For the next part of the class, the ambassador encourages us to become master blenders, like the guys in Scotland who blend forty different kinds of whiskey to make the blend this company is most famous for.

We are instructed to take our favorite scented Scotch and pour it in the first glass, thereby making it the base for our personal blend.

I immediately dump all of the vanilla Scotch test tube into my glass, and sniff.

"What do you think?" Jim asks me as he pours the honey Scotch test tube into his first glass and puts his nose to the top of the glass.

"I think it's perfect," I say, sniffing happily.

"Next," the ambassador says with this thick Scottish brogue, "add a bit of any of the other flavors you liked, swirl it around in your glass, and have another sniff."

"What are you going to add to yours?" Jim asks as he opens his smoky test tube.

"Nothing. This is perfect. Are you using your vanilla test tube?" I ask him.

As Jim starts to say, "I'm not sure because . . ." I quickly reach over him, take his vanilla Scotch test tube, and dump it into my glass. Jim gives me another sexy smile. "You know how a guy knows a woman is comfortable enough with him to sleep with him?" he asks me.

"No," I say, smiling back.

"She takes food off of his plate."

I turn away, blushing a bit.

Then I continue the mating dance. "What if she takes his test tube?"

"Oh, well, I think that at least means she'll give him her phone number."

We spend the next half hour or so drinking our blends, then comparing them to blends from the company. I'll admit, their twelve-year-old blend was smoother than mine.

Jim couldn't get any smoother, but he got even more charming and fun.

When the tasting is over, George, Jim, and I walk out of Sound Stage Nine and into the night air.

"So, now that we've had our booze, who's up for dinner?" George asks us as he pulls out his phone. "There's an amazing steakhouse just down the street. Let me make a call."

Jim smiles at me as he says to his friend, "That sounds great." He turns to me, "Are you free? Or have we already taken up too much of your evening?"

"No, that sounds wonderful," I say shyly. The truth is, I would have preferred having dinner with just Jim. But one man in my hand is worth more than two men in a bush without me.

"Perfect," George says, then calls his favorite steakhouse for a reservation. Jim and I continue to make "I want to kiss you" eye contact while George gets off the phone. "We have a reservation for three as soon as we can get over there," George says. I notice he types in a text as we walk toward the exit of the studio. "So Mel, what do you do for a living?"

"I'm a physics and math teacher at Cornwell High School. How about you?"

"Oh, I own this place," George tells me as he gestures around the studio with his hand.

"Good night, Mr. Gideon," a security guard calls out politely to George as we walk out of the main gate.

Both George and Jim respond, "Good night Hank."

Several pieces of information just zipped past me. I do a slight double take. "Wait, are you guys related?" I ask them.

"That's my dad," Jim says.

"Oh," I say, now wildly embarrassed. A girl is normally on her best behavior when it comes to meeting the parents. Instead, I have already shown this man both that I'm a drunk and a slut who flirts with men by suggesting a bubble bath of Scotch. Damn it.

The other bit of info that hits me—this is George Gideon. *The* George Gideon. The guy who owns a movie studio, a baseball team, and probably half of the LAPD. (Just kidding.) And I'm flirting with his son. How the Hell am I going to impress George Gideon enough for him to approve of me for his son?

George's text beeps. He checks his phone. "It's your mother," he says to Jim as he reads the screen. "I'm going to have to take a rain check." He looks up at us. "You guys will still go, though, right?"

"Um . . . sure," we both say, rather awkwardly.

"Wonderful," George says, suddenly pulling away from us and heading toward a Mercedes just pulling up to the curb. "Mel, it was lovely to meet you. Jim, we'll see you tomorrow morning for brunch."

I say, "Nice to meet you as well." At the same time, Jim flashes George a suspicious look and says, "Okay, Dad."

And George opens the door to the Mercedes, where I see a

beautiful blond woman who doesn't look a day over forty driving. She smiles and waves at Jim, who forces what can only be called a smirk, and waves back. The two pull away.

"Was that your mom?"

Jim nods. "Indeed."

"Wow," I say, audibly impressed. "She looks good for her age."

"She had me at sixteen."

"Really?"

Jim snorts a small laugh. "No. She just has a good dermatologist." Jim turns to me. "So . . . that was my ride home. Subtle, aren't they?"

I smile. "Well, I could give you a ride home."

Twenty-eight

Nicole

There are currently over seven billion people on the planet, and they all have one thing in common.

They are all at Disney World today.

I am so tired, I think as a writer I need a new word for tired.

Exhausted, drained, worn out, bushed.

Nope. I got it: motherhood.

Seriously, at one point in the day, between the thirty-minute line to take a picture with Cinderella and the ninety-minute line for the "It's a Small World" ride, I almost stopped a pregnant woman who was pushing a stroller, being tugged by a toddler on a kid leash, and telling a manic three-year-old to quit tackling her hyper five-year-old brother so that I could ask her "Why?"

And if she didn't answer immediately, I planned to grab her by the collar, look at her with crazy eyes, and reiterate my question with a very desperate "Seriously! Why?!"

What the Hell am I doing in Orlando today?

Paying for something bad I did in a past life. I mean, I don't think I was Hitler or anything, but maybe I jumped the line early during the Oklahoma land rush. Or invented the stiletto heel.

What no one tells you on these cruises is that six nights means just that—six nights. Not seven days and six nights, like a normal vacation. Six days and six nights. As in, we did get a sixth night: our departure time from the boat was at 8:00 fucking A.M.

And no, I did not use that expression in front of my lovely new bonus daughters. But honestly, on your honeymoon, anything that happens at 8:00 A.M. that doesn't involve the horizontal hokey-pokey is just wrong. (Oh, God. Did I just use the word hokey-pokey?)

Our flight home to Los Angeles isn't until late Sunday night. This was done intentionally: we thought we'd give the girls a day at Disney World and Epcot, so that we could see both Disney World and a fake rendition of Italy. Only now we're giving them two days.

Yup. I get to spend the last few days of my honeymoon at Disney World. On Labor Day weekend. You can imagine my unbridled excitement.

Cost of two adult and two child tickets for two days: over seven hundred dollars.

Cost of two adjoining hotel rooms, with reservations made last minute, on Labor Day weekend: at least two pairs of Christian Louboutin shoes. And a lunch at Le Cirque.

Total time spent on first day at the first park: twelve hours.

Total time waiting in line in ninety-four-degree heat and a billion percent humidity: I'm guessing ten hours.

Seeing your two bonus daughters happy and (much more importantly) asleep after a ridiculously long day: priceless.

Taking advantage of your first night alone as a married couple, only to emerge from your bathroom in a sexy red lace bustier to see your new husband out cold and snoring (snoring!) on the bed: ridiculous.

He didn't even get naked to wait for me: he's still in his clothes from today.

So much for my magical kingdom.

I sigh, walk over to the silver champagne bucket, and open the bottle of Dom Perignon I ordered from room service while he read the girls their bedtime stories. The loud pop of the cork makes Jason stir. Hoping he'll get a second wind, I immediately pose in my negligee.

Nope. Nothing. Slightly angry yet resigned, I pour myself a glass of champagne. I take a sip and stare at my lump of a husband.

"What? This old thing?" I say playfully, pointing to my lacy lingerie and pretending to talk to Jason. "I had it made especially for our honeymoon. Only had to diet for six weeks to get it to fit. Thanks for noticing."

"Daddy?" Malika says, walking in through our (what I thought was locked) connecting door.

"Ah!" I scream, immediately putting down my champagne flute and throwing the curtain around my barely there lingerie.

Malika turns to me. "I had a nightmare. Can I sleep with you guys?"

I look over at Jason. He is snoring so loudly, he sounds like he just oinked. There will be no joy in Mudville tonight.

"Knock yourself out," I tell her.

Malika's face lights up. "Yay!" she yells, as she runs to our bed and leaps onto it. "You're the best bonus mom ever."

"And you're the best bonus kid," I tell her from behind the curtain. "Now could you do me a solid and go get me one of the hotel robes from the bathroom?"

Twenty-nine

Melissa

An hour later, Jim and I are in the middle of dinner at one of the city's premier steakhouses, and the conversation is flowing even easier than the bottle of Opus One cabernet Jim has chosen for us. I've learned that Jim helps run the studio his father owns, in that he handles all of the money. He plays hockey—as in ice hockey—on Saturdays in a league, loves to travel, and has a wonderful sense of humor.

If I'm not in love, at the very least, I'm in heat.

"So, where do you see yourself in five years?" Jim asks me, as he tops off my wineglass.

"Wow. I'll take 'conversation killers' for a thousand, Alex," I say.

"Why?" Jim asks, taking a sip of his wine. "I can tell you where I see myself in five years."

"You're a good-looking man with a ton of money," I point out. "You can see yourself wherever you want in five years."

"I don't have a ton of money," Jim corrects me. "My parents have a ton of money."

"Now see, that's something only rich people say. Although I do appreciate it. My ex-boyfriend used to brag about his money all the time. It was so . . ." I search for the perfect word. ". . . degrading."

Jim tilts his head to the side. "Degrading? How so?"

"Well, for example, where he lived. He used to tell people he owned a house in Brentwood. In reality, it's a very nice condo south of Wilshire. But that's not Brentwood, and it's not a house. Or he used to name-drop the kind of car he had, but he'd say it was a 2010, when it was a 2008. Little things like that."

"Okay, so he wasn't trustworthy," Jim says, taking a small french fry from his plate. "But why is that degrading?"

"Because it means that whatever he had was never enough. Therefore, I was never enough."

Jim reaches over and takes my hand. "I think you're enough."

I smile and squeeze his hand.

"Well, isn't this rich?!" I hear a woman snarl next to me. I turn to see a voluptuous dark-haired beauty with a body and an attitude that could make Eva Mendes feel like a skinny fifteen-year-old wallflower.

"Sarah!" Jim stammers, immediately pulling away from me and standing up. "What are you doing here?"

"Having drinks with friends," Sarah hisses. "We've only been broken up for two weeks. How could you be dating already?"

"Dating? Sweetie, this is Mel. I just met her tonight."

Waiter, check please.

"Is that true?" Sarah barks at me.

"Huh?" I say, surprised she'd address me directly. My experience with this kind of situation is that the slut who's trying to break up the relationship (Shit! This time, I'm the slut, aren't I?) doesn't ever actually speak to the girlfriend. "What?" I say. Then I trip all over my words. "No. I mean, yes. What? You thought I was with *him*?! Lord no. He's soooo not my type."

Sarah eyes me suspiciously.

So I finish my word jumble with, "I'm gay."

"Wait a minute!" Jim says to Sarah, suddenly growing a backbone. "Why does it matter anyway? I thought you never wanted to see me again."

"I never said that," Sarah tells him quickly. "I just said I didn't want to marry you."

Jim throws his cloth napkin down on the table in frustration. "You know what? When someone you've been dating for four years says they don't want to marry you, what they really mean is they never want to see you again."

"You want to get married that much?" Sarah says angrily. "Okay, FINE, I'll marry you."

And the backbone turns to jelly. Jim suddenly gets all weird and doormattish. "You will?"

"Even though I'm not ready to get married!" Sarah practically spits out at him. "Even though I'm only doing it to keep you from dating some slut who only wants you for your money."

"Thank you," Jim says to her. He pulls Sarah into a hug, then turns her back to me so that he can silently mouth over her shoulder, "I'm sorry about that." Then he starts shaking his head madly as he mouths, "Nobody thinks that."

Sarah pulls away from the hug, grabs his hand, and angrily says, "Let's go plan this fucking wedding."

"Yes, dear."

"I want it in Hawaii and I want it in June."

"Anything you want."

"And we're getting a surrogate," Sarah tells him. "There's no way I'm destroying this body just because your father wants an heir."

And they're out of the room, leaving me to sit at the table by myself. I stare at my half-eaten rib eye, and avoid eye contact with any of the restaurant's horrified patrons.

Plus I get to pick up the check. Great. I wave to a seventy-something couple at a table near me, then take a big gulp of wine.

Yup. I love it when a plan comes together.

Jim comes racing back in. "Mel, it was so nice meeting you. Here's my card. Please come to the wedding. Check's taken care of."

And he races out the door just as quickly as he came in.

I look at his business card. On the plus side, maybe he knows some single man . . .

Oh, fuck it. I rip up the card, finish my steak, and go home.

Thirty

Seema

Right after Britney left a few hours ago, I opened with the most failed attempt at nonchalance. "So that was quite a kiss. Did your heart charm come true?"

Scott smiled downright bashfully and said, "Maybe. I don't know."

"Wow," I said, pretending to be happy for him. "I had no idea it had gotten so serious so quickly. How come you haven't been talking about her more?"

Scott took a bite of tempura shrimp and told me, "Don't do that. I don't want to jinx it. If I talk to you too much, you'll jump ahead and assume we're getting married, and for right now I'm having a lot of fun just . . ." he takes a sip of beer, "discovering her."

"I don't always jump ahead in your relationship," I say a bit defensively.

"Sure you do. And I'm glad you're always so optimistic that everything will work out. But it makes me all . . . I don't know, weird. Men don't go on dates thinking it's going to lead to marriage. We go on dates hoping it leads to bed. When you start acting like this is the one, it makes me have to think long and hard—is this the one? And this girl might be the one, but I don't want to put any pressure on anything. It's like, you don't decide to have a baby thinking ahead to the day he moves out to college. You shouldn't start a relationship just to see if there's a wedding involved."

I could feel my shoulders tensing up. "Hmm."

"Hmm," Scott repeated, amused. "That's a very judgmental 'Hmm.'"

"No, it's not," I insisted, quickly taking offense. "In fact, I would say you're the one being judgmental. I don't always jump ahead."

"Sweetheart, you treat every date like it's an international summit," Scott said only half jokingly. But before I had time to take offense he put his hand over his heart and said, "I love you, and it's all good. But let's face it—if you have sex with a guy, he better be committed. He better be onboard, he better not look at other women, he better have his shit together. You're like ninety-nine percent of the women out there. I love being with the one percent who's not seeing a future me, she's just seeing me."

At the time, Scott rendered me speechless. I kept trying to have a sentence come out of my mouth, but depending on the moment, I was either angry, hurt, or confused. Finally, I said, "I don't think wanting a commitment from someone before sex is a bad thing."

"It's not a bad thing at all. But it's not always a good thing," Scott answered at the time. "For example, you're amazing, and you deserve an amazing guy. But he better be on point—no screw-ups. You're not the kind of girl who allows a guy to have a little fun now and figure things out later."

I didn't know what to make of anything Scott said at the time, and I still don't hours later. He called me amazing, and he basically said I'm not a slut who jumps into bed with a guy on the off chance he'll have enough fun to stick around. Neither of these things were insults, yet somehow the way Scott said them made them sound like insults.

"You know what? You're right," I conceded, taking a bite of tuna sushi. "If a guy doesn't know for sure he wants me, I can't be wasting my time."

"Exactly," Scott agreed. "And that totally works for you. But for me, it's been nice to have a woman around who I'm not worried is going to think I'm screwing up. Who pursues me once in a while. Who's in my field and gets what I do for a living, gets my passions. Who shows up at two in the morning, drunk, horny, and happy to see me. I love that. It's really working for me. And, you may very well be right, this is the one. But I don't want to think about it yet."

I smiled, took another bite of tempura, and said, "Fair enough."

I decided to drop the subject of Britney, mostly because where else were we going to go with it? He's happy with her. She's everything I'm not.

So, we ate Japanese food, I drank wine while he drank beer, and then we worked on *Chode* as well as another installation, *Anticipation,* which is a collection of children's toys dating back to the 1950s set among Christmas decorations from various decades.

Finally, around midnight, once we were emotionally spent from re-creating his work and a little tipsy from his booze, we settled in on Scott's bright red couch to watch a Blu-ray of *When Harry Met Sally.*

Normally, Scott hates it when I talk during a movie, and he always wants to see the whole thing before either of us says anything. But I have told him in advance that I want to hear his reaction to various opinions being said by the characters, and he has agreed to oblige me, provided that I oblige him with not talking the next time we watch reruns of the British version of *Life on Mars*.

Scott throws some microwaved popcorn into a bowl and we take our drinks to the couch and settle in for the night.

I begin grilling him after the scene in the car where Billy Crystal tells Meg Ryan that a man and a woman can never really be friends, because the man still always wants to have sex.

I hit pause, and while I walk over to his kitchen to grab him another beer and get myself some more wine, I ask, "Do you agree with what he said?"

"About what?" Scott asks me.

"That a man and woman can never truly be friends."

Scott grimaces as he looks at his sixty-five-inch plasma TV. "No, of course they can."

Rats.

"But when you're twenty-two, you don't know that yet," Scott continues.

Huh. I decide to dig deeper. "So, when you were twenty-two, would you have secretly wanted to sleep with me?"

"Not secretly!" Scott says immediately. "I banged pretty much all of my female friends back in college." He thinks about his statement for a moment. "Oh. I suppose that proves his point, doesn't it?"

I am in love with a man who uses the term "bang" to refer to sex. Perfect. When exactly did my life veer so off course?

"Hey, is there any wine left?" Scott asks me. "I think I want to switch."

"I just killed the bottle. Should I open another?"

"Depends. Are you spending the night?"

"Um . . . Isn't Britney spending the night?" I say awkwardly.

"No. She texted me when you were in the bathroom to say she wanted to stay over at Roger and Roger's."

Britney isn't spending the night, even though she knows I'm here? This relationship is way further along than I thought.

"I'd love to. But I don't have any pajamas."

"I'll loan you a T-shirt and boxers," Scott assures me. "Open the Australian one."

We're splitting a bottle of wine, and then I get to spend the night. That's a good sign.

Oh, who am I kidding? That's not a good sign. That just means it's Saturday.

I open the bottle of red, pour Scott a drink, then bring the bottle and the filled glasses to the coffee table.

Scott hits play, and we begin the movie again.

The next time I hit pause is after Harry explains to Sally that after sex all he's thinking about is leaving.

"Do you think that's true?" I ask Scott.

"Of course not!" Scott practically belts out. "What kind of an idiot doesn't spend the night after the first time?"

Yay!

"A woman who's just started seeing you is still good to go in the morning," Scott continues. "Sometimes even for round three."

I give Scott my facial expression for a heavy sigh. "Oh please," he says to me. "Like at three months in, women don't start treating the flag at full mast at seven A.M. as an annoyance. A guy's gotta take that seven A.M. lovin' when he can get it."

Well, he's not wrong. I shake my head, and turn the movie back on.

I spend the next ten minutes watching Scott as he watches the movie.

He looks so beautiful. I wish I could move over, lean my cheek against his chest, and relax into the warmth of his body.

My God. Has there ever been a guy I felt more excited to be with? If there has been, I can't remember now. Somehow, high school boyfriends just seem like playtime to me now. Even men who broke my heart seem so insignificant. More like some story I watched happen to someone else. Could I have really cried caring about what some other guy thought of me? Could I really have pictured myself spending my life with any man but the guy sitting next to me?

Scott turns to me. "What?"

"What . . . what?" I ask.

"You're looking at me funny."

I'm caught off guard. "Oh, I was just thinking about how nice it would be to snuggle."

The look on Scott's face says it all. "Did you just use the word 'snuggle' in a sentence?" he asks me teasingly.

"I meant because I'm cold," I quickly add.

Scott smiles and jumps off the couch as he pauses the TV. "I'll grab a blanket."

Scott pulls the red bedspread from his bed, then carries it to me. He makes a show out of leaning back against the couch, then patting the spot on the couch next to him, signaling me to move in.

I scoot over to him almost timidly. Scott opens his left arm out and pulls me in toward him.

It's a friendly gesture. And yet . . .

I'm in!

Scott turns the movie back on, but from that moment on, all I can focus on is how he smells, how he feels, and how nice it would be to kiss him.

I try to focus on the scene at the bookstore, but instead I just inhale the Calvin Klein cologne for men I bought him for his birthday. Without thinking, I burrow my head farther into his chest.

Scott responds by pulling the blanket in closer, then slowly stroking my back.

I completely forget the movie. His fingers feel amazing.

I can't look at him yet. If I do, I'll want to kiss him, and I have to figure out how best to do that.

Hm. Look up at him and let him kiss me? Begin kissing his neck (since that's where my lips are anyway?) then work my way up?

Turn my body one hundred and eighty degrees, straddle his lap, put my arms around his neck and brush my lips against his . . .

The buzz of his building's intercom breaks my concentration.

Scott turns to me. "What time is it?"

"A little after one," I say, trying to control my inner panic as I pull away from him. "Do you think that's Britney?"

"Nah," Scott says as he gets up from the couch. "She already told me she wasn't coming over."

I watch Scott walk up to his intercom, press the button, and speak into it with the voice of Lurch from *The Addams Family*, "You rang?"

"It's me!" I hear Britney's slurred voice announce through the intercom. "Are you decent?"

"Some say I'm kind of cute," Scott jokes, then presses the button to let her in.

Shit.

Scott unlocks and opens his door, then walks back to the couch. He sits back down, smiles at me, grabs my knee playfully, then turns the movie back on.

Wait. Are we going to watch the movie with a drunk, horny blonde glaring daggers at me?

Britney stumbles through the door just as Billy Crystal tells Meg Ryan she may be the first attractive woman he has not wanted to sleep with in his entire life. "Hiiiiiii . . ." she slurs happily. "Did you miss me?"

"Always," Scott says. "We're watching *When Harry Met Sally*. Come sit."

"Can't sit!" drunken Britney tells him as she points her fingers up to the ceiling. "Too drunk. Must go to the kitchen and get more beer."

Scott glances at me with one of his unreadable expressions, then asks Britney, "So, how was Library Bar?"

"Good. Crowded though. Much more fun with you on a Monday night," Britney says casually as she pulls a bottle of beer out of Scott's refrigerator, and pops the top with the bottle opener she effortlessly fishes out of his top drawer. "Roger and Roger both said I was too drunk to drive," she slurs as she avoids our couch to head to his bed. "They told me I could stay with them tonight. But their place is a loft like yours, and I'm pretty sure they're going to have sex, so I had Roger drop me off here instead."

She falls onto Scott's bed, somehow keeping her beer from spilling. Then she says to the ceiling, "Unless you're working. I can go if you're working."

"No. We finished around midnight. We're watching a movie."

Britney does something with her throat to allow her to guzzle twelve ounces of beer in one gulp.

Then she burps. "Okay. You finish your movie, I'm gonna pass out."

And she dangles the empty beer bottle over the side of his bed, and lets it fall with a thud on the hardwood floor.

Charming.

Scott turns to me and smiles. "I guess it's just us again."

"I promise I'll rock your world tomorrow morning!" Britney assures the ceiling.

An hour later, I am standing outside of Scott's building, waiting for Mel's car to pull up and drive my drunken ass home.

"I'm sorry Britney was being weird," Scott says as we wait for Mel. "But you can totally stay."

"It's fine," I tell him for the millionth time. "She obviously wants to be with you, and I am obviously cockblocking."

"That's not true."

I turn to him in astonishment and furrow my brow. "She got up from your bed, took off her T-shirt, straddled you on the couch, then asked if I wanted to have a threesome."

Scott gives me a weak smile. "I feel like you guys haven't gotten off on the right foot. She's really sweet once you get to know her."

"I know," I lie. "I just don't want to know her biblically."

"Tell you what?" Scott suggests. "I'll bring your car to your house tomorrow, Britney can follow me in her car, and we'll all have lunch. Okay?"

I know I should say no. It's hurting like Hell to see him with another woman. I should get as far away as possible and let the relationship run its course without me in the bleachers watching every move.

But he's asking with those beautiful eyes, and I have to leave him now, and I miss him already.

"Okay."

Scott smiles at me as Mel's car pulls up. "It's a date," he tells me, his voice awash with relief. He kisses me good-bye—a little more softly than usual, and gives me a warm hug.

I climb into the car as Mel and Scott wave to each other. The moment the door is closed, I turn to her and declare, "Okay, I'm in."

"What?"

"Your lists. Your online dating. All of it. I'm in."

Thirty-one

Nicole

The first day of school went beautifully.

Jason didn't have to be at work until ten that morning, so we set the alarm for five-thirty, had a little sumpin'-sumpin' to start our morning, then effortlessly woke the kids at six. I made pancakes. The girls put on their uniforms (brand new and clean for the new school year) without a fuss, excitedly carried their new backpacks with all of their new school supplies to their father's car, and we left as a family at 7:00 A.M. for the thirty-minute car ride along Mulholland Drive, and over to Waxell, a private elementary school for mentally gifted children.

That morning, I had a leisurely coffee with Seema, walked around the L.A. County Museum of Art, then drove back to Waxell in the early afternoon to pick up the girls. We went to Coffee Bean and had ice blendeds. They gave me their thumbs-ups and thumbs-downs for the day. We went home and did homework: one page of English and one page of math for Malika. More for Megan, but not out of control or anything.

I was in Heaven. All of that worry about me getting in over my head was ridiculous: this mothering stuff was fun.

We are now one week, one day into the school year, and I am officially in Hell.

First off, the first day of school was apparently an anomaly. Jason does not normally like to wake up in the mornings. As a matter of fact, no one in this house does but me.

I don't know why that man thinks setting his alarm for five-thirty, and then snoozing it seven times at nine-minute intervals, somehow gives him more rest than, say, just setting the God damn thing once for six-thirty and then waking up. But every night before bed he claims tomorrow will be different, and he will get up. And every morning he treats the snooze button like an obese rat treats the bar that dispenses food pellets in a lab. He hits it often, and with a desperate smack.

The second morning of our first week of school Jason woke up late, so I offered to take the girls to school. This way he could beat the grueling traffic getting down to El Segundo, in the South Bay, where his team practices in the morning.

I learned something that second morning: if you leave our house at 7:00 in the morning, you can get to school in plenty of time to be at the drop-off gate by 7:30, which gives the girls plenty of time to play and hang out with their friends before the bell rings at 8:00. If you leave at 7:15, you are going to be in hideous, one-lane traffic all the way to the west side and barely get to school at 7:58 for the 8:00 A.M. bell. Then you get to slog through hideous traffic going home (what is it about L.A. traffic at 8:00 A.M. that there is never a good way to get anywhere?).

By that second night, I had forgotten all about the morning debacle, Jason was so grateful to me for taking his place that morning, he thanked me with champagne, a romantic dinner after the girls went to bed, and mind-blowing sex. Which made it all worth it.

Unfortunately, my love of champagne, sex, and a grateful husband is how I accidentally assigned myself the job of sleep warden in the mornings.

This morning began pretty much like every morning except the first:

5:30 A.M.: Jason's alarm goes off, and Ryan Seacrest blares into my bedroom with the latest interview with some singer I've never heard of, or some inane story about his love life. The alarm doesn't gently go off—it blasts. Sound waves are ricocheting off our bedroom walls so fast, I swear we're having an earthquake.

One might ask, why set the alarm so loud? Well, because Jason, the love of my life, is a very heavy sleeper. Very. So he needs his alarm clock to blast at decibel eleven so that, three or four minutes into the interview, something in his unconscious mind stirs that it might be time for wakey-wakey.

And why has he set it for 5:30 in the morning? Because every night he plans to wake up bright-eyed and bushy-tailed, wake the girls, feed them breakfast, then take them to school, leaving himself plenty of time to commute to work in the South Bay before traffic gets bad.

Hah!

Other than the first day, this has yet to happen. But hope springs eternal in our house around eleven at night when Jason is setting the alarm.

So from 5:30 until 5:33, I am treated to blasting verbal abuse from his radio.

Which is followed by him hitting snooze.

Which he will now do seven times in a row.

Like he does every freakin' morning.

I may kill him in his sleep.

Unlike my darling husband, I cannot hit snooze, then fall back into a coma. The moment I hear an alarm clock, I am wide awake and ready to start my day. Even if I don't want to. Even if I desperately want to hide in bed with the covers over my head and avoid writing and job hunting and stepkids by sleeping the day away, I can't. It is not physically possible for me to do so. If the alarm goes off, I'm awake. So from 5:33 until 5:39, I begin my daily ritual of trying to go back to sleep knowing full well I'm up for the day.

5:39: the alarm goes off again. This time, Jason is faster—his hand pounces down on the clock within thirty seconds, and he falls right back asleep.

The rest of the morning goes as follows:

5:40: I give up and get out of bed. I walk past Malika's room and check to see what bizarre sleeping position she has finished with for the night. This can be anything from her head at the foot of the bed, to her head being on her nightstand, to once having her head on the floor yet somehow the rest of her body managing to stay connected and comatose on the bed. This is how the Washington family sleeps—like the dead. I walk in and whisper, "Honey, it's time to wake up." She doesn't move. She's so cute when she's asleep. I decide not to roust her just yet.

5:42: check Megan's room. Her head is on the pillow. The moment I open her door, she yells, "I'm up!" This, despite the fact that her eyes are still welded shut.

"Good. I'll get breakfast ready," I say cheerfully, knowing that once I leave her room, she will grab a pillow to throw over her eyes and grab ten more minutes.

5:45: I putter downstairs to our enormous kitchen and wonder once again why anyone would spend so much money on a house with such a grand kitchen. I walk over to the coffeemaker, whose timer has allowed me to pour myself a fresh cup of joe.

5:48: while sipping coffee, I hear the alarm blast off upstairs, then just as suddenly be silenced.

5:57: same deal. I decide it's time to begin rousing the troops.

6:00: I walk into Megan's room. She once again yells, "I'm up!" I tell her she better be, and that I will not have another morning like yesterday. I cross my arms and try to look stern. She doesn't move. I yell, "Megan!" She sits up and gives me her best preteen *I am so over you* voice, "Okay, I said I'm up." I smile and tell her that I put the Frosted Flakes on the table. Then I leave.

6:01: Malika always looks so confused when she first wakes up—like an amiable drunk trying to figure out how she got to Seattle and, wait, what is she doing in pink hot pants? I tell her her Froot Loops are on the table downstairs, etc.

6:02: I walk into our bedroom. I sweetly tell Jason that I have a day planned, and that I really need him to wake up today and take the girls to school. He smiles, tells me how much time he still has, and pulls me onto the bed and into a spooning position.

I must concede, I very much like this part of the morning. Until . . .

6:06: fwap! He is going to break that clock one of these days.

"Seriously, Jason, if you don't get up soon . . ."

"Baby, just one more snooze, I promise."

6:15: fwap!

And I get up to leave my husband out cold and begin another round with my bonus children.

Megan is back asleep. I grab her covers, rip them off of her like I'm shucking a cob of corn, then run like Hell out of her room with her blankets balled up in my arms. I let her chase me and the blanket ball all the way down the stairs and into the kitchen, where we see Malika, bleary-eyed, staring at an empty cereal bowl. Megan stomps off to the bathroom. I pour cereal for Malika, and we talk about whatever she feels like monologuing about today. (*iCarly*? Build-A-Bears? How had I lived so long without knowing the nuances of the game Club Penguin?)

6:24: This is Ryan Sea . . . fwap!

6:28: I tell Malika to finish up her cereal, then I trot upstairs to discover that Megan has fallen back asleep, this time on the cold tile of the bathroom floor. I walk in to ask her, "Honestly, how are you ever going to get through college if you can't wake yourself up in the morning?"

To which she responds, "No classes before noon."

Then I say, "Okay, so you got college covered. But what kind of career do you think you'll have if you can't stay awake in the morning?"

"I'm thinking bartending or go-go dancing."

6:33: I hear Jason yell, "Oh fuck! I did it again!"

As I stare at the carcass that is my eldest stepdaughter, I yell to him, "Honey, can you help me in here?"

Jason runs in his pajamas over to the girls' bathroom, then screams at his firstborn, "Get the Hell up or Nic is leaving without you!" (As if that would ever happen. What am I going to do? Spend forty-five minutes driving Malika to school, then forty-five minutes trudging through traffic home, only to return to a house with a sleeping child on the bathroom floor?)

Jason turns to me. "I am so sorry to do this to you, but can you just take the girls one more time?"

"It's fine," I assure him. (Which, for the most part, it is.)

Jason continues to oversell me, "It's just that we have a big meeting this morning with one of our point guards, and I need to get in early so I can review some of his—"

I smile. "I said it's fine."

Jason smiles and tells me for the millionth time, "We really need to get a nanny."

"We do *not* need a nanny," I assure him.

"But I feel bad. I keep messing up your day."

"So you'll wake up tomorrow," I say, giving him a friendly wink.

He gives me a quick kiss, then heads back to our room for a shower.

The girls and I run to my car at 7:13. Like every other morning, Jason is tremendously grateful, and the girls are being sweet now that they're actually awake.

The morning routine is frustrating, but it is nice to be needed.

Plus that, what the Hell else do I have to do that's so important? It's not like I have a job to race to.

By the time I drop off the girls, they look great—hair brushed, uniforms clean. My hair is unbrushed and in a ponytail. I am still wearing my flannel pajama bottoms, but have changed into an oxford cloth shirt. This is a trick I figured out on the third day of drop-off. You don't actually have to get out of the car when you drop off your precious cargo. You wait in a long line of cars leading up to the school gate, and then once you're at the front of the line, a parent volunteer opens the back door and leads your kids out. So if I wear a normal shirt on top, I could get away with wearing nothing but a thong and a tutu on the bottom, and no one would be the wiser.

"You need to go to the office to pay for my field trip," Malika announces to me as I inch the minivan up toward the head of the line.

I look down at my flannel pjs and sigh. "The one to the aeronautics museum?" I ask.

"Uh-huh," Malika tells me in her sweetest voice.

"Isn't that included in your tuition?" I ask.

Megan lets out a guffaw. "Nothing is included in our tuition. We have to pay for lunches, books, field trips, everything."

I sigh again, signal to the volunteer that I will be driving ahead to the main parking lot up front, and park my car.

The girls immediately race out of the car and head off to the playground, and I trudge into the front office in my L.L. Bean pajama pants.

Swank.

"Good morning," I say to the pleasant-looking older woman at the front desk. "I'm Nicole Eaton . . . sorry . . . Washington. I need to give you a check for Malika's field trip."

"You're Megan and Malika's mom?" she says to me, a little surprised.

"Stepmom," I force myself to say in a happy tone, even though her reaction grates on my nerves. People take one look at blond little me, and just assume I'm only the stepmother. Or, worse, the nanny—I got that from Malika's ballet teacher earlier this year. People always quickly backpedal or change the subject. I know no one's being malicious. But that unspoken assumption is one of those things that consistently makes me feel like a second-class parent.

The woman smiles at me warmly as she hands me a form. "It's sixty dollars, cash or check. And you need to sign this permission slip."

I write out a check for sixty dollars, then begin madly filling in all of the blank spaces on the permission slip. (Name, date of birth, reason why if we accidentally shoot your kid off into space, you can't sue us . . .)

I hear a man's voice coming from one of the offices. "Julie, do you know what we did with the Friends of Waxell budget? I can't find a thing on this desk."

I look up at the sound of the voice—my heart jumping into my throat.

Nah, couldn't be. I look back down at my work: no, she's not allergic to anything (other than alarm clocks). I write a note telling them that she may *say* she's allergic to any kind of sauce, including plain butter, and vegetables, but that's bogus.

"It's in your top right drawer. Pink sheet," Julie yells to the man in the other room. "Kevin, have you met Mrs. Washington yet?"

Kevin???

I look up, my eyes opening wide in fear. I'm pretty sure I resemble a terrified sorority girl in a B slasher movie, right after she insists on taking a walk alone in the forest to look for her scantily clad roommate, and two seconds before she is confronted with her executioner.

Obviously, I am discussing an ex-boyfriend. What else would inspire such a spirited reaction at 7:55 in the morning?

Kevin Peters walks out of the principal's office looking fucking amazing. His brown hair is still short and wavy but now has a few flecks of silver that I can see. His eyes are just as clear, warm, and brown but now have a few small lines to show off all of the laughter in his life. His jaw is still just as chiseled as it was when we were twenty-two, and he still looks exactly like Prince Charming in the *Sleeping Beauty* cartoon.

And I'm in a pair of flannel pajama bottoms, an oxford cloth shirt I only ironed in the front, no makeup, and sporting a ponytail.

God. Fucking. Damn it.

Why is it that when we run into our ex-boyfriends, we always look like crap? I think back to any woman I've ever known. I have never once heard of a story where the woman is dressed in an evening gown, makeup done, hair perfect, and he's a beat-up mess walking into a Chinese restaurant on a Saturday night in his battleship-gray sweatpants to pick up lo mein for one.

Kevin's face lights up when he sees me. "Nic?"

I force a smile as he walks up to me. "Hi, Kevin."

"You look fantastic!" he says, pulling me into a bear hug.

"Thanks," I say. "So do you."

He pulls away, his brown eyes sparkling at me. "So, do you have kids here?"

"She's the Washington girls' mom," Julie tells him.

"Stepmom," I correct her. "I mean, bonus mom. I mean . . ."

Great. Now I sound like a nervous wreck. "What are we calling ourselves these days?"

"So you're Jason's fiancé," Kevin asks, my reputation apparently having preceded me.

"Wife," I say a little too quickly, holding up my engagement and wedding rings.

I know this is petty, but right now I'm very happy Jason spent too much money on my engagement ring. At the time I thought it was a gigantic waste of money, a ring that just screams, "Trophy Second Wife." But at this moment, it is the only thing I have going for me. Because I notice Kevin isn't wearing a wedding ring.

Hah! I win!

"How's Heather?" I ask him, hoping to hear that the trollop dumped him after he dumped me for her.

"She's good," Kevin says, scratching his neck self-consciously. "Won the Kennedy Award last year."

The Robert F. Kennedy Journalism Award. I fucking hate her. I smile. "Tell her congratulations."

"Wish I could," Kevin says. "We're divorced."

"Oh," I say, "I'm sorry to hear that."

"It's fine," he says, giving me his best self-deprecating smile. "So, are you still writing?"

"Well, I was working for the *L.A. Tribune,* but I decided to take some time off to write my novel."

Kevin's face lights up for the second time in a minute. "Oh my God! You're finally writing *Tales from My Happy Place.* Good for you! Do you have a rough draft? Can I read it?"

"It's still very rough," I say, noncommittally. Then I add, "But I'll let you look at it once I'm done."

Why? Why did I say that? Just treat him like a fire: lay low and crawl on your elbows and knees to the nearest door to get the Hell out of there.

"I would love that," Kevin tells me, while flashing me a smile that still melts my heart. He walks over to the office coffeepot. "So, do you have a couple of minutes for coffee?"

As if on cue, Malika comes tearing through the office and over to me. "Nic," she whines, while grabbing me in a forceful hug. "I forgot my space journal. You have to go and get it. Pleee-assseeee . . ."

And now I have a five-year-old hanging on me. I don't think I could be less cool if I tried. "Honey," I whine right back, "it'll take me at least an hour to go home, find it, and then come back."

Her bottom lip starts to quiver. "But I can't go on the field trip without my journal."

I sigh. Damn it, I can just feel myself about to cave. "I'm sure your teacher can give you another journal to write . . ."

As Malika looks up at me with those doelike brown eyes and pleads, "Please, please, please . . ." I can feel Kevin's eyes on me. Judging me. Thinking I'm a bad mom.

"Okay," I sigh.

"Yay!" Malika says, giving me a great big hug. "You're the best bonus mom ever!"

I force a smile to Kevin. "Duty calls. Rain check?"

And then my little love pushes me out the door, and farther away from my old life.

Thirty-two

Seema

"I am a woman aged . . ." I say aloud as I read my computer screen, "thirty-two. Seeking a man aged . . ." I think about the question for a moment. "What should I write?"

"Type in thirty to thirty-eight," Mel tells me as she types in her profile.

"Wait a minute," Nic argues from our couch as she leafs through her wedding proofs. "Why is it that the man can only be two years younger but up to six years older?"

"Men mature slower than women," Mel tells her as she clicks away at her keyboard. "Therefore, Seema probably wants a guy who's older."

"Don't be ridiculous," Nic says to Mel, then turns to me. "Men never mature. Grab a young one."

"This from a woman whose husband is six years older than she is," Mel points out.

"Yeah, but he'd be perfect if he were my age," Nic tells us. "Start out looking for perfect. Better to shoot for the stars and hit the moon rather than aim for the gutter and get a bull's-eye."

"I think that might be this Web site's motto," I quip as I type. "What should I say my desired annual income for a man would be?"

"Ask them how much money can they print in a year," Nic jokes. She hands me a black-and-white proof. "I can't see the fire extinguisher glop on your dress in this one. Can you?"

I look over to see a very nice picture of Mel, Nic, and me. Nic is radiant. "Nice, and no I can't see anything. But will it be in color?"

Nic looks at the picture. "I'm not sure."

"Have it retouched if it is," I say to her. "How would you describe my job?"

"Put that you're in the arts," Nic says at the same time Mel says, "Say you're an executive."

"If she says she's an executive, she'll catch an actuary," Nic tells Mel.

"There's nothing wrong with an actuary," Mel points out. "And if she says she's in the arts, she'll wind up with a broke artist who lives with his mother."

It's Wednesday night, and the three of us are back together as a group for the first time since the wedding. While Nic goes through her wedding proofs, Mel and I begin our quest for the perfect man via a leading dating Web site for singles in Los Angeles. Mel has put out her silver chili pepper for good luck. I leave my silver shovel in a drawer.

"How has the stepmothering been going?" Mel asks Nic.

"Better," Nic says, although her slightly weak tone of voice makes me wonder if she's questioning it. "Although with Jason working such long hours, this is the first night I haven't been with the girls in over a week."

"Well, at least you have the weekends," I say to her.

"Well, I will soon," Nic says, sounding a bit worn out. "Unfortunately, the governor was in Washington last weekend, and Jacquie went with him. This weekend, we have time off, but the following weekend is a governors' conference, and she'll be out of town again."

"I love how you say 'time off' like you're serving a jail term," I say as I debate whether I should fill out the box saying I'm curvy, or if that's some online code for "fat."

"Actually, being stuck at home with sleeping kids and unable to leave does feel a little like I'm under house arrest some nights. Oh, and I'm not allowed to use the 'what the' words anymore. That's been a challenge."

"The what words?" Mel asks, furrowing her brow.

"No, not the 'what' words, the 'what the' words," Nic clarifies. "You know: what the fuck, what the hell, what in the God damn fucking Hell are you doing? Malika's classmates call them the 'what the' words. And I'm not allowed to use them. Particularly while driving." She looks at my screen. "Who's Seema562?"

"I am," I say.

"I see," she says, clearly not seeing at all. "And why?"

"On the first question, when they asked me what I wanted my username to be, I typed in Seema. I thought that one advantage of being Indian is that at least no one has my name. But then it said that name was already being used. Makes sense, I figured. Even if Seema isn't a common name, I gotta figure at least one girl in this country would have it."

"Have there really been five hundred and sixty-one other Seemas trying to hook up online?" Nic asks, surprised.

I shrug as Mel says, "At least you got a number. When I gave the name Mel, it suggested I take the name WittyMel."

"What's wrong with that?" I ask her.

"Seems like lying," Mel admits.

"At least they didn't suggest DesperateMel or LonelyMel," Nic jokes.

"I don't know," I counter. "Maybe that's the way to go. Reverse psychology." I check out a few pics of the guys that fit my parameters so far. "I mean, there's a guy here called Whatacatch. As if."

"Let me see what he looks like," Nic says, happily walking over to my side of the table. "I mean, if he has the confidence to . . . oh, yuck."

"I know! Right?" I say, shaking my head and checking a box that allows me to delete him.

"Maybe you should fill out the whole questionnaire, then start making choices from the available pool," Nic advises.

"Fair enough," I say, then read the next question. "Oh fuck. What are you saying for exercise?"

"I put five or more times per week," Mel says.

"Yeah, put that," Nic tells me.

"I can't," I say. Mel actually does exercise five or more times per week. My idea of exercise is that excruciatingly long walk from the couch to my freezer. "How about I say once a week?"

"Once a week sounds a little fat," Nic explains to me.

"Hey, for this drinking question, what's the difference between a social drinker and a moderate drinker?" Mel asks.

"Put social," Nic suggests. "So did I mention I ran into Kevin yesterday?"

Both Mel and I stop typing and turn to face Nic. She looks back at us innocently. I'm the first to say something. "Sweetie, you've been here twenty minutes. You buried your lead."

"No, it's not like that," Nic says, brushing off the information with the tone of her voice. "Turns out he's the principal of the girls' school. I saw him a couple of days ago when I was dropping them off . . ."

"A couple of *days* ago, and you're just mentioning it now?" I say to Nic suspiciously.

"Oh, it was barely worth mentioning," Nic says, shrugging. "I mean, I called Jason the minute I got in the car. But he didn't seem fazed by it, so why should I be?" She walks over to Mel's screen. "Okay—this is the fun part: what do you want in a guy?"

"How'd he look?" I ask just as Mel asks, "Is he still married?"

"He looked great. No, he's divorced. And before you ask me the next question, no I don't still like him." Nic reads the screen. "Mel, you've said you'll take a guy three feet zero inches tall."

"Wait. Really?" Mel says in surprise as she moves her face closer to the screen. "Oh, look at that. All right, I'm five-foot-two, so what can I get away with height wise for the guy?"

"What brings me to this site?" I read from my computer. "Well, isn't that a loaded question? 'I am in love with my best friend, and he won't have me. Thanks for asking.'"

"What is going on with Scott?" Nic asks, having heard the latest during a recent late-night phone vent.

"He's called twice this week, and texted a few times, but he hasn't seen me since he brought my car back Sunday. One would assume it's because he's with *her.* That's the main reason I'm doing this—I need a fantastic date for his show a week from Saturday."

Mel jumps back from her seat. "Oh, God no!" she yells as Nic simultaneously winces at something they see online.

I get up and walk over to look at Mel's screen. "Which one?"

"The Fu Manchu guy with the nose ring and the tattoo of the butterfly around his eyebrow." Mel gasps in horror. "I specifically said no body piercings, no facial hair, no tattoos."

I point to a different picture, this one of a cutie with red hair and blue eyes. "How about him? He's cute."

She sighs. "I don't know. I guess."

"No," Nic says, shaking her head. "Don't go on a date with someone who makes you sigh before you've even met him. Let me scroll through."

Nic quickly scans through several pages of potential mates, stopping at a handsome dark-haired man. "His job is listed as medical/dental or veterinarian. He doesn't smoke, drinks moderately, diet is meat and potatoes. Send this guy a note."

Mel scrutinizes his picture. "Okay. What should I say?"

"I want to have a meaningless relationship with some guy for a few nights so that I can forget all about my problems with my current guy," I answer immediately. "Must buy me dinner first."

Nic and Mel look at me disapprovingly. "What?" I ask. "Just me then? Okay."

My home phone rings. I check the caller ID. Scott. I pick up. "Hello?"

"Wanna go get drunk Saturday night?" he asks, sounding angry.

"Okay," I say hesitantly. "What's up?"

"Britney not only broke up with me, she just totally laid into me about how I was basically a douche bag for sleeping with her without a commitment. Even though she specifically told me we should just hang out and discover each other and see where things go. And even though I was actually thinking about making a commitment. Why is it that women say they want something, yet then they hold it against us when we give it to them?"

"Because, no matter what we say, if we're dating you, the something we really want is for you to be madly in love with us," I tell him truthfully. "Anything else just messes up our master plan. You want me to come over?"

"No. I'm working now. Which is what started this whole fucking fight in the first place."

I signal to the girls that I'm going to go into my bedroom for some privacy.

"I mean, *you're* not upset that I haven't called all week, are you?" Scott asks me as I walk.

He's not really asking me a question so much as stating emphatically, "You are not upset, and that proves me my point." So I lie and say, "Of course not."

"Thank you!" he belts out. "That's because you have respect for my career. You know how much I have to do between now and a week from Saturday. Oh, and she told me I couldn't ask you for your shovel."

He practically spits out that sentence, so I immediately say with (albeit feigned) outrage, "Well, that's just ridiculous. Of course you can have my shovel."

"Really?" Scott says, his voice softening immediately. "I can borrow it?"

"Of course," I insist. Then I have to clarify, "We are talking about the shovel from Nic's shower, right?"

"Yes. See, I wanted to put it in this piece I just started that may or may not be done by next week. But the place that sells the sterling charms are back-ordered on shovels, and they won't be able to send me one for at least three weeks. So Britney and I got into this STUPID argument because I told her I wanted to borrow your shovel, and she said it's a fortune, I can't steal your fortune, so I said . . . well, you know me . . . that fortune stuff's all bullshit anyway, you make your own fortune. And somehow she turns that around to, I must have meant that she doesn't work enough on her stuff, and that's why she's not as successful as me. Which . . . I'm sorry, but why the fuck do women do that?"

Before I can answer, Scott says, "Shit. She's calling me again."

"Of course she is," I tell him. "She wants you to win her back."

"Wait. You cannot be serious."

"Dead serious. Ostensibly, she's calling to say she's sorry, but really she wants you to admit that she's right by giving you a different perspective of why she blew up at you, and why, really, this is all your fault."

I hear Scott make a clicking sigh noise, followed by, "All right. That's it. I don't have time for this. This ends now."

And he's off the phone before I can even say good-bye.

I walk back into Mel's room to watch her madly typing away on her keyboard as Nic watches the screen over Mel's shoulder.

"What's going on?" I ask.

"Doctor guy e-mailed her back," Nic tells me proudly. "They're chatting right now."

"I have a date tomorrow night!" Mel says excitedly as she finishes typing, then reads the guy's response.

"And apparently I have a date Saturday night," I say as my text beeps. I grab my cell phone and read from Scott:

Good God woman—you were right! On the phone with her now, she's saying exactly what you said she'd say.

Saturday: plan for Jack and Cokes, taxi home, and spending the night.

By the way, did you know the shovel also has another meaning?

So many parts of that message to obsess about for the next three days.

Thirty-three

Melissa

That Thursday, my date begins promptly at seven o'clock at Monsieur Marcel, a lovely French restaurant at Third and Fairfax. Knowing it's still warm in the evening in September, and that the restaurant is outdoors, I wear a modest yet form-fitting BCBGMAXAZRIA long-sleeve dress in a breathable jersey knit and some killer strappy sandals that make me look tall. My makeup is good, I have doused myself with the right amount of Chanel No. 5, and I am ready for a night of romance.

Or at least good sex.

My online conversation with Max last night was flirty and fun, and went until almost midnight. I knew from the dating sites and self-help books I've read that I shouldn't be so available, but sometimes things are just effortless, and you gotta grab those rainbows when they magically appear. (Or grab a potential chili pepper, in my case.)

When I walk into the restaurant, Max is already sitting at a table, a bottle of white wine open, my glass already poured. He's even cuter in real life than his picture. (Whew!) He stands up, smiles warmly, and takes my hand. "Mel," he announces.

"Max," I respond back as I shake his hand firmly, but not too firmly.

He kisses me on the cheek, which slightly startles me, then has a seat. "Since it's such a warm night, I took the liberty of ordering a white Bordeaux I think you'll find exquisite."

"Thank you," I say, taking my seat. "So what's good here?"

"If you're coming here for the first time, you must go with the fondue. Although I like to start with a nice salad," Max tells me. "So, why would you say you're single?"

I haven't been back in the dating scene long, but my Spidey sense is telling me something is amiss. "That's an odd conversation starter, don't you think?" I say, taking a sip of wine. (Which I will admit is delightful.)

"You alluded to something being wrong with the man in your life during our chat last night, but you never actually said what it was," Max tells me. "Why would you say you're single? Is it because you're too picky? Or maybe you pick the wrong guys? You have a tight little body and fantastic skin, so it's not like your options aren't wide open."

"Um . . . thank you?" I say, trying to make it sound more like a statement than a question. "I was in a long-term relationship that didn't work out."

"Did he cheat?" Max quickly asks. "Did you cheat? Were you thinking of cheating? Have you ever thought about cheating with a woman? And, if so, have you ever thought about using any toys with her?"

Red flag! Red flag! Abort mission. I turn my head slightly, yet maintain eye contact. "I don't get it," I tell him. "Are you gay? . . . Married? . . . Just weird?"

"Oh, sweetie. Some days, all three," Max says, brushing off my accusations with a wave of his hand. He hands me a clipboard with a form for me to fill out. "I think you are the perfect candidate for a reality show I'm producing: It's kind of like *The Bachelor* meets *Temptation Island*. We're shooting the pilot next week in Hawaii—all sixteen of you living in the same mansion. Sun, surf, a hot tub, and more mai tais and daiquiris than at a happy hour in Maui. One girl dropped out last minute and I need a hottie who doesn't sound like a Laker Girl. Are you in?"

I stare at him blankly. Blink a few times. Max smiles at me warmly as he puts his hands over mine and tells me in all sincerity, "Sweetie, during our chat last night you explained the difference between the words salacious and salubrious, and you used the word 'twee' in a sentence. I . . . LOVE YOU. I must find a man for you."

I stand up. "Thank you so much for the wine," I say through gritted teeth. "It was great to meet you."

Max hands me his digital camera to show me a picture. "This is Chad. He's one of the men who will be at the welcome dinner tomorrow night."

I look at the picture. My lips scrunch together like an accordion as I check out the photo. He's so hot that Taylor Lautner would aspire to be his wing man.

But, no. It's not worth my dignity just to . . .

"Click to the next shot," Max tells me. "Sven is even yummier."

Sven is indeed even yummier.

I slowly sit back down again.

"Well . . ."

"One fun twist," Max tells me. "Half of the men and half of the women are gay—but you won't know which half until day five."

I swear, at the end of one of these dates, I'm just going to punch the guy dead in the face.

Thirty-four

Nicole

You know a private little joke that parents play on themselves? Bedtimes. Because no matter when you tell your kids they must go to bed, they can always stretch that out by at least thirty minutes—two hours on a weekend night.

"Megan!" I find myself screaming Thursday night, "It's nine o'clock. Go! To! Bed!"

"Just one more minute," Megan tells me as she madly types something on the computer in the family room.

"Not one more minute. Now," I say, trying to summon up a threatening voice that she knows has more bark than bite.

"I know, I know, I know," Megan says as she finishes typing. "Okay, I'm done."

"Great," I tell her, trying to keep my voice on an even keel. "Now get upstairs, brush your teeth . . ."

"Wait."

I sigh. I wonder what it would be like to get through a bedtime without at least one "Wait."

"What?" I ask her.

"I forgot to do my math homework."

I let my shoulders slump down as I exhale a deep sigh. "Megan . . ."

"I'm sorry," Megan says to me quickly. "I'm sorry, I'm sorry, I'm sorry."

I heave another deep sigh to make my point, then give in. "Ten minutes. I'm not kidding."

"Thank you. You're the best bonus mom ever."

Malika comes charging out of her room wearing a powder-pink bunny suit with light blue ladybugs on it. "Does that mean I can stay up?"

"No," I say firmly as I charge up the stairs. "I read you your books more than twenty minutes ago. What are you still doing up?"

"I had to go to the bathroom," Malika tells me.

That kid gets up to go to the bathroom so many times in one night, you'd think she was a sixty-two-year-old man with an enlarged prostate. I shake my head. "Go quickly," I tell her.

Our home phone rings. I run into our room, check the caller ID, and pick up immediately. "Hey . . ." I say sweetly to Jason. "Are you almost home?"

"I will be soon. I promise. Dave and I are just going out to have a quick beer and discuss a couple more things, and then I'll be right home."

Nooooo . . . I think to myself. I've either been with the girls, chauffeuring the girls, or running errands for the girls all day. I love them, but I've been up and running since five-thirty this morning, and I was desperately looking forward to Jason coming home an hour ago to do the nighttime routine and give me a break.

"How are the girls doing?" Jason asks.

"They're fine," I say. "Bedtime's running late, and I'm sure they were looking forward to seeing you before bed."

"Is that my dad?" Malika asks, appearing in my doorway.

"Yes."

"Oh, oh! Can I say good night?" she asks me as she runs in, and throws her hand out to grab the phone from me.

I hand her the phone and say, "One minute. He's still at work."

"Hi, Daddy," Malika yells into the phone excitedly. "Wanna know what happened on *iCarly* today? . . ."

I walk out of the room to go check on Megan, who I overhear saying, "No, the answer is forty-two."

"Megan!" I yell, leaning over the banister and toward the downstairs. "Are you Skyping?!"

"I'm just doing homework," she yells back.

"Turn off the Skype!"

"Got it," Megan says.

I turn back around and walk into my room, where Megan is still monologuing into the phone. "And then Sam's sister, who's her twin, wants to kiss Freddie. But he doesn't believe she's not Sam, so . . ."

"Honey, your dad needs to get back to work. Say good night."

"Night, Daddy," Malika says sweetly.

I reach out my hand to take the phone, but she hangs up. "Daddy said to tell you he had to go," Malika says, handing me the now dead phone and walking out of the bedroom.

Of course he did, I think to myself dryly as I put the phone back in its charger.

"Can you lie down with me?" Malika asks.

"Okay, but only for a minute," I say, then head into Malika's room.

Where I spend the next twenty-five minutes lying in her bed, waiting for her to fall asleep (something she cannot seem to do without a grown-up by her side) and replaying the Eagles's song "Wasted Time" in my head over and over again.

After two false starts of slowly and silently sitting up, getting out of bed, then tiptoeing over to the door only to hear a bloodcurdling, "Nicole!" come out of Malika's mouth, I am finally able to escape.

I walk out of her room, and peer into Megan's room. Her door is wide open, her light is on, and she is nowhere to be found. "Megan?!"

"I'm done!" she yells proudly from downstairs.

"Then why aren't you in bed?"

"I'm hungry!" Megan answers back.

I head down to the kitchen. It's now almost nine-thirty.

I think the girls have a little experiment going to try to figure out which activity stalls bedtime the longest: nocturnal trips to the bathroom or to the kitchen. Megan is definitely a fan of the latter: she eats like a hummingbird, and by that I mean twice her weight in food every day.

I walk in to see her eating a bowl full of Rise Krispies with milk. "Will you please remember to throw that in the sink when you're done?" I ask her.

"Okay," Megan says with a full mouth.

Then she silently eats her cereal.

Something's off. A stepmom can feel these things. "Are you okay?"

Megan doesn't answer me. Instead she nervously eats a big bite of cereal. I place my hand on her arm. "Honey, are you all right?"

"Yeah. I guess. It's just . . ." She looks over at me. "Is it true that when you marry a guy, it means that he can put his penis in you anytime he wants?"

The immediate answer in my head goes like this: *"No, dear. You marry him so he can put his penis in you anytime* you *want."* But something tells me that in later years, I would pay dearly for my answer—in therapy bills.

"Because, if that's true, I'm a Thespian," Megan tells me.

The next hour went . . . Well, it didn't go horribly. I think that's the most any parent or stepparent in my situation can hope for.

At eleven o'clock, Megan is finally in her room and I am avoiding writing by going through Facebook.

Carolyn, my friend who got the money bag charm and then won the lottery, has posted pictures of herself and her boyfriend at the Hotel Gritti Palace in Italy. It looks exquisite from what I can see, and she looks like she doesn't have a care in the world.

I don't mean to be jealous, but I am. I longed for that trip. I know what I have is more important than a trip to Italy. But it sure looks pretty.

And soothing.

And bedtime argument free.

Jason's ex, Jacquie, she of the typewriter charm, posts an impassioned speech from the governor's office. I'm torn in my jealousy of her. On the one hand, I wish I was still following my dreams with the tenacity she has. But on the other hand, I get to spend time with her kids, so I don't envy her too much, as I know she is wracked with the kind of guilt that only a working mother can have. (Sorry, dads—but, yeah, I said it.)

And finally, a quick note from Mel:

> You know how Scott just told Seema last night that her shovel might not mean a perpetual life of work, but might mean something else? Well, what if my red hot chili pepper doesn't refer to a hot sex life? What if it is just trying to tell me that I'm going to keep getting burned by men?

I am about to write back to her to ask what happened, when up pops a friend request from Kevin Peters.

I puff out my cheeks as I stare at the request.

How the Hell did he find me? There are over a hundred other

Nicole Eatons on Facebook. (I always thought I had a distinctive name until I got on Facebook.)

I click on our two mutual friends: two friends from college, no parents from the school.

I click over to his friends list: several parents' names I recognize from school. Jacquie and Jason aren't on the list, but I'm not sure if that means anything.

Having done what little investigative journalism I get to do these days, I click back to the friend request, then stare at the screen.

Okay, on the one hand, what's it going to hurt if I'm friends with Kevin? Jason's on Facebook with at least one ex (his ex wife) and probably way more. I'm not threatened by that, nor should he be threatened because I'm friends with an ex. I am not a retrosexual looking for a fling, I am a happily married woman, as my status clearly states and all of my photos show.

On the other hand—he has been sneaking into my thoughts ever since I ran into him at the school the other day.

It's nothing bad. It's not like I'm thinking back on my life with him and wishing I was with him instead of Jason.

But, like just now . . . without meaning to . . . I let my mind drift back to the night in the haunted house. Our first Halloween. We had been dating for a few weeks, and were going to some local haunted house, a makeshift tent decorated by some high school students to raise money for a class trip or something. At some point I had accidentally walked ahead of him, and ended up in a graveyard filled with zombies trying not to be buried by the local villagers. I turned around to search for him, only to be confronted by a teenaged Dracula, who made me jump a foot. I backed up, ran into someone, screamed, and turned around.

There was Kevin, giving me an amused smile. "Hi," he said softly to me.

"I . . ." I stammered, still jumpy. "I thought I'd lost you."

He smiled and leaned in to kiss me. "You'll never lose me."

And we kissed in the middle of the phony graveyard. And all was absolutely perfect in my world until . . .

Get your head out of the clouds, Washington. Until you dated for almost three years, and he wouldn't put a ring on it. So when he he moved to New York, you "took a break." And instead of calling you a month later to propose, he called to announce his new girlfriend.

Which is good.

Because if I hadn't broken up with Kevin, I wouldn't be married to Jason. And Jason is, by far, the hottest man I've ever been with.

I am about to click the ignore button. After all, what good can come from exes being friends?

Then I stop to reconsider.

How is it going to affect Malika and Megan if I reject his Facebook request? It's not like he's asking me out; he's just asking to be able to e-mail me. Am I overreacting?

I'm overthinking this. I click the confirm button.

I am immediately roped into chat by Kevin:

KEVIN: Are you avoiding writing?

My head jolts back in surprise. Why is he roping me into conversation? I decide to go with humor.

NICOLE: Nice opener. Do you walk up to strange women in bars and ask them if their thighs really need that third glass of wine?

KEVIN: Hah! No, I asked because I'm on here avoiding writing.

NICOLE: Wait. You're writing now?

Since when does Kevin want to be a writer?

KEVIN: **Just a TV spec idea I had. Probably nothing will ever come of it, but writing is something I always wanted to do, I just never had the nerve to follow through on it. Probably why the women I fell in love with were writers: I loved living vicariously through them.**

Whoa, whoa, whoa. What the Hell is that? Flirting? Getting the past out of the way so we can have a clean start for our future? I stare at the screen, wondering how to respond.

NICOLE: **Well, good for you! Can I read it when it's done?**

KEVIN: **Sure. So, what's up with you? You looked great the other day.**

NICOLE: **Yeah—when trying to impress people I always go with pajama pants, no makeup, and unbrushed hair.**

KEVIN: **You look better with no makeup. So, are you still with the *Tribune*? I haven't seen any of your articles lately.**

Again, I am startled by what I'm reading on the computer and I don't know what to make of it.

NICOLE: **No. Got laid off earlier this year, decided to take some time off to be with my new family.**

KEVIN: **You remember Howard, my editor friend? He's at the *Globe* now. Do you want me to see if they're looking?**

NICOLE: Actually, he offered me a freelance gig after I was laid off, but I decided not to move to Boston. Thanks, though.

KEVIN: Just a thought. You're such a good writer.

"Daddy!" I hear Malika yell from upstairs.

"Your dad's still at work, sweetie," I yell back.

I wait for the pause, followed by the predictable, "I had a bad dream! Can you come upstairs?!"

NICOLE: I'm sorry. I gotta go. Malika just woke up. She had a bad dream, and I need to get her back to sleep.

KEVIN: Okay, go. Let me know when you want that coffee.

I look at the screen and debate. What would it hurt to go get coffee?

Then again, something in my gut is telling me that's a bad idea.

"Nicole?!" Malika whines.

"Coming!" I yell back. Then I type.

NICOLE: Soon. Gotta go though. 'Night.

KEVIN: Good night.

I click off Facebook, walk out of my office, and head up to Malika's room.

Thirty-five

Melissa

It's not speed dating if you actually have dinner. Yes, I'm a bit defensive about this idea—it seems so nineties. But I have a friend who met her boyfriend through this service, so I'm willing to give it a shot.

"Six at Six" is a dinner/dating service where twelve people meet for dinner at a lovely Italian restaurant and exchange conversation over food courses: predinner cocktails, appetizer, salad, soup, entrée, dessert. Because you're not limited to five or seven minutes at a time, you actually can have a conversation that doesn't consist of saying "I'm a high school math teacher." And "No, I haven't seen that movie" over and over again.

This extended conversation, it turns out, can also be a bad thing.

"I think an addiction is an addiction, not a disease," Bill, the man across the small table, spits out at me angrily. "I don't decide to drink cancer."

I haven't said a word since he started his tirade twenty minutes ago. It started with a diatribe on women with cats, quickly moved on to why he hates the Los Angeles Zoo, then segued into an attack on all things yogurt.

"Uh-huh," I say innocuously.

And then, for the first time since Bill sat down, we have silence.

Uncomfortable, lengthy silence.

"You seem angry," I say diplomatically as I lift my glass of sauvignon blanc up to my lips, then put down the glass self-consciously before drinking any.

"You can drink that," Bill tells me. "It's your body."

"Oooooo-kay," I say, taking a sip of wine.

Bill eyes me disapprovingly. "That said, I don't understand why you would intentionally put poison in your body, knowing your meninges can't deal with it."

The words spill out of my mouth before I have a chance to edit myself. "Actually, it's my liver that can't deal with it."

"What?"

"The meninges cover the brain and the spinal cord," I tell him awkwardly. "It's the liver that removes alcohol from your body."

Bill stares at me.

I'm probably in trouble, but I couldn't think of anything else to say to hold up my end of the conversation.

Bill continues to stare at me in silence. Finally, I start talking again. "The liver produces an enzyme called dehydrogenase, which—"

A bell rings.

"Oh, thank God!" we both say in unison.

A perky blonde walks up to the front of the room. "Our cocktail course is over. Gentlemen, please move to the table on your right, so that we may begin eating our appetizers. Ladies, stay in your seats."

Bill stands up and runs away from me as I take a big ole gulp of wine and prepare for the next guy, an older, darker-haired gentleman who didn't bother trying too hard with his choice of clothes when he got dressed this morning. "Hi," I say as he sits down. "I'm Melissa."

"How old are you?" he asks me right off the bat.

I hate him already. "How old are you?" I answer back.

"It doesn't matter," he tells me as the waiter puts down our shrimp cocktails. "A man can impregnate a woman well into his eighties. By the time women are thirty-five, genetically their eggs are inferior, and their ovaries are starting to shrink."

I force a smile. "In the first place, that's biologically incorrect," I tell him. "But the point is moot, since you won't be getting anywhere near my ovaries anyway."

The minidate during the salad course starts out fine, albeit a bit strange. A nerdy, slightly overweight gentleman introduces himself as Chester (are men still really called Chester?), then begins to talk to me. "So what would you do if you won the lottery and never had to work again?"

I start off with a joke. "Well, in the first place, I don't play the lottery, since I figure my odds are the same of winning either way."

This falls flat. Chester looks at me, confused. "That's not true. In the California Lottery, your chances of winning are one in forty-one million, four hundred and sixteen thousand, three hundred and fifty-three. Therefore, if you played eleven tickets per game, your chance would be one in less than four million. Not great odds, but certainly not the same as not playing."

I have no response to that. "True," I finally concede. "I don't know. Travel, maybe? My friend just won the lottery. She's traveling."

"Really?" he says to me, fascinated. "So, is your friend single? Because, let's face it, we have no heat here."

Soup guy opened with, "Have you heard the word of Jesus?"

Entrée dude opened with, "So what political party are you registered with?" (By the way, never answer that. No matter what political party the guy is in, you are just encouraging an angry monologue.)

By dessert, my ego wasn't yet shattered, but it was definitely cracked. So when my date said to me, as I put the spoon of chocolate mousse up to my mouth, "Are you really gonna eat that? Because, you know, a moment on the lips, an eternity on the hips," I responded with an irate, "You, sir, just blew any chance of spending an eternity with these hips." And proceeded not only to eat my chocolate mousse, but his crème brûlée as well.

At the end of the night, I decided to chalk up the evening as an amusing aside for my future memoirs.

Thirty-six

Nicole

In the dead of night that Friday, lightning is flashing through my bedroom, thunder is booming, and I have just been awakened by a colossal kick in my stomach.

"Ugh . . . Son of a . . . bitch," I call out, the wind knocked out of me.

I open my eyes. Attached to my stomach is Malika's foot.

She's terrified of thunderstorms, so I told her she could sleep with me tonight.

No good deed goes unpunished. That tiny girl has managed to stretch out her entire body across our bed to lie in an odd little asterisk position to take up most of the king-size bed, leaving me to move my body farther and farther out to the side, until I look like a car halfway over a precipice.

I sit up in bed, move Malika's head onto Jason's empty pillow, and her feet down to the foot of the bed. "Honey, wake up," I say to her sweetly.

She's out cold, her mouth is slightly open, and she's doing this little snoring thing that makes me worried she needs to have her tonsils and adenoids removed.

"Honey," I whisper. "The storm is passing. You can go to sleep in your own room now."

BOOM! pounds the thunder.

Malika sits bolt upright, but with her eyes still closed. As I start to softly repeat, "Sweetie, you can move back to your own room," her whole body plunges down diagonally right at me, full force. I scurry out of the way, leaping out of bed just as her head hits my pillow with a thud.

Great. Now I'm standing outside of my own bed, trying to figure out a way in.

First, I try Jason's side of the bed, empty due to a road trip. I slowly and silently lie myself down, trying not to disturb her royal highness. Malika immediately whips her body around to me, then throws her entire body on mine.

It's like in the middle of the night, she becomes a heat-seeking missile. Owww . . .

I give up, get out of bed, and putter down to the kitchen to have a glass of wine recommended by the guy at Wine Library TV.

I open the refrigerator to look for the rest of a bottle of chardonnay Jason and I shared last night after he got home. It's not there. Sigh. Jason must have had the last glass before the car picked him up to take a red-eye to New York for some NBA Cares charity event.

He doesn't even like chardonnay.

I pour myself a mug of milk, stir in some Hershey's syrup, then throw it in the microwave. As my hot cocoa heats, I walk to the desk in my office and turn on my computer. Then I walk back to the kitchen and retrieve the unopened mail from our mail bowl. A letter that I didn't notice earlier today from the *Toluca Lake Post*, a (very) local weekly paper. I open it and read:

Dear Ms. Eaton,

Thank you very much for your inquiry for our new opinion column. I was very impressed with your reporting in the Tribune, *as well as with your writing sample on the Pros and Cons of Charter Schools.*

Unfortunately, we are not able to use you at this time. A woman of your caliber should be at a large daily paper, not at a small independently owned weekly like ourselves.

Best of luck with my future endeavors, blah, blah, blah.

I rip it up and throw it in the trash. Man, when you can't even get a weekly column at a paper that pays pretty much nothing, your life is definitely not on plan A.

The microwave beeps. I grab my cocoa, head back to my office, then check my e-mails. This week, I was really trying to get my career back on track, so I sent out inquiry e-mails to every reporter and editor friend I had. My efforts so far have led to twelve incredibly nice rejections, each one filled with flattery and accolades but no job leads.

So this evening's e-mail rejection from an old editor friend who now lives in San Francisco shouldn't have come as a surprise.

To: Nicole
From: Gerry
Subject: I'm sorry

You know I adore your writing, and we love you over here, but there are just no openings—even for freelance. What are the odds that we could get you to do a blog for the paper's Web site? No pay, but sometimes that leads to something.

Please don't take this personally. Our business is just in shambles right now, and my priority is to keep what few staffers I still have left.

Give the blog some thought.

Hang in there baby,
Gerry

Sigh. I go to Facebook to click on Mafia Wars—I'm ready to shoot something or someone, even if it's just online.

KEVIN: **What are you doing up at 2 A.M.? I thought you were a lark.**

NICOLE: **Malika is afraid of thunderstorms, so she's in our bed tonight. She was kicking in her sleep, probably from all the thunder. What are you doing up?**

KEVIN: **Playing Farkle and avoiding writing. How are you?**

I stare at the computer screen. How am I? How *am* I?!

NICOLE: **Not a great day to ask. How are you?**

KEVIN: **Boing!**

NICOLE: **What's that mean?**

KEVIN: **Boing! That's you deflecting my question. What's wrong?**

NICOLE: **I'm just having a bad day. Jason had to leave town for the weekend for this charity event. I couldn't go because the girls' mother is in Sacramento for work until tomorrow morning and someone had to stay with them, and it's raining so hard I feel like I should be looking up blueprints online for an ark. Whatever. It's fine. I am very lucky, I know that. I have absolutely no right to complain.**

KEVIN: You do remember I was a psych major, right?

NICOLE: Yeah. So?

KEVIN: So then you know that I'm going to point out that when people think they have "no right" to complain, what they're really saying is they have no right to have their feelings.

I read that sentence over and over. Decide to let his hint drop. Eventually, I see the little icon pop up that tells me Kevin is typing. Then this comes up:

KEVIN: So start your next sentence with "I feel like . . ."

I take a deep breath. Okay, what could it hurt to tell someone who, in effect, is a total stranger these days a bit about how I'm feeling? And frankly, it would be nice to vent.

Before I realize it, my fingers are flying over the keyboard.

NICOLE: I feel like I don't even recognize my own life anymore. It's like I made all of these decisions that I thought would make me happy, and I put all this work into doing things that I thought would make me happy and . . . I don't know. I'm not unhappy. It's just—things aren't what I thought they'd be. It's like I was on this path, and I zigged when I should have zagged. Or maybe I stopped when I should have run, or run faster when I took a break. I don't know. And the worst part is, I don't even know how to get back on track. I don't even know what my life's purpose is supposed to be anymore. Plus there's this charm I pulled from this cake that told me my fortune was to have a baby. Which is fine, it's good even. But I had rigged my

charm to be one of work. And then I pulled the wrong charm, and that charm is so symbolic to me that life isn't working out the way I planned.

And if I say any of this to Jason, it's just going to cause a big fight. The guy is working really hard at his job and he's raising his kids without much help from their mother. I can't be one more problem for him to deal with, you know?

And I can't tell my friends, because they have all these things going on in their own lives. Mel just had to dump Fred because he's been cheating on her for years. What am I going to say to her? "Yeah, I know you desperately want what I have, and you probably have a bit of frenemy jealousy over it, but hey, feel sorry for me because I'm not happy, even though my life is perfect."

I hit send without even thinking. Kevin doesn't write back for a while.

Why did I do that? I spent years fantasizing about running into Kevin, looking amazing, having a fabulous career, and proving to him that moving on from him was the best thing that I ever did. Now I've just gone ahead and shown him that all those things I demanded and planned for when we were in our twenties didn't pan out anyway. He was right, I was wrong.

KEVIN: I'm going through a lot of those same things myself. Tell me more.

And so I did. Until about six in the morning, when the sudden September storm cleared up just as quickly as it had come. For those four hours I got to tell someone all of the worst things going on in my mind, all of my self-doubts, all of my failures to date, and all of my flaws. And I got to hear from an ex-boyfriend (an ex-enemy, if you will) that his life hadn't turned out the way he planned either—and that maybe some of what both of us were feeling was just an early midlife crisis.

Albeit, if we die at sixty-four, but still.

Thirty-seven

Seema

"Whoa!" Scott exclaims approvingly as he opens the door to greet me at his loft that Saturday night. "Planning on hooking up with some dude later?"

Indeed, I think to myself as I walk in, happy that he has noticed my red minidress and red strappy high heels.

I am pulling out all the stops tonight. I spent the whole day getting ready: I got my legs waxed (below and above the knee) and bought a new dress at a little shop off of Melrose and some fabulous new shoes I couldn't afford on Rodeo Drive. I even bought new lingerie—just in case.

"What do you think?" I ask, spinning around to show off all of my assets.

"I think my end-of-the-day T-shirt and jeans look like crap, and I better take a quick shower and throw on some new duds."

"Like your gray suit?" I ask him, hopefully.

"Don't push it, Singh," Scott says jokingly as he closes the door behind me. "So, what are you drinking?"

"Champagne," I say, pulling out a bottle left over from Nic's shower.

"Wow. Okay," Scott says, walking over to his kitchen to get us some glasses. "By the way, did you remember to bring—"

"My shovel," I say, finishing his sentence as I pull it out of my purse. "Yes. Now what else can it mean besides a lifetime of hard work?"

An enigmatic smile creeps onto Scott's face. "I'll let you know next week, when my show is up and my piece is finished."

He sets the charm down on his kitchen counter, then pulls two beautiful new wineglasses from his cabinet as I take a seat. They're interesting: both glasses have a purple mask with gold accents hand painted on the bowl, purple, green, and gold feathers painted on the rim, and three masks painted on the bottom of the stem of the glass. Also on the stem is a purple and gold feather. A real feather. The glasses are very silly, very fun, and totally Scott.

"Those are cool," I say.

"You like them?" Scott asks me distractedly. "The pattern is called Masquerade. Hand painted by a former advertising executive who decided to shuck her old job and follow her bliss."

"They're really funky. I like the colors."

He holds up the wineglasses. "So they don't bother you?"

"Um . . . no," I say, wondering where he's going with this. "They're beautiful. Why?"

"I bought these earlier in the week when I was with Britney. She said you'd hate them."

"I don't hate them," I say, hating her more all the time.

"Even though they're wineglasses, and not specifically champagne flutes?" Scott asks me.

I eye him suspiciously. "Am I in trouble just because I own champagne flutes?"

Scott smiles at me. "You're not in trouble for anything," he assures me, his voice softening. "I'm sorry. I'm in a weird mood." He gives me a kiss on the forehead, then pops the champagne.

As Scott pours the champagne into his cool new glasses I ask, "You wanna talk about it?"

Scott seems to be debating whether or not to answer my question. As he hands me my glass of champagne, he asks me, "That movie we were watching last week before Britney came over. How does it end?"

"*When Harry Met Sally*? They get together, just like you predicted," I tell him. Then I take a sip of champagne. "Why?"

Scott pauses again before he answers me. It's only a pause of a few seconds, but I think it means something. He has a drink of champagne to stall a few more seconds before telling me, "Britney said you and I have an unhealthy relationship. We actually got into a big fight about it. She said our watching that movie in the middle of the night on a Saturday night was either me trying to put the moves on you without taking responsibility for my actions, or you hinting to me that you wanted me to get rid of Britney so that I could be with you, not her."

Spot on, Britney. "I'm sorry she thought that," I say noncommittally. "What did you tell her?"

Scott shrugs. "In fifty words or less, I said that I have a lot of beautiful women friends and that she needed to get over it. She said she couldn't. So we broke up."

"I'm sorry," I tell him, sympathetically.

"I'm not," he assures me.

Scott takes a swig of champagne, then puts down his glass. "So, obviously you are not dressed for a sleazy dive and Jack and Cokes. What do you say I rinse off and change, we quaff the champagne for a bit, cab it over to Little Tokyo for sushi, then down to the Ritz-Carlton for some fancy drinks?"

"That sounds perfect," I say, surprised that he has suggested such a romantic evening.

"Great. Have some more champagne. I'll only be five minutes."

And with that, Scott turns around and walks into his bathroom for a quick shower.

There's no Britney anymore. No Conrad, no Sherri, no Greg, no five-foot-ten bimbo whose name escapes me.

For the first time in our relationship, we're both free and clear. If I wanted to, I could walk into that shower and join him. Just unzip my dress and let it fall to the floor while I open the door and . . .

Oh, for God's sake—I am not Charlize Theron in that perfume commercial. I can't pull off the attitude or the dress.

Thirty-eight

Melissa

With Jason out of town, and the girls finally with their mother, Nic called me that Saturday evening to see if I wanted to go out. Since it was Saturday night, I suggested a hip new club with a velvet rope, eighteen-dollar drinks, and paparazzi outside to snap pics of young Hollywood starlets leaving the VIP room.

Nic politely suggested that I get my head examined. "We'd be the oldest ones there."

"We would *not* be the oldest ones there," I said to her firmly. "There'll be a film producer in the corner in his late fifties who will offer to buy everyone a car."

"Nonetheless," Nic said, "I'm more in the mood for a Kobe burger, craft beer from a tap, and, most important, not dressing like a slut and hitting on men like an idiot."

"Easy for you to say. You're married now. The hunt is over."

"Oh, I still dress like a slut and hit on Jason from time to time. But tonight I want to be in jeans," Nic told me dryly. "I'm hungry. Pick you up in thirty?"

"Done."

So the two of us went to our favorite beer joint, Blue Palms Brewhouse in Hollywood. She had the Kobe beef burger with the sweet potato fries, I went with the fish and chips. Then we perused the selection of beers. For me, there was only one choice: the beer from the cask is a vanilla bean porter from Stone Brewing Company—it's ice cream in a glass. Nic opted for the five-beer sampler—which is five four-ounce tastings of any of their twenty-four beers on tap. Besides a few standards, she opted for a coffee stout, a hefeweizen, and one beer that smells and tastes like a Christmas tree.

I'll admit, it was nice not to go to any great efforts for a change. The food and drink are gourmet, but Blue Palms is casual. The patrons here are mostly dressed in jeans (as are we). There are plasma screens around the room, and a game is on, but it's not so loud as to be distracting. Plus, there are more men here than women, which is very nice.

Except that none of them are hitting on us.

"Which is fine," Nic tells me as I complain to that effect. "You're trying too hard. Give it a rest."

"Of course I'm trying too hard," I say to Nic as I bite into a perfectly battered piece of tilapia. "You have no idea how much of a crush it is to the ego to realize NO ONE wants to have sex with you. I might as well be a fifteen-year-old boy."

"You're exaggerating."

"Wish I was. I have tried online dating, blind dating, and one very bad night of speed dating. I have trolled the Home Depot, the farmers' market, two churches, and a temple."

"What do you call that?" Nic asks. "Praying for prey?"

"Very funny. I set up camp in the frozen food section of Whole Foods and joined a softball league. At one point earlier this week, I even followed a hearse and a caravan of cars into a cemetery because the driver of the third car in the line looked particularly yummy. Seriously, who does a girl have to fuck to get laid around here?"

Nic shakes her head. She takes a bite of her burger. "Honey, if you really wanted, you could have any guy in this bar. The thing is, you don't really want any guy. You're holding out for something better."

"Not true," I insist.

"True," Nic counters.

"No. I can't hold out for anything better, because I already know they're all fuckers," I say. "They will cheat, they will lie, and if I keep them for more than one night, I will regret it." I take a sip of my girlie beer. "So how's married life?"

"Nice segue," Nic says, dryly.

"Sorry. How is it going?"

"For the most part, it's good," Nic says, nibbling on a french fry. "Not quite what I thought it would be, but good. Jason is working all the time, because he really wants to move up to head coach somewhere in the next few years. Which is great. He has an amazing job that he loves, and I totally support him in that. And I am in love with the girls. But I'm wondering if I've made an active choice of dedicating my life to them for now, which I do think is important, or if I'm only doing it because my career . . . What are you doing?"

"Hmm?" I say, jolted back to reality. My mind had wandered. I have just noticed Mr. Perfect is in this bar.

He's beautiful. I guess you're not supposed to call men beautiful, you're supposed to call them handsome, but he is stunning, exquisite, and exotically beautiful.

From where I'm standing, he looks half Japanese, half Caucasian. High cheekbones, short black hair, tall, but not too tall. An athletic build, but not obsessively so. Wearing jeans, and a San Francisco 49ers jersey that I'll bet I could get off of him in two seconds flat.

He sits with his (male) friend at the bar, looking relaxed, nursing a pint of dark beer and chatting with his friend and Brian, the owner of the bar.

"You're not listening to me," Nic says irritably.

"Sorry," I say. "Real quick, do you think he—" and I point right at the guy, "would sleep with me?"

Nic rolls her eyes.

"I saw that," I say to her, accusingly.

"You were meant to," Nic tells me. She shakes her head. "And I'll go on record as saying yes he would. But having sex with a guy is not going to get your mind off of Fred and everything he did to you. Why do you think it's taken you this long to have sex? Because you know it's a bad idea, and it's only going to make you more depressed."

"I'm not depressed," I correct her. "I'm angry. And on a mission. And that guy," I say, pointing right at him again. "That guy could do a lot for my ego. That is the kind of guy I have never, in my life, had the nerve to approach, much less ask out on a date. That is the kind of man I want to have the guts to go across the room and introduce myself to. That's the guy I want to have the nerve to lean over flirtatiously and kiss. That man isn't one of the Freds of the world—a man who was in my range and who still rejected me. That is a guy who is totally out of my league. And for just one night in my life, I want to be totally out of my league."

I grab Nic by the arm. "Oh!" I say, my eyes bugging out as I come up with a plan. "His friend! You can go talk to his friend!"

"What are we? College freshmen?"

"Seriously, you can be my wing girl!" I say, very excited about my plan.

"Please don't use that word in a sentence again," Nic pleads with me as she shakes her head.

"Sorry. I'm just trying not to sound like a math teacher."

"Doesn't work," Nic assures me as she takes a sip of the fifth beer in her sampler. "Remember when you tried to say 'hookup' with a straight face? Or 'Z'up'?"

"Fine," I say, getting irritated. "Just please go over and talk to his friend."

"I'm married."

"I said to talk to him, don't offer to cook him breakfast."

Nicole looks over at the two guys. The friend is blond, decent looking. Not Jason handsome, but easy enough on the eyes that having a conversation isn't going to kill her.

"Okay, fine," Nic says, sighing loudly. "Maybe once we're done with our dinners we could get a drink at the bar so they can approach . . ."

Her sentence drifts off, because I have already marched over to Mr. Perfection and his Brad Pitt look-alike friend.

I put my drink down between their two pints, and look right into Asian dude's eyes. "Hi. I'm Mel," I say, on a mission, but smiling.

The guy looks a little surprised. Not startled exactly, just . . . caught a little off guard. "I'm Danny," he says, giving me a warm smile.

As Nic chases after me to the bar, I say to him, "Hey, Danny. Do you want to go somewhere and make out?"

"Oh God!" Nicole blurts out. "Danger, danger, Will Robinson. Abort mission! Repeat: abort mission!"

Danny darts his eyes suspiciously around the room. I can tell he's convinced someone's playing a joke on him. "Um . . ."

His lag time is annoying me. "What? Do you have a better offer on the table?" I challenge.

Danny looks over to his blond friend, who is starting to crack up at my antics. "Is this some kind of joke?" he asks his friend.

His friend puts up the palms of his hands to signal, *I have nothing to do with this.*

I say very matter-of-factly, "It's no joke. I was talking to my friend Nicole here—" I point to Nic. "Nic, introduce yourself."

"Z'up," she says dryly to the two men.

Blondie smiles at Nic, trying to solicit the same offer from her that Danny is getting from me. "Not much. I'm Nick."

"Seriously?" Nic says.

"Why would I lie about that?"

"You know what? I can think of, like, a gazillion reasons why you'd lie in the middle of a bar . . ."

"Gazillion is not a real number," I say to Nic, warningly. (Really, my tone of voice is telling her to be nice.)

"Fine. A zillion reasons why you'd lie . . ."

"Also not a number!" I say sternly, talking over her.

Nic squints her eyes at me, then puts out her hand begrudgingly to Nick. "Nice to meet you, Nick."

While they shake hands, I set my sights back on Danny. "So here's the thing, Danny. You are godlike. And I'm sure you eat mead for breakfast out on Mount Olympus. For once, I am throwing caution to the wind and going to try and make out with the best-looking man in the room. That would be you. So . . . how 'bout it? Wanna go outside and make out?"

Danny still seems stunned. He blinks several times as he stares at me.

Which is not an answer.

Which is pissing me off. "You know what? I'm in a mood, and I've got no time for deliberation. You're either in or you're out. And I mean that figuratively, not literally. Try anything funny, and I'll hit you so hard, your children will be born dizzy."

Danny smiles. He seems oddly charmed by this strange woman

(that would be me). "If I bought you dinner, could I be in literally?" he jokes.

I smile. Take him by the hand and gently pull him away from Nic and Nick. "You don't have to worry about driving me home," I assure Nic. "Danny will make sure I get back safely."

Nic promptly grabs me by the elbow and pulls me back to the table. "I am not letting you go home with some strange guy," she says under her breath. "He could be a serial killer."

Danny leans in to whisper to Nic. "What if I gave you some collateral?" he asks her. "Like . . . say . . . Nick."

Nic (my Nic) ignores him and pleads her case to me. "Or married. He could be married."

"I already thought of that," I say to Nic as I hold up Danny's left hand. "No tan line."

"I could bring her to my house," Danny suggests. "That would prove I'm not married."

I hit Nic on the arm excitedly. "He's bringing me to his house!" I say proudly. "I am SO making out with the best-looking man in the room tonight!"

"How much have you had to drink tonight?" Nic asks.

"Not enough," I tell her in all honesty. "Two Diet Monsters, three cups of coffee, and half a beer." I grab Danny by the hand and drag him away. "Good night! Wish me luck!"

(Nic later told me that after she watched us leave, she could feel Nick's finger go under her chin and push her mouth shut. Apparently, her jaw had literally dropped from witnessing my successful pickup.)

As I drag Danny out of the bar and onto the street he asks me, "So, how do I know *you're* not a serial killer?"

I turn around. "I'm, like, a hundred pounds soaking wet."

"You could have a gun or a knife hidden in those jeans."

I look down at my jeans. "These are my 'Trying Too Hard' jeans. I wouldn't be able to sneak a Tic Tac into these, much less a weapon."

Danny smiles and asks me flirtatiously, "Can you fit underwear in those jeans?"

And my jaw drops. "You're flirting with me. Wait, are you flirting with me?"

"Didn't you ask me to go make out with you?"

"Yes."

"Well, then I'm flirting with you."

"Oh. Right. I guess that makes sense," I say, furrowing my brow. "So, how do we do this? Do I kiss you? Do you kiss me?"

"I could kiss you," Danny offers.

"Okay, that would be good," I say.

Danny leans over to me and kisses me sweetly.

I lift up my hands and intertwine them behind his neck as I kiss back.

He's a REALLY good kisser. My lips just felt a spark.

And then I almost fall to the ground, completely light-headed. He slips his arm around me and catches me. "Are you all right?"

"I'm fine!" I say quickly. "I just . . . um . . ." And I realize as I'm looking down at the cement that "My knees kind of gave out. That's all."

Weak knees. A kiss that gave me weak knees. Wow. It's been years.

So maybe that cake charm was right. Maybe I am going to get a night of red hot romance.

Danny slowly and seductively pulls me into his chest, and hugs me.

He feels good. Warm, soft, comforting. Secure.

Secure. That's a weird feeling. I haven't felt secure around a man in so long, and I'm feeling more self-assured and confident around this total stranger than I have been with Fred, or any other boyfriend, in years.

Danny kisses me again, and we make out for a while, instantly becoming the idiot couple on the street you want to yell to "get a room!"

He's brushed his teeth, but not so recently that he tastes like Colgate. His tongue moves around nicely—not so much that I feel like he's trying to find my tonsils, but not so timidly that I feel like I'm in this all by myself.

I eventually pull away from the kiss. We look deep into each other's eyes. I realize I'm grinning. And we just stand there, hugging, looking into each other's eyes, and saying nothing.

"So are you done now?!" I hear Nic yell from the front door of the bar.

I turn to look at her pleadingly to go away. She ignores me. "Yeah, right. Like I'm going to let you go home with a total stranger. Both of you, get back in here. Danny, buy the girl a drink. Maybe ask her her last name."

Danny takes my hand, and we follow Nic back into the bar.

Okay, so maybe I haven't gotten laid. But I just kissed the best-looking man I've seen in years. And I feel positively triumphant.

Thirty-nine

Seema

The sushi restaurant was fantastic. I don't actually eat raw fish (I figure a few turns over a heat source does both me and the fish a lot of good), so Scott took me to a small sushi restaurant that served their sushi on a conveyor belt.

That's right—a conveyor belt. Like a giant supermarket belt of rubber mechanized to flow around and around the restaurant, carrying on it whatever the chefs are preparing that moment, everything from tuna to octopus, and allowing the patrons to grab whatever they want from their seats. I grabbed three ebi (cooked shrimp) plates right off the bat and didn't have to endure the chef making snide comments about my limited palate. I was also able to order vegetable tempura and a bottle of sake.

Which meant I was a bit tanked by the time we hit the bar at the Ritz-Carlton.

"This place is awesome!" I say to Scott after he orders a glass of cabernet for me and a designer beer for him.

"I thought you'd like it," Scott tell me, smiling proudly. "I discovered it last week with . . ." His voice trails off. "Well, when I was here last."

"You can say her name," I assure him. "It's not like if you say Britney three times, she'll magically appear."

"I never take that chance with exes," Scott jokes as the waitress brings us our drinks. He scrunches up his nose a bit. "Actually, we dated for such a short period of time, does she even count as an ex?"

"I don't know," I admit, as I take a sip of my cabernet. "You had sex, right?"

Scott looks almost insulted. "I always have sex with the women I date."

"Charming," I say dryly.

He shrugs. "Right, like I'm suddenly offending you. I'm a pig. You know that. Why, Britney just said so herself this week."

"You're not a pig," I promise him. "You're the most loyal, honest guy I know. As a matter of fact I'm surprised you've gotten as far as you have in your career, considering you have scruples."

"Wait, that's a compliment, right?"

"Indeed."

Scott shrugs as he takes a sip of his beer. "Well, that just shows where having scruples gets me. I'm thirty-one and alone."

"You're not alone, I'm right here."

"Not having sex with me," Scott says jokingly. "Doesn't count."

I drink a bit more wine for courage, then decide to go for broke. "So, how come we've never had sex?"

Scott seems surprised by my question. "You didn't want to, remember?" he reminds me amicably.

I'm shocked by that answer. Genuinely shocked. Granted, in a way that comes from half a bottle of champagne before you leave for dinner, and sake with dinner, but still shocked. "What?!" I blurt out. "That's not true!"

Scott looks at me, amused. He smiles as he insists, "It is too! I asked you for your card, and you gave me your work number. That meant you weren't interested."

"No, I asked you for your card," I correct him.

"No, I asked you for your card," he assures me with 100 percent certainty.

I think back for a moment. Did Scott ask me for my card first? Am I remembering the story wrong? Have I been sabotaging myself this whole time? And if so, now what?

"Well, even if you did ask me first, I gave you my card, didn't I?"

"Yee-ah," Scott says, acknowledging my point, but not conceding the argument. "But if you had wanted a love connection, you'd have jotted down your home number, or at least your cell. I had to call your assistant before I could get to you—that's not a woman letting me past the red velvet rope anytime soon."

"I was kind of interested," I say coyly. (Yeah, kind of—that's right. As in I kind of like to breathe.)

"Right," he says sarcastically. "So 'kind of interested' that it took meeting with you in your office, a coffee, then a lunch, before you gave me your home number."

It did?

I got nothing. I take another sip of wine. "Well . . . just because I'm not as aggressive as some of the women . . ."

"Sweetheart, it's fine. I got over it. You asked a question, so I answered it. You weren't interested."

"Oh," I say, saddened.

"And I'm okay with that."

"Oh."

I have played this all wrong, and now I have passed the point where I can fix it.

"Of course, Britney thought you wanted to sleep with me," Scott says, countering his own argument, then taking a sip of beer.

And so did Sherri, apparently. What the Hell am I supposed to say to that?

"Well, I'm not saying I would want to now—you know, since we're such good friends. But I'll admit there was a time when the thought of making out with you crossed my mind."

Scott takes a moment to decipher my statement. He squints his eyes and points to me. "Making out. That's a girl's way of saying 'sleep with a guy,' right?"

"Pretty much, yeah," I say, covering my flushed, embarrassed face with my wineglass by taking a big drink.

Scott nods to himself. "Good to know." He points to my wineglass. "Now take it easy with that stuff. We want you tipsy when we get home to watch the rest of *When Harry Met Sally*. We don't want you slurring and passed out. I plan to continue our debate tonight on male-female relationships."

Really?

An hour later, we cabbed it home to Scott's apartment. I changed into a pair of Scott's sweats and his COME TO THE DARK SIDE—WE HAVE COOKIES! T-shirt, Scott went to his kitchen to make us decaf lattes with his espresso machine, and we sat down on the couch to watch the rest of the movie.

Some of our discussions were predictable. For example: "That wagon wheel table is not that bad."

"Are you out of your fucking mind?" I said as I brought a freshly opened bottle of wine and two glasses into the living room.

"I'll grant you, you don't want it in the middle of your living room," Scott conceded as I poured him a bottle of red from the BevMo! nickel sale. "But as a piece in and of itself . . ."

"It's still ugly," I insisted.

Some moments were awkward: when Meg Ryan leaned in to kiss Billy Crystal for the first time, I snuck a glance at Scott. He was staring right at the screen, his face pensive, his eyes narrowed. I have no idea what was going through his mind, but that was definitely not the time to move in for a kiss. And the dinner scene afterward where they both admit their one-night tryst was a mistake made me certain that nothing would ever happen between Scott and me.

So the two of us watched the rest of the movie in silence. The wedding fight, the prolonged days when a lonely Harry tries to apologize, and finally the scene where Harry realizes he's in love with Sally and says to her, "I love it that it takes you an hour and a half to order a sandwich."

Of course—that scene never happens in real life.

In real life the guy goes on his merry way and leaves you to haul the Christmas tree home all by yourself.

As the credits roll, Scott turns to me, his face still very serious and pensive. "I love that you read a new novel every other week."

I don't know what that means. Scott continues, "I love that you put rainbow sprinkles on your ice cream every chance you get, because it reminds you of being a kid. I love how shiny your hair is, even when it's the end of the day and you have it twisted up in a bun with nothing holding it up but two chopsticks. I love how you look up the lottery numbers every week, to make sure the numbers you didn't play didn't get picked. I love that you stay up on the phone with me until all hours of the morning, even though you have to go to work the next morning. Because you are the last person I want to talk to at night. I love—"

I fling myself across the couch and pounce on Scott, giving him a giant kiss.

And lo and behold, he's kissing me back.

He's kissing me! Right now Scott has his arms around me, and his tongue is in my mouth, and I'm getting light-headed at the thought that the man of my dreams actually wants me too.

I pull away from him, a surprised smile plastered across my face. "Oh my God—it worked! You actually let me kiss you!"

Scott leans in, his face serious and sexy.

And this time I let him kiss me.

It wasn't the last time I said "Oh my God!" that night, but it was the last time we actually talked.

Forty

Nicole

Around eleven o'clock that night, Mel and Danny (his real name—I soooo checked his driver's license)—were still making goo-goo eyes at each other, Nick (also his real name) had told me his life story, and I was ready to head home for a pint of Häagen-Dazs and a bag of Chips Ahoy!

I got home, had a quick call with Jason, who was still hanging out with some former players at the NBA fund-raiser, then settled in for the night.

The first thing I did after talking to Jason was check Facebook to see if Kevin was on.

It's not like how it sounds. It was just such a relief to get to talk to him last night. To get to be honest with my feelings about my life, no matter how ugly they were. I tried talking to Mel tonight—her response was to check out and hook up with a guy.

And that is fine—she is allowed to have one night where we focus on her. God knows we focused on me for months on end leading up to the wedding, and she gets major points for not only coaxing me out of the bathroom that day, but never breathing a word about it to any of my guests.

But I need to talk some more. I need to figure stuff out.

I click on Facebook.

KEVIN: **You're home early.**

NICOLE: **Mel hooked up with someone. You know what they say: two's company, three's kinky. What did you do tonight?**

KEVIN: **Watched six episodes of *The A-Team* back-to-back while eating a balanced diet of Hot Pockets and potato chips.**

NICOLE: **Still blocked, huh?**

KEVIN: **Indeed. And now I plan to weep in the dark because I'm not hooking up with someone tonight. I'm jealous of Mel. Ever miss it?**

NICOLE: **What? Hooking up? Nah.**

KEVIN: **The first kiss? Really. Oh, I missed it when I was married. That excitement of everything being new, everything having possibilities. Remember that place in Malibu?**

I know exactly what he's referring to and quickly type:

NICOLE: **Barely. It was a lifetime ago.**

KEVIN: **Hold on. My microwave burrito is ready.**

As I wait for Kevin to come back, my mind wanders back to the fish restaurant in Malibu he referred to. A memory floods through me of him pulling me into a kiss on our first date.

We had gone to this little seafood place just over the Ventura county line, a funky run-down shack on the Pacific Coast Highway with amazing views of the ocean and even better food. We were drinking beers and eating fried fish, and somehow I was so comfortable with him that I brought up the subject of first kisses.

"Oh, there's so much to worry about," I had complained at the time. "As a girl, you have to do the lean-in thing, so he knows you're interested. But you don't actually want to lean in and kiss him, because then you look too easy . . ."

"You look easy giving someone a kiss?" Kevin had asked, amused.

"Well, no, I mean, not easy," I clarify. "It's not like you're sleeping with the guy. But you have to let the guy make the first move, because if he doesn't then he's not interested, so you don't want to waste your time on a second date. But then—"

"Wait," Kevin stopped me. "Why do you think a guy would ask you out on a second date if he wasn't interested?"

I knitted my brows and thought about that. "You know, I'm not really sure. Why do guys do that?"

"I don't know any men who do that," Kevin admitted. "If we ask you out on a second date, it's because we're interested. So maybe if the guy doesn't kiss you that first night, he's just being a gentleman."

"No, he's being a wuss," I blurted out. "I mean, it's bad enough we have to play with our keys and kill time waiting in front of our locked door."

"Stop," Kevin commanded again. "Why are you in front of a locked door? If you like the guy and want to kiss him, why not invite him in for a drink?"

"Because then I look like a slut," I said succinctly.

Kevin's eyes bugged out. "Over a drink?"

I looked up and stared at the seagulls hovering over the restaurant while I thought about his question. "Well, maybe I could get away with coffee or something," I decided. Then I looked back at him again. "I don't know. See, but this is what I mean by how awkward and awful first kisses are. I mean, you just can't—"

And Kevin promptly shut me up by leaning in and kissing me.

As I think back to that moment, I realize that I am smiling and a little short of breath. A man who was my absolute idea of perfection back then kissed me. That moment of shock and excitement and the thrill of the conquest all mixed into one . . . it was perfect.

Turns out I do miss first kisses.

And I know I'm not supposed to feel this way, but I guess I am a little sad that I'll never have the thrill and excitement of a first kiss again.

KEVIN: I'm back. Okay, so you don't miss first kisses.

NICOLE: No.

I type back instantly.

KEVIN: Fair enough. Back to what we were talking about last night: best and worst part of marriage. Start with best.

I think about the best part of marriage for a moment.

NICOLE: I love him.

KEVIN: That's not a best.

NICOLE: Sure it is. I love him. I love how I feel when I'm around him. I get to feel like that for the rest of my life because I'm married to him.

I hit send, then ask Kevin:

NICOLE: What about you? Best part of marriage?

KEVIN: Better tax status.

NICOLE: Sweet-talking devil.

KEVIN: What can I say? I'm not a strong supporter of marriage. Maybe if I had married you, things would have been different.

NICOLE: Yeah, but if you had married me, you never would have had the nerve to follow your dream and move to New York.

KEVIN: True. But as I pointed out last night, sometimes the path to happiness isn't what you thought it would be. Sometimes it doesn't go directly forward, it curves around, doubles back, hits a tree . . . Anyway, worst part about marriage?

NICOLE: That's easy. Somehow that ring on his finger is a magical tourniquet that stops the flow of blood to the part of his brain that knows how to put dishes in the sink and throw socks in the hamper. You?

He takes a moment before he writes back.

KEVIN: No more first kisses.

That's all he types. I let it lie there for some reason.

KEVIN: Wanna go meet me for a drink somewhere?

NICOLE: I shouldn't.

KEVIN: Why not?

He has a point. Why not? No one's home, no one will miss me, and I'm still wide awake. What's it going to hurt to have a drink with an old friend?

KEVIN: Why not?

Kevin types a second time.

NICOLE: I have stuff to do around here. Maybe I'll get some writing done.

KEVIN: Come on! If Mel hadn't hooked up, you'd still be out, right?

NICOLE: Yeah, but Mel's not an ex. Plus, I'm an old lady. I'm going to bed soon.

KEVIN: Don't think of me as an ex, think of me as a friend. And quit being such an old lady. Plus, with all of your responsibilities these days, when is the next time you're going to have the opportunity to be out until past two?

I think about Kevin's question for a moment. He's right: when will my next opportunity be? And the truth is, I would like to see him. And it would be nice to be out late. I was disappointed that my big night out was over by eleven.

NICOLE: Okay, one drink. But nowhere trendy, and it has to be somewhere near my house. Thoughts?

KEVIN: My place.

NICOLE: Good night.

KEVIN: I'm kidding! Don't leave, I'm totally kidding. How about that little place in the Valley on Ventura with the lounge couches?

NICOLE: Going to be mobbed on a Saturday night. Oh! Bowling! What about that bowling alley on Ventura above the deli?

KEVIN: Eaton, are you seriously suggesting bowling?

NICOLE: It's Washington now. And I like bowling.

No response from Kevin for a while.

NICOLE: So, are you in, or what?

KEVIN: I'm in. See you in thirty?

NICOLE: Awesome.

Kevin clicks off. I click off, then run upstairs to grab my bowling shoes. (Yes, I have bowling shoes. It is the fabulousness that is me.) I'm so excited! I haven't been bowling in I don't know how long. In Los Angeles, bowling alleys tend to be booked by leagues until ten at night, and by then the girls are in bed and I can't go. So it's been months and months since I've been bowling.

Come to think of it—maybe even years.

My home phone rings. It's Jason. Damn it. I really love him, but I really want to go bowling.

I pick up.

"Hey," I say quickly, hoping this is a one-minute call. "How's the event going?"

"It's done for tonight, and I am exhausted and in bed. How are you? What have you been up to?"

"Good," I say, nervously looking at the clock. "Nothing much. I miss you."

"I miss you too," he says sweetly. "Listen, Jacquie called. She wanted to know if she could drop the girls off at four, instead of six."

I audibly sigh.

"Problem?" Jason asks.

"You know? Kinda, yeah," I admit. "I planned a day tomorrow. I know my job isn't as important as everyone else's, but I . . ."

"Whoa, whoa, whoa. Sweetie," Jason interrupts. "Your job's not less important than ours. If you have plans, it's fine. I'll just tell her no."

"No. Because if you do that, then she'll just show up at five all stressed out, and then the girls will pick up on the stress, and then they'll get all stressed . . ."

"The girls have had a career mom for a long time. They'll be fine. Don't worry about it."

"You know what? It's fine," I say quickly. "I can be done with my stuff by four. It's fine."

"You don't have to be," Jason insists.

"No. I want to be. I need to take Megan shopping for a new leotard anyway. It'll be fine."

Jason pauses for a second. I take the time to grab my iPhone and text Kevin:

Don't leave yet. Jason's on the phone.

"Are you okay?" Jason asks me. "You sound weird."

"I'm fine," I insist. "I'm just thrown at having my plans changed."

Which is true. So I don't quite know where it's coming from as I blurt out, "I just . . . it would just be nice if someone acknowledged everything I do around here. I mean, Jacquie doesn't even call me, she calls you. You don't even know Megan needs a leotard, you certainly won't know I got her one unless I point it out, which I'm doing now, which I know even as I'm hearing myself talk just sounds petty and insecure, but . . ." my voice trails off. "I don't know. I guess maybe I'm having a bad day."

"Did something else happen with the job search?" Jason asks me.

I sigh. "Man, I don't even want to talk about that."

"Is that a 'I don't want to talk about it, ask me questions'? Or a 'I don't want to talk about it. Seriously, if you bring it up again, I'll rip out your throat'?"

I smile. "Second one."

"Okay," Jason says, and I can hear the smile in his voice.

I miss him. I can just see him right now, lying in the hotel's king-sized bed with a pair of flannel pajama bottoms on but no top (a quirk of his; his lower half gets cold, but not his upper half), drinking a glass of milk that he always orders from room service, even though it's got to be ten bucks plus tip.

"You want to stay on the phone with me for a while?" Jason asks me.

"Sure," I say softly.

"Sweetie, what's wrong?"

"I don't know," I answer honestly. "I just wish I knew what I was supposed to be doing with my life. I wish God would send down a lightning bolt: this is your place. This is where you belong. This is your path. Now knock it off, I've sent you enough signs."

"You do know your path is with me, right?" Jason asks me.

"Of course."

"Okay. Just checking. Because I can go down a lot of roads, but I plan to be with you no matter which one we choose."

It's nice to hear that. With all of the craziness of his work, his parenting, and my coparenting, I think maybe I had forgotten that.

I spent the next hour talking to Jason. I texted Kevin a few times, finally telling him I couldn't go out tonight because I was talking to my husband.

But there was still a small part of me that wanted to go. Wanted the excitement of someone paying attention to me, and not just because I could be home by four to make everyone's life a little easier. And I will admit when Kevin wrote his final text of the night:

Sorry I missed you. Coffee at school Monday?

A small part of me was excited for Monday.

Forty-one

Melissa

Nothing quite makes you feel as self-loathing as a one-night stand. Particularly if you've never had one before (seriously).

I open my eyes, and sigh. Crap. This is so not how I thought I'd feel the next day. I thought I'd feel empowered. Now I just feel clueless.

I look over at Danny, naked next to me in his bed. He's a very fine-looking man. That chest is perfect. Muscular, but not overly so. And his face is exquisite—perfectly chiseled features and flawless skin. Much more handsome than Fred.

Why am I thinking about Fred?

I try to figure out how to politely extricate myself from this situation. I am a fucking idiot—I have no idea what you're supposed to do the morning after a one-night stand. Maybe I should have looked that up on Bing or something.

I lift the sheets, and look down at my own body. Yup, naked all right.

Crap, crap, crap.

I slowly peel the blanket off of Danny and step out of his bed, careful to keep myself completely covered. Then I start a vain search for my underwear.

Yeah—this is a good place to be in my life. When I was a teenager just discovering boys, this is exactly where I pictured myself at thirty-two.

"Morning," I hear Danny say behind me.

I jump a foot, startled, then turn around, and try to act nonchalant. "Good morning."

He rubs his eyes. Checks his watch on the nightstand. "What time is it?"

"I'm not sure," I say, my eyes madly darting around the room in search of my black satin underwear.

Danny reads his watch. "Wow. It's almost ten. Do you want to go get brunch?"

"Brunch?" I repeat. "I'm not sure what the protocol is here. Are we supposed to get brunch?"

Danny sits up, and the sheet over him slides down to reveal his perfect, naked torso. "What do you mean 'Are we supposed to'?" he asks me.

I sigh. "I know this is going to sound like a line, but I've never done that before."

Danny smiles. "Never done which part before?"

"Oh God!" I nearly shriek as I cover my reddening face in embarrassment. "I've never had a one-night stand before. You can believe me or not believe me, but I haven't."

Suddenly I notice my panties are draping the lamp on his nightstand (good Christ). I race over to his side of the bed and yank them off.

Danny slowly rubs my stomach through the blanket. "Come back to bed."

"Come BACK to bed?" I repeat incredulously. Then I try to figure out how to shimmy into my underwear while keeping the blanket completely covering me. "Oh, no, no, no."

I watch his sheet slip down below his hip as he says to me, "You know, you can put your underwear on in front of me. I have already seen you naked."

"That was at night," I say, a bundle of nerves as I try to slip my underwear over my feet without dropping the blanket. "Plus, I was drunk."

I manage to get my underwear completely on before Danny slowly (and sexily) pulls me back into the bed. He kisses my neck for a moment. Which I will admit feels ridiculously excellent. "You didn't drink much," he points out.

I try to push him off of my neck. I need to get out of here. "I was drunk on power and intoxicated by your beauty."

"Intoxicated by my beauty?" Danny repeats.

I continue, "I needed to know that I could talk someone out of my league into wanting me. I have. Now I need to leave."

Danny moves his left arm over me, straddling himself slightly on top of me. He smiles. "So . . . what made you pick me?"

I do give in a little by leaning back. I'm tempted just to do it with him one more time, then leave.

But, instead, I sigh loudly. "Oh please—I'm embarrassed enough without the Monday Morning Quarterback."

"The what?"

"The Monday . . . Don't you watch football?"

"Nah. I'd rather play sports than watch them," he tells me seductively. He takes my hand and kisses my palm ever so lightly. Then he begins moving his lips up my arm. I could get used to this if I didn't think he'd be dumping me later today. "Do you have a girlfriend?" I ask.

"No," he mumbles while his hot breath caresses my neck. "Why? Do you have a boyfriend?"

Danny begins licking my neck as I try to continue my sentence. I take a deep breath and try to forget the hormones coursing through my body. Or the fact that I'm suddenly remembering how last night he was very . . . Um, what's a polite way to say this? . . . how adept he was in the boudoir.

"Why would I be with you if I had a boyfriend? What kind of girl do you think I am?"

Before he can speak, I say, "Don't answer that. I'm the type of girl who picks up random boys in bars. Oh God, I'm someone I hate."

Danny stops kissing me. He looks me in the eye. "Are you going to relax at all?"

"Not until you dump me. No."

He looks away, then blinks several times. My comments seem to inspire blinking in him. It's not something I'm proud of, but he's not the first.

Danny stands up and gets out of bed. "Okay, let's go."

"Where?"

"I don't know. What's your idea of a perfect outing on a Sunday?"

"What? I have to pick what we're doing? It's not enough that I asked you out last night . . ."

"Asked me out? Is that what that was?" Danny jokes.

"Stop it. If we're going to go on this date, which I'm not even sure is a good idea, I am not picking where we go. You need to make some decisions here."

"Fine," Danny says, sliding back into bed. "I choose bed day."

He moves in for a kiss, but I crane my neck back, pulling away from him. "I do love the beach."

Danny smiles to himself.

"What?" I ask.

"Nothing," he says, climbing out of bed for the second time. "The beach it is. I have a brunch place I want to take you to first." He turns to me. "Promise me one thing?"

"What?"

"At the end of the day, I am getting sex again, right?"

"Are you sure you want to?" I ask.

That makes Danny laugh. He takes my hand. "Come on, you goof."

I let him lead me by the hand. "Where are we going?"

"Shower."

"What?! Together?!" I ask.

"Yes. A shower together is the first step in the, quote, 'protocol' for the 'morning after date.'"

"Are you making that up?"

"Well, since you've never had a morning after, you'll never know, will you?"

I must admit, the hot shower relaxed me somewhat.

And, for now, I am liking this whole "morning after" thing.

Forty-two

Seema

This is weird.

He's going to wake up, and everything's going to be wrong.

Let the arm chewing commence. Or maybe not. Maybe this is the beginning of the rest of our lives. Maybe if I can just relax, and not overthink this thing, everything will turn out the way it's supposed to.

I glance over at Scott.

And he's . . . not there. The bed is empty.

I sit up. "Scott?"

Nothing. His loft is eerily quiet. "Scott?" I say again, a little louder.

No . . . he couldn't have ditched me. He wouldn't have made me feel totally abandoned on a morning when he knew I would need reassurance that what I did the night before was okay.

I get out of bed and head to the bathroom. "Scott?" I yell.

He did. He fucking left. Oh. My. Fucking. God. I don't fucking believe he did this.

Shit. What the hell am I going to do? Clearly this should not have happened. It was a giant mistake.

In my head, I already know exactly how it's going to go down. When he gets back, he'll act like nothing happened last night: we were just a couple of friends who made a drunken mistake. No big deal. He'll call me tonight and see me next Saturday at his show, where he'll be sure to bring a date: a perfect ten, blond, big breasts, little waist, no brain. And he'll treat the whole thing like it meant so little to him that I'll want to stay in bed for a week, and not in the good way.

Or, worse, I'm going to get lectured. He'll tell me that what he meant last night with all the "I love you because"s was really just that he loved me as a friend. I took it the wrong way, and therefore it's all my fault that we've gone down this path.

I grab my matching bra and panty ensemble, then his WE HAVE COOKIES T-shirt and sweats from the floor, and quickly throw them on. Then I grab my purse, minidress, and shoes, and head out the door.

I'm already on the 101 freeway when Scott calls. I click on my Bluetooth, "Yeah."

"Where the Hell are you?" Scott asks me (seemingly in confusion).

"I'm driving home," I tell him angrily. "Where the Hell were you?"

"Picking up croissants. I was only gone for fifteen minutes."

Oh, I fucking hate it when he lies about time like that. "I've been on the road for fifteen minutes," I point out. "You were gone for at least forty-five."

"No I wasn't—"

"Yes, you were! And, by the way, very classy abandoning me after our first night together."

Scott gets very quiet. "Seema, don't do this," he warns me quietly.

"Don't do what?"

"Act how you're going to act. Just please, for one God damn day, can you act like a normal person?"

"Act like a normal person," I repeat angrily. "I see, because I'm being so abnormal."

"Actually, in this case, you're being crazy," Scott clarifies. "As in 'girl the next morning who has all these thoughts in her head of what she's expecting of me now that we've had sex and there's no way I can live up to it, so I get to be the bad guy, *bat shit*' crazy."

"Wow," I say dryly. "Bat shit crazy. Nice. So not only do you make me feel bad about myself when I'm not sleeping with you, apparently I get to feel even worse about myself now that I am. Perfect. I'm hanging up on you now."

"Oh for God's sake, I knew you would pull this!" Scott explodes. "I knew it! We should have never slept together!"

"Agreed!" I yell back.

"You don't get to agree!" Scott yells. "You kissed me, remember?"

"I knew you'd say that!" I spit out.

"Oh, you did, did you?" Scott answers back sarcastically.

"Yeah. It's why I'm not surprised you snuck out on me this morning, and why I needed to get out of there."

"I snuck out to buy you breakfast!" Scott yells in exasperation. "I never would have bailed on you."

"You just did. Because you thought I was going to be bat shit crazy this morning."

"That's not what I said."

"It most certainly is."

"No. I said *please* don't act bat shit crazy."

"I'm sorry. And the difference is?"

"Well, apparently, there's no difference, because you're acting exactly like I thought you'd act!"

He may have a point (sort of), but now I can't figure out a way out of this fight. I go with a soft (yet begrudging), "I'm sorry."

"It's fine," Scott says, his voice softening a bit as well. "I should have known when you kissed me that we would—"

"There it is again!" I interrupt. "I kissed you first. What kind of passive-aggressive Los Angeles single-male bullshit is that?! You started it with your whole 'I love you because,' and if you really felt that way, you should have had the balls to kiss me a long time ago."

"Why? So we could be at this moment earlier in our relationship?" he asks dryly.

"I'm gonna go," I say angrily.

"Wait," Scott says. "Why don't you come back, and we'll have breakfast?"

I know that's a bad idea. I should quit while I'm behind. Nothing good is going to come from the next hour.

But I can't help myself—I desperately want this to work out. "Okay," I say.

So I come back, and we head out to brunch at a funky little downtown diner that under normal circumstances makes me happy to be alive and in the company of bacon.

Only we don't talk. Instead, we avoid each other's glances, and stare at other people in the room. I can't eat—I think I ate two bites of bacon before my stomach rebelled.

Scott asks me several times if there is anything wrong with the food. I say no. Other than that, there is no talking. Just awkward postfriendship silence.

When we get back to his building, he doesn't ask me up. Hoping to find a way to salvage this, I decide maybe a little time and distance could do the trick. "So I should let you work," I tell him as he puts his key in the lobby door.

Scott looks beaten down. "Probably a good idea."

"All right," I say awkwardly. "So, um, can I call you?"

Scott shrugs. "Sure."

I nod. "Okay then," I say, and I turn to head back to my car.

As I beep the alarm, Scott asks, "So does that mean I don't call you? Or is this girl talk for 'You better call me'? What?"

I think about the question. It's a fair question. "Um . . . this is *uncharted territory, one of us should call when we know what we want to happen next* I'll call you," I tell him.

Scott nods grimly. "Fair enough."

I get into my car, and we wave good-bye to each other.

When my car comes to the first red light, I burst into tears.

This isn't what I thought would happen. It's even worse. It's bad when everyone is yelling. But when no one has anything left to say, it's over.

Forty-three

Mel

Danny is laughing aloud as I continue my story, "So then I end up answering, 'Pi. 3.14159265.' "

As Danny continues laughing, I say, "Okay. Your turn. What's the worst question you've ever been asked on a blind date?"

" 'Have you ever been with a man?' " Danny says without hesitation.

"Oh God! How did you answer?"

He gives me a look like I should know the answer. Then he tells me, "I said, 'No. Although I will concede that if Bono serenaded me, I might at least let him get to first.' "

"Ew!"

"Yeah, she didn't think it was funny either. I was kidding. I have no desire to be with a man."

"Not that! You like Bono? Ew! What is it with guys and the man-crush on Bono? His voice sounds like a cat in heat scratching up against a chalkboard."

"Okay, you know what? You're wearing a Spice Girls T-shirt. You can say nothing."

This is true—I am wearing my old Spice Girls T-shirt. Nicole insisted we not dress up at all last night, that we not put out any effort whatsoever before we went out. Nothing says "No effort" quite like a Spice Girls T-shirt.

Danny has taken me to Santa Monica, where we plan to spend the day at the beach. But first, he brings me to a brunch place on Main Street, where the omelettes are huge and the coffee is excellent.

"So, is Spice Girls your favorite group?" he asks me.

"No," I say as I take a big bite of ham and cheddar goodness. "Although if they were an all-male group, they could be, and I wouldn't have to be embarrassed telling men I like their music."

"What? Is this another one of your theories on dating?"

"No. I just have a theory that bad music by women disappears over time, yet bad music by men seems to stay with us forever," I say, taking a bite of hash browns.

"Not true."

"Please. Otherwise, why do men still listen to Sir Mix-A-Lot?"

"Because we like big butts, and we cannot lie."

I laugh, surprised at his sudden singing rendition.

"Oh, I got another bad first date question!" I say, snapping my fingers. "How many people have you slept with?"

"Yeah. See, as a guy, I would never answer that. I can't win."

"You can't win? Try being a girl. If you answer 'Three,' to some men that means you're just some innocent who's lousy in bed. Yet fifty percent of women in this country have only been with one or two men, which means statistically you're a slut."

Danny smiles. "So, you've been with three?"

"I didn't say that," I respond quickly.

Although in reality, yes, it's three. Wait, no, I guess now it's four.

Danny continues to smile. "You didn't have to." He has a sip of coffee and says, "If I were to admit to seventeen I'd be in trouble one way or another, too."

Gulp.

"I'm at four," I blurt out, then take a nervous sip of my coffee.

Danny smiles at me, looking positively charmed. "I think four's the perfect number."

I smile back, surprised by his acceptance. It's been so long since I wasn't defensive about my choices in life. It's nice to be able to blurt out something about myself and not have the man look at me with quiet disapproval.

"Oh! I just thought of another bad question," I say to Danny. "How come you're still single?"

"Oh, now, see, I don't think asking a girl that is so bad."

"Sure it is. It's another way of saying 'What the Hell is wrong with you that no one wants you?' "

"Huh," Danny says, considering my statement as he takes a bite of eggs Benedict. "As a guy, I don't see it that way. I see the question more as an incredulous, 'What the Hell is wrong with the last guy that he let her get away?' "

"Really?" I ask him dubiously. "Why are you still single?"

Danny pauses.

"Hah!" I say, pointing to him. "See? Sucks, doesn't it?"

"You know what? I'm being silly not wanting to tell you. I broke up with my girlfriend because I wasn't in love with her. She was great, and I loved her, but she wasn't who I was supposed to be with. So we broke up."

I shake my head. "Man, I wish I could give a breakup speech like that. So cool, so loving, so nonjudgmental. Plus you get to be the windshield."

"I'm sorry?"

"You know. Sometimes you're the windshield, sometimes you're the bug. I was the bug."

"So, what happened? Why are you single?"

I take a deep breath. I don't want to admit this. Not to a guy

I'm trying to impress. But here it goes. "He was cheating on me."

I watch Danny watch me, which is making me self-conscious.

"What?"

"He was an idiot."

"You don't know that. Maybe if you dated me for six years, you'd cheat on me too."

Danny shakes his head slowly. "No. He was an idiot."

As I open my mouth to say something else self-deprecating, Danny leans in and kisses me.

It's such a sweet kiss. We begin to make out a bit.

Maybe this chili pepper was onto something.

"Didn't take you long to bounce back, did it?" I hear a voice say bitterly.

I break the kiss and look up to see Fred, standing at our table, by himself. "Fred! What are you doing here?"

"Having brunch and watching you make a spectacle of yourself." He glances briefly at Danny, then asks me, "So who's this?"

"Fred, this is Danny. Danny, this is my ex-boyfriend, Fred."

Danny stays cool and pleasant, even putting out his hand. "Nice to meet you, man."

Fred glares at the extended hand, then turns to me. "So while I'm proposing marriage and wanting us to spend the rest of our lives together, you had this asshole just waiting in the wings."

Danny starts to stand up. "Dude, there's no call for that—"

But before Danny can stand up, I'm already on my feet screaming at Fred. "Are you out of your fucking mind?! You cheated on me with not one but like, twelve HUNDRED women, and you're going to try and turn this around on me?!"

Fred gives me the same condescending look that he gives me every time we have a fight. Like I'm the crazy one, and he'll indulge me in my little fantasies, but that, truly, this is beneath him. There's a patronizing tone of voice that goes with the look, and I hear it now as he says to me, "Oh, please, I made one mistake . . ."

"One mist . . ." I turn to Danny. "This is the idiot," I say, angrily thrusting my thumb in Fred's direction. "This is the one who dumped me."

Danny, now standing, puts a comforting hand on my shoulder. "I know. And he's not worth it. Let's get out of here."

Fred pushes him backward. "This doesn't concern you."

"Hey man," Danny says calmly but warningly. "It's over. Walk away."

Before I even realize what's going on, Fred takes a swing at Danny, who blocks it effortlessly, then punches Fred in the stomach.

Fred goes down hard. I cover my mouth. "Jesus!"

I start to bend down to help Fred up, but I stop myself. Fred doesn't deserve my help. He never did. I turn to Danny and weakly ask, "Can you take me home now?"

A while later, Danny and I are parked in front of Seema's house. "He's an asshole," Danny tells me for the fortieth time.

"I know," I agree sadly.

After we left the restaurant, Danny asked me to go to the beach with him, but I said no. I can't do this. Fred has me all screwed up about myself. I don't feel worthy of Danny's attention. I feel like if he got to know me for six years, he'd do the exact same thing to me that Fred did.

The person who knew me best in the world eventually realized I wasn't good enough. I can't go through that pain again.

"Thanks for the ride home," I say to Danny.

"Offer for the beach is still open," he tells me, trying to sound upbeat.

I shake my head. "No. But thanks."

Danny keeps his tone light and cheerful. "Movie? Picnic? A quick jaunt to Las Vegas, perhaps?"

I laugh politely. "I really did like meeting you. I'm sorry it was the wrong time for me."

"Don't say that. I'll call you later this week. Then maybe it'll be the right time."

"Okay," I say to him, halfheartedly.

I already know I'm not going to return his call.

If he even does call. Which he probably won't. If I were him, I wouldn't call me.

Danny leans over and kisses me good-bye. It's a very nice kiss, but a lot sadder than our other kisses.

"Last chance for Vegas," he says.

I laugh. "How are you single again?"

He smiles as I get out of the car. I close the door and wave good-bye.

Then I watch him drive away.

I open my purse and look for my house key.

And there, mocking me, is my silver chili pepper.

I walk over to Seema's big black trash can at the side of the house and throw it away.

Forty-four

Nicole

That Monday morning, I wake up a little extra early and take the time to brush my teeth, throw on some nice clothes, and even put on a little perfume. I have to admit, I am a little excited to see Kevin for coffee.

First, I wake up Malika and send her downstairs to breakfast.

Then I begin the half hour dance routine that is waking up Megan.

I walk into Megan's room. She is completely under her covers. "Megan, wake up."

Megan throws off her blanket, rolls over, and looks at me through half-closed eyes. "I don't feel very good. My stomach hurts."

"Please don't do this to me this morning," I beg her. "We're already late. I put out your uniform."

"Nicole!" Malika yells from downstairs.

"Ye-ah?" I yell back.

"I had an accident with the milk!"

God, can't we have one morning where things go smoothly? I run downstairs to see Malika holding up a half gallon of milk in a one-gallon plastic milk jug. The other half gallon of milk is in her cereal bowl, on the table, and all over the floor. "Malika?" I sigh, my shoulders sinking. "I told you I'd do that for you."

"But I wanted to do it myself," she explains.

Then she bursts into tears. "Honey, don't cry," I say, giving her a hug with one hand as I grab a dish towel and begin cleaning with the other. "It's just milk, it'll be fine."

Two minutes later I have raced upstairs and back into Megan's room.

Megan's eyes are shut tight, and she is grabbing her stomach. I feel her forehead, which is hot to the touch. "You're burning up. How long has your stomach hurt?"

"I don't know," Megan nearly whispers.

"Well, think back," I say, pressing down on her abdomen.

She gives me a half shrug. "I guess since I woke up in the middle of the night. Ow."

"Okay, when I pull my hand up . . ." I say gently.

"OW!!!!!" She yelps as I take my hand off of her stomach.

Appendicitis.

Fuck.

I try to stay calm as I ask her, "Honey, why didn't you tell me last night that your stomach was hurting?"

She looks away from me, ashamed. "I don't know. I figured I'd wait until Daddy got home."

I slowly and gently try to help her out of bed. I wrap her arm around my neck and shoulder and pull her up. "Okay, sweetie, I think I know what this is, but I need you to try and jump for me."

She looks dazed. "What?"

"You need to stand up, and then try and jump as high as you can. Okay?"

"Okay."

I stand Megan on the floor, then pull away from her. She is

standing pretty well. Maybe I'm overreacting. "Okay, now I need you to jump."

She bends her legs, then tries to jump. Nothing—her feet don't even leave the floor. "Ow! I'm sorry, it hurts too much."

"All right. Well, maybe we can try—"

Megan then pukes all over me.

Five minutes later I am driving down the hill to Cedars-Sinai hospital, and on my headset, leaving a message on Jason's cell. "Hey, it's me," I say as calmly as possible, even though I'm freaking out inside. "No need to panic, but I'm pretty sure Megan has appendicitis. I've called her pediatrician, and she's meeting us at Cedars in the Emergency Room. I dropped Malika off at her friend Rachel's. Rachel's mom will bring her to school. I have all of the insurance cards and everything, but I need you to call me back as soon as you get this."

I hang up the phone.

Damn it. They played an exhibition in New York last night, and play in Philadelphia this evening. God knows what city he's in at this hour, much less which hotel.

I call Jacquie's phone. Of course I get her voice mail, too. "Hi, it's Nic," I say, once again trying to sound casual. "I just wanted you to know that everything's fine, but that there's a chance that Megan has appendicitis. But everything's fine, don't panic. I just wanted you to know that we're meeting her doctor at the hospital now, and that everything's fine, but to please call me back."

I leave her my cell phone number, and also suggest she call Jason.

I hang up the phone and look in my rearview mirror at Megan in the backseat. "Are you okay back there?"

"I'm fine," Megan lies. "But can we not talk?"

"Oh. Okay, fine," I say.

She's not fine. She could die.

Oh God, please don't let her die. I will never complain about mornings or Italy or my lack of a job again. They mean nothing to me, I swear.

I want to burst into tears but don't want Megan to see me lose it. I don't want to but my mind keeps picturing one of those awful tiny coffins.

God, I can't stand this. My whole life would be over. Jason would never get over it. I would never get over it. Please God—why can't it be me back there?

"Can I lie down?" Megan asks me weakly.

"It's safer to sit up," I tell her. "Otherwise, the seat belt isn't as effective."

I hear her say, "You're driving carefully," then lie down. Within seconds I hear her dry heaving into a small trash can I brought along. As I speed down Coldwater Canyon, I ask her, "Do you want me to pull over for a minute?"

"No. I'm fine."

My mind jumps to the future again, even though I can't bear the thought: no college graduation, no wedding, no grandchildren. Spending the rest of my life not being in the company of this amazing woman who I can't wait to watch grow up.

I realize tears are streaming down my face. I wipe them away quickly.

Please God, whatever you do, please don't take her away from me.

Half an hour later, we're in the Emergency Room at Cedars-Sinai, and Jason is finally calling me back. I pick up my cell on the first ring. "She's fine," I say without preamble. "But can you come home?"

"I thought you couldn't have a cell phone on in the hospital," Jason says, sounding shell-shocked.

"Just not in the hallways," I tell him. "Can you come home?"

"I'm packed and will be out of here in five minutes," Jason assures me. "Are they prepping her for surgery?"

"Not yet. They've done like a million blood tests, and they're gonna do a CAT scan. But I've had appendicitis, I know what it looks like."

"Okay," Jason says, trying to sound clinical and rational (and failing miserably). "Can I talk to her?"

I hand the phone to Megan. "Your father wants to talk to you."

Clearly in pain, Megan forces herself to sit up in her hospital bed. "Hey, Daddy."

I watch her listen to him for a minute and hope he's saying something reassuring. "No, I'm fine," Megan says through a pained breath. She listens to him more, then says, "No, I'm not scared. The doctor was here, and she says I'll be fine. Plus Nic's here, and she says they do stuff like this every day. It's totally routine . . . I know. . . . I know. . . . Okay good. . . . I love you more."

Megan hands me the phone and flops back down. "He wants to talk to you."

I take my phone back. "Hello."

"How are you holding up?" Jason asks me.

"I'm fine," I lie through my teeth, knowing Megan is within earshot and not wanting her to know how worried I am. "Just want to keep things moving along."

"What can I do on my end?" Jason asks. "Do you want me to track Jacquie down?"

"Already tracked her down."

"Through her cell?"

"No. I left a message. When that didn't work, I called Carolyn, my old friend from the paper, and got her to track down the governor. He's in Albany. His team found Jacquie, I talked to her, and she'll be on the next flight home."

"Wow," Jason says, impressed. "What about Malika? Should I get someone to—"

"Her dance class is at three-thirty, school is out at two-thirty-four. I've already talked to Seema. She's on the girls' emergency cards, so she's going to leave work early, pick Malika up from school, take her there, and then, depending on where we are in the day, bring her here to see her sister or take her out to get the biggest ice cream sundae of her life."

"Do you need to call—"

"Jason, I'm on it," I assure him. Then I whine, "I love you, but just let me deal with the details like I do best, and get your butt home."

There's a pause on the other end of the line.

"I am so glad you're there," Jason says to me, relief in his voice. "I'm just . . ." I hear Jason struggle to complete his sentence. My amazingly eloquent husband is at a loss for words. "I love you very much."

"I love you more," I promise. "Come home."

"I'll be there as quickly as I can."

And he's out.

Forty-five

Seema

I walk into the hospital waiting room to see Nic slouched in a chair, staring into space. A flat-screen TV blares war coverage from CNN, as though the tone of the room weren't somber enough.

I sit down next to Nic. "Can I interest you in a full-fat venti mocha with real whipped cream and a pumpkin cream-cheese muffin?"

Startled, Nic turns to me. "When did you get here?"

"Just now," I say, pulling a venti mocha out of the beige cardboard Starbucks holder and handing it to her. "I thought you could use some breakfast."

"I told you you didn't have to come," Nic says, taking her mocha from me.

"Yes, you did," I agree, as I open a brown paper bag to show her two muffins. "And you also sounded like you were going to have a brain aneurism over the phone. Do you want pumpkin cream cheese or blueberry? Because I can go either way."

"You eat them," Nic says. "I don't think I could keep anything down right now."

"I'll take the blueberry, and we'll save the other one for if you change your mind," I tell her, pulling the blueberry muffin out of my bag. "So how's it going in there?"

"I have no idea," Nic tells me as she pulls the white plastic top off of her paper cup. "It took them a few hours to determine for sure that it was appendicitis, but then everything moved at light speed. They had her prepped and in the O.R. within, like, fifteen minutes."

"How long has she been in?"

Nic takes a big slurp of the whipped cream on top of her coffee. "Almost an hour since they wheeled her in and I had to leave her." She pops the plastic top back onto her cup. "So how are things going with you?"

"You're kidding, right?" I ask her.

"I need a distraction," Nic tells me. "Some other person's problems for me to think about and solve. Have you heard from Scott?"

"He sent me a text this morning saying he loved me. I texted him back the same thing. Other than that . . . we're at an impasse."

"What do you want to have happen?" Nic asks me.

I smile self-consciously and shrug. "If I knew that, we wouldn't be at an impasse." I shake my head. "It just . . . it didn't look like how I thought it would look, you know?"

"Honey, it never does," Nic tells me.

She gives me a sympathetic smile, then nervously looks toward the double doors leading to the operating rooms.

"She's going to be fine," I assure her. "I'll bet the surgeon does five or six of these a week."

Nic stares down at a crumpled-up tissue in her hand. "The whole drive down I just kept thinking: why can't it be me? She was lying down in my backseat, writhing in pain and trying so hard to act like nothing was wrong, and I just . . . wanted to feel all that pain instead." Nic's eyes get wet, but she stops herself from crying. "If anything ever happened to her, I don't know what I'd do. I know I don't have the right to love her so much, but I do."

"The right?" I ask. "What? Is there some law I don't know about on how much you're allowed to love a child?"

"It's an unspoken law," she tells me. "You wouldn't understand, because you're not living it every day. I'm just the stepmother."

"My God, you're hard on yourself," I say, sipping my coffee.

"Oh really? I guarantee you that whenever one of the nurses comes out to give me an update, she'll take one look at me and assume I'm the stepmother. It happens almost every day."

I shake my head. "No, it doesn't."

"Yes, it does," Nic insists.

"It might happen occasionally," I concede. "But did it ever occur to you that that might just be because you're blond and Megan's—"

"She's mixed race," Nic interrupts, defensively.

"Honey, you're talking to an Indian girl. Maybe people are just being ignorant."

"No. We live in Los Angeles. That's not it," Nic says dubiously.

"Really?" I say to her dryly. "Let's see . . . In the time I've lived here I have had very friendly people ask me in the most loving tone, 'What the Hell are you anyway?' I've had people just assume I am whatever they're comfortable with, then make comments on my being everything from black to American Samoan to Hawaiian. And then there was my favorite question, 'So, what are you? French?' "

Nic knits her brows at me. "Why would they ask . . ."

"He thought I was from the French West Indies, apparently."

Nic thinks back. "Was that the night you adopted a Caribbean accent?"

"I thought he was cute, and I thought it was funny. And frankly, humor is the only way to get through such assumptions. My point is, no one is assuming you're not her mother. You just have this massive insecurity chip on your shoulder because you're not. And you really need to let that go."

Nic thinks about my statement for a few moments. "Fair enough," she concedes. She takes a sip of coffee, still thinking. "But I'm still not her real mother."

"You know what? The minute this planet can agree on what a 'real mother' is, you let me know."

A black woman of about forty walks into the room wearing scrubs. "Mrs. Washington?"

Nic jumps up. "Dr. Shaw, how is she?"

Dr. Shaw gestures to a small private room off to the side of the room where we are sitting.

"Can I see you in here for a minute?" she asks.

Nic gives me an absolutely petrified look, then turns back to Dr. Shaw. "Of course."

Forty-six

Nicole

Terrified, and temporarily unable to breathe, I quickly head into the small room off to the side of the waiting room. Inside, I see two empty red plastic chairs, a clean, empty, blue table, and nothing else.

This is the bad room. I'm sure of it. If everything had gone great, she'd be smiling and telling me how wonderfully it went.

Dr. Shaw walks in behind me, then quietly closes the door behind her.

I turn around to face her. "Oh God. How bad is it?"

The doctor gives me a reassuring smile. "No, no. Megan's absolutely fine. We're just not legally allowed to discuss a patient's medical history in the waiting room anymore."

"Oh," I say, suddenly remembering how to breathe again. "So, how did it all go?"

"The surgery is over, and everything went great. Your daughter's just waking up now, and the nurses will call you when she's in recovery, so you can be with her."

"Calling where? Calling me on my cell phone, the waiting room . . ."

"I'm sorry. There's a phone in the waiting room. Just give them a few minutes. They just need to hook her up to all of the monitors and make sure everything continues to go smoothly."

I realize my eyes are red rimmed. I nod quickly to the doctor. She gives me a gentle smile. "So, do you have any questions?"

"Was it ruptured?" I ask in a panicked tone. "Was anything else wrong? Did I get her here in time?"

"No, it wasn't perforated. And you got her here in time, and that should make her recovery go pretty quickly."

"Really?" I ask. "So she's totally okay?"

"She's going to be fine."

"Thank you so much, Doctor. I can't . . . Just thank you so much. When can I take her home?"

"Probably tomorrow. We'll see if she keeps running a fever, and how quickly she can keep food down. But I don't foresee any problems."

"Thank you," I say.

And then I do something I don't think patients are supposed to do: I pull Dr. Shaw into a bear hug. "Thank you, thank you, thank you."

Dr. Shaw is nice enough to hug me back. I know it sounds sexist, but I am glad Megan had a female surgeon. I think we need more of those.

I tell Seema that the surgery was a success, and insist that she go back to work.

About fifteen minutes later, once I get the go-ahead from the nurses, I head over to the recovery room to see my daughter.

Okay—so I lied. It was a lie of omission. She has the last name Washington, I now have the last name Washington. So maybe I wasn't completely clear on my relationship when they said only parents were allowed inside the recovery room. I know I'm being petty, but it's nice to have people assume I'm the mom for a change. Like Seema said, are there rules about how much you can love a kid?

I walk into the recovery room to see Megan wearing a paper gown and shower cap and lying on a small bed with the covers up to her chin. She's groggy but looking around.

"Hey," she says, in a drug-induced slur, as I walk up to the bed.

"Hi," I say, gently stroking her head. "How are you feeling?"

She winces a bit. "I feel like I'm going to throw up again."

I pull out a sick bag. She immediately pukes her guts into it. It's yucky and awful, and I wish I could go through this for her.

After vomiting two more times, Megan stops throwing up, and gasps for breath.

"That's from the anesthesia," I tell her, softly.

"Let me get that for you," a nurse tells me, switching out Megan's sickness bag for a new one.

Megan continues to look around. "Is my mom here yet?"

I take her hand, the one that doesn't have the needle poking out of it, and force a smile. "She'll be here any time."

"Is Dad here?"

"They're both on their way," I assure her quietly.

I lie down in the six inches of space between Megan's body and the side of the bed. "But I'm here."

Megan tries to move her head onto my shoulder. "I'm sorry," she says, sleepily.

"For what?" I ask her in a whisper.

"For telling you to grow a pair. At the wedding. I just found out what that means."

I smile. "That's called a euphemism. And you were right, by the way. I needed to."

Megan smiles at me, then drifts back to sleep. I pull her body closer to me, then snuggle next to her. She feels soft. Cuddly. And mine.

Megan's eyes pops open, and her body jolts upward. "Nicole?!"

"I'm right here," I say gently.

Megan lies back down and relaxes her body. "Sorry," she whispers.

Megan drifts off to sleep again.

I hug her some more and wonder how I ever got so lucky to get to be in this moment, hugging this amazing kid. How did I ever get so lucky that I got to be in this future woman's orbit?

"Do you know how much I love you?" I whisper in her ear.

Megan smiles slightly, but her eyes stay closed.

And then I whisper, "I am so lucky to be your bonus mom."

An hour later, we are in room 413, and Megan is sleeping comfortably. I'm sitting in the chair next to her, watching her intently. We've both talked to both of her parents to let them know she's fine. Jason is the first to get to the hospital. He races in. "How is she?"

"She's doing great," I whisper to him as I stand up. "The doctor said it couldn't have gone smoother. They don't foresee any complications and she can go home tomorrow."

He starts to tear up as he pulls me into a hug. "God, I was so worried."

"Me too," I admit. "But she's fine now."

Megan opens her eyes. "Hi, Daddy," she says weakly.

Jason rushes to her bedside. "How are you feeling?"

"Okay. I guess." She looks past him to see me. "Are you staying?"

Jason gently takes her hand. "Yeah. I took a couple of days off, and then the team is back in town so . . . yeah."

I think the question was directed at me. But I let Jason have his moment.

I decide to give them some time alone. "I'm going to go get . . . a cup of coffee or something. I'll be back in a bit."

"Are you going to Jerry's Deli?" Megan asks me, referring to the delicatessen across the street from the hospital.

"Um . . . I can."

"Then I want a ham and Swiss on whole wheat with french fries," Megan says. "Oh, and a chocolate milk shake."

"Are you hungry already?" I ask her, stunned. "I don't think you're supposed to be hungry yet."

"Well, I am," Megan counters.

I smile. "Then ham and Swiss on whole wheat with french fries it is," I say, turning around.

"Nicole," Megan continues.

"I know," I say by rote, "no mayonnaise. A small bit of honey mustard, lettuce, tomato, no onion, and ask them to toast the bread."

Megan smiles. "Thank you," she says weakly. "Oh, and—"

"Steak-cut fries, no string, and for God's sake, no curly," I finish.

She smiles again. "Thank you. I love you."

"I love you more," I say.

And I do. I mean really, what parent doesn't?

That night, Jason and Jacquie spent the night in the hospital with Megan, and I spent the night with Malika.

Around eleven that evening, I checked my e-mail and Facebook for the first time all day. It didn't take long for Kevin to rope me into conversation:

KEVIN: Heard about Megan. Is she okay?

NICOLE: She's fine. They got the appendix out before it burst, and she'll be home tomorrow.

KEVIN: **Good to hear. So . . . when's coffee?**

I look at the screen. Debate what to type.

NICOLE: **I think maybe that's not such a good idea.**

KEVIN: **Why not?**

I look at the screen and just think to myself, *Oh sweetie, let's not play this game.*

NICOLE: **Because I'd be tempted to get a giant ice-blended mocha without the girls and I just can't do that to my kids.**

Subtext is fun.

Kevin doesn't write back for a while.

KEVIN: **Fair enough. Can I still read your book when it's done?**

NICOLE: **I would love that. Can I read your script?**

KEVIN: **Of course.**

And we don't Facebook again.

Boom! I hear a thunderbolt crack as I turn off my computer for the night.

These freakin' fall thunderstorms—they're making me nuts.

Wow . . . even in my head, I just said freakin'.

"NICOLE!!!!!" Malika yells from her room. "I'm scared! Can you come up?"

"I'm on my way," I yell as I head back upstairs.

I walk into Malika's room. She looks adorable in a bunny suit with pink bunnies on it. "I hear someone here is famous for her cuddling," I tell her.

Malika smiles, lies down with me with a giant smile on her face, then burrows her head into my chest.

Okay, so maybe I'm always going to envy women in their twenties a bit. I'll miss the promise of the first kiss. I'll miss the excitement of dreaming of what my future will be. I'll miss cleaning my house and waking up and having it still be clean. I'll miss going to the bowling alley at midnight, and happy hours at elegant bars, and not having to schedule my life around a 2:34 pickup time.

But in exchange, I have something more.

For better or for worse, I have a family.

Forty-seven

Seema

Once again, I am in front of Scott's building, ready to press his buzzer and ask to be let in. Once again, I feel like I'm going to throw up.

I take a deep breath and press the little white button. Several seconds pass. Nothing.

This is a bad idea. I turn to leave, and I hear Scott's muffled voice say, "Hey."

I look up at the building camera. "Hey," I say meekly.

The door buzzes.

Moments later, I am walking down the long gray hallway, heading to apartment 441. It's a long walk. I should have called first. Actually, I shouldn't be here at all. I need to go find someone safe. Maybe an accountant from Encino. Or an actuary from Newport Beach.

Scott turns the corner of the hallway to meet me halfway. "Hi," he says awkwardly.

I nod.

Desperate not to lose him, and not thinking about the consequences, I grab him in a hug.

And he hugs me back.

We stay that way, entwined in our hug, in the middle of the cold hallway, for what seems like hours. Scott finally asks me quietly, "Are we okay?"

I pull away from him and look at him with sad eyes. "I don't think we are."

Scott sighs. He nods in agreement, then asks me gently, "You wanna come in? Maybe have a glass of wine or something?"

I nod.

Back in Scott's loft, I watch him pull out a bottle of Clos Du Val cabernet. "Wow," I say as he gets a corkscrew and begins opening. "That's, like, Nic-quality wine."

"Wanna know a secret?" Scott asks.

I nod, so he continues. "I bought it a few days ago. I knew you liked it from the wedding. Thought it might serve as a peace prize or something, but then I didn't have the nerve to go over and see you."

"Peace *offering*?" I correct. Then, off his look, I quickly say, "Sorry. I'm nervous. Sorry."

Scott's features harden a bit as he pours me a big glass. "So why are you nervous, and why aren't we okay?"

"Be . . . cause . . ." I begin, dragging out the word to stall.

Oh, just say it. Get it over with.

". . . I'm in love with you. And I can never have you. And I can't live like this anymore."

Scott puts the bottle down. He crosses his arms, furrows his brow, and asks, "Why not?"

"Why not what? Why can't I live like this . . ."

"Why can't you ever have me?"

"Because being with you makes me feel bad about myself," I say, truthfully.

Wow, now I do think I'm going to throw up. God, what do you do when you tell someone the worst thing in the world about yourself? "You know, I think I should go."

Scott looks stunned by my statement. "I make you feel *bad* about yourself?" Scott repeats. His tone gets a little more angry as he says, "I, who went out and bought you your favorite bottle of wine because . . . oh wait . . . I actually *know* what your favorite bottle of wine is. I, who routinely tell you how you don't need to lose weight, or get Botox, or dye your hair. I, the guy who has been your last phone call for the past eight or nine months. I make you feel bad about yourself?!"

Boy, now he does look angry.

I respond by getting angry in return. "Oh come on!" I say. "I watch women who are much better than me throw themselves at you on a regular basis. All kinds of women! I watch size-four blondes with fake breasts hit on you and get shot down. I've watched artists who are world renowned for their work hit on you, and you have no interest. I watch a woman who speaks seven languages flirt with you in French, then get rejected. A few months ago, I saw an heiress offer to sponsor you the first time she met you, and you couldn't get away from her fast enough. They're all tens, and with those reminders regularly around, I cannot help but notice that I'm a seven."

Scott looks at me. "Did it ever occur to you that *you* might be the reason I keep finding fault with all of *them*?"

"No," I say. "Because we don't fit, and you make that clear all the time."

"I most certainly do not."

"The checkbook argument?" I immediately say.

Scott throws up his arms. "Because it is ridiculous to balance your checkbook by hand when there is a computer program and online bill paying to do it for you."

"I like doing it my way," I tell him for the millionth time. "Just because something is new doesn't make it better."

"Right. Let's go get our horse and buggy and try that out."

I shake my head. "Here we go . . ."

"No, no. I'll get my quill, and we can write texts to each other, then wait three days for a mailed response."

I try to defend myself with a good offense. "You know, I'm not crazy about the way you run your life sometimes either. Why don't you try an alarm clock sometime? Maybe start your day before the crack of noon."

"Another good invention: the electric lightbulb," Scott says. "Now the day people don't get to be in charge."

"The day people are still in charge!" I raise my voice. Then I stop. "God, we're both talking, and no one is saying the hard, ugly truth!"

Scott stops talking, and so do I. We have thirty seconds of silence.

"And that's what?" Scott says.

"That we don't fit," I tell him sadly. "We just don't. I like order in my life. I hide behind it. I'm too afraid to let it go. I don't take risks. You do. It's why I fell in love with you."

I shake my head. "And I finally took a risk, and all it's done is led to fighting."

Scott just stands, not responding. Eventually, I turn on my heel to go.

"It's not supposed to be this hard," I tell him, as I head for his door.

"You can balance our checkbook," Scott says before I leave.

I turn back to him. "What?"

He shrugs, "I'd at least like the online bill paying part, but if you want to take a ballpoint pen and do the register by hand, I can live with that."

Before I can figure out how to respond to that, Scott walks up to me. "You're right. You don't take risks. You suck at it. It's all me. I'm the one who takes risks." And he grabs me in his arms and kisses me.

The first few seconds, the kiss is tentative. I'm scared, I'm nervous, and it feels weird.

And then I begin to relax, and so does he.

And the kiss becomes comforting, yet sexy. Exciting, yet safe.

And, mostly, not hard.

Any girl who's ever been kissed by *the one* knows that the second he kissed me, my arguments were all out the window. I don't think he's going to win every argument by kissing me like that—just the ones for the next ten years or so.

I pull away from him to ask, "Wait, did you just say 'our checkbook'?"

Scott smiles. "I did. And I have something I want to show you."

He gently takes my hand and walks us over to his walk-in closet.

"I've been working on a small piece for a while. It's still in the 'Oh, God, it's crap' phase. But do you want to see it?"

Before I can answer, Scott opens his closet door. "I call this piece *Love Takes Work*."

As I look at the installation, Scott confides in me, "This was actually in the middle of my living room until you buzzed, and then I quickly hid it. I've been working on it ever since the night of Nic's bridal shower."

I walk around the piece, completely stunned that he has thought about me even one tenth of the time I've dreamed about him.

Scott continues, "I don't know if you remember, but that night you were complaining about your shovel, and how it wasn't what you wanted because all it meant was hard work, and you wanted a different one, and then I got the heart, and I thought to myself, 'Yeah—this is the universe trying to tell us something. But I'm too much of a douche to ever do anything about it.' "

The installation has rendered me speechless. The background is a series of pictures: one of us at Nic's wedding, another of me holding the penises the night Britney was here, another of us at the beach the first weekend we spent as friends. Then there are various souvenirs from our adventures together strewn around in what looks like a random fashion—but I'm sure he thought out their exact placement to the millimeter. My business card with my home phone number written in Scott's handwriting, in black pen. Tickets to a suite at Staples Center to watch the Kings play ice hockey. The copy of *Ulysses* I bought him for his birthday. A book of matches from a restaurant in Ventura.

And, in the center of the installation is his silver heart charm, next to a silver shovel, next to a small velvet box.

"Is that my shovel?" I ask Scott.

"Yeah," Scott says, donuting his arms around my waist from behind and resting his chin on my left shoulder. "Only you were wrong about what it means. According to my research, the shovel doesn't stand for a lifetime of hard work. It symbolizes nurturing and caring. The theme of the piece is: relationships take nurturing and caring. And, yes, sometimes hard work. Some people don't want to acknowledge that. They want the red hot chili pepper romance. And that works great for about ten of us on the planet. There are some people who just happen to be totally available when they find the person they want, and there are no complications. No boyfriends or girlfriends already in the picture, no money or career problems, no getting used to the other person's habits or quirks. People totally ready to lose their last Trader Joe's vanilla bon bon from the freezer, even though they were waiting for it all day."

Scott moves his head over to my right shoulder to declare, "I hate those people."

Scott reaches around me to take the velvet box next to the shovel off of its clear plastic stand. "I need this for one sec, then I'll put it back."

He gets down on one knee and opens the box to show me a beautiful amethyst ring surrounded by a diamonds. "Will you . . . ?"

I can't breathe. I can't take it! This is exactly how I pictured it in my mind—him on bended knee, the ring, a perfect little jewel tucked in a blue velvet box. It's even more perfect than I imagined.

Naturally, I do what any woman in my position would. I interrupt him. "Are you fucking kidding me? We've slept together once."

Scott rolls his eyes, stands back up, and corrects me. "Three times."

"One night. That's once! Which technically means we've only been on one date," I say, as Scott slips his arm around my waist. "You can't ask someone to marry you after only one date. That's crazy."

Scott shakes his head. "I *knew* you would say that."

"There's no way you can know if we're compat—"

Scott pulls me into a kiss. Which lasts for at least five minutes.

And, again, he wins the argument.

When we finally come up for air, he makes a show of popping the box closed, and slipping it into his pocket. "You are *such* a pain in the ass," he says, smiling as he takes my hand and pulls me toward his bed.

"No, no, no. Maybe I was too hasty. Maybe I should take the ring."

Scott shakes his head. "I'm sure I'll ask again at some point."

"Don't be like that," I plead. "It's just that I would feel bad if you were only proposing because the sex was so good. I mean, I have a *lot* of issues."

Scott pulls me onto his bed. "True. Plus, how the Hell are we going to raise kids with a king-size mattress in the middle of the room, and paint, glue, and metal instruments all over the place," he says in a mocking tone of voice as he lies down.

"Yeah—there's that too!" I answer back, propping myself up with my right elbow. "And I have a mortgage, and in this market, I think I'm stuck. I can't really move . . ." I stop talking for a moment. "Wait," I say, "You didn't actually propose, did you?"

Scott smiles at me, very proud of himself. "No. Kinda knew what you'd say if I did."

I make a show of looking into his pocket for that box. "Well, then, what was that?"

"A promise ring," he says, pulling out the amethyst ring again. "One year from today, I want you to promise me we'll talk about it."

I smile. My voice catches as I ask him, "Yeah?"

"Yeah."

I kiss him once, and then fall back onto his bed. "So, the charm was right," I say. "This is going to take nurturing, caring . . ."

"And hard work," Scott says.

I look over at him. "So, now that we're dating, that means I can have you Sunday morning, right?"

Scott looks at me lasciviously. "What do you have in mind?"

Ah, this is perfect. I am now at the point where I can allow myself to be happy. To be hopeful about the future. Which means I am comfortable enough to say to him, "I want to buy you a box spring."

Scott laughs. "But I love this bed."

"Why?" I whine.

Scott leans over me and, right before he kisses me again, tells me, "Because you're in it."

Forty-eight

Melissa

So I'm sitting in my calculus classroom after school, a yellow notepad on my beat-up wooden desk, staring at a blank sheet of paper and wondering if this is going to help me.

Danny has called me three times. Fred has called me twice. I haven't returned any of their calls.

Tempted though I may be to go back to my old life, I'm never calling Fred back. I blocked his phone number from our home phone and my cell phone and blocked his e-mails.

Danny is another story. I desperately want to call him back, but I know I shouldn't. That would be like an alcoholic going to the bar for one last drink—might feel good at first, but I'll pay for it later.

The romantic girl inside of me wants to fall into the trap of thinking that my prince has come. But the thirty-two-year-old woman with the series of failed relationships under her belt knows better.

I decide that it's time for me to just focus on me for a while. Not try to have a man save me from my life, and not focus on a man's happiness to bring me my own.

To just focus on what makes me happy.

It's been so long since I asked myself what makes me happy, I decide to take pen to paper and just write down any thoughts I have on the subject.

I pull a blue fountain pen from my desk drawer and begin scribbling:

Am I happy?

I may be doing what I set out to do when I graduated from college, teaching math. But now that I've reached my goal, is it still something I want? And for how long? Ten more years? Next Tuesday? A lifetime? And at what expense? I don't like that I'm thirty-two and still single. I hate that I just wasted six years on something that ended up meaning nothing.

Am I moving forward, backward, or staying in one place? I start to get nervous when I go home for Christmas and I don't have any exciting news to tell everyone that they didn't already hear last year. One of the worst things you can be in life is stagnant. Am I stagnant?

Where am I compared to other people my age? Most of the people I went to high school with are married with children. I used to justify my lack of marriage by thinking that I had chosen a demanding career. But now I have friends who graduated from medical school and who are married and pregnant and home owners, which makes me start to question my own priorities and timeline. I know it's taboo to compare yourself to others, but I do it ALL THE TIME.

Is there a balance in my life? I usually think of life as a struggle to balance three things: my health (physical and spiritual), my profession, and my relationships. I usually can only seem to manage to keep two of these balls in the air at once—every once in a while I get all three in the air at the same time, but it's never for long. And when there's a particular leap in one area, sometimes I wonder if it means as much without the other two parts of my life in order. (Is a promotion at work worth something without a partner to share it with? Is it worth it if it means I'm tired and run-down all the time health-wise?)

Am I getting the most out of life? Am I taking enough chances? Am I traveling enough? Am I opening myself up to new experiences? Are my morals on track? Am I appreciating my family while I still have them? Am I learning as much as I can? Am I doing things I'm afraid of? Do I have too many regrets already? Or not enough? Am I being too easy on myself? Too hard?

Am I happy?

"I don't ever remember the teachers being this hot when I was in school," I hear from my doorway.

I look up to see Danny, looking amazing in a plain gray T-shirt and jeans, standing by my door and holding a bouquet of silver roses. "Seriously, do the boys just play Van Halen's song 'Hot for Teacher' all day, every day?"

"What are you doing here?" I ask him.

Danny smiles and lets out a large sigh. He shrugs as he walks into the room. "Well, you wouldn't return my calls. I would have stalked you at home, but that's not nearly as creepy as coming to your work."

"How did you find out where I worked?" I ask him, as I flip over the notebook to hide my innermost thoughts.

"You told me where you worked. Honey, it's not rocket science," Danny says as he walks to my desk. "Although you probably actually teach rocket science, which means I should grab every time you look impressed with my intelligence and hold onto it like a poodle holds onto a tuggy toy."

Danny holds out the flowers for me. I take the roses and sniff. "They're beautiful," I say, genuinely surprised. "My favorite color too. How did you . . ."

"Again, you told me," Danny says kind of mockingly. "Do you not listen when you talk?"

I smile and sniff the flowers. "They smell amazing. But you didn't have to do that."

"I know. But I figured it was the only way to get you to have sex with me again."

I frown, mad at myself once again for being such a slut. Danny quickly says, "I'm kidding. I brought you flowers because I thought it would be nice to bring you flowers. And to apologize for punching your boyfriend."

"Ex-boyfriend," I correct him.

"Good. I'm glad to hear that. Because I also want to ask you to a wedding."

I'm confused. "What?"

"My friend Dave is getting married this weekend. I need a date."

I look at the roses, and debate. "I can't," I finally say.

"Sure you can!" he says lightly. "You can put on that ugly aquamarine dress you told me about, tell the bride you actually wore it again, and you're good to go."

I laugh politely, and maybe a little sadly. "Danny, you're a great guy, but this isn't going to work out."

"So you'll have sex with me, but you won't go to a wedding with me?" Danny asks, only half joking.

"Right."

"Man, suddenly I know how girls feel."

"You have no clue how girls feel," I assure him. "Look, I really like you, but I think you should leave."

Danny gets this look on his face like he plans to fight for me. He leans against my desk. "Why?"

"Honestly? I can't go out with someone who's going to cheat on me."

"Why do you think I would cheat on you?"

"Because you already have," I say.

Danny looks totally confused, so I clarify. "A random girl walked up to you and asked you to sleep with her—and you did!"

"Yeah, but . . . you're the random girl."

"That's not the point. How low are your standards that you would sleep with some slut you just met?"

Danny looks like his head is going to explode. "Wait a minute. You're the slut. You're mad at me for sleeping with you?"

"Yes."

"Even though you propositioned me?"

"You didn't know it was *me* propositioning you. You just knew some desperate girl was propositioning you."

"I knew a *hot* desperate girl was prop—"

"Did you just call me desperate?!" I interrupt.

"No. I mean yes. I mean . . . no, you called yourself desperate. I just said you were hot."

"Well, you're hot too," I concede, but now I'm getting angry. "You're a hot guy who will cheat on me. You've already proven it."

"Wait," he says, putting up his hands in a T to signal time-out.

I stop talking.

"So you're mad at me for cheating on you . . ." he struggles to finish his thought, ". . . with you?"

"Yes!" I say immediately. I realize how stupid it sounds, but I know exactly what I'm talking about. "You slept with some random woman who just walked up to you and asked you to have sex with her!"

"Uh-huh . . ." Danny says, staring at me like he's trying to figure out where I'm headed with this.

"Well, who's to say you won't do it again?" I argue.

Danny blinks several times. "I don't know. Casino odds. It's not like random women normally come up to me and offer me sex."

"I don't believe you," I say, crossing my arms. "You could have any twenty-year-old supermodel you want. And don't think I don't know you'll leave me the second she shows up."

Danny squints at me. "It sounds like you're complimenting me. And yet, really, you're insulting me."

He's right. My anger isn't really directed at Danny. It's at Fred. I slowly walk up to Danny and give him a hug.

"I just can't do this again," I tell him apologetically from inside the hug.

He rubs my back. "Do what?" he asks. "I'm just asking you to a wedding."

"No," I say, pulling away. "You're asking me to care about someone again, and I can't do it. You seem like this really amazing guy. And you're gorgeous, and smart and funny, and great in bed . . ."

As I stumble over my words Danny nods and says, "Well, I can see why you need to get rid of me then. I'm a menace."

I sigh. "I'm just so tired of hurting."

"Oh, honey," Danny says sympathetically. "I'm just asking you out on a date."

"But to me, it wouldn't just be a date. I'd fall in love with you. And then you'd dump me, and I'm not strong enough to handle it anymore. I've been dating since I was fourteen years old. It's a battlefield, and I'm tired and want to lick my wounds and go home."

Danny pulls me into a hug. "Go home with me instead."

I eye him suspiciously. "And then what?"

"Then you use me for sex. Again. And I let you, because that's the giving kind of guy I am. Although we have to go to the mall first to pick a wedding gift, because you're going with me to this wedding, if only for the promise of getting more sex from me.

Which, because I so desperately need a date, I am willing to give you. Then . . ."

I can't help myself. I start laughing. "Please stop being so charming and cute."

"Not until you agree to come to the wedding. Where, by the way, you will get to know me and discover, I am (a) a pretty nice guy and (b) not even vaguely all that cute."

Dem's fighting words. "You're *so* cute."

"Please," he counters. "People at the wedding are going to think the beautiful lady lost a bet to the geek. And I already want to ask you to my high school reunion to prove to those jerks that the head of the chess club can go on to date the prom queen."

My face lights up at the coincidence. "I was in chess club!"

"You were not."

"I was!"

"No. Girls who looked like you did not join chess club. They were too busy dating college students who were premed."

My smile widens. Ah, Hell, what's one more trek into battle? "Your house is only a few miles from here," I tell him sexily. "Want to fool around?"

"I promise you, this is the only time I will ever say this, but mall first," Danny tells me firmly. "I really do need to go get this wedding gift. I'm not kidding—the bride is a bitch, and if I don't have something for them by the rehearsal dinner, she'll make *me* wear an aquamarine dress to the wedding."

I laugh. "Well, at least it would be something you could wear again."

An hour later an escalator whisks us up to the third floor of the Bloomingdale's in Century City.

I love the third floor of Bloomingdale's. It's so inspirational—if

I could figure out a way, I'd be buried there. (Or maybe they could cremate me and put me into one of the beautiful Baccarat crystal vases on display.)

"Doesn't this entire floor just reek of hope for the future?" I say, beaming, as I look around.

Danny gives me an amused smile. "How so?" he asks.

I shrug, grinning like a five-year-old in a candy store. "Well, unlike the clothing floors, which always make me feel like I should jog off those last five pounds, or the shoe department, which inspires in me a deep-seated insecurity about my teacher's salary, the third floor of Bloomingdale's represents all that I have to look forward to. Dreams about my future, and how great it's going to be. The sparkling china reminds me that one day I can have eight people over for a fabulous dinner. The glittery crystal reminds me of the champagne flutes I will toast with my gorgeous husband on our wedding night, and every anniversary thereafter."

I watch Danny smile at me, then I look down in embarrassment. "Never mind. It's stupid. I know."

"Personally, I like the linen department," Danny tells me.

"Really," I say, surprised that he has an opinion about this kind of stuff. "How come?"

"Looking at the beds makes me dream that, one night soon, I will have you back in mine."

I smile, and we kiss.

Danny takes my hand and walks us over to the registry computer. Danny types in a name: David Devereaux.

"So, when's the wedding?" I ask.

"This Saturday. Rehearsal dinner's Friday. Wanna come to that too?"

"Don't you think the bride might get mad that you're bringing a date on such short notice?"

"If so, the bride can bite me."

"You don't like her?"

"She's okay," Danny says, shrugging. He reads from the registry list. "She told me she wants a place setting of . . ." He looks farther down the registry page. "Of William Yeoward. The pattern is called 'Avington Magenta.' "

We walk over to the wall displaying an assortment of plates in the various William Yeoward patterns. When I find the plate, I gasp in delight. It is a stunningly beautiful solid magenta china, with a thick gold border around the rims of each piece. I take a deep breath and once again feel the inspiration of hope for the future. I know I'm jumping ahead, but maybe Danny is the one. Maybe one day the two of us will be engaged and picking out china and saying things to each other like . . .

"Christ. That's hideous," Danny says behind me.

"It is exquisite," I counter. "It's stunning. It's sophisticated. It's . . ."

Danny picks up a plate and reads the back. "It's two hundred dollars for a salad plate!"

"Close your mouth, dear," I admonish. "Your Y chromosome is showing."

"You cannot seriously tell me you *like* this pattern," Danny blurts out.

"And you cannot seriously tell me you don't," I contend. "What's wrong with it?"

Danny's eyes bug out. "What's wrong with it? Well, for one thing, it's pink."

"It's not pink," I correct him. "It's magenta."

"Dishes aren't supposed to be magenta. They're supposed to be white and silver, maybe a little black or gold. But not pink."

"Who says?"

"Who says?!" Danny repeats. "Everybody says. What kind of a

girlie girl picks pink china? And what the Hell is Dave thinking that he agreed to it?"

"Yeah, like the groom cares what the china looks like."

"The groom cares. What kind of a sexist statement is that?"

I'm mad at myself for allowing the thought of Danny being my groom to creep into my brain. But it makes me smile. I look at him engagingly and say, "Okay. So let's say you're the groom. What china would you pick?"

"Something that matches whatever else you put on the table," he says, glancing around the room. "Like this one." Danny walks over to the Bernadaud section and takes a white and platinum plate from its rack. "This one is simple, elegant . . ."

"Boring," I say, not bothering to suppress a mild sneer.

Danny gives me a pretend glare. "I see registering with you is going to require a lot of compromise."

"Wow. I'm impressed," I say, eying him flirtatiously and giving him my best *kiss me* face. "You managed to go from talking me into another date to registering for china with me."

Danny smiles back. He puts his arms around my waist, flashes me a captivating smile, and tells me confidently, "It's charming as Hell, you gotta admit."

And he pulls me into another romantic kiss.

In the middle of the china department at Bloomingdale's.

Maybe that cake charm was right—maybe it is my turn for a red hot romance.

I smile at the thought as Danny and I pull away from our kiss. "I've changed my mind," Danny says seductively. "You want to go back to my place?"

Yes, I do. But instead of agreeing right away, I tease, "Don't you want to get your shopping done?"

He moves his hand down my thigh and pulls me closer as he says, "You know, I really don't right now. I want to . . ."

And he whispers into my ear, and my knees give out slightly.

Still smiling, Danny takes my hand and begins to lead me out of the store.

Then he stops dead in his tracks. "Oh, shit," he says under his breath.

I follow his gaze to see a strikingly beautiful Asian woman looking in our direction. I say "striking" because right now I want to strike him.

My God, I am a fucking idiot. Of course he's dating other people. I knew this would happen if I let my guard down even for a second.

The woman notices us for the first time. Her face lights up at the sight of Danny.

"Will you excuse me for just one second?" Danny says, dropping my hand like a hot potato and touching me lightly on the arm before he runs across the room to get to the girl.

As he runs toward her, I want to throw up. She's so gorgeous, she makes Fred's new girlfriend look like Cinderella's wicked stepsister. Five-foot-ten, although six-foot-two in the five-hundred-dollar suede heels she wears. Impeccably dressed—the woman's got money, and style . . . I'm definitely going to throw up.

I watch Danny as he kisses her on the cheek quickly and clearly tries to talk his way out of something. She looks over at me curiously.

I need to leave. Just put one foot in front of the other, walk purposefully out of the store in a self-righteous huff, and never see that motherfucking two-faced little weasel again.

Wait—she's walking over to me. No, no, no! I will not have my hair ripped out and be in a catfight in one of my favorites places in the world. I clench my jaw, keep my hands down at my side as I ball them up into fists, and prepare for combat.

"Hi, I'm Scarlett," the woman says to me cheerfully as she puts out her hand. "You must be Mel."

I watch as Danny stands behind her with a pleading look. An apologetic look. A look that says, *Yes, I'm sleeping with both of you. Can't we all pretend we're French and get past this?*

"I must be," I say, shaking her hand tentatively and having no clue about how to act. (I'm just not that cosmopolitan.)

"My brother has told me so much about you," the embodiment of female perfection tells me, excitedly. "So are you coming with him to the wedding?"

My jaw drops slightly. I blink several times as I stare at her. I think maybe I can breathe again. "I'm sorry. What?"

"My wedding," she clarifies, smiling brightly at me. "I know it's last minute, and who the Hell wants to meet their future mother-in-law this early, right? But are you going?"

I look at her blankly. She turns to Danny. "You *have* asked her to the wedding, haven't you?"

He glares at her. "I have. But I hadn't quite gotten around to the family part—I was leading up to it."

"Why? Are you embarrassed by us?" she asks.

"Constantly," he answers. "By the way, thanks for the 'future mother-in-law' comment. Couldn't have nailed that better myself."

Scarlett waves her hand at him. "Please. You told me yesterday this could be the woman you want to marry. I'm just greasing the wheels. Faint heart never won fair lady."

"I'm not so sure 'Wildly obvious heart' did much better . . ." he tells her, irately.

Scarlett grabs my hand, her face beaming. "I notice you were coming from the china department. What did you think of the William Yeoward?" she asks me.

"It's pink," Danny says, disapprovingly.

She turns back to him. "No one's talking to you," she says with a dismissive wave of her hand. Then she pulls me back toward the china section. "Come on. Let's go make him buy me a place setting. I think my man of honor should do that, don't you?"

Forty-nine

Nicole

Some things never work out the way you thought they would.

Well, okay, probably most things. I mean, does anyone really plan to grow up to become a crab fisherman, a radiologist, or a *Dancing with the Stars* contestant?

And if we met the person we were going to marry when we were five, that would ruin all the fun we have making such bad decisions about dating.

Another example of things not turning out the way you thought they would—and I'm just pulling this out of thin air—pregnancy tests.

I've always had this *I Love Lucy* idea of what it would be like to tell my husband that I was pregnant. I'm not delusional—I never really thought the father would be a bandleader who could sing "We're having a Baby, My Baby and Me" to me in front of a national audience. But, I have to admit, I did not think he'd be three thousand miles away either.

Or that he'd hear the news from my stepdaughter.

The week after Megan had her surgery was awful. The good thing about laparoscopic surgery is that a kid can go home the following morning and recover in the comfort of her own room.

The bad thing about laparoscopic surgery is that a kid can

come home the following morning and spend the next week of her life driving her stepmother crazy.

I had never seen a person eat so much ice cream. Somehow, Megan had confused an appendectomy with a tonsillectomy and ate us out of house and home.

And she hogged my laptop computer for a week playing Club Penguin, refused to so much as bring a dish to a sink because she "needed to stay on the couch or in bed to recover," and TiVoed so many *iCarly* episodes and Taylor Swift specials the she filled up our machine and I missed the latest episodes of *30 Rock*.

And I could not have been more content, or felt more blessed.

So I did something I thought I'd never do. I asked Jason if I should go off the pill. We figured we wouldn't be trying, but we wouldn't be not trying either. I was in my thirties, I had read the statistics: it could take me a year to get pregnant, maybe more. Plus, I had been on the pill for over a decade. Who knows how long it would take my body to get back to being fertile after being chemically infertile for so long?

Plus, in October, basketball season officially began. My husband wouldn't just be working long hours prepping for the season, he'd be in the season. Games until ten o'clock locally, plus the road games. We'd never have time to schedule sex, so keeping track of my ovulation cycle would be fruitless. (Pun intended.)

I should have known my plans would go awry. It's been five weeks since I got off the pill, and I haven't had my period.

So, I pee on the stick and wait three minutes.

Naturally, that means Malika starts pounding on my bathroom door. "Nicole! I need you to pour me milk!"

I look at the stick to see my urine creeping through the white window and the first pink line starting to form. "Can you do it yourself?" I yell to her through the door as I watch and wonder if a second pink line will show up and tell me I'm pregnant.

"I can. But it's the one-gallon milk, and the last time I did it myself . . ."

I've already raced to my door to open it. "Right. Don't do that again," I tell her gently. "I'll do it for you."

I quickly head downstairs, pour her some milk, throw the jug back in the fridge, slam the door, then start to head back upstairs.

"Nicole!" Megan yells from upstairs. "I can't find your ChapStick!"

"Where are you looking?" I yell to her, as I start up the stairway.

"Your bathroom!" Megan yells back.

I pick up my pace and take the stairs two at a time. "Hold on!" I say in a mild panic. "Let me find it for you!"

I run into the bathroom to see Megan holding the stick and looking a bit confused.

"What is this?" she asks me, intrigued.

Crap. We have not talked to the girls yet about siblings. I figured we wouldn't say anything to them unless something was definite. Otherwise, we'll either get their hopes or their anxieties up. Either way, why do it? But I can't lie either. "Um . . . it's a pregnancy test."

"Are two lines good or bad?" Megan asks me.

I smile.

Wow.

"They're good," I tell her. "They mean you are going to be a sister again."

Malika, who has apparently followed me up to the bathroom, starts screaming excitedly. "I get to be a big sister!" I start screaming, too, and she and I dance around the bathroom like idiots.

Megan is smiling, but dignified. "Cool," she pronounces.

The phone rings. Malika runs to get it while I look at the test.

Two lines, all right. Two very dark pink lines. I look at Megan. "So are you really okay with this?"

"Why wouldn't I be?" she asks.

"Well, a baby changes everything. You might wake up in the middle of the night when the baby cries. You may have to drive around with me doing baby errands. Plus, someone else might hog the TV when you want to watch something."

"Kind of like what you do for us?" Megan asks me.

I smile. "Indeed."

Megan shrugs. "Like I said: cool."

"Nicole's having a baby!" I hear Malika scream excitedly into the phone.

"No!" I yell, running into the bedroom. "Gimme the phone! Gimme the phone!"

Malika hands me the phone, then dances around the room yelling, "I get to be a big sister!" as I try to talk to her dad. "Honey . . ."

"You're pregnant?" Jason asks me in a stunned stupor. "Already?"

"Um . . ." I stall, not sure how he's going to react. "Yeah, but I'm really sorry she told you right before the game. I figured I'd tell you tonight when you got home."

Dead silence on the other end of the line. "Are you okay?" I finally ask.

A moment later, I hear Jason's choked-up voice. "Yeah." And a sniffle. "I guess I'm crying." And then I hear him yell to the locker room, "Nicole's pregnant! I'm gonna be a dad again!"

And from the other end of the phone I can hear a locker room full of basketball players screaming, "Hooray!"

Fifty

Seema

"You should not be throwing a party in your condition," Mel says to Nic, as we watch her finish frosting a chocolate cake with gobs of white buttercream.

"Women have been in my condition since . . . well, since there were women. I'm fine," Nic insists, as she cleans off a white satin ribbon dangling between the two frosted layers.

Mel hands me a glass of champagne, then pours one for herself.

"You've got it straight this time, right?" I ask Nic dubiously, as I take a sip of my champagne.

"I have it straight," Nic says, irritably. "Mel, you wanted the antique phone, it's right here. Pull."

"No, I didn't want the antique phone," Mel says as she pulls on a white satin ribbon and pulls out a sterling silver phone charm. "I wanted the passport."

"But the phone means good news is coming your way," Nic tells her.

"Not specific enough. I want the passport."

"Fine," Nic says, exasperated. She points to a different ribbon. "Passport's right there."

Mel yanks out the ribbon.

"Pull gently!" Nic admonishes. "You're going to get the cake all messy."

"Better the cake look messy than I get the wrong fortune again!" Mel insists.

"Was it really such a bad fortune?" I ask Mel knowingly.

Mel shyly turns away from me and shrugs. "Fair enough. But I still want the passport this time."

As Mel carefully pushes the passport charm back in the cake, Nic points to me. "Seema, you want the baby charm, right?"

"Yes!" I say, admittedly uncharacteristically for me.

"It's right here, under the four o'clock position from the heart cake topper," Nic tells me.

As I pull out the baby carriage charm (just to be sure!) Mel asks Nic, "Why do we need a cake topper?"

"It's just another insurance policy against getting the wrong charms," Nic says. "Not that we got the wrong charms last time, but this time I want to control my destiny a bit more. Based on the angle of the topper, I can point to each ribbon around the cake and know exactly what charm is hidden inside. Check out this ribbon. That's mine."

Mel pulls out a . . .

Actually, I have no idea. "What is that? An earring?" I ask Nic.

"No, it's not an earring. It's a picture frame. It means a future with a happy family."

Can't argue with that.

The doorbell rings. "Your guests are here," Nic says. "Can you guys go greet them while I finish tucking these charms back in?"

"Okay," Mel says, hopping off a seat in Nic's kitchen to greet the guests in Nic's front hallway. "Just remember the passport . . ."

"One o'clock position. After I place the topper directly in front of Seema!" Nic assures her. "Seema, you're midnight."

So an hour later I discover the problem with putting a cake topper on your circular cake as a marker.

If you turn the cake upside down, the cake topper looks exactly the same.

Which means the midnight position becomes the six o'clock position, and the six o'clock position becomes . . .

"What the Hell?" I blurt out after we have grabbed our white satin loops and pulled.

"No . . ." Nic groans.

"Okay," Mel asks, upon seeing her charm. "Can we trade this time?"

For glamorous Charlie Edwards, nothing comes easy in Hollywood—especially not love

"A hilarious cast of characters and the funniest, coolest heroine since Stephanie Plum… you will not be able to put this one down."

—MARYJANICE DAVIDSON, AUTHOR OF *UNDEAD AND UNAPPRECIATED*

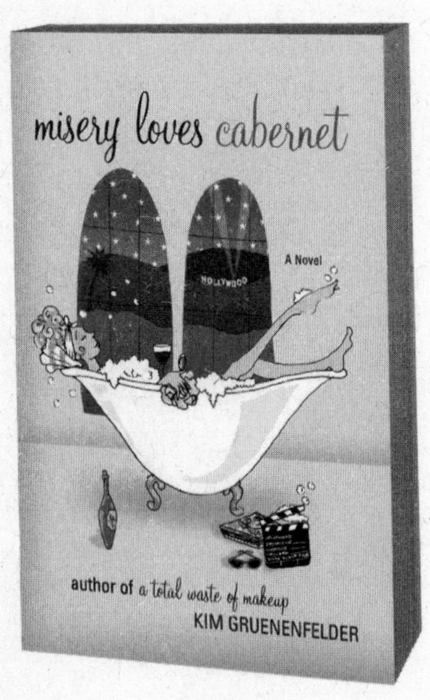

"Delightfully funny…loaded with hilarious one-liners…[and] filled with tips for the heroine's future great-granddaughter that are insightful and witty."

—***ROMANTIC TIMES*** **(4 STARS)**

Escape with *SheLovesHotReads.com*

www.stmartins.com

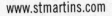

ST. MARTIN'S GRIFFIN